Also by Jean Davis

The Last God
Sahmara
A Broken Race
Destiny Pills and Space Wizards

Chain
of Grey

Mike -
Thanks for all the
inspiring words!

- Jean Dm

Chain of Grey

The Narvan • Book Two

Jean Davis

All characters, places and events portrayed in this novel are fictional. No resemblance to any specific person, place or event is intended.

CHAIN OF GREY: Book Two of The Narvan

www.jeandavisauthor.com

ISBN-13:   978-1-7345701-2-0 (print)
              978-1-7345701-3-7 (ebook)

First Edition: February 2020

Printed in the United States of America
Published by StreamlineDesign LLC
Distributed by Ingram

Chapter One

I didn't think my shipping business was overly successful, not to the point where anyone would want me dead because of it. But as I lay there on the floor, observing the fine spray of my blood on my office wall, I had to consider that I might be wrong.

Heavy footsteps drew closer.

Damn. I knew I was rusty, but it was still disappointing to know that I'd not done any serious damage with the two knives I'd managed to throw before toppling from my chair. I tried to peer around my desk, but my body wouldn't cooperate.

Rhaine was going to be pissed when I missed dinner yet again.

The footsteps stopped. Something tingled inside my head. The telepathic barriers I'd erected years ago dissolved as my strength faded. The tingle came again as someone invaded my mind. It was a familiar touch, one that sent my head reeling as much as the blood loss.

The blurry form of my killer loomed over me. "Oh Fuck! Vayen? Is that really you? You're alive?"

ॐ

Whispers told me I was dreaming, but I ignored them in favor of enjoying a quiet meal with my family. We sat around the table in our little house on Veria Minor, Ikeri shoving sweet yellow fruit into her mouth until her cheeks were bulging, Daniel looking guilty, and Rhaine giving me a look that said I should ask why. I didn't. Instead, I slowly ate the meal I'd made after coming home from my day at Dugans, savoring this normal moment I'd never thought to have.

A moment that wouldn't exist if the High Council hadn't drugged me into forming a bond with my partner. If they hadn't demanded that I kill her. If we both hadn't had to give up what we'd worked so damned hard for and ended up here, around this table.

Ikeri giggled. Juice dripped down her chin. I laughed, ignoring the pressure in my head that was likely the warehouse informing me of a late shipment. Rhaine and I had agreed on no work or datapads at the table. I'd deal with it in the morning.

Except, it occurred to me that it wasn't a message on a datapad. I tried to will the pressure away. I'd closed off all my telepathic contacts from my previous life. Other than Daniel, who was sitting right there picking at his dinner, no one else in our colony was telepathic. Beyond that, my link was gone. No one should be in my head in any manner.

My hand itched for a gun, but I hadn't used one of those in five years. They were safely locked away in a chest in a closet under the armored coat I'd folded up upon arriving on Minor. For peace of mind, I allowed myself two small knives when I left the house, but I was home now and they were put away. I didn't need weapons anymore, certainly not in my own home.

We were safe here. I picked up my fork and ate another bite.

Ikeri slid off her chair and grabbed my hand, tugging me toward the common room where we sat most nights to watch the local vids. Rhaine was talking as I stood. I had the sense that she was telling me what trouble Daniel had gotten himself into, but the words I heard were wrong, muffled, confused. It wasn't her voice, but a familiar man's voice. One I didn't want to think about. Ikeri tugged at me again, more insistent and with more strength than I expected. I started to fall.

I woke with a gasp to a view I never thought I'd see again. I prayed to Geva I'd stepped out of one dream and into another, but when I blinked for the tenth time, the cold metal room was still there. The grey metal ceiling, metal walls, crisp white sheets on the narrow bed, my old clothes on the shelf beside me—my room on the buried ship on Frique.

Merkief stood over me with his hands clasped together as if he'd been praying. "I'm so sorry. If I had had any idea you were Isnar K'turoc, I would never have taken the job. I swear. It wasn't one of your known aliases, and it was just a quick and easy contract, no setup." He grimaced. "Sorry, not to make you feel insignificant."

"It's all right. That's what I was going for."

Had I ever really been gone? Being on the ship again made my years on Veria Minor seem almost surreal.

He burst into a grin. "We thought you were dead. I mean, Kess killed you. Or he claimed he did. We didn't want to believe it, but he had proof."

"Why the hells were you taking contracts in the Verian Cluster anyway?"

"We need all the credits we can get without Merchess to help finance the system. I spot a good contract, I take it."

At least someone had put enough credits on my head to make me a worthwhile target. Though, was that a bragging point in my new life? I supposed not.

The life I'd left behind hadn't treated Merkief well. He'd acquired deep lines on his forehead and around his eyes, and his hands and face revealed a gauntness hidden elsewhere by his armor. The armored coat was the same, the weapon lumps were in the same places, but his stance had changed, more wary, guarded. The good-natured grin I fondly remembered faded as the silence between us grew.

Not that I wasn't happy to see that he was also alive and well, but we'd received little news of the Narvan System on Veria Minor, and for my own sanity, I'd done my best not to look. I was done with that life. With my link implant removed prior to our going into hiding, I had no way of knowing or even guessing at Merkief's current affiliations.

"So where does this put us?" I asked.

He glanced at the door. "In a Geva-forsaken mess, I suppose. Jey will be here in a minute."

At least they were still partners. Knowing my people were well-cared for brought me a measure of relief.

"How long have I been out?"

"Six hours maybe seven? It was a clean shot. Honestly, I was too busy hoping the tank would heal you using your old profile to pay much attention to the time."

Alarm plowed through my momentary nostalgia at seeing Merkief and the ship again. Rhaine would be beyond pissed and into panicked territory by now. Merkief might have been polite enough not to come out and ask about her, but Jey would. Now that they knew my current alias, they could search Veria Minor's network to determine our exact location.

The peace of the past five years began to unravel.

If Merkief and Jey had developed a tight allegiance to the High Council, blackmailed or otherwise, Rhaine and I were in serious trouble. And so were our children. I rubbed my hands over my face, loosening a thousand tiny flakes of tank gel.

I hadn't missed that crusty feeling at all.

Daniel could calm his mother so she wouldn't leap to any further conclusions over my absence. I opened my mind to his fledgling telepathic abilities, nudging him as I did during our lessons, rather than speaking right away.

Distress flooded from his five-year-old mind into mine.

I sent a wave of calm. *"Daniel, can you hear me?"*

"Yes." The strain of his effort made his voice waver. *"Mom is scared."*

The room closed in around me as two worlds that never should have met collided. I wasn't supposed to be there on the ship with Merkief and Jey, covered in tank gel. I was supposed to be home, tucking my kids into bed, composing a memo about productivity at Dugans and listening to the colony gossip Rhaine picked up from her Seeker sessions.

Reluctantly taking my eyes off Merkief, I closed them to focus on the fragile voice in my head. *"I need you to do something important for me."*

His sense of distress was dulled by excitement. *"Sure!"*

I took a deep breath and pushed the anxiousness from my mind. *"Tell your mother that I had a problem at work, but I'll be home as soon as I know you're all safe. Can you tell her that for me right now?"*

The door to my room opened, allowing the entrance of heavier footsteps that I recognized as Jey's. Merkief went to meet him by the door. I kept my eyes closed and focused on the task at hand. If I needed to send out a warning to Daniel, I wanted to be ready.

Nothing sharp pressed against my bare skin and there were no sounds of weapons being drawn or clicks of guns being set. Merkief and Jey murmured to one another but came no closer than the foot of my bed.

When Daniel's voice came back, it shook. *"Mom is crying.*

She's making us go to bed. Ikeri has to sleep with me."

He might not like it, but I was glad she was keeping them together. I wished I could talk to her directly, but her telepathy was only a small fraction of what it had once been. All we had was the bonded connection and that now only relayed feelings. Even then, she only picked up hints of me unless she was very focused.

As upset as she was, she'd not notice anything I sent. She didn't unravel often, but it sounded like she was dealing with the situation in spite of it.

"Listen to your mother and give your sister a kiss for me. I'll see you in the morning."

At least I hoped I would.

Our connection faded as his stamina wore thin. I opened my eyes to see Merkief watching me.

"Vayen, are you feeling all right?"

It sounded so odd to hear my name again. Even Stassia, who now went by Rhaine, hadn't called me Vayen since the first few days after we'd arrived on Veria Minor. Our aliases were ingrained for our own protection.

"I'm just tired. It's been awhile."

I sat up slowly, pulling the sheet with me. It had also been a good long while since I'd been naked around anyone other than Stassia, let alone armed men with uncertain allegiances.

The pinched look on Merkief's face eased.

Jey stepped to the side of the bed and clapped me on the shoulder. "You had us worried." His face split into a grin that went all the way to his bright blue eyes. "I can't believe you're really alive. And here."

"Me either."

The years had been kinder to Jey than Merkief. He wore his blond hair just past his shoulders and bound back much like I used to wear mine. Only a few fine lines at the edges of his eyes revealed themselves with his smile.

"Geva, this changes everything," said Merkief.

Jey nodded, still grinning.

I wanted to smile back, but my thoughts had flown far beyond our reunion. "How are things in the Narvan?"

Merkief and Jey exchanged glances, likely in private conversation through their links.

"The Council handed the Rakon Nebula to Kess. He's acting as a good deterrent for any adventurous Fragians," Merkief said.

Not surprising that Kess had been rewarded for offing Stassia and I. An advisor position was beyond adequate payment for the favor I'd asked of him and then some, the promotion he'd been dreaming of.

Keeping the Fragians in line sounded like good news. The constriction in my gut eased a little with the confirmation that I'd left the Narvan in capable hands.

Jey returned to Merkief's side at the end of my bed. "Trade and development are on track within the Narvan."

They should have been proud, but neither of them would meet my gaze.

"So what's the problem?"

"The High Council," said Jey. "They liked you and me working together, but you were always in charge. At least, according to them. With Merkief and I, we split the planets. They don't like it."

"Too bad for them. I set it up this way for a reason. They can't have you and me working together. I'm dead."

Again they looked at each other, no doubt noting that I'd neglected to mention Stassia.

Merkief cleared his throat. "There were some repercussions when you and Kazan...died."

My heart began to race. I'd thought I had it all worked out. There shouldn't have been any of the mess Stassia had thrown at me when the Council had locked her away. Sure Merkief and Jey had lost a few hours of memory and would think we were dead and Kess was to blame. But they should have had their hands full with advising the Narvan rather than acting on their anger. Kess was supposed to leave them alone. He had his own advisory position now, for Geva's sake.

"What kind of repercussions?" Not that I really wanted to know. I wanted to be home, and maybe to go back a year or so and rethink a few of my more aggressive expansions of trade territory that were probably what had ticked someone off and gotten me killed.

"Kess took you and Kazan out," said Jey. "His reputation skyrocketed. They handed him the Nebula territory the same day he offed you, no trial or probation, just gave it to him, along with Merchess, which should have remained ours." He shot me an annoyed look. "They gave the two of us a chance to fill your boots, but with Kess shining his glory all over the Nebula and us missing a large portion of our funding from Merchess to hold things together neatly, some of the High Council found him more alluring."

"They wouldn't pit Kess against you. That would be Kryon against Kryon. And Kess and I had a deal. He promised to leave you two alone."

Merkief's eyes narrowed. "A deal? With Kess? Why would you make a deal with that bastard?"

"Someone had to kill us. He was the logical choice."

They both looked at me as though I'd made my deal with Hewr himself.

Jey grasped the metal end of my bed in a white-knuckled grip. "They're funding him through extraneous sources, feeding him restricted information, enough to make sure we're all on a level playing field. I'm guessing whoever takes the other out won't get hit with any charges."

"And they'll happily scoop up the winner, knowing the best option won," said Merkief.

I struggled to get back into the mindset of the High Council. "But if they wanted one advisor, why not just pit the two of you against one another?"

"They tried," Jey said.

His hold on the foot of the bed didn't ease up in the least as he stared down at me. Merkief stood beside him with a less than friendly curl to his lips.

"Is that what you wanted, the two of us fighting one another?" asked Merkief.

"Of course not. I split the Narvan between the two of you so you could hold it equally. The Council liked the idea of a Jalvian and an Artorian working together, and that's exactly what I left them with."

"Left. After you made a deal with Kess." Merkief sounded more menacing than I remembered. "That means he knew you were alive, but you both chose to let us think you were dead. Him, I can understand, but how could you do that to us, to our people?"

"What did I do to our people? I left them in your perfectly able hands." Hands I'd thought could handle the Narvan, but now I had the sinking suspicion that I was wrong.

"I had to protect Kazan. That was our job, wasn't it? Above and beyond all else?" I asked, imploring them to see reason.

Jey let go of the bed and paced the four stride width of my room. "She wasn't able to hold the Narvan any longer, but you were and we'd done a damn fine job of it. We all wanted her back like she had been, but that wasn't going to happen. Not after what the Council did to her. You were just too blinded by your fucking bond to see it."

"They demanded that I kill her! You, of all people, must understand that I couldn't do that. What would you have done?"

Jey, who had been her almighty protector from day one, stammered and scowled and tapped his fists together several times. "I don't know," he said eventually.

"If I had stayed, the High Council would have moved down the line and held your lives over my head the next time they wanted me to do something I disagreed with. They were ready to off Merkief just before they gave up on me and tried to take Kazan out themselves."

It surprised me the Merkief didn't appear particularly stunned by my revelation. If anything, he shrugged it off.

"I vaguely remembered speaking to you before you...died, but I could never remember what we talked about or exactly when. I always wondered if it was my imagination toying with the hope that you weren't really dead," said Merkief.

"The drug I gave you made you forget. How much time did you lose?"

Great Geva, I wanted a shower and to go home and for both of them to remember those last days and hours we'd had together so we could at least go back to being happy to see one another. I had never expected to see them again, and that would have been better for all of us, because clearly, the truth wasn't improving anything.

Jey surged to my side. "You drugged us?"

I held up my empty hands and wished I had my armor rather than a sheet. "If I hadn't, the Council would have killed Kazan either by forcing my hand or with someone else's. I had to protect us from discovery and from either of you being probed or inadvertently saying something to make the Council doubt Kess's story."

"You mean, you had to cover your own ass so you two could slink off and play happily bonded couple while the rest of us picked up your mess," Merkief said.

"You both knew how the Council worked. Jey had half the Narvan in his hands already. There shouldn't have been a mess."

Merkief crossed his arms over his chest. That did nothing to relax me even though his hands were now farther from his weapons. His gaze was intense. And angry. And it made me acutely aware of my unarmed and unlinked position.

"You're forgetting Kess," said Merkief. "He showed up on Sere with your links, looking like someone beat the shit out of him. We got called in to witness his report." A muscle under his eye twitched. "We had to sit there and listen to how he killed you and Kazan and there wasn't a damn thing we could do about it. Do you have any idea how hard that was? Did you even consider that when you drugged us and scampered off into the sunset with Kazan?"

As much as it had pained me to let them think we'd been killed, I'd needed their grief to be believable. That and Kess's performance had sold our demise to the Council. However, stranded on the ship and at their mercy, it didn't seem wise to point that out.

"I'm sorry. We spent months after we left trying to think of a way to let you know the truth, but anything one of us came up with, the other shot down. Neither of us were happy with how we left you."

Merkief's arms fell to his sides, his fists clenched. Jey took half a step away from him, allowing either of them ample room to make a move on me.

"Here you sit, alive and well. You could have come back at any time to help us out," Jey said. "You have no idea how much we could have used you."

"The Council would have used me too. I knew where she was."

Jey shook his head. "You could have gotten her settled somewhere and then taken whatever drug you fed us."

Without being obvious, I worked my legs as close to the edge of the bed as I dared. If I needed to run, I wanted to be ready. Not that there was very far to go on a ship buried underground. My best hope was to barricade myself in another room until Merkief and Jey were more sensible. Assuming I could make it past them.

I employed my most reasonable tone. "I could have wiped my memory too, and I had planned on it, but she was in no condition to protect herself after having her damaged link implant removed. The Council tried to kill her during the surgery, for Geva's sake. She barely made it onto our flight before the stim wore off. She slept almost all the way to Minor. It took her weeks to recover as much as she did and then there were further complications. She wouldn't have survived on her own."

"All you had to do was let us know you were alive," said Jey.

"I told you-"

Jey slammed his open palm against my chest, driving me against the unforgiving metal headboard. "We thought he'd killed you. Did you think we were just going to stand there and smile with the Narvan in our hands? Do you have any idea how many times we almost died attempting to kill Kess for what he did to you and Kazan?"

"I'm sorry. Really."

If they'd gone after Kess, it was little wonder that he'd reneged on his promise to leave Merkief and Jey alone. Kess had a habit of working for the most advantageous boss of the hour and he'd been courting the Council before my offer. Not that I could blame Merkief and Jey for going after him. Hells, part of me was flattered that they'd been so devoted to avenging us. However, they were supposed to be advising the Narvan, not repeatedly going off on a private hunt that kept putting them in the tank.

Merkief stood over me on the other side of the narrow bed, removing any hope of escape. "The Council gave us your ruined links after Kess cashed in on the two of you. They were legit. Your head is intact. I'd like to think Kazan's was too, so how the hells did Kess manage that?"

Jey had me pinned so hard that I couldn't quite catch my breath. I wondered if they meant to kill me or if they wanted to get ahold of both of us so they could discredit Kess. We'd be at the Council's non-existent mercy. I couldn't let that happen.

"You handed him our links after we had them removed."

"I most certainly did not! Did you give him your links in exchange for a stab at the Narvan without either of you in his way?" Merkief punched me in the jaw.

It had been a long time since anyone had punched me. I hadn't missed that either.

"Our deal only included him making a convincing show of our deaths and leaving you both alone." I rubbed the side of my face and glared at Merkief.

Jey eased up a fraction. "Do you or do you not currently have a link?"

If I told him no, would they ditch me and go after Stassia, knowing I couldn't Jump? Bluffing could leave me stranded here, helpless.

Merkief drew a gun and aimed it at my head.

Shit. I opened my path to Daniel, ready to scream a warning, but I hit a soft wall. He was sound asleep. I squirmed under Jey's hold, but he'd remained in top form, and I'd spent a good deal of the past few years sitting behind a desk.

"No link." Merkief slid the gun into a holster under his coat. "So, how about Kazan. Dead or alive?"

I couldn't breathe, and it wasn't just because of Jey holding me down. "Why?"

"Because we want to know. Why do you think?" Jey drove his fingers into my chest with a quick jab and then backed off.

I swallowed hard and glanced from one to the other. If I told them anything, the knowledge would be there for the Council to find. Even if Merkief and Jey were actually on our side, the High Council could use Stassia and our children against them or to punish me.

The thought of my daughter pierced with the blue creature's claws as he digested her alive, brought bile surging up my throat. Memories of Sonia's screams filled my head. Would they be Stassia's screams next? Sweat soaked into the sheet clenched in my hands.

"Look at him. She's still alive," Merkief said.

Jey nodded. "Get him into the shower and dressed. I'll get a jump point."

I tried Daniel again but got nowhere. Stassia's mind was nothing more than a swirl of panic. For that matter, so was mine.

"We can't have Kazan thinking we mistreated you. She'd never let us in the door."

Merkief hauled me out of bed by my arm and shoved me toward the bathroom.

My hands shook so bad I could barely turn on the water. If they were concerned about my appearance, at least I was assured they weren't so pissed that they planned to kill me. Not yet, anyway.

The hot water didn't ease the chill inside me. A quick scrubbing dislodged the majority of the tank gel. After what was likely the shortest shower of my life, I stepped out to see Merkief waiting.

He shoved a handful of clean clothes at me. "Hurry up."

Not that I was out of shape exactly, but I had to fight to get the pants fastened. The shirt also fit tighter than I remembered.

Merkief raised a brow. "Somebody's been living the good life."

The clothes felt all wrong, too constricting and the synthetic fabric too smooth. I'd grown used to the natural fibers of the long free-flowing tunics and pants of the Verians we endeavored to fit in with.

Merkief shook his head. "I didn't recognize you at first with that short hair."

"Seen many long-haired Verians?" Not that it was that short. It still went down to my collar, but a far cry from the long locks I'd left with.

"I don't usually see many Verians at all, but no, I suppose not." He looked me over from head to toe. "Not that an Artorian would ever pass for one of those tiny Verians in any way."

Jey barged in. "I found where they live. Minor is tame enough. I think we can chance using the satellite image for a jump point. Is he ready?"

Merkief nodded.

Jey clamped his hand down on my shoulder. The void of the Jump swallowed me. I couldn't count how many times in the past few years I'd secretly wished to still be able to do that—to be able to pick up dinner from anywhere in minutes, be home in an instant instead of taking the transport, or to see Artor again. And now. If I could have Jumped myself home, I would have had time to run upstairs and haul my weapons chest out of the back of the closet. Better yet, I could have Jumped my family to safety elsewhere and started over again.

The black void vanished, disgorging us outside my home on Veria Minor. Thankfully we had a good sized piece of land with trees between us and our neighbors or they would have been glued to their windows. The only hulking person in the colony was me and they were used to that now. Stassia's partial training as a Verian Seeker, which she used to bring peace and therapy to the citizens of our colony, earned us a great deal of tolerance for our non-Verian presence. However, the arrival of more like me would push the little Verians past their limits of tolerance.

"Go on, open it." Jey shoved me toward the door.

In the spirit of getting them out of sight before we were seen, I deactivated the lock. The door swung open. Stassia stood inside with one of my guns in her trembling hands.

There was a time she could have dropped two threats in a heartbeat, and I wouldn't have worried about my own safety standing next to them while she did it. But that was years ago and this was Merkief and Jey. From her wide-eyed gasp, I gathered she wasn't about to go for a headshot without further information.

I hoped that once they saw she was alive and well, we could get past the resentment about us lying about our deaths. Then maybe we could figure out a way to move forward that didn't involve any of us getting eaten alive by the Council.

"Put the gun down," I said.

Uncertainty and relief warred on her face. Her hands dropped to her sides.

I took the gun from her and led her away from the door. "Sorry I'm late. I got killed today."

"What?" Her voice cracked.

Merkief cleared his throat. "Hand it over."

Though Stassia's death grip on my arm begged me not to, I didn't have much choice. I placed our one bit of defense in his hand and prayed I'd not just killed us all.

Chapter Two

A scowl grew on Jey's face as he glanced around our house. "You run off with Kazan and this is the best you can do for her?"

Ours was a simple home, yet one of the more affluent of our colony. Certainly a far cry from the mansion we'd all shared on Merchess and more like Stassia's house that I'd always despised on the tiny, sweltering planet of Frique. But this house was mine and my family lived in it. My children's feet ran up and down the stairs, their toys littered the floors and their laughter filled the rooms. I didn't need prism glass windows, expensive rugs, or prantha hide furniture and neither did Stassia.

I pulled her behind me. "We're trying to fit in."

Jey shook his head. "I get why you did it, but your vacation is over. It's time to fix the mess you made."

Stassia's lips brushed against my ear. "What is he talking about?"

"They started a pissing war with Kess over our deaths, and now the Narvan is on the table."

Stassia dodged around me. Unmindful of the physical discrepancy between her smaller human frame and their much larger forms, she approached them as she always had when she was our boss, with utter confidence. She strode past Merkief to plant herself in front of Jey.

"You did what? You idiots!" She smacked Jey in the chest.

He grinned for a moment and tried to hug her but she shoved him away.

"Isnar," she shook her head, "I mean, Vayen, handed you everything and now you're fighting over it with Kess? Rebelling against the High Council's wishes, I could see, but you had the upper hand. How the hell did you lose it?"

Despite our situation, warmth welled up within me. I'd not seen her so fired up since a few months after we'd left the Narvan behind. Rhaine was a much more peaceful and subdued woman than Kazan. I'd missed this.

Merkief leapt between Jey and Stassia. His lips twisted into a very un-Merkief-like snarl.

"They tried to turn us against one another. Our attention was a little divided." He took a step, and then another, driving Stassia backward. "I hope you two have been enjoying yourselves here. We haven't been so fortunate."

"We were, until you two burst in, intent on blaming all your troubles on us. How about you leave now?" I said.

"When we leave, you'll be leaving with us," said Merkief.

"I don't think so." I signaled for Stassia to run.

She stayed put. Damn woman.

Merkief lunged forward, grabbing Stassia and swinging her into Jey's awaiting grasp.

My heart seized. The inbred bond that bound me to Stassia screamed in my head, demanding that I protect her.

Jey wrapped his arm around her squirming body. "We don't want to hurt her, Vayen."

Even though he sounded sincere, he was still holding her against her will. I punched Merkief in the gut, intent on getting past him to reach Jey.

My efforts elicited a mere grunt from Merkief as he slammed me up against the wall. The rough fabric of his armored sleeve scraped against my neck. I knew I was out of practice, but Merkief had never been a match for me. Running the Narvan had made him harder and far more aggressive than the man I'd known before.

"You will come with us to Sere, and you will show your face and reveal Kess's triumphs as lies. Once he's discredited, you can go," Merkief said.

"They'll never let me leave. You know that."

Little feet thudded down the stairs. "Daddy?"

Merkief paled. He wrenched his head around to see where Daniel had halted halfway down the stairs. Ikeri stood beside him, her hand in his.

His voice dropped to a whisper. "You didn't tell me you had children."

I tried to pry his arm away. "Where between your threats was I supposed to do that?"

Uncertainty filled Jey's voice. "Merkief."

Merkief bowed his head. He let me go. "Put them back to bed."

I glanced at Stassia, still in Jey's grasp. Her eyes were squeezed shut. I scrambled for the right name to use in front of our children. "Rhaine?"

Her hands shook and her lips quivered.

"She needs to lie down. Please." I pointed to the stairs. "Hurry."

Jey took in her condition and looked to Merkief, concern plain on his face. Merkief nodded. I didn't have time to explain. I darted up the stairs. Daniel and Ikeri followed on my heels. Jey scooped Stassia into his arms and followed.

I should have known she'd have a headache from dealing with my disappearance. Jey and Merkief showing up had been enough to escalate it into a near full blown attack. She hadn't had one of those since giving birth to Ikeri three years ago.

The injector lay next to the medicine capsule in the bathroom cabinet. Thanks to our cover, we were stuck with what medicine the Verians had to offer. It probably wasn't as effective as what Strauss or an Artorian doctor would have used, but it worked.

I grabbed the supplies and ran to our bedroom, Daniel and Ikeri still trailing behind. It would ease her mind to have them nearby so I didn't stop them. I really didn't need her going into a seizure along with everything else going on.

Merkief stood in the hallway. Jey knelt on the floor next to Stassia, mumbling Geva knows what to her while I got the injection ready. She kept her eyes shut tight.

Our children scrambled up onto the bed to wedge themselves in around her. They clung to their mother, Daniel keeping Jey in his fearful and uncertain gaze.

Once I got the medication into her bloodstream, Stassia fell asleep within minutes. The pain on her face eased as her breathing fell into a steady rhythm.

With Stassia sleeping and the children safe and in bed with her, I had the leisure to dwell on the fact that Jey had invaded our private place.

"Get out."

Jey nodded and joined Merkief in the hallway.

"Everything will be all right," I assured Daniel. "Make sure your sister stays in bed and get some sleep."

He glanced at Ikeri, who was already closing her eyes, too young and tired to understand the situation. "I will."

I covered my family with a blanket, pausing a moment to land a kiss on Ikeri's forehead and ruffle Daniel's hair. He smiled sleepily and closed his eyes. After one last look, I turned off the lights and closed the door behind me.

Merkief and Jey waited for me by the stairs. They were deep in a conversation that died the moment Jey's gaze met mine.

"When I said, get out, I meant get out of my house."

"I'm sorry, but we can't," Jey said as he again looked to Merkief.

Merkief was calling the shots? I couldn't imagine what would have brought Jey to heel when I'd left him in the dominant position.

"What's wrong with her?" Merkief nodded toward the closed door.

"Complications from the damage the High Council inflicted on her link. The surgeons did what they could, but there was a lot of injured tissue. The attack during her surgery didn't help matters. She gets worse when she's under a lot of stress. Thanks for that."

"We didn't know." Merkief straightened his coat. "How about we try this again?"

"Try what again? The part about killing me, invading my house, scaring my kids, or almost sending Rhaine into a seizure?"

Jey grimaced. "The part where we ask for your help."

"I don't remember you asking. It was all accusations, threats and demanding."

Merkief said, "Then let's have a seat and discuss how you will be helping us."

"That still doesn't sound like asking."

"That's because I wasn't." He headed downstairs.

Jey hung back and waved for me to follow Merkief. I didn't know this new Merkief, and I certainly didn't trust him.

"Vayen." Jey inclined his head toward the stairs, his tone more pleading than demanding.

"Yeah, I'm going."

I didn't remember the single flight of stairs being so long. Jey's booted footsteps thudded along behind me, giving voice to the pounding in my chest.

Merkief stood in the common room, gazing at the latest still frame of Ikeri that I'd hung on the wall a week ago. My dark eyes peeked out from a tangle of brown curls. A rosy-cheeked smile lit a younger version of Stassia's face.

"She's beautiful," he said in a hushed tone.

"Thank you."

His head snapped toward us as if he hadn't realized we were in the room. He cleared his throat and pointed to the still frame of Daniel that hung next to Ikeri's.

"They're very different," he said.

Daniel was all my brother, Chesser. Or all me. We had always looked so alike. Beyond a loose curl to his hair that Stassia claimed was from her family, what little I'd discovered of her in him were the troublesome bits, stubbornness and a wicked temper. Then again, that could have also been Chesser. Whoever was to blame for Daniel's personality, I had a feeling we were in for trouble when he got older.

I wondered if I could jog Merkief's memory and recover the man who used to be my friend. "Do you remember him? You held him for me when I had my link removed."

He gave me a blank stare. "How could I hold him for you? He wouldn't have been born yet. I think I'd remember Kazan being pregnant, and that certainly couldn't occur during the few hours you claim I lost."

The admission was painful, I'd raised Daniel after all, but only the truth would help me here. "He's my brother's son. He and Kazan were to be joined, but he died."

Jey snorted. "Keeping it all in the family, are we?"

"How is that possible?" Merkief said. "You told me your brother died long before we were even hired."

Jey sat down in one of the chairs across from the couch. Since it was clear they weren't leaving any time soon, I took the couch and settled in.

"Anastassia had put Daniel in stasis on the Verian station shortly after his birth. I had him revived before we disappeared. He was sleeping, and you held him while I was in surgery to have my link removed. Both of you saw him when we parted ways on Artor. Jey, your eyes about popped out of your head."

Jey shrugged. "I don't remember."

"Me either." Merkief remained standing, though he came

closer. "So the bond, was it real, or are you merely fulfilling your brother's obligation since she bore his son?"

Before I could defend myself, Jey did it for me. "You saw him when she returned from serving her sentence and afterward. Even I could see he was bonded to her. You were the one that laid the stupid Artorian bond out for me for Geva's sake! Why are you being such an ass?"

Merkief's eyes narrowed. "You know exactly why."

For a second, I thought he would leap over the empty chair and attack Jey. His fists clenched and unclenched several times before the tension eased.

"If you have truly bonded to Kazan, why can't I find any record of your joining?" Merkief asked.

My mouth dropped open. Invasive bastard. "We don't live on Artor or any version of an Artorian world. There isn't even another Artorian within four colonies of here in any direction."

"She wears your joining gift, why do you bother with that and not follow through? You claim to care about our people, but you disrespect our traditions."

I looked to Jey, hoping for some hint as to why Merkief was hounding me like a raving grandmother. He sat back in his seat, staring at the plain rug on the floor between us. No help there.

"The neckband she wears is Chesser's gift, a replica of it actually. The original was stolen. I used my chit to have this one made for her. Besides, Anastassia isn't Artorian. She likes how things are right now, and I can accept that."

Not that it didn't bother me to see her touch the band around her neck from time to time when she gazed at Daniel. But after a year of hard debate, she'd agreed to bear my child, and every time I caught her smiling at Ikeri, she smiled at me too. That had to be more meaningful than memories and a hard metal band. Didn't it?

"So you proposed a joining," Merkief said.

"Not exactly, no." I sighed.

We were both making the best of the life we'd made for ourselves here, but the best wasn't always the happily bonded couple Jey had accused me of running off to. Stassia had been thrown into our Verian life far more so than I had. It wasn't at all by her choice, a fact she'd tossed in my face on a daily basis early on, and later, whenever she was pissed. She'd been quite adamant that joining wasn't on the table from the moment she'd learned about our bond, and I spent enough time sleeping on the couch or being ignored without pressing matters I knew would set her off.

Merkief stared at me long and hard. I wondered what he saw that made him so angry.

"Your credit stashes, are they still active?" he asked.

"As far as I know. I haven't wanted to attract any attention by checking."

He nodded to Jey. "So we can assume at least half are still available. That should help us a little."

I sat forward. "Wait, you can't just have my credits. I worked damn hard for them."

"You want to help our people? Remember them? The ones you walked out on?" Merkief asked.

"I didn't-"

He cocked his head and gave me a look that dared me to say another word. It wasn't like I was using those credits, or that I had planned to for the same reasons I'd left them untouched. Still, his demanding tone grated on me. I was the boss at Dugans and thereby, to at least a minor degree wthin our colony. And dammit, I'd been the boss in the Narvan. I was the one who made demands. Submitting to anyone else felt far too much like working for the Council all over again.

"You'll hand over your credits. We need everything we can get to combat Kess's efforts. Speaking of which, you're going to spend the next few weeks getting back into form, and then you're going to go talk to him. You created this mess. You can end it," Merkief said.

"I like this better than your going-to-the-Council plan, but it still gets me killed." I shook my head. "You think Kess would let me walk out of the room? The deal was status in exchange for my death. I prefer fake death, thank you very much. He's not going to call off his bid for the Narvan if he has any degree of Council backing."

"Then I'll go with you so it's two against one," Jey offered.

"Yeah, how about you and I both walk into his personal territory and make things easy as all hells for him?" I rubbed a hand over my face and sighed. "If I agree to go anywhere, it will be alone so you don't lose what little edge you have left. And if I go talk with Kess, Jey will stay here to watch over my family."

I couldn't believe I'd just uttered those words, but I didn't see any way of getting rid of them without agreeing to something. If

Merkief was willing to give me a couple weeks, I might be able to talk some sense into him before I had to act on my suicidal offer.

"Good. Jey will be here in the morning to begin your reintegration." Merkief walked back over to Ikeri's still frame.

"I didn't actually agree to anything yet," I pointed out.

He ran a finger over her cheek and turned to me with a smile that forced my fingernails into my palms. "I don't recall you giving me that luxury either."

Chapter Three

Daniel sat at the table, ignoring the bowl of fruit I'd set out for his breakfast. "Who were those men?" he asked.

Ikeri slurped the juice from her bowl, her innocent eyes peering over the top as if she was also waiting for the answer.

"Old friends."

I took Ikeri's bowl and put it in the sink before she could cover herself in sticky juice.

"What happened to Mommy?" asked Ikeri.

"Just one of her headaches. A bad one." They were familiar enough with those to not be too alarmed.

"The doctor only gives us shots when we're sick. Are you a doctor?" asked Daniel.

"No. Eat your breakfast."

I had enough to think about without having to formulate safe answers for my kids. The pale green walls had seemed safe yesterday, fresh and clean like the needles on the trees surrounding our home. My sanctuary had been invaded and it would never be secure again.

The soapy smell of the tank gel lingered in my nose. I'd never noticed it before, but compared to the crisp air of Minor, it was artificial. Even the tangy fruit I normally liked tasted wrong because of it.

Stassia's soft footfalls came down the stairs. A few seconds later, she walked in and sat next to me.

I slipped my arm around her shoulders.

She rested her head on my arm and closed her eyes. Her hair draped over the long loose shirt I wore. I couldn't put on the clothes I'd worn when I'd returned from the ship. They were from someone else, someone I wasn't anymore. They didn't belong here on Minor where I was the owner of Dugans, a shipping company that might arguably have grown a little too successful. Other than my two small knives, my pockets held a datapad and maybe a rock or a piece of candy one of the kids was sure I needed before I left for the day. If I wore a coat, it was because it was cold rather than providing a cover for a host of weapons or keeping bullets at bay.

"How are you feeling?" I asked.

"Like I've just had the most horrible nightmare, and I ache all over." She peeked at Daniel and forced a smile. "I'll be fine. You're just like your father. Quit your worrying and go play."

Which father? Why was I second-guessing her light-hearted comment? Damn Merkief.

"Does that mean I can go play too?" I asked.

Stassia's smile turned genuine.

Ikeri cheered and jumped out of her chair to grab my hand, her delicate fingers making mine seem giant.

"In a few minutes." Stassia sat up and turned her smile on Ikeri. "I need to talk to your father. Why don't you and Daniel go play upstairs? Nicely." She aimed the last word at Daniel.

He nodded and deserted his breakfast without hesitation. The two of them bounded up the stairs. Light and dark, side by side. They were so different. Stassia assured me that they were both far ahead of normal children of her race, so they both favored mine there, but Ikeri had Stassia's frame and coloring while Daniel bore mine. The size difference made the age gap seem much larger than the two years that separated them.

She turned to me, tired and pale, all momentary vibrance gone. "What happened? All of it. Did I really almost lose you yesterday?"

I explained how Merkief had attacked me, thinking he was fulfilling a quick and simple contract on a nobody.

Stassia reached over to squeeze my hand. "I told you Dugans was growing too successful for a colony this size. This isn't Rok, able to hide Cragtek amidst a hundred other shipping operations."

"It hasn't grown near as large or successful as the that."

Though that would have been easy to do so. The Verian Cluster lacked a decent trading company to compete with the large commercial combines on Armin. Learning as much as I had from Gemmen, it was frustrating not to use that knowledge when it could have really put Minor on the trade route map and boosted the local economy.

"I've bent over backward to keep everyone happy, my customers and my employees."

"Who would even-"

My fist pounded on the table. "I don't know, but when I find out..."

She covered my fist with her other hand. "You'll what? Run off and hunt them down?"

I rested my head against the hard wood of the chair back. "What should I do?"

"Let Merkief and Jey take care of it."

"They have far bigger problems than offing some nobody who wanted another nobody killed."

She sniffed. "I'd say they owe us for barging in like they did."

"I highly doubt they'll see it that way." I told her of Merkief's sudden swing from being overjoyed at seeing me to accusations and anger and how they wanted me to talk to Kess.

"Jey is coming back? What are we going to do?" Her voice turned hollow. "We can't run. They'll find us now that they know we're alive. What about the kids?"

"Stassia."

She bowed her head. "No use pretending anymore, is there? Rhaine and Isnar are over. Merkief and Jey want you back, and there's nothing I can do about it."

"I don't want to go back."

"You say that now, but wait until you get back into the swing of things and feel the rush of a job again. You'll visit Gemmen, step into your old office, and it will be like you never left. Once you get a whiff of the Narvan-"

"I left it all behind, remember? I'm happy here."

She released my hands to get up and dump the contents of Daniel's bowl.

"And you should remember that I can still feel you." She tapped her temple. "You've been regretting the choice to remove your link since we got here, and I don't care how much you deny it to my face, Dugans is a poor substitute for Cragtek, which you'd much rather be running, if not the Narvan itself."

Denial sprang to my tongue. I managed to stop it before it left my lips. She'd know I was lying.

Stassia sat down again, this time across from me, out of reach. "Can we trust them?"

"Jey, maybe. Merkief, I don't know. I don't want him around you or the kids."

Upstairs, Ikeri squealed. Daniel laughed. Something rattled and rolled along the floor, ending in a thunk. We both waited, holding our breaths until it was clear neither of them was going to cry.

"I don't want either of them here, but they're not going to just go away," I said.

Stassia rubbed her temples. "What should I do? You can go back, I can't."

Cragtek was one thing, but I had no desire to get back into Kryon or deal with the High Council.

"I don't know yet."

She scowled. "It was more of a rhetorical question. I might not be Kazan anymore, but don't start thinking you can tell me what to do now that you're back in the business."

Hearing her admit she wasn't herself, the woman I'd admired, hurt. I'd seen the change, gradual in some ways, sudden in others, but that she didn't even think of herself as Kazan anymore...I'd never considered that. Maybe it was more that I'd expected her to deny it, to assume she could step back into our partnership like nothing was different. I wished nothing was, but my wishes rarely counted for anything.

Her illness and the Council's demands had prevented us from finding out if we could overcome the changes between us before we'd left. She'd come to accept the limitations they'd inflicted upon her, but could I? I'd never been faced with the need to until now. I cursed Merkief again.

"I'm not back in any business, dammit."

"I beg to differ." Jey strode into the kitchen and sat down at the end of the table.

Stassia turned her glower on him. "Forget how to knock?"

"I didn't figure you'd want anyone to see me standing on your doorstep. If you'd prefer I knocked..."

Her glower darkened further. "Nevermind. What are you doing here?"

"I'm taking Vayen to my house on Jal for a few weeks so we

can get him back into shape."

"You're not taking him anywhere. I need him here and so do our children. He has a job. He can't just disappear for days on end." Her voice took on a hard edge I hadn't heard in a long time. "Get out. Leave us alone."

Five years ago, Jey would have acquiesced without argument. Today, he only offered her a look of mild apology before glancing to the ceiling as if he could see through it to where our children played.

"Thousands of other children would like the chance to play with their fathers, but those men aren't home. The Council wants us out there, exploring and conquering. Kess is willing to give them more than we are, and he's trying hard to prove it with our people and our resources."

He sat back and sighed. "You both have to understand, this isn't like the conflict with the Fragians. It's not outright. The High Council won't allow us to turn the fleets on Kess's holdings or his on ours. But there are too many pairs of hands on the Narvan."

"They've openly acknowledged that there is a power struggle between you and Kess?" I asked.

"Not exactly. Our contracts have changed. They're demanding our fleets take jump gates to systems we've never seen before and subdue them. We've allowed a few small exploration missions to satisfy them for now. Kess's excess ships are being bled off too. Neither of us has the military resources for an all-out war. It's like they're keeping us both reined in. We're stuck picking away at each other."

Stassia's head dropped into her hands. "I thought I'd talked the Council out of this. Why can't they just leave the Narvan be?"

"I thought I'd talked them out of it too," I said. "Defeating the Fragians should have bought peace."

Damned High and Mighties. We'd all be better off without them. Hatred twisted into a tight knot deep within my stomach.

"Both of you might have done as you said, but neither of you is sitting in on their private meetings anymore, are you? You left that to us, and we don't have the leverage either of you did."

Jey pointed an accusing finger at me. "We need to get rid of Kess so we can concentrate on dealing with the Council's demands before they slowly deplete our fleets to the point where the Fragians see us as an easy target again. Vayen can fix this. He had a deal with Kess. He can make him honor it."

"It was more of a verbal agreement."

Great Geva, did he really expect me to say a few stern words and the problems they had with Kess would just disappear?

"You can't seriously hold me accountable for your actions or the whims of the High and Mighties. That's insane," I said.

"You were pretty insane when you held the Narvan before. I'm sure you'll adjust."

Stassia cast me a desperate glance. "You can't leave us here. What if-"

I nodded. There were too many what-ifs.

However, I didn't want my children seeing Jey and I go at it, nor was there room to train in our house. I'd set up a gym at Dugans for me and Stassia to use under the guise of a benefit for my employees, but I didn't want Jey seen there either.

If I was going to face Kess at any point, or wanted an edge over Merkief again, I was going to have to do some intensive training to get back to where I'd been. Jey and I had worked well together during Stassia's imprisonment. If he was willing to help me, I couldn't have asked for a better physical match.

"I want a link first. Until I have the assurance that I can Jump back here to protect my family the moment I feel any threat to Anastassia, I'm not agreeing to anything."

"I've already set up an appointment for you this afternoon. Would you rather I stay to observe the operation in case one of the Link Experts is on someone's payroll or come back here and watch over your family?"

"I want you here." LEs with alternate agendas were not out of the question, but unlike when Stassia had her link removed, the High Council wasn't expecting me in the operating room.

Stassia shook her head. "You're staying with him."

Jey looked between us. "I can't be in two places at once. How about Merkief stays here, and I go with you?"

"No," Stassia and I said in unison.

"Fine. But you have about thirty seconds to figure out which one gets me. We have a lot to do."

With a pang of loss, I reveled in the mask of authority and control that made a momentary reappearance on Stassia's face. "You're sticking with Vayen. I want him back here in one piece, or I'm holding you personally accountable. Got it?"

He glanced at me.

"Are you sure?" I asked, thinking of all the horrible things that could go wrong during my absence.

"I'll keep the kids inside, and I haven't forgotten how to use a gun." The mask lifted, leaving only Rhaine behind. "You'll be home at your regular time though, right?"

If I was to attempt a meeting with Kess, more than a few people were going to be made aware of my status as a living individual. If they knew I was alive, they would come after me. Eight-hour shifts for a few weeks wasn't going to cut it. I knew it, and Jey's apologetic smile showed he agreed.

Stassia's shoulders slumped. She knew it too.

I raked a hand through my hair. "I need to make some arrangements at work, a leave of absence or something. But I'm checking in here for a couple hours every night. That's the deal."

Jey sighed. "That's not really what I had in mind, but we'll see how it works for a few days. Fair enough?"

I looked to Stassia. She stared sullenly at the table.

"Nothing about this is fair, but yes," I said.

Knowing I would be spending some significant time away from Minor if I was going to accomplish anything, I spent the next hour at the vid terminal in the common room. After a couple meetings and signing a few documents, I changed myself to a silent partner and promoted my assistant, Roshonomen, to take over daily operations. It was quietly acknowledged that Rhaine and I had a good deal of credits. After all, ours was a small colony and everyone knew everyone else to some degree. So it hadn't come as a shock to those I'd met with that I might step back to spend more time with my family when we could easily afford it.

After a private farewell upstairs with Stassia, Daniel, and Ikeri, I reluctantly changed back into my old clothes. The boots were heavier than the plas clogs I was now used to and my coat was stiff from disuse. I shook out the folds and opened the chest to load a few weapons into the inside pockets. I hoped I wouldn't need any of it but it would be in my favor to get used to the weight again in case I did.

With a heavy heart, I went into the kitchen were Jey was waiting.

"That's more like it," he said, smiling.

I didn't share his enthusiasm, but he rested a hand on my shoulder regardless. Jey Jumped us both to his house on Jal and just like that, my retirement was over.

❧

Jey's version of training entailed showing me everything they'd picked up in the time I'd been sitting behind a desk and knocking my ass on the mat with it.

"You don't have to hit so hard." I picked myself up for the tenth time in fifteen minutes.

"I wasn't." He grinned. "You're just old and sore and out of practice."

"You're the one who needs me to come back. Where does that put you?"

He adjusted his stance. "Wishing you'd stop talking and knock me down for once."

By the time we took a break for lunch, I'd managed to knock him down all of twice. I doubted that suitably granted his wish. There had been a time when I would have had his back on the mat in less than five seconds, and I would have held him there, dammit.

I peeled my sweat-soaked shirt off and sat on the bench beside the training mat. "I can't believe you kept Anastassia's home here."

With Jal in his hands, I'd assumed Jey would have picked up something more in keeping with his own personal style, like a top floor suite in one of the prestigious plexes. Then again, I'd also envisioned him with a couple wives by now, as most Jalvian men often did once they'd outgrown their zealous, early years. But the house was quiet as we walked up the stairs from the basement, and I'd seen no evidence of other life when we'd arrived.

"With the two of you gone, I wasn't in the mood to sell it," he said without turning around.

The lights came on when we reached the main floor. He'd bought new furniture. It looked comfortable and more what I would have expected from him, the high-end stuff Stassia hadn't bothered with except on Merchess. I noticed one of Stassia's candles on the table next to the couch. It was half burnt down. The handful of firestones that had been in her room on the Verian station were arranged in a circle around it.

"Your room is still the same one if you want to settle in a little. As long as you stay inside, no one will know you're here. You'll be safe and so will Kazan."

"I do remember how that all works. I haven't forgotten

everything."

Jey clapped me on the shoulder. "You didn't forget; your body just needs time to remember. I'll be back with lunch." He Jumped.

After a quick shower, I took the opportunity to look around a bit more. The walls were the same too blue shade but he'd upgraded the rugs in keeping with the new furniture.

Jey's bedroom door was closed. The rest hung open. I walked down the hall. Stassia's room stood just as I'd last seen it. Her minimalist and orderly style greeted me as I walked by, reminding me that she was likely sitting at home, either worrying or growing angrier by the minute, or both. I went in and, out of curiosity, opened her closet. As I suspected, Jey's shrine to Anastassia also included her armor that I'd left on the floor of the destroyed operating room at the Artorian University. He'd cleaned her coat and hung it at the forefront of the few clothes hanging inside.

I ran my hands over the hard surface, wishing she was wearing it and standing there in the Jalvian house with me like we'd never left. Like everything was how it used to be, and we could go do a contract together. To see her move like she used to, hear her barking out commands and threatening anyone who displeased her. I didn't realize until just then how much I missed that woman.

With a wistful sigh, I stroked the top latch, toying with the idea of removing it from the hanger, of taking it home with me once I could Jump. But that wasn't yet, and Jey would be back soon. I closed the closet door and went back out into the hallway.

Hoping for some clue as to Merkief's demeanor, I peered into his room. The walls and floor were bare. Not only did he no longer live there, he no longer stayed there. I left the vacant room and went to my own. I'd never been as neat as Stassia, but when I walked in, my mouth dropped open.

Fist-sized holes littered the walls. My mirror hung from one corner, shattered. Three jagged shards remained in the frame. The ever-efficient bots had begun to clear away what debris had landed on the floor, but there was a lot of it. By the amount still present, I guessed the damage spree had occurred the night before. Bedding lay strewn in the opposite corner and a long tear severed the top of the mattress. The closet doors hung open, crooked and half off the hinges. My clothes lay in a tangled mass.

One of them had had a meltdown, and my bet was on Merkief, who had once been a good friend and now... Now I didn't know what to make of him.

I sat on the edge of the bed with my head in my hands. All the bases should have been covered when I'd left. I'd never wanted any of this to happen. My years as a High Council puppet were over.

Dammit. They were over.

I swore to Geva I'd be content with my little shipping endeavor if she'd just erase the past two days and let me go back to my life as Isnar.

As usual, Geva chose to ignore me.

An aroma I'd not enjoyed for too many years taunted my nose. My mouth watered.

"I figured I owed you for hauling you out of retirement," Jey called out. "I hope Verian fare didn't turn you away from Artorian food because there's a lot of it here, and it's not really my preference."

I got to my feet and paused there as my muscles berated me for sitting down after my first major workout in years. I stumbled toward the kitchen like a sleepwalker. A feast of spiced flatbread, cheese and shellfish awaited me. A meal I'd taken for granted in all my years in Kazan's service, and now it was like food from Geva's own table. I sat down and breathed deep.

Jey cracked open a green shell with his hands and fished out the tender meat inside with his fork. "Been awhile?"

I shoved a hunk of bread into my mouth and savored it. "You have no idea how sick of bland Verian food I am. There's a reason Verians are so small. They don't know what real food is."

Importing food from outside the Verian Cluster had not been a shipping priority for merchants dealing with Veria Minor, no matter how many times I'd asked.

A bite of cheese melted on my tongue, filling my mouth with its savory tang.

"Doesn't look like you've suffered too much. Kazan must be a pretty good cook."

"She's gotten better." I did most of it, but there was no helping the lack of good ingredients.

He set the empty shell on his plate and proceeded to pick at a piece of bread. "What's it like?"

"Her cooking?"

A chunk of bread bounced off my forehead. "Living with Kazan and being away from all this."

"Oh. Good. Different, but good."

"That's it? You set the entire Narvan aside for good?"

"What do you want me to say?" I asked.

"You're bonded to her. Merkief made it clear that was a major event. He's furious that you haven't formally joined, to the point where he's doubting your bond and your intention for disappearing with her. If you really do love her, why didn't you two make it official?"

"I told you yesterday."

He set the bread down. "Come on, Vayen. Give me something to defend you with."

"To Merkief? He should understand. Anastassia isn't Artorian."

"And?"

"And she doesn't want to join. Do you have any idea how long it took me to get her to acknowledge we were even in a relationship before we left?"

I picked up an empty shell, running my fingers over the prominent ridges. It was aggravating enough that the two of them demanded that I help them. Now they were compelled to examine my personal life too?

"You don't understand," I said. "Neither of us wanted this, to vanish, to settle down peacefully. It was never our intention. You want someone to blame for us vanishing? Thank the fucking High and Mighties for that."

Jey's eyes widened. "What did you want? Either of you?"

"What I want never seems to matter to anyone." I quelled the obscene gesture I'd queued up for Geva. I needed all the help I could get, especially now. "Like I said, I'd intended to run the Narvan with her or you, all of us, whatever. I'd guess Anastassia had planned to barrel forward until a bullet stopped her once and for all."

"For all of that, you two looked pretty settled in together, kids, jobs, the whole deal."

"We were making the best of the life the Council forced us into. It beat one or both of us being dead for real." I shrugged. "Look, I mentioned joining once after we got to Minor. She nearly bit my head off. I tried again a year later, and she didn't talk to me for two weeks. I settled for asking for a child, which we fought about long and hard. She finally agreed. Isn't that close enough?"

"Making the best of it, my ass." He leaned back and crossed his arms over his chest. "So tell me, is it close enough?"

The meal lost its taste. I tossed the shell down. It bounced off my plate and onto the table, spinning over the smooth surface.

"What does it matter? You two are demanding I leave her behind and go have a faceoff with Kess that I'll likely not walk away from. If I survive Kess, there will be others once word gets out I'm alive. Why in all nine hells would I want what little time I have left with her to be filled with more arguing and angry silence?"

"Maybe she wouldn't argue this time."

I snorted. "You know her better than that."

His gaze dropped to the table.

"What's going on?" I pushed my chair back and stood. Opening my mind to Stassia's, I was met with seething. "What did you do?"

"Merkief was supposed to wait until I'd talked to you. I take it he didn't?"

My entire body shook. I used the natural path Merkief had reestablished when he'd tried to kill me at Dugans. *"What are you doing in my house? What did you say to her?"*

"What needed to be said." He slammed our connection shut.

"Take me home. Now."

Jey shook his head. "I have to take you to Artor to get your link. Once it's operational, you can go home. I won't stop you."

"I need to go home now."

"I'm sorry. I can't."

I tried to keep the tremor from my voice. "Jey."

"He won't hurt her, if that's what you're thinking."

Surely he had noticed the difference in Merkief. "How can you know that?"

"Did you look at Kazan's room?" he asked.

I nodded.

"Did you notice yours?"

"How could I not?"

"If Merkief is going to hurt anyone, it's you."

And there was no better way to do that than to hurt her. I took a deep breath and let it out slowly. Panic wouldn't help me.

"What did I do to him?"

Jey bowed his head, dropping his gaze to the remnants of the meal that lay between us on the table. "You have a family."

"And that's a bad thing?"

He sighed heavily.

If Jey really was the ally he seemed, I was going to have to give him something to help them both understand. Stassia was already set off. It couldn't get any worse now.

"The family wasn't planned, well, other than Ikeri, but the rest, far from it. You remember that drug I got hooked on years ago?" I pushed my plate away to make room for my elbows so I could massage my forehead and look at the table rather than face him.

"How could I forget?" he said.

"That was the Council's doing. It lulled me into forming the bond with Anastassia. Again, not my plan. We hadn't even talked about it. The Council wanted it in place so they could manipulate me. Some of them, anyway. Like you, Merkief, and Kess, I got caught between two factions."

Jey was so quiet I glanced up to see if he was still there. He sat staring at me, his mouth gaping.

"The faction that was more on my side wanted Anastassia dead, which would have freed me from the bond they'd tricked me into. Their version of doing me a favor."

"Remind me not to ask any favors of the Council," he said quietly. "Does she know this?"

"Not the details, but that it wasn't intentional, yes. It sort of came out when we were fighting. We were separated for a while early on."

His eyebrows rose.

"Yes, well, remember the fights we had when we were still around?"

Jey nodded.

"They got worse. We got better at getting along, eventually." I took my time picking the meat from one of the remaining shells in reach. "The Council didn't do Anastassia any favors either. When she left us all, before the Fragian war, she thought the High and Mighties were going after Daniel in order to manipulate her. She was protecting her son and it cost her everything."

"It would seem that we've all been screwed over by the Council," he said.

"Indeed. What I'm trying to say is, we're not a blissfully joined couple. Most days it's great, but it's not traditional by any Artorian standards, and she never wanted kids."

Jey snorted. "Then maybe she should have-"

I cut short his off-color comment with a wave of my hand. "Ikeri was a damned selfish request on my part. Anastassia was miserable for six months straight. For the record, compatible does not mean recommended."

"But she did it anyway," he said. "She had to know how it would be after the first one."

"Yes, well, she didn't divulge exactly how bad it had been the first time until it was too late. I wouldn't have asked it of her if I'd known."

"Things must not be that bad then if she still put herself through that for you."

I felt sick all over again, just like I had when she'd said the words herself. "She said she owed me."

He cringed. "Was she angry when she said that? She did always have a habit of flinging out biting retorts."

"She was angry most of the first couple years, so probably. Whether that makes it any less true in her mind or not, I couldn't tell you."

"But she's okay with the kids now?" he asked.

"More now, yes. I did most of the work when they were little."

"You?" He laughed until tears welled in his eyes. He wiped them away and exhaled deeply. "Sorry. All right then, I suppose that helps, but do you want me to share all of that with Merkief?"

"Would it get him to back off?"

"No. When we told you the High Council tried to pit us against one another, we meant it." Jey's voice grew quiet. "He had found someone, and they were joined. They were happy, had a baby. A girl. He kept them hidden as well as he could, but I knew where they lived. I'd visited many times. I'd held his daughter."

He rubbed his eyes. "The Council called me in for a private meeting."

I knew all about private meetings. I clenched my hands on my lap to keep them from shaking. Lunch churned in my stomach. I could see the blue creature, hear its abrasive voice in my head, feel its hard shell pressed against my cheek, its claws digging into my back. The digestive acids burned my skin and its putrid stench filled my nose.

"The Council wanted to know how I rated Merkief's loyalty to them. They wanted to know about his family and if they posed a security risk. I answered their questions. Then they sent me on a contract to take care of a minor dignitary on Rok."

Jey clasped the edge of the table as though he wanted to fling it across the room. "After I filed completion on the contract, I went to the little house I'd picked up on Karin and dropped into bed. Merkief and I had been arguing over policies between Artor and Jal for weeks, so when I got a message from him through my link, I ignored it."

His voice broke. "I'd barely fallen asleep when the security grid went off. My eyes snapped open to see Merkief shoving a pulse pistol in my face. He rammed his way into my brain and made me see what they had done, what he thought I had done."

Had I found a way to remain in the High Council's service, it could have been either of them offering information on Stassia or Daniel, thinking they were doing their duty to the Council. Kryon didn't act against Kryon. But the High and Mighties weren't us. They'd made that abundantly clear. Good operatives followed orders and didn't ask questions no matter what the contract was.

"Was it Kess?" I asked. "You said they are feeding information to him."

"I don't know." He got to his feet and turned away. "Oh gods, Vayen, the blood, the baby. Merkief thought I'd killed them. He thought I would do such a thing."

I couldn't imagine what Jey and Merkief had seen, nor did I want to. Ever.

"I'm sure the Council planted that thought in his head, if not directly, through more subtle means. He wouldn't have leapt to that conclusion on his own."

They'd been close friends, and though I suspected the duties I'd thrust upon them had fractured that to some degree, I still didn't think Merkief would leap to Jey as his number one suspect. Clearly he'd not been sure, or he'd have pulled the trigger. But blinded by grief and with a severed bond, I couldn't fault him for being blind to the Council's manipulations.

"You didn't see him before. Before it happened." Jey's voice was ragged. "Dealing directly with the Council changed him. He's not made of the same stone you are. You became the position, thrived in it, embraced it. He was never meant to bear the weight of the Council's demands."

"It changed me too, you know."

Jey shrugged. "Kazan changed you. The High Council merely finished the job. I got to work with you, but Merkief never had the benefit of that gradual lead-in. You just dropped the Narvan in our laps and disappeared."

"If I had managed to stay, to hide Anastassia—with her link removed and the Council still considering her a loose end in need of tying up—her death could be on either of your shoulders in the same way Merkief's family ended up on yours."

He looked at me with a condemned man's eyes. "So you consider that my fault too?"

"Not intentionally. But had you given the Council information on her or Daniel that led to their deaths, I'd have pulled the trigger without question."

"If you'd never left, Merkief and I wouldn't be in this position. His family would still be alive. I wouldn't have their blood on my hands. He would have been the one to step away to be with his family. Not you. You were supposed to stay. Kess respected you enough to have minded his own business. The Council would have never bothered to look in his direction."

I slammed my fist on the table. "And Anastassia would be dead. Would that be better? Would you rather have her blood on your hands?"

His jaw tightened. "No, of course not, but it was going to be you and me running the Narvan. You'd just not admitted that to her yet. That much I do remember."

The old Jey, the hulking-Jalvian-who-hadn't-liked-me Jey, stalked forward. "Dammit, Vayen, it was Kazan's time to step back. It was your time to be in charge. Our time. You knew how to handle the Council, Kess, and all the rest of it."

"I told you, she wouldn't have survived on her own and even if I'd forgotten a few hours or days, I'd still be bonded to her."

"You buried it before. I'm sure you could have done it again," he said.

"I'd planned on it, but the Council fucked up that option too. What about when she died on Minor, if she even made it that far? Would you really want to see me in Merkief's place? He handled a broken bond so well."

Jey halted his approach. "I don't have a magic answer. Every option is shit." His fists clenched.

I rather hoped he'd take a swing at me. This wasn't the practice mat. I'd been frustrated when we were downstairs, but now I was irate and the surging energy inside me wanted an outlet.

Jey's voice went flat. "We should get to Artor to get your link."

Home. The thought swirled around in my head, and I savored it. I'd resigned myself to never seeing Artor again as part of the cost of saving Stassia. I'd also come to accept that I'd never host an implant again. Now, I was getting both things in one day.

I blew my anger out my nose with a heavy exhale. There would be time for that later—when I was better equipped to do something with it and had a more deserving target in front of me, be it Merkief, Kess, or the High and Mighties themselves.

৵

Jey Jumped me into what I recognized as the heart of the University, depriving me of the chance to see the deep blue Artorian sky over my head once more.

"Merkief set up a new jump point inside for us. He didn't want to chance you being seen yet."

"Remind me to thank him for that later." After I finished beating the crap out of him for whatever he'd said to stir up trouble between me and Stassia.

The maze of hallways were just as I remembered them, and the guards we encountered took a look at Jey and waved us through. I followed him to a small, square room, just big enough for a single cot and a chair.

"Sorry for the lack of opulence. This room was easier to secure," he said.

"How long will I have to wait?"

"The LEs be here for you soon. Why don't you get ready? I'll step outside." Jey left me alone and took up guard duty in the hall. His boots shuffled on the tiles.

I got undressed, slipped on the loose-fitting robe and sat on the bed. Within the next eight hours, I'd wake up with a new blank link implant. It would take a time to reestablish all the connections I'd had before, but I'd have the ability to Jump right away. I was getting my life back. My pulse raced.

Why was I so excited? My conscience warred with my ambition. I didn't want this, not with the cost that came with it, anyway.

A Link Expert came in with an assistant who went about getting me prepped while the LE explained the procedure and what I would feel afterward. He acted as if it were my first time. Wealthy businessman, Isnar K'turoc was getting a link implant—a nobody from Veria Minor, off in the distant Verian Cluster. If either of them wondered why Jey was watching over me, they kept their questions to themselves.

By the time I'd reached the operating room, I was half-sedated. The last thing I was aware of was that the room wasn't the same one where Stassia and I had been attacked years before. Thankful for that, I fell into a dreamless sleep.

⁊

When I woke, I found Jey sitting beside me in the little room. His eyes were distant, as if he were deep within his link. Had I been in his place, I'd likely be doing the same. I distinctly remembered there had been no downtime for those who advised the Narvan.

I let him be and tried out my new link. Like a welcome wave of cool water on a hot day, networks washed over me. It took some digging but slowly I started to reconnect with my old life. Credit accounts, inquiries from old acquaintances and contacts that had been waiting for my attention before my supposed death filtered in as I worked. Records, maps, anything I wanted to search for, it was all back within my grasp.

And the ability to Jump.

I closed my eyes and pictured the foyer of my home—the missing chip of paint on the front door where Daniel had thrown a toy, the security pad on the wall beside it and the rug with the red juice stain mostly hidden in the pattern of grasses. I willed myself to go there.

Jey's heavy hand landed on my chest, breaking my concentration.

"Impatient bastard. You should give yourself a few hours before you try to Jump. You just got the damned implant for Geva's sake."

I shoved his hand away. "You said you wouldn't stop me from going home."

He crossed his arms and looked me over, clearly thinking I was crazy. "If you expect me to keep my word, I expect you to keep yours. My place, tomorrow morning. No excuses. If I have to waste my time hunting you down, you'll be spending even more time on your ass than you did today."

I closed my eyes and Jumped.

⁊

A small body barreled into me. "Dad!" Daniel wrapped his arms around my legs and squeezed tight.

In light of the operation just hours before and completing my first jump in years, dizziness overtook me. I pried Daniel off before I collapsed on him and lurched my way to the couch.

Stassia hovered over me. "Are you all right?"

"I just need to lie here a minute." Or for the rest of the night. My aching body melted into the soft couch.

"Good, because I need you on your feet so I can knock you on the floor."

"Jey did that enough already." I covered my face with my arms to block out the lights. "Where's Merkief?"

"He left about an hour ago." Tension pulled her voice taut. "He had a lot to say."

At least he was gone. I wasn't up to facing him just then.

She paced the length of the couch, her feet marking a steady rhythm as she stepped off the rug onto the hard floor at each end.

I knew I was in real trouble when she sent Daniel upstairs to watch over Ikeri, who I could hear playing in her room. Giving up the hope of recovering in peace, I sat up and faced her.

"I told you I didn't want Merkief here."

"And what did you expect me to do about it?" She glared. "I told him to leave. Repeatedly. Beyond that, I couldn't exactly gun him down in front of the kids or Jump the three of us to safety."

She had a point.

"I need to move you and the kids somewhere Jey and Merkief don't know about. I don't want a repeat of today." Or the past. If the High Council got it in their heads to question Merkief or Jey about me and my family, would they answer? Would they have a choice?

"I'm going to find somewhere safe for you tomorrow."

"Uproot the kids? I can't just leave, I have obligations here."

She sounded far too much like Sonia when I'd yanked her from the life I'd ruined. And then I'd fed her to the blue creature. Her death was on my shoulders just like Merkief's family was on Jey's.

"I know, but your clients will have to get by. The kids will adapt. You know what we have to do, Stassia. Next time the unexpected visitor might not be Merkief. Or maybe it will, and he'll have a less friendly agenda."

"His agenda wasn't all that friendly today." Her pacing picked up speed. She pulled off her neckband and shook it in my face. "Did you assume we were joined because I wear this?"

"No. That was Chesser's gift to you, not mine. I made it quite clear that my giving that to you had nothing to do with joining. As if you would have accepted it if it had."

She set the neckband on the table on her way past and resumed her route. Her neck appeared bare without it. She'd worn it since we'd arrived on Minor when she'd found it in the bag I'd packed for her.

"You and I were rarely clear," she said through clenched teeth.

"I never thought of it as a joining gift between us. If people here saw it and assumed we were, then that further helped our cover."

"So our being together is all about cover?" Her green eyes narrowed. "This is our life dammit! Or is it just mine? Perhaps to you, it has always been a cover."

"What do you expect me to say to that? I have a job here, just like you. Hells, I was the one asking you for another child! Does that sound like I'm biding my time?"

Damned Merkief, barging in here trying to make up for his own issues by supposedly fixing ours and then demanding I walk away from her in the same fucking breath.

"No, it doesn't." Stassia collapsed into the chair opposite me, staring at the band on the table.

"I tried to ask you about joining before, but you didn't want to hear a word of it, even here," I gestured to our house, "away from everything. I would have never considered asking were we still in the Narvan, but we aren't. No one knows who we are. It would just be between you and me."

I shifted around, hoping for a more comfortable position, at least physically. Her intense gaze seemed to be teetering on the edge of actually listening or deciding how many nights I'd be on the couch this time.

"From your extreme opposition, I gathered it wasn't something you felt was important between us, and I was willing to let it rest," I said quickly.

"Is it?"

I wished we could have had this conversation years ago, without Merkief laying on the guilt and threats, without my having to leave, and without my head throbbing and every muscle in my body aching.

"If we lived on Artor, it would mean we'd share social benefits, our children would be legal citizens, we'd be respectable, we'd be officially bound on record, which is what Merkief is looking for."

"But we're not on Artor," she said.

"No. We're not."

Her face softened. "We don't need the benefits of your government. We've got plenty of credits. And we've never been respectable, in a society sort of way, have we?"

Still unsure if I was talking myself into a trap, I tried a hesitant smile. "No?"

"Our children will never be legal citizens, will they? What with my not being Artorian and both of us being dead and all." A smile tugged at her lips.

"Probably not," I said. "And being dead also negates the whole legal record aspect, so Merkief would have to deal with it."

"So this comes down to your crazy bond again, doesn't it? Does it demand that we get joined?"

"Is that what Merkief told you?"

She shook her head and sighed. "He told me a lot of things. Mostly ranting and raving about us not following the traditions of your people, and how either I was defying them to spite you or you were turning your back on them." She stared at her hands. "You've noticed how different he is?"

"Hard to miss, yeah."

"I never imagined he'd be this way. He was the optimistic one, smiling and joking. Not that we didn't argue now and then but he was respectful about it. When he was angry, he was the silent treatment type, not outright furious, not like this."

Stassia could handle herself in the face of pretty much anything, including a raging Merkief; I knew that from experience. But that didn't mean I liked that she'd had to endure whatever he'd said. Or how he'd said it. I flexed my fingers, attempting to remain calm. Me getting angry wasn't going to help. Not until I had Merkief alone, anyway.

"Did he tell you about his family and what happened?"

Her gaze wavered. She nodded.

A fulfilled bond broken, would it be more devastating than if something were to happen to her today? I wasn't sure if that's what Merkief intended for me to find out, or if he merely felt that by us not joining, he'd lost his family for us to run off for nothing sincere. Did we cheapen his loss or was I going to pay for it? Only time would tell.

"If you don't want to, I'm fine. I've said from the start that I didn't expect that of you. Not to mention, you made it quite clear since that first day I walked in on you and Chesser arguing that this was never what you wanted."

"I certainly owe you for all you've done for me. So if it means that much to you..."

Not the owing again. My stomach clenched.

"I don't want you to join with me because you feel like you *owe* me. I had my link removed, turned my back on the High Council and walked away from the Narvan to keep you safe. That was my choice. I'm not going to guilt you into this or make you feel like it's something I'm going to resent you for if you don't want to do it."

I found myself getting rather worked up despite the fact that I kept repeating 'it doesn't really matter' over and over in my head.

She'd accepted my bond to her before we'd disappeared, but we'd never completed the ritual. Half the reason, if not more, she'd even accepted the bond in the first place was because she had needed protection for Daniel. And I hadn't given her a choice in the matter when we'd run off to our new lives on Minor.

She studied me for a long moment. "This is a big deal to you isn't it?"

"I'm good with what we've got. It's far more of a big deal to Merkief."

This wasn't at all how I'd imagined this conversation happening in all the times I'd played it out in my head, but at least she was still talking to me.

"You're still a terrible liar, but I appreciate you sticking to our agreement." Stassia shook her head slowly and smiled. "I suppose the past few years have worked out well enough for us, and to be honest, you may have changed my mind. Slowly, but still. We had a rough start, but this is better than I thought it would be."

I'd changed her mind? Maybe Geva had a little mercy for me after all.

"We might as well make it official and get Merkief off our backs so he'll leave us alone," she said.

"Stassia, our joining might make him less angry, but I highly doubt it would get him to leave us alone."

She got up and came over to sit next to me. "Less angry means more reasonable. We can both work on him." She looked at me expectantly. "So let's do this. Gift away."

I wanted to freeze that moment and remember it forever.

That was it, the one thing I'd been waiting to hear for so many years, even if the motivations behind it weren't for the typical reasons. For a second, things between us were as perfect as I could imagine them to be, given who we had been and were now. I took a deep breath, savoring the warm feeling of being complete. Then I let the second go.

"I used my chit to replace Chesser's joining gift. I don't have one of my own."

"So we'll call it yours then. Not a big deal."

"That's not how it's done."

"Oh come on, who cares?" she asked.

"Merkief will care." And really, if we were going to do this, so did I. Chesser had chosen the neckband for her, not me.

She wrapped her arms around my shoulders. "Then you'll have to figure out a way to make it work that will satisfy him."

"I suppose I could convince a jeweler to make a new gift for me under my name, but it would set off alarms in the governmental system because I've already had the correction procedure. Not to mention that it could take weeks for them to finish a gift. These men are busy, and I need to train with Jey. For all Merkief's ranting about our joining, I doubt he'll offer me any downtime to make it happen."

"Oh come on! You're Vayen Ta'set. You'll figure something out."

Hearing my real name uttered from her lips after all this time, and in such a playfully provoking way, I couldn't help but grin.

"Are you sure?"

The kiss that followed was all the confirmation I needed.

Chapter Four

I left Stassia sleeping in bed and slipped out for my second day of training with Jey. It was better than the first, but I had a long way to go. By the time we stopped for lunch, Jey looked suitably worn, which made me feel better about my efforts.

"Why don't you spend the rest of the day getting back up to speed on the Narvan? I have a few meetings I need to attend in person, but I'll be back by dinner. We can get back to work then."

It seemed I wouldn't be getting a good night's sleep beside Stassia this time. As soon as he left, I took the opportunity to dig into the details of Rok.

The Jalvian-ruled planet had been in Jey's hands when I left, and from the news feeds and government reports, it appeared to be doing well enough, if not excelling, at least maintaining. I didn't expect more in light of the issues with Kess and the High Council.

The one thing I really wanted was a report on Cragtek, but other than the legal front I'd set up, they didn't exactly publish public reports or statements on the information I wanted to know. I'd seen to the policies on hiding their data myself—changing codes and procedures every couple weeks. I was years out of the loop.

There was only one way to learn my standing with Cragtek. I had to go there. In person, I could surprise them and get a truthful reaction from the start.

But where to Jump to? The warehouse seemed like a bad

idea. Too much could have changed there, and I didn't know the employees like I once had. They'd likely shoot for my head first and identify me later. My best option was the office I'd kept there. That was secure. Or it had been. If it was still even there and hadn't been turned over to someone else.

I checked the contents of my armored coat, made sure it was latched shut, and Jumped to Rok.

Since I wasn't still standing in Jey's house on Jal with a pounding headache, I could only assume the Jump worked and that the pitch black place I found myself in was my old office.

"Lights."

The cold glow of artificial light filled the room. Before I'd left, I hadn't had much chance to appreciate the repair efforts since the Council faction had blown my original furnishings to bits. Uncertain of everything as I was, I very much appreciated the familiarity of the room. The Moriekian marble of my desktop and the vid terminal that sat on it showed no sign of dust. My high-backed, black prantha hide chair sat in the same position, as if I'd just gotten up. The Artorian weaving that hung on the wall behind my desk reminded me of the sunset colors of home. My couch was well worn, the only original piece in the room. I'd spent many a night on it when not speaking to Kazan—back before I'd known her as Anastassia, or intimately as Stassia and then as necessity dictated, Rhaine.

The thought of Stassia brought a smile to my face. She would love to see my office, one of the small parts of me I'd managed to keep private during all our time together. My space. I would have loved to share it with her now, knowing beyond a doubt that she no longer posed any threat to me. But there were too many other threats that did, and I wasn't willing to leave our kids with someone else to give her a private viewing. That couch also had its share of bullet holes and blood.

I needed my family safe. I opened the door.

A single guard stood halfway down the hall, between the six rooms that separated Gemmen's office from mine. He raised his gun and shouted a warning as he fired.

The bullet hit my coat, driving the pinpoint impact into my chest but failing to penetrate the armor. I'd forgotten how much that hurt.

I held up my empty hands and shouted loud enough that I hoped others who might recognize me could hear. "Is Gemmen here?"

He raised his gun a little higher. "Don't move or I go for your head."

It was good to see Cragtek employees still took security seriously and were prepared for the likes of me, who might make an unexpected appearance. I'd made sure all of our security force had access to black-market projectile weapons. Legal-issue stunners did little good in instances like this.

"What's going on out here?" Gemmen's door flew open. The barrel of a gun preceded the silver-haired man whose shoulders were hunched further forward than I remembered.

His gaunt and creased face paled as recognition lit blue eyes that had lost their luster. He gestured for the guard to lower his gun and slid his own into the holster on his thigh.

"You're dead."

"Not exactly." I lowered my hands.

"Can we go inside?" I nodded to his office. "I'd rather not be seen just yet."

Gemmen turned to the guard. "Get Gamnock then return to your post."

The guard nodded and jogged off.

"Let's have a seat, shall we?" Gemmen motioned me into his office. "We have some catching up to do."

I sat across from his desk and scanned the chaos of datapads, hand-written notes, and the edge of a report I could barely make out on his vid. Nothing jumped out at me as a solid indication of how Cragtek stood.

He sat back, resting his empty hands on the desk. He wore no armor and his shirt did little to hide the fact that his once strong arms had grown thin. Veins stood out on the backs of his hands. I didn't remember Gemmen being old. Past his prime maybe, but never old.

My mouth went dry and explanations to cover my absence vacated my mind. Gemmen had never seemed to age since the day Stassia had introduced me to him. But here he was, looking frail, and now that the shock had subsided, tired.

"You were dead," he said with a hollow voice. "Merkief, Jey, they were both so torn up about it. They wouldn't have lied about something like that. Couldn't have put on that convincing of a show. And they knew I could keep a secret. You knew." His hands trembled. "Why?"

Gemmen didn't know about the High Council, no one outside Kryon did. I'd died and left the company we'd built up together, his homeworld, his star system, to be plagued with problems while Kess clashed with Jey and Merkief. Yet another person with a legitimate grudge.

"To protect Kazan. I was here. You gave me the memory wipe drug the Fragians use. You took one yourself." I was sick of trying to explain my actions. I left it at that. It should have been enough. For all of them.

"She's alive too?"

"Is this room secure?"

He scowled. "Of course it's secure."

"I need a safe place. A very safe place. Somewhere I can hide some very important people until I find somewhere better."

Now he looked really offended. "Better than our security? We haven't slipped just because you died. We still have our own families to protect."

"Then I hope you can handle protecting mine."

"Your family, is it?" His scowl wavered and turned into a full-fledged smile.

"That's all you need to know for now."

He nodded. "I thought seeing you alive would be reason enough for celebration, but this news is even better. I never imagined you would settle down. With Kazan? How many children? Am I a grandfather or an uncle? I should get to be one or the other, you choose. When can I meet them?"

Seeing someone honestly happy at my good fortune made it hard not to let the relief wash over me and spill everything he wanted to know. But he was just one man and there too many who would not share his joy. I needed to keep my guard up, even here.

"Two children. How soon can you have a location ready?"

A patterned knock sounded on the door.

Gemmen called out, "Come in."

I turned to see a much younger version of Gemmen, his face smooth, eyes bright and blonde hair close-cropped just like the man who had to be his father.

"This is Gamnock. He's in the process of taking over Cragtek for me. Gamnock, this is Vayen Ta'set."

Gamnock raised a single blond brow and looked me over with the usual dismissiveness I'd come to expect as an Artorian from an unknown Jalvian.

"Wasn't he dead?"

Gemmen waved his skepticism aside. "We need to celebrate."

"Father, it's been years. You were positive he was dead, and now he's sitting here looking healthy as can be. You said-"

"Never mind what I said, and quit looking at me like I've lost my faculties. He's here and that's all that matters. Bring us a bottle and have a drink with us. You'll need to be in on this."

Gamnock gave me another once over, this one far more calculating than the last. "You're in luck. I was just going through our current acquisitions and located a case of this." He pulled out a bottle from under his arm and handed it to Gemmen. "I was heading here to show you the model for the newest proposed ship upgrades and thought I'd bring you a bottle."

Gemmen opened a cabinet behind his desk and pulled out three glasses. Gamnock poured the amber liquid and passed the glasses around.

"I'm glad your back, kid. I've missed you." Gemmen raised his glass and met my gaze with moist eyes.

While I'd missed Gemmen too, I wasn't exactly glad to be back. I managed a smile and poured a mouthful of the sweet liquor down my throat. Warmth rushed through me a second later.

"Is the suite available? We're going to have important guests," Gemmen asked Gamnock.

I shook my head. "I don't want anything special. Something easy to secure. Small and understated is better. Less attention that way."

"I think I can manage that," Gamnock said. "How soon?"

"Today. As soon as possible."

I didn't want to take any chances with another visit by Merkief or anyone else. Once he discovered I'd moved them, he might guess I'd come to Cragtek for help, but if security was as good as it used to be, I'd have enough time to find somewhere safer to move them before they were actually found.

Gamnock nodded. "I'll see to it." He pulled out a model ship from his pocket, slim and flat, it fit perfectly in the palm of his hand. He handed it to his father. "This is what the Artorian manufacturers are willing to give us. I'm still in negotiations over price.

"You shouldn't have to negotiate a price," I said.

I'd set a flat rate when I'd worked out the original deal with the Artorian University. Cragtek stole the tech and handed it over in return for the first choice of modified upgrades at a deep discount.

"Your deal died with you," Gamnock informed me. "I don't need another of your negotiations falling through when you decide to die again, leaving our company in the hands of a grief-stricken mess. I'll take care of this, just like I have with every other damned thing since you left."

Gemmen stared at his desk.

Gamnock tossed back the remaining contents of his glass. "So what exactly do I need to be in on? Are you expecting to walk back in and take Cragtek from me?"

"Hardly. I have bigger things to deal with. All I need from you is what I already asked for. If you decide you want my help with anything else, ask, and I'll do what I can. Right now, that's not very much since I'd prefer everyone thinks I'm still dead."

"Good," Gamnock said. "Give me two hours, and I'll have a security team in place and get you the location." He set the model on the desk in front of his father and left.

I finished my drink. "Looks like you're leaving the company in capable hands."

Hands that had little use for me, but I had little time for Cragtek at the moment so it didn't bother me too much. What did, was the man before me.

"Did you want to hand Cragtek over or did he make a play for it?"

"He stepped in for me when I needed time-" Gemmen cleared his throat. "He's been beside me ever since. There's really no need for me to be here anymore. Gamnock's got a handle on the business now. He gives me work to make me feel busy."

Gemmen gestured to the mess on his desk. "My wives want me to spend more time at home." He grimaced. "I never really expected to live long enough to retire."

"I know someone who would love to spend time with you that will not include nagging or complaining. She saves that for me."

His face lit up. "So it is her. You'll let me know as soon as you're settled in, won't you?"

"Of course. I need someone I can trust to keep an eye on this security team your son is setting up."

"You're just as bad as Gamnock, you know that? Trying to make an old man feel useful." He shook his head and chuckled.

"I better get going. Anastassia didn't know she was going to have to pack today."

"I'm glad I'm not you then." He waved me off. "Go on. I've got work to do."

⁓

"What do you mean we have to pack right now? You expect me to pack everything for us and two children in two hours?" Stassia stared at me like I was speaking Fragian.

"Not everything. Think of it as a long vacation."

Ikeri squeezed my hand. "Are you coming too, Daddy?"

"Yes, but I'll be at work a lot. You'll get to meet your grandfather though. He's very excited to see you tonight."

"Since when do they have a grandfather?" Stassia whispered.

I shrugged "Gemmen."

She grinned as if this upheaval suddenly meant nothing compared to gaining access to a piece of her previous life.

"Let's pack!" She herded the kids upstairs.

I walked around the kitchen and living room, packing up a few small things so our temporary home would feel a little more normal for the kids. It reminded me of the last time I'd had to pack, when I hid Stassia and Daniel here for their own safety. Now I was bringing them back to the Narvan.

"You want anything else packed from the weapons chest?" Stassia called down to me.

"I've got what I need for now. Don't worry about my stuff. I'll come back for it later." I already didn't know if I could handle Jumping all three of them and their things. I'd not done a complex Jump since I'd given up my old link.

The kids had never Jumped before and would likely feel sick on the other side, but I didn't want to leave them here alone while I Jumped Stassia first. At least Gemmen could help them when we got all there.

I contacted him through my link. "Meet me in my office in five minutes."

"Will do," Gemmen said.

When Stassia finished, she stood before me with the kids. Several bags sat at her feet. She looked at me and shook her head.

"We're ready," she said, almost daring me to be foolish enough to do what I was about to do.

I took them all in, every detail of them and of the bags, and

formed the Jump. We stepped out of the void and into my office.
I immediately went to the couch and collapsed onto it. What the
hells had I been thinking, Jumping the three of them and several
bags at once? My head pulsed with every heartbeat. Daniel and
Ikeri looked a bit pale, but I was the one who retched into the
garbage can Stassia thrust at me.

"You're going to have to slow down," she said quietly.

"I can't afford to." I shoved the can aside and sat up. The room
spun.

Stassia sat next to me, half holding me up. "Find a way."

"I'd love to. Any suggestions?"

"Not at the moment." She threaded her fingers around mine
and looked around the room. "So, this is nice. I always wondered
what it looked like."

Daniel hopped up into my chair and tapped away at the terminal. I hoped he wasn't pulling up anything he shouldn't be seeing.
Ikeri wandered over and climbed into my lap. She snuggled up
against me as the door opened and Gemmen walked in.

He froze in the doorway. "Kazan?"

Stassia extracted herself from me and stood. Her loose-fitting,
ivory clothes softened the sleek, muscled body underneath and
her unbound, light brown hair hung to her waist.

"You were expecting someone else?" she asked.

"No, it's just...you...I didn't expect..."

Was she blushing? I nearly laughed out loud despite still feeling sick to my stomach.

His brow wrinkled. "Why can't I-"

"No link," she said. "Let's just go with Anastassia, shall we? I'll
never be up for being Kazan again."

"Look at you." His gaze fixed on the band at her neck and then
leapt to the children. "Look at them!" He started toward Daniel
and stopped. "They're not armed are they?"

Stassia laughed and so did I.

"They're a little young for that yet," she said.

"Never know with you two for parents," he winked and
crouched beside Daniel. They began to chat like long lost friends.

As much as I enjoyed seeing this side of Gemmen, and Stassia
beaming next to me, I really wanted to lie down and there were
too many people in my office. "Is that house ready?"

"Yes." Gemmen stood slowly, stretching his back as he did
so. "Gamnock has assured me it's all set for you. We can take the

tunnels if you'd prefer."

"Sounds good." The less we were seen, the better. I picked up half the baggage and Gemmen took the rest.

With Daniel oogling every crate and scrap of metal and plas as we skirted the edge of the main warehouse, and Ikeri in Stassia's arms, we followed Gemmen as unobtrusively as possible. Thanks to the company workers' families being housed nearby, the appearance of a man and his family didn't raise many eyebrows. Still, my skin crawled with each passing glance.

Once we entered the tunnels below the complex, we encountered very few people. Robotic movers shuffled inventory between storerooms as they buzzed by us.

"Those are just like yours," Daniel said to me as if that revelation was a great disappointment.

"It's a common model." Not that I was about to explain that the ones I had in my warehouses were several versions older than the ones here. The fewer clues anyone else had about where we had been the better. I still wanted to go back and retrieve my things, and hopefully, once this was over, return to live there, or at least on Minor somewhere. It was home to our children. Our home.

"But you don't have those," he pointed to the crate of thick milky-colored cables on the mover passing us as we stood off to the side.

"I suppose I don't."

As if he had a running tab on the company inventory. Although, maybe he did. Daniel had come to work with me a lot, mostly to keep him busy while Stassia had been occupied with Ikeri or her clients.

"So how far is it to this house of yours?" asked Stassia as she walked beside Gemmen.

"Ten minutes or so, well within the compound walls, but far enough from immediate activity to offer some privacy."

I couldn't imagine Stassia stuck inside a house with the kids all day. She'd want to send them outside to run off their excess energy and to have a few hours to herself. I wouldn't be able to take either of them off her hands for the foreseeable future.

"Air surveillance?" I asked.

"The usual. We still have the government to deal with, though not as much as before. We've managed to plant a few of our own in positions as they've opened up over the past few years. That's helped keep the eyes off us, even with the precautions you put in place before you left," said Gemmen.

"Good to know. Anyone high?"

"Mostly assistants, aides, a few secondary positions. Nothing too ostentatious, just enough to lose reports or alter figures if we need it."

"Whose idea was that?"

"Gamnock's."

"His son," I said to Stassia in response to her unspoken question.

Industrial lighting filled the tunnels with a harsh glow, nothing like the calm sunlight of Minor. I found it oddly exciting to see Stassia's hair lit by a similar light as on the ship, as Sere, as so many of the places we'd worked together in the past. For a few moments, she could have been Kazan. Except she wasn't wearing her armor, nor was she armed, and her hair was free of a braid. And she was carrying our daughter. I sighed.

"It's not too much farther," Gemmen announced.

We paused before a lift entrance. Movers buzzed past us, oblivious to our presence except as obstacles to be avoided. The doors slid open and we all squeezed into the tube that would have comfortably fit two men. An uprush of air signaled that we'd shot up a level. The movement did nothing to ease the turmoil in my stomach. I couldn't afford to be sick again.

"Gemmen, you wouldn't happen to have a stim on you?"

"Gamnock insisted I stop taking them." He dug into his pants pocket and pulled out a tiny tin. "I cut back. Close enough, right?" He chuckled as he handed me one.

"Close enough for me." I tossed it back and swallowed, savoring the rush that sped through me seconds later.

The doors opened, revealing a yard of red-brown grass and a winding walk that threaded through rows of buildings. At the end of the walk stood a lone structure. It was small, smaller even than the house on Frique.

"That's it?" I asked.

"You said…"

"I know. Let's just get inside." Even with friendly surveillance from above, I didn't like being out in the open. Not here, not yet.

"Is that our new house?" Daniel asked.

"For a little while. Stay on the walk." Stassia directed his wandering feet back onto the plascrete with a tug on his arm.

"We get to play on the grass at home."

"This isn't home," she said firmly.

Did she want it to be? She'd sure acted happy enough to pack, but now our bonded connection didn't yield anything solid from her one way or the other.

"So this is it." Gemmen opened the front door.

We followed him inside. The imported wood flooring echoed our footsteps throughout the main room which acted as both a dining and common room. A set of stairs led upward and two doors on either side of the big room led to what looked like a bedroom to the left and a bathroom to the right. Two men stood between them.

"This is Neko and Harmon," Gemmen said. "They'll be your guards, one per shift. They're both linked. We don't have many men who are, but I figured you'd want that. You can also contact me if you need anything, or Gamnock, but I'd start with me."

One guard on duty. It wasn't enough. Not near enough. I didn't know either of these men. That Gemmen vouched for them was one thing, but the fact that there were only two of them made me think that Gamnock didn't fully understand just who I was. Though, I supposed that was my fault. Gemmen didn't know either, but he'd always acted as though he'd guessed Anastassia and I were more than he knew for sure.

Gemmen and I set the bags on the floor. Stassia put Ikeri on her feet but held her hand. Daniel ran up the stairs.

His shrill voice called down, "There's only one room up here. I have to sleep with Ikeri?"

"For now," I said, wandering up the stairs after him. The second floor was only a small section of the main floor footprint, just enough to give us a little space from the kids. Not near enough room for an argument out of earshot. Maybe small was a good thing after all.

Someone had put two beds in the room. One was likely there previously while the other was new, the metal framing still shining.

The bedroom looked safe enough. I left Daniel to his exploring and went back down the stairs to join the others.

"I know it's small," Gemmen said. "But you said easier to secure was better."

Stassia eyed up every corner and surface as if mentally assigning a place to everything we'd brought with us. I had a feeling there wouldn't be any chance for me to have a single bit of space to myself, no little corner of chaos to set my mind at ease.

"It will do," declared Stassia as she turned to Neko and Harmon. "Which one of you is on?"

Harmon, a typical burly, young Jalvian stepped forward. Both men wore armored coats, though of what grade remained in question as did what weaponry they carried and their skill with it. He met her gaze with his bright blue eyes, cool and bland, a man just doing his job. This was the man who would be protecting my family while I was gone?

"Take Ikeri upstairs," I said.

Stassia cast me a questioning glance.

I put a hand in my pocket, one at my side that was merely a slit for weapon access.

She nodded and nudged Ikeri toward the stairs. "Let's go see what your brother is up to."

As she disappeared upward, the tension in the room rose. I pulled a gun from my coat in a long-missed fluid move that felt so natural, that for a moment, it was as if I'd never been away. I fired into Harmon's chest. A bullet flew at Neko a second later. Both men were knocked back against the wall, but they recovered in short order and found steady footing with guns in their hands in half-way decent time.

Gemmen waved his arms. "Could we not fill the house with bullet holes, please? Execs don't like bullet holes."

I kept my gun and gaze locked on the two guards. "I rather doubt you house many high-end buyers here."

"True, but still. The mid-grades aren't fans either."

"Then your men better be good at absorbing bullets because I'm not impressed. I thought you said they were good."

"Of course they're good. Their ours." Gemmen looked insulted.

"Do they have families of their own?"

Gemmen looked to Neko and Harmon. Harmon nodded. Neko shook his head.

"Got anyone important to you, Neko?" I asked.

He stepped forward. "A sister. Parents, the usual. Why?"

"If anything happens to my family, it happens to yours. Got it?"

They both nodded.

"Good." I turned to Gemmen. "Where would you prefer we used bullets because I'm not leaving until I am confident they can do their job."

Gemmen balked. "You think I'd leave Anastassia in incapable hands? Or those children?"

"No." I slid my gun back inside my coat. "But I don't think you realize how capable the hands are that I'm up against. Now, where can we go?"

I left Neko with Gemmen and followed Harmon back into the tunnels. He spent the next hour proving himself with assorted weapons and going hand to hand against another man we came across in the training room. Harmon wasn't Jey. He wasn't even near the old Merkief, but he was formidable enough that I felt he had a fighting chance against a Kryon member. At least enough of one that he could buy me time to get there to take the threat out. So fodder. Harmon made good fodder.

I figured I'd spent most of my first weeks at Anastassia's side in much the same capacity and I'd survived. He might too.

Harmon swapped places with Neko, sending him down to the training room to meet me. Neko may have been part Jalvian, but I couldn't guess what else littered his genes. Taller than me but lanky, with medium brown hair and green eyes, he didn't fit any immediate mold. His guttural accent placed him outside the systems I knew.

He folded his arms and narrowed his eyes. "What was that all about back there, firing at us like that?"

"Just seeing how fast on your feet you are."

"And?"

"Tolerable."

"I didn't really need any more bruises." He smacked himself in the chest. "This might be armor, but it still hurts like hell when I get shot at."

I laughed. "Get used to it."

"Look, I get that you want to appear important to the bosses around here, but if you think I'm going to stand for threats and getting shot at for your amusement, it's not going to happen. All I have to do is put a word into Gamnock and you'll find yourself without any guards at all. We're not playthings, dammit. Save the tormenting for your own employees."

I had Neko by the collar and slammed against the wall behind him before the man could make a move to stop me.

"Until a few years ago, I was the boss around here. I could very well be again if you and Gamnock don't give me what I need. Got it?"

Neko nodded.

"Good. You have half an hour to impress me or I'll find some-one else." I let him go.

He shook out his coat. "What if I say find someone else right now?"

I took a page out of Anastassia's threat manual. "You already know too much. I'd have to kill you."

Doubt floated in the depths of his eyes. He stood there staring, almost daring me to try.

"I'd rather not injure the man I'm relying on to guard my family unless I have to. That would mean I'd have to replace him and Gemmen said he was short on linked men. So I'd seriously consider your next move before you do something stupid."

"How do I know you're not just a big bag of threats?"

"You could find out, but I wouldn't recommend it."

Neko's gaze darted over the lumps inside my coat, taking in the slits like the one from which I'd drawn my gun earlier.

"Well then, let's see what impresses you," he said.

The wiry man turned out to be a whirlwind on the sparing mat, as his unlucky opponent discovered. He wasn't bad with a gun either. Satisfied that Gamnock hadn't saddled me with cast-offs, I established a link connection with Neko as I had with Harmon after his own demonstration. After I dismissed him, I returned to the house. If I didn't continue updating myself with the Narvan, Jey would know I'd been up to something when he returned.

Gemmen and Harmon looked up from the meal Stassia had set out for them. Ikeri and Daniel sat on either side of Gemmen, beaming with excitement. Stassia got up and came to meet me at the door.

"How are they?" she asked.

"No worse than me on day one."

She grimaced. "That's not good enough."

"Are you saying I wasn't good enough?"

Stassia snickered. "Affronted and smirks don't go together." She slipped her hand into mine. "Tell Gamnock we need more men."

"We do, but maybe it would be better to keep the knowledge of our being here to a minimum of people."

She bit her bottom lip and glanced at the table before turning back to me. "I suppose you're right. It's just that I-"

Inspiration hit me. "Yes, you. Train them. You're as out of

this as I am. Get back in there and show them what they need to know."

She dropped my hand and stepped back. "I can't. I'm not her anymore."

"An implant didn't make you Kazan. You did." I pulled her close and wrapped my arms around her. "Just because you can't Jump doesn't mean you can't fight."

"I didn't plan on just standing here, taking on bullets if we were actually attacked," she said.

"Then get yourself some decent backup. Gemmen can watch the kids for a couple hours a day. There's a gun range and training center accessible through the tunnels. I'm sure Gemmen could arrange a time for you to have a private session with Harmon and Neko."

Her lips brushed against my neck. "You think so?" A wave of very pleasant thought washed through our natural connection.

"Uh huh." If I hadn't had an audience, I would have sent the kids upstairs and fully revelled in what she'd started, but I settled for a kiss.

Stassia broke away, her eyes sparkling. "Weren't you feeling ill? Maybe you should go lie down."

"I'd love to, but I have to get back to Jey's."

"Hmm, yes. No rest for the wicked. I do remember that distinctly. You will be back tonight though, won't you?"

"If I can."

I kissed her again, very much wishing I didn't have to leave. It had been a long time since I'd had any aspect of her but Rhaine in my arms. Belatedly remembering we were in full view, I broke off before we got too carried away.

"Listen to your mother," I told Daniel, knowing he tested her at every opportunity. Stassia always seemed to ease off when it came to him. Keeping him in check fell to me.

Ikeri sprang up from her chair and wrapped her arms around my legs, the top half of her vanishing underneath my coat. That wasn't a particularly safe place for a three-year-old to be. I extracted my daughter from my otherwise hidden web of weaponry and knelt down to give her a proper hug. A feeling of peace washed over me, not as strong as the bond I shared with Stassia, but there as it always was when Ikeri was near. She smiled, dimples forming on her round cheeks.

"Be safe, Daddy," she said and then she climbed up in Gemmen's lap without hesitation.

I'd not expected the words of parting so often shared between me and Stassia before our lives on Minor to come from my daughter's lips. Maybe she'd overheard them. I stood up to see Stassia looking oddly at Ikeri and then me. I shrugged.

"I'll be back as soon as I can. Harmon, if anything comes up, contact me immediately." I left them and returned to Jey's house on Jal, praying he'd not discovered my absence.

Chapter Five

Jey found me on his couch, deep in my link as I researched all that had gone on in the Narvan during my absence. A kick to my leg alerted me of his presence. Once the information faded and I could focus on my real world surroundings, I discovered he didn't look happy.

"Where were you?" he asked.

"Catching up on the Narvan?"

"No shit. I mean earlier when I dropped by to check on you and found you gone. You weren't at your house, and neither was anyone else, interestingly enough."

"Huh." I stood.

He shoved me backward. I dropped back onto the couch.

"Cut the shit. Where the hells were you?"

I searched for a lie that he would want to hear.

"Putting my family somewhere safe. And if Merkief wants Anastassia and I to join so badly, the two of you have to allow me a little time to make that happen."

"So you were out shopping for your gift."

"Something like that, yes."

I stood again, this time making sure I was out of reach.

Jey grew distant for a moment. "Merkief doesn't see any mention of you on Artor."

"Oh Great Geva! Maybe no one saw me. Maybe I was inside, or just maybe I covered my tracks. How about that? If the two of you want my help, you're going to have to trust me a little."

He didn't look much happier, but he backed off.

"We'll let this one go, but check in before you take off next time. We can't have you off on your own, wandering the streets. What if someone killed you before you talk to Kess? We'd be no better off than before."

"I don't need a fucking babysitter."

Jey sighed. "Vayen, I get it, this isn't where you want to be, but please don't make this more difficult than it already is."

"Fine." At least it would be, until I had to Jump to Rok unexpectedly while one of them was hawking over me. "What's on the agenda for the rest of the day?"

"We need to go over the resources for the Narvan and figure out where we can satisfy the High Council, sell enough to finance the explorations they want us to make, and yet build up our fleets enough to keep Kess at bay. Oh, and the citizens can't notice that anything is different or riots will break out. We tried that. It was ugly."

"Just how I wanted to spend my evening." I settled back onto the couch.

We spent hours debating resource allocations. Merkief joined us shortly thereafter. There were moments, when we were deep in discussion, that he was the man I remembered. He even smiled a couple times as though he might have been grateful for my assistance. But every time I thought we were onto something good between us, his mood would change. I couldn't pinpoint what Jey or I had said to cause the shift. In the end, I tried to ride out the goodwill as long as I could, enjoying the companionship I had genuinely missed while it lasted.

Seven hours into it, I almost asked if Merkief ever slept but then I remembered my relentless couple years of work while dealing with Stassia being gone and kept my mouth shut. At least I'd gotten Stassia back. Merkief was alone. Painfully and miserably alone, and he didn't visibly regret taking that out on either of us.

"You're with me tomorrow," Merkief informed me when we'd hit a wall in our productiveness.

"I'll be back in the morning then." I consulted my link for the standard universal time. Four hours to sleep in my own bed before it was technically morning. Not long enough, but I'd take it.

"I'd suggest staying here. She won't miss you."

Damn, he'd taken a downward shift again. "What do you

mean by that?"

"You'd just wake her up getting there and wake her up leaving. Stay here," Merkief said.

"Maybe I don't want to."

"Then maybe you won't mind me accompanying you to wherever you hid your family."

I gritted my teeth and fought back the urge to express myself with my fists. Lucky for him, I wasn't confident of the optimal outcome of that quite yet.

"I have eyes on your house, and it's what I would have done," he said.

I felt his presence sidle up to mine over the link and our natural connection, attempting to skim my thoughts with quick, light probe. I slammed my defenses down.

"You were never subtle, were you?"

Merkief glared at me, looking very much like he'd enjoy getting in a few hits on me too.

Jey stepped between us. "Leave him alone, Merkief. He's helping us. That's what we need. Aggravating him is only going to slow us down."

"Of course you'd side with him." Merkief let out a growl and Jumped.

"Even when I help, I get shit. What's my incentive again?" I asked.

Jey shook his head. "You don't want to know."

"When you say it like that, you're probably right."

It was night on Rok anyway. Everyone would be asleep, and I really did need to rest. I dragged my tired ass to the bedroom. This one time, I'd let Merkief have his way.

The bots I'd reprogrammed were nearly done with their full cleaning of my room. Now it was too clean and not my space at all.

I wanted to leave a message for Stassia, but Daniel was sound asleep. There was nothing of vast importance to say that would necessitate using whichever guard was on duty, but it grated on me not to connect with her in any manner.

In the interest of attempting to get some quality sleep, I flipped the sliced mattress over and settled into the sagging middle for a restless few hours of trying not to think about what I was missing out on in my own bed with the deviously excited woman that I'd left.

Jey woke me up half an hour early to get some practice in. We hit the mat, and having knocked him down more than once, I felt good with the results.

"I think you're getting back to your old self," Jey said as he peeled himself off the mat.

"Slowly," I offered him a hand up. "Do you know what Merkief has in mind for today? I really do need to get to the jeweler to get my gift going, but I'll attempt not to piss Merkief off if I can help it."

"I would appreciate it." He grinned. "You're crazy, you know that? It would be utterly draining for me to Jump three people and baggage, and here you go doing it the day after you get your new implant."

"Not like I'd never used it before."

"But your tolerance has to be lower. Much lower. You're out of practice there too. Don't even try to fake it with me. I can see how tired you are. You used to live on a few hours of sleep. Now missing a single full night is killing you."

"I wouldn't go that far." Though, I wasn't surprised that my exhaustion showed.

He came at me again.

We wrestled hard for a few minutes before he pinned me.

"All right fine. I'm not used to this anymore, and I really didn't want to be."

He froze, then quickly helped me up. "He's here."

We went upstairs. I stopped in my room to grab my coat before meeting Merkief in the common room.

"So what are we up to today?" I asked.

"You're meeting with Kess."

My heart dropped to my feet. "Today? Now?"

Jey wasn't wrong. I was drained and tired. Very much so, in fact.

"The sooner the better. He's got men attacking Karin. Sabotage. Are you okay with that? Just sitting around here, shooting the shit with Jey while our people lose crops and factories go dark? I'm not. You had a deal with the man, call him off."

I looked to Jey, hoping for a voice of reason.

"He's not ready," Jey said.

"Tough."

Jey shook his head. "Do we really need to do this today?"

"Will tomorrow be better for you? How many days will people go hungry or production sit at a standstill while Mr. Not-quite-ready-yet takes another day to catch up?"

It sure didn't sound like Merkief cared if I lived through the attempt to patch things up with Kess. This was a matter of making me pay one way or the other. I had no idea what to do to make things right with him. As Jey had said, all my options were shit.

"Can I at least stop home first?"

"No," Merkief said.

"Come on. I'll be right back."

It killed me to think that I was nearly begging him for what I could take if I dared. But I didn't put it past one of them to grab me before I Jumped, or worse, pick up on where I was going and then my family wouldn't be hidden at all.

"What part of no, don't you understand?" Merkief's once friendly face had turned hard and implacable. "You have a job to do. We're leaving now."

He marched forward and grabbed my arm. The void swallowed us both.

I stood in the hallway in front of Kess's office at what had been the assassins guild. From the level of bustling activity in the hallway, I had a feeling he'd consolidated his endeavors.

"What do you expect me to do that you couldn't do?" I asked Merkief, hoping he'd snap out of this malicious streak before I did in fact get killed.

"Walk in there and make this end. Don't come back until you do." He Jumped, leaving me there alone.

Opening the connection to Kess that I'd formed back when we'd aligned to make Stassia disappear, I found myself faced with a wall. Blocked. I settled for knocking on the door.

It slid open with Kess standing behind his desk, a gun in his hand. He seemed mostly unchanged, his white-blonde hair still past the shoulders of what appeared to be a new deep blue armored coat. His wary stance and suspicious gaze was just as I remembered from our last in-person meeting.

"This is unexpected," he said with a slightly raised note.

"Tell me about it." I kept my hands empty and walked in.

"You shouldn't be here."

"I couldn't agree more."

"Don't sit. We're going somewhere else." He kept the gun in his hand, walked over, and slapped his other hand on my shoulder. The void swallowed me again.

I stepped out of the Jump into a dimly lit and deserted factory only Geva knows where. We eyed each other up.

"You're looking pretty good for dead."

"Thanks."

I noted he looked nearly as tired as I felt and was limping slightly on his left side. He was also heavily armed.

"How is she?" he asked.

"Next topic."

"Why are you here? I thought we had a deal?"

"We did. We do. However, there seem to be a few grey areas, and I'm here to make them black and white."

"So you're here to mediate for them."

I gathered my nerve and plastered on my work face. "Or end it, yes."

Kess smothered a snicker, shifting his position until he struck one that seemed to take the weight off his left leg. The gun remained in his hand. I wondered if I could get one out and fire before he took my head off. He was the only one with nothing to gain by keeping it intact.

"You're a bit late for that. I've got backers now. Powerful ones."

"I've heard. So do they. The three of you are doing the Narvan no favors while you play the High Council's games."

"Why the sudden interest? She toss you out?"

"You've got Merchess and the rest of the free territory beyond the Nebula. Why do you need the Narvan? Strike at Fragia. Expand in that direction. The High and Mighties should reward you for their destruction or assimilation," I said.

"You already played that card. The Narvan is a neat package which includes my homeworld. Why would I want Fragia when I could do something great for my own people?"

"But you're not doing anything great. You're making life miserable for the general populace."

"Only in the short term. Your friends are no better. You could just as easily throw in with me, silently of course," he offered.

"I don't think so." My hand hovered over one of the false pockets in my coat.

"If you wanted to do something for the Narvan, you would have stayed. You had the Council behind you. You had everything right in your hands but you let it all slip away. You left those two to blunder their way in and out of the Council's graces. The Narvan was stagnant. Your friends had their chance. The Council wasn't happy and they approached me. Me." He thumped his chest. "They asked me to make a move, and I am."

"Then make the right one and step aside."

"For them?" Kess laughed.

"For me."

What the hells was I saying? I couldn't take the Narvan back. Could I? I strangled the guilty, outspoken subconscious spark that had made those words slip off my tongue. If the Council had a third option, would they go for it? But how would I erase the last five years from memory? There wasn't enough of Gemmen's mind wipe drug for that, not reliably anyway. And dammit, I didn't want to forget. Not even for the good of the Narvan.

Kess's sputter of laughter broke through my racing thoughts.

"You can't just walk back in. It was your death that got me back into Kryon. Killing Kazan was just a bonus." He stepped forward. "Here's a piece of friendly advice since you did me that favor: Stay dead."

"What if I could get the High Council to overlook our charade? Would you be willing to work with me on this?"

"I don't know what kind of ego trip you're on, but the High Council doesn't even know you're alive." Kess shifted his weight again, keeping his gaze and gun on me at all times. "Do you really think they'll be overjoyed to learn you lied to them? You've been out of the limelight for years, out of contact, and out of the business. When was the last time you had a good fight? I dare bet it was before you vanished. Just how confident are you that you can hold your own against me?"

I didn't like where this was going. And no, I wasn't feeling all that confident. I had been hard pressed to hold my own with him on a good day. The only thing I had going for me at the moment was a rush of adrenaline, and while I had certainly missed that, it was no match for speed, talent, and skill.

Kess lunged at me. While I was able to jump aside, I belatedly realized he had still managed to sink a knife into my right hand. I groaned and pulled the thin blade out. I wasn't near as accurate with my left, and he knew it. With grim determination, I set out to prove to myself that I still had it.

Under a hail of gunfire, my mind and body began to remember what they were supposed to be doing. I did manage to repay him a few bruises but I wasn't at all pleased with my performance. Going at it with Jey and firing on the two hapless Cragtek guards was one thing, but a rapid-fire, every second counts, fight for your life attack from an enemy was quite another.

As I spun around to find better cover, two bullets sunk into my leg, making a fine bloody mess of my thigh. It gave way. I dropped down ungracefully, banging my head on an unforgiving pipe and wrenching my arm around as I tried to catch myself. All in all, not one of my finer moments.

Kess's voice rang out, "I'm going to give you one chance. After this, all favors are off."

His footsteps drew closer. "Jump now and stay dead. You've been out of it for too long. Go back to whatever life you've made for yourself, and for Geva's sake, stay out of this."

His footsteps were just on the other side of the hulking machinery I'd fallen behind. Spots floated in front of my eyes and my leg and hand burned. Feeling none too happy with myself, I knew he was right. I couldn't hope to take him out in my condition.

I Jumped to the ship, not wanting anyone else to see what a failure I had been. Merkief sat at the terminal, as if he had been waiting for me.

"I take it that didn't go well?" he asked.

My patience was gone, my ego sorely bruised, and I hurt. "Shut the fuck up and get the tank going."

I stripped off my ruined pants along with everything else. It was a blessedly short dip as far as time in the tank went. After only a couple hours of recovery sleep, I found myself no better off than the last time I'd woke up in that damned bed.

Merkief sat beside me. He called Jey in once he snapped out of his link enough to realize I was awake. The only consolation was that his scowl was gone.

"Kess pulled out of Karin," Jey announced. "Whatever you did, it worked at least to some degree."

Merkief nodded. "I knew you could do it."

I sat up and rubbed the tank crust from my face. "Don't get too excited. He's probably just regrouping. He knows me well enough to realize I'm not going to walk away until this is settled."

"I'm glad we have an understanding." Merkeif appeared at ease as he clapped me on the shoulder.

"He's not backing down. He's got the Council behind him. Which of you has their majority vote?" I looked between them.

"It's a pretty even split. Our half knows we have at least some of your knowledge," Merkief said. "The other half knows Kess worked with Kazan so he's also in the general know."

"But he was out of the loop for years before he returned to Kryon work. He never advised the system other than in a supporting role. Did they really welcome him back with open arms?" I asked.

Jey nodded. "He killed you. That was a pretty impressive feat in the Council's eyes. Enough so that they were willing to overlook his hiatus."

That outspoken spark reared up again, demanding my attention. Having given it voice once seemed to have given it strength. I didn't like what it kept saying, but it felt like the right thing to do.

"So who would I have to kill to have them overlook mine?"

Merkief's mouth dropped open, and if I'd thought he'd looked pissed before, it paled compared to the fury on his face now. "You can't come back. That option isn't even on the table."

I slipped out of the bed and put some distance between us. Jey moved in, as though he was ready to break us apart.

"You left. You walked away," Merkief's face turned red as he spoke.

I'd never seen him like this. I was glad Jey was close by because I had no idea what to expect. Even dealing with Stassia's mercurial moods during our first couple years on Minor hadn't prepared me for the intensity of these shifts.

"You don't get to waltz back in and become the Council's chosen one again. That's over."

"So you merely want me to hand the Narvan to you a little more neatly? Did I make you work too hard the first time around? I seem to recall Kazan leaving us in a huge ass lurch, and we came out of it shining."

"You came out shining. We were stuck in your shadow."

"Speak for yourself," Jey muttered.

Merkief turned on him. "And I suppose you have this all worked out with him. It'll be the two of you at the helm again just like old times. And me? I'll take the back seat. Well, you know what? I've lost too much to sit back and take that shit again."

He spun back to me. "You threw the Narvan at us and we're keeping it!"

"Then have the Narvan. Slowly let it slip into Kess's hands like you've been doing. Maybe the Council will take one or both of you out once things tip far enough in his favor, or maybe they'll let you watch it all fall away until Kess does the job himself. I'll gladly go back to my little house on Minor and let you two get back to it."

I half expected to see shattered teeth fly out of Merkief's mouth from how hard his jaw was clenched, but eventually, he swallowed and the fire in his eyes died back.

"Maybe you aren't ready to finish the job yet. You've got two weeks to work with Jey and then you'll try again."

"To actually take Kess out? I don't know that two weeks is enough," I said.

"Make it enough. And take care of things at home. You'll want everything in order before you face Kess again."

A chill ran through me. "Would that make you happy? To have Anastassia lose me and for my kids to grow up without a father? Would my death make things even between us?"

"It would be a start." His dark gaze met mine. "But don't worry, getting men was never a problem for her. I'm sure she'll find someone else to be a father for your children. The one of them that's actually yours, that is."

Despite the fact that I was naked and he was fully armed and armored, I leapt over the bed and knocked him to the floor. I'd done a good number on his face before Jey pulled me off.

"Get dressed and get out of here. Be at my place in five hours, or I'll come looking for you," Jey growled in my ear before shoving me away.

I must have done better on Merkief than I'd realized because he wasn't moving.

Jey dragged him from the room. "Too bad you didn't fare as well with Kess," he said on his way down the hall.

Maybe I just wasn't as angry with Kess. Maybe I'd hoped he would see reason. But that had been stupid, wishful thinking, and I should have known it would never happen. All three of them had tasted the Narvan and none of them was willing to starve.

At least Jey didn't mind if I went home.

I pulled on some clothes without bothering to look at them. Pants, a shirt, my boots. I stuffed my wad of weapons and holsters into my coat which I threw under my arm and then realized I'd not set a Jump point in the house where I'd left my family. Idiot. I Jumped to my office instead.

The tunnels took longer than I wanted them too, but overland wouldn't have been any faster. At least I generally stayed out of sight. When I strode up to the house at a half run and threw open the door, Neko was on his feet with a weapon in hand in good time.

"Oh. It's just you," he said, tucking his gun away. "Someone behind you?"

"No. Everything's fine." It wasn't though. Not by a long shot.

"You're home!" Daniel leapt down the last two stairs and bulleted toward me, knocking into me with all the force of a solid torpedo.

As glad as I was to see that he was fine, I needed to see Stassia. I gently pried him off me and set him aside. "Where is your mother?"

"Upstairs with Ikeri."

"Go watch your sister for me and send your mother down."

Daniel's face turned serious as though he sensed something was wrong. "All right." His ascent was far more solemn.

Stassia ran down the steps and came to a sudden halt in front of me. She glanced at Neko over my shoulder.

"You want me to leave?" he asked.

"No, stay," I said.

I nodded Stassia toward the bedroom.

Once she shut the door behind her, her gaze instantly dropped to my hands. "Who?"

My red and swollen knuckles had given me away. "Merkief. He said some things he shouldn't have."

"Was that a good idea? What if he comes looking for us?"

"Then we have Neko or Harmon. And hopefully me. How about you?"

She grimaced. "I don't know about you, but I'm far more out of the groove than I'd anticipated."

"I knew I was damn rusty." I pulled her close and held on tight. "I have a feeling I'll be gone for a while."

"Why? What are they asking you to do?" She tried to back away, but I didn't let her. My work face was shattered and she'd guess the truth.

"Intensive training. Jey and Merkief have made quite a mess of things. They need me."

"So do we. Dammit, let me go."

I did and sat down on the edge of the bed. It was harder than the one we'd shared on Minor, and smaller. If I managed to get a night in it with her, we'd be side by side whether she was speaking to me or not.

"Is that tank gel in your hair?" She brushed her fingers along my scalp. Concern whispered along our bonded connection.

"Maybe." The fight with Merkief must have dislodged most of it from my face.

"Don't maybe me, Vayen. What the hell happened?" She stood inches in front of me, her arms crossed and a Kazanish demand for the truth in her eyes.

"Kess."

"You went against Kess? Like this? Already?" Her open palm slammed against the wall. "Get me to Merkief."

"Why?"

"So I can yell at him. It's about all I'm good for anymore, but dammit, he needs to know." She let out a frustrated growl that morphed into a string of profanity. "He's wasting you, and for no damn good reason other than he's got a chip on his shoulder. I'm not okay with it. Not in the least, and he's going to hear about it. Take me to him. Now."

A smile crept onto my face. "I love it when you're mad. At other people, I mean."

She punched my shoulder. "I'm serious."

"I know." I grabbed one of her hands and pulled her onto my lap. "Last I saw of Merkief, Jey was dragging his unconscious ass down the hall. I'd rather give him a little time to cool off if you don't mind."

"See, you're not near as rusty as I am." She brushed her lips against my cheek. "Take me to Jey then."

"I'd rather not."

"Tough. If you expect me to sit here while they're out there throwing you at Kess until it gets you killed, that's not going to happen."

"How about you lay here." I flipped her off my lap and onto the bed.

"Only if you're lying here with me." She tugged me down next to her and gripped the collar of my coat.

I enjoyed the feeling of her pressed against me, hoping it wouldn't be the last time.

"Stassia, I should go see the kids."

"How long do you have?"

"A few hours, and I need to sleep for most of it."

Stassia nodded and kissed my forehead. "Go on then. I'll get Gemmen in here to watch the kids when you're done. If I only get you for a few hours, I'm spending them with you, even if you're sleeping."

Warmth flooded through me. "Thank you."

She kissed me and then sat up, allowing me to get out of the bed. "You're still taking me to see Jey, but I'll let you sleep first."

"You're so patient."

She threw her pillow at me as I walked out the door.

Ikeri met me at the top of the stairs, her big green eyes filled with sadness. I picked her up.

"What's wrong?"

Her thin arms wrapped around my neck. "Stay."

"Who said I was leaving?" I was pretty sure our room was soundproof enough that the kids couldn't have overheard us speaking at a regular volume.

She rested her head of curls on my armored shoulder.

"Your coat is scratchy," she said.

"Only on the outside."

"Are you cold?"

"No, why?"

"Then why do you and Neko and the other man wear coats in the house?"

"To keep us safe."

She picked up her head. "I want to be safe too. Where's my coat?"

"I don't think your mother packed one for you." I carried her into the room she shared with Daniel. "Neko and Harmon will keep you safe. And Grandpa and your mother."

"Not you?"

"Yes, me too."

"Who will keep you safe?"

That was a very good question. "My friends will." At least that's what Kess had called them. Jey would. Merkief, that depended on the moment.

I carried her into the bedroom and put her down. Daniel sat on the floor, a selection of battered blocks scattered around him. A box containing the rest sat within reach. Gemmen must have brought them. We hadn't packed much in the way of toys in our rush to leave.

"What shall we play?" I asked.

"Tower." She stuck her tongue out at Daniel. "And I get to knock it down."

"How about we all build it and no one knocks it down?"

"That's no fun," Daniel complained.

"Sure it is." I grabbed him and tickled him until he was laughing so hard he got hiccups.

Well into our tower masterpiece, I caught a glimpse of someone in the doorway. Stassia smiled down on us all. "Your father needs to sleep. Tell him goodnight."

Daniel's brow scrunched. "It's the middle of the day here. We don't have to sleep too, do we?"

"No." She carefully skirted our block tower and held out her hand to me. "But someone needs a nap."

Daniel laughed. "And it's not me."

He jumped up and down until the blocks gave way and our tower crumbled.

Ikeri scowled at her brother then gave me a hug. "Stay."

"I wish I could."

She sniffed, tears welling in her eyes.

"You're leaving again?" Daniel asked. "I want to look at the warehouse, but Grandpa said I had to wait for you to come with. He said there's lots of stuff there to see. I want to see! I want to go outside. Can I at least go outside?"

"Not yet," Stassia said.

"When?"

"When I say you can. Now, be good for your mother and Grandfather," I said.

He let out a long-winded sigh. "I will."

"Good." I gave him a quick hug.

I took Stassia's hand and got to my feet. As I walked out of the room I caught a glimpse of Daniel handing Ikeri a block.

"They'll be fine," Stassia assured me.

I nodded, hoping she was right.

We went downstairs. While I got undressed, I could hear Stassia talking quietly with Neko, asking him to have Gemmen watch the kids. When she returned, she closed the door quietly behind her.

"Can you do me a favor before you get in bed?" she asked.

"What?"

"Take a shower. I don't want the sheets covered in gel flakes."

I laughed at the absurdity of it. "How many times have we slept in sheets covered in this crap? Come on."

She shook her head. "This is different."

"How so?"

"Just do it."

A wave of urging flowed over our bonded connection. I wasn't sure what she was up to, but the playful gleam in her eye got me on my feet. I shrugged at Neko on my way to the bathroom.

I made quick work of showering, looking forward to spending a few hours in bed before getting the shit kicked out of me by Jey. I was just about to turn the water off when Stassia came in and locked the door behind her. She quickly stripped and joined me in the steam.

"Feeling dirty?"

She smirked. "Feeling like you're going to be missing from our bed for awhile and like you better make it up to me."

"I don't know if we have enough hot water for that."

"It will be a good start, I'm sure." Her mind opened to mine, caressing all the right places, while her hands did the same. I did my best to reciprocate.

After her last not very muffled moan, I was pretty sure everyone in the house knew what we were up to. "Am I clean enough to be allowed in the bed now?"

She nodded, still catching her breath.

"You still plan on joining me?" I asked, handing her a towel.

"After that, even I could use a nap."

"Good, because I really do need some sleep. The few hours I had after the tank didn't really make up for the couple hours I got last night."

Stassia looked into the mirror and grumbled.

"What's the matter?"

"My hair is all wet."

"That's what you get when you get naked and stand under running water."

She rubbed the towel over her hair as if it would magically dry in an instant. "I told them I was bringing you a change of clothes."

"That was twenty minutes ago. If that wasn't a big enough clue, all the moaning and groaning cleared up any doubt."

"The water was supposed to cover that."

I shrugged. "I suppose that was more privacy than we would have had with Neko sitting ten feet away from our bedroom door."

"That's what I was thinking." She gave up on her hair and threw the towel on the floor. "I'm not used to having other people in the house anymore."

"We may have to get used to it again." I wrapped my towel around my waist and picked up my clothes.

"You're going out there like that?"

"Yep." On second thought, I dropped my clothes, picked up the towel she'd dropped and wrapped it around her. "And so are you. We're together. No need to tiptoe around it anymore, is there?"

"I suppose not," she said, but she still looked uncertain as she held on to the towel and shook out her long wet hair to cover more of herself.

We were both used to hiding our intimate moments from Merkief and Jey, but those days were gone. Beyond keeping our more vocal activities relegated to the hours when our kids were sound asleep, we'd been free to do as we wished. That wasn't something I was willing to give up when we weren't in our own home. And Geva only knew when we'd be back there again. She was just going to have to learn to be comfortable with it.

"Come on." I swept her up and managed to open the door without dropping her or losing my towel. Or hers.

Neko did his best to look elsewhere as I dashed across the common room with Stassia in my arms. I wasn't sure what Gemmen was doing upstairs with the kids but all three of them were stomping and singing at the top of their lungs.

Stassia laughed and didn't even stop to glare at me when I hit her head on the doorframe as I carried her into the bedroom.

"How long have they been doing that?" she asked.

"No idea, I wasn't paying attention to them."

"No, you certainly weren't." She smiled as I set her down on the bed.

"You're not going to let me sleep yet, are you?"

"Not quite yet." She turned off the lights and pulled me down with her.

Chapter Six

Jey reached down to help me up off the mat. "You were sup-posed to sleep."

"I tried."

I'd arrived at Jey's house on time but far more exhausted than I had been when I left, although for much more enjoyable reasons.

"I doubt that. You're too used to being the one in charge. That's not the case anymore. You're going to have to follow directions."

"At least you're smart enough not to call them orders." I lunged at him.

He dodged out of the way. "That would just be asking for trouble."

"Mind if we add some weapons? That's how Kess got me."

"Tomorrow maybe. You're in no shape for anything beyond me smacking you on the mat today."

"Maybe it will be the other way around." I reached for him and managed to pin him for a few seconds before he reversed our positions.

"But probably not." He got up and helped me to my feet.

We went at it for another hour. Sweat soaked my clothes and my muscles were quivering before Jey called a break. At least he looked like he got a good workout out of the deal too. "I'm going to Rok for a meeting. Not that I don't think you'll stick around if I leave, but I'd appreciate it if you'd continue with getting up to speed with the Narvan."

"How long do you plan on being gone?"

"You think I'm going to tell you?" He snorted. "Nice try."

He headed to his room to change. I headed for the shower. It wasn't nearly as fun as the last one I'd taken. After a change of clothes, I made sure Jey had left and then parked myself in a chair in the common room. I reached out to Daniel.

"What are you doing?"

"Nothing," he said begrudgingly.

"What is your mother doing?"

"I don't know. She was mad this morning. I'm staying in here."

I knew she'd be mad. I'd left without waking her. However, I didn't expect that she'd take it out on the kids.

"I'll take care of it."

I got the sense he was grinning smugly.

"And I'll find out why you're in your room."

His end of our connection slid closed as if he could hide from me. I Jumped back to the bedroom I'd left that morning, having remembered to set a point there this time.

Harmon nodded to me as I walked into the common room. Stassia caught sight of me from the kitchen and came storming over.

"You said-"

"That's why I'm here. I thought one of us should get some actual sleep."

She had the grace to give me an apologetic smile. "Is he expecting me then?"

"No. I had a feeling you'd get more enjoyment out of surprising him with your tirade."

"Are you sure you can't read my mind?" She kissed my cheek.

I chuckled. "Come on, I don't know how long he's going to be gone."

"What about the kids?"

"Tell them to play in their room for awhile. Harmon can let me know if there's a problem."

"They're kids. Of course there will be a problem. You wouldn't believe what Daniel already did this morning."

I sighed. "Try me."

"I caught him in our bedroom. He had one of the guns you'd left for me in his hands."

My heart leapt into my throat. "How the hells did he get his hands on it? Why was he in our bedroom?"

"It's a small house. He's going crazy being stuck in here all day," she said.

"Then you should have been keeping a better eye on him. He could have hurt someone or himself."

From the tightening of her jaw and thinning of her lips, I knew I'd pissed her off, but this was serious.

"Don't even think about blaming me." She planted her fists firmly on her hips. "You're the one who started wearing guns again. He just wants to be like you."

"Really?" I ignored her angry stance and pulled her close, running my hands down her back. My gamble paid off when I hit metal just above her waist. "So this isn't a gun you're wearing then."

"He can't see it." Anger blazed in her eyes. "He doesn't even know about it."

"Hmm. So this coat I'm wearing. Can you actually see any guns?"

"Of course not."

"But you know they're there," I said.

"Well, yes."

I let her go and stood there, waiting.

The spurt of whispered profanity told me she'd reached the wall of blame and come back empty-handed.

"So what are we going to do about him?" she asked.

"Have Gemmen bring in a safe, something you can lock the dangerous stuff away in. As for the rest, teach him the basics. At least if he ends up with one in his hands again, he might be safe with it."

"*Might?*" She shook her head. "He's way too young."

"I didn't say to give him a gun, Stassia. Just explain a little safety to him."

Anger still raged on her face. I didn't need it aimed at me. "I doubt Jey's going to be gone long. We need to go."

She scooped up Ikeri from in front of the vid and carried her upstairs. After a few minutes, she returned and talked quietly with Harmon.

"Let's go," she said to me, looking every bit as annoyed as she had when I'd walked out of the bedroom. I prayed Jey wouldn't keep me waiting for long.

As usual, I wasn't in luck. Stassia stalked through the Jalvian home that had once been hers. She scowled at the pieces of furniture Jey had replaced, and poured over everything he'd hung on the walls or set on counters and shelves. When Stassia disappeared into her old bedroom, I let her be and sunk into my link to continue my updates on the Narvan while keeping in contact with Harmon.

Jey interrupted my prowling around old investments on Artor by sitting down across from me.

"I hate to say it, but I'm surprised you're still here."

"You said to stay here."

"And I can count the times you've listened to me on zero fingers."

Stassia's door opened. Jey sprang to his feet with a gun in his hand. I knocked it away before he gave any further thought to firing.

He spun toward me as if he wasn't sure if I was betraying him or about to explain what the hells was going on. It wasn't until he realized it was Stassia that he unwisely relaxed.

Oh Geva, she was wearing her armor. I wanted to grab her and jump her back to our bedroom, but that was going to have to wait.

She jabbed an accusing finger into Jey's chest. I stood aside and let her have at him, enjoying that view too.

"You sent him against Kess? What were you thinking?"

He stood there, sputtering.

"If you want his help, I'm not wild about it, but I'll accept it. However, if you even consider doing something that stupid again, I'll find a way here myself and you can be sure, I'll make you regret it."

"It's not really up to me," he said, finally finding his tongue.

"Like hell it isn't. Since when do you take orders from Merkief?" She held up a hand. "Yes, I know, shit happened. But come on, while Merkief was good at a lot of things, commanding wasn't one of them. That was the two of you." She looked between us.

"He's made some bad decisions," she said. "The Narvan has suffered for it. The Council isn't happy. We get it. But don't you dare get Vayen killed just because Merkief's got a grudge." She hit him in the chest again, her voice on the edge of breaking. "Don't you dare, do you hear me?"

"I won't." Jey's voice didn't sound much more solid than hers. He glanced at me, seeking silent permission. I nodded. He hugged her, whispering Geva knows what that I couldn't hear.

The possessive end of the bond I shared with Stassia bared its fangs. I stepped away, hoping that by not seeing or hearing them, I could keep my jealousy under wraps. My eyes closed, lingering on the edge of forming a Jump where I could escape what was going on in the room. I'd not felt threatened by the attention she paid anyone else since we'd disappeared. No one on Minor had triggered my ire. Then again, Stassia wasn't as emotionally connected to anyone else as much as she was to the three of us. And there she stood in her armor, a sight I'd so longed to see. The fact that her hair was long and loose made an even more alluring combination of Rhaine and Kazan.

It wasn't until her fingers slipped into mine that I returned my attention to my immediate surroundings. She stood there, gaze darting from us to all corners of the room, her grip tightening with each second.

"Take me home."

But I didn't want to. Seeing her, here in a house we shared when she alone was in command make me ache inside for what had been taken from us.

"Vayen." She tugged on my hand. "The kids are waiting."

"Are you sure?"

"What do you mean?" Her eyes glistened with tears that threatened to fall.

That was the thing that shattered the illusion—the thing that made her Kazan in my eyes: her work face, the one that hid all the intimate pieces that made her Stassia. But I loved that woman too. I couldn't have them both.

"Nothing. Sorry, yes, I'll take you home."

She shed her coat and handed it to Jey. "Thanks for keeping that for me. One of us in armor is enough for the kids to take in for now."

I latched onto the words *for now* and Jumped her back to Rok.

❧

After Stassia had been safely returned to Rok, I returned to Jey's house. I remained there for eight days that ran together in continuous cycles of sweat, headaches, and restless sleep.

I spent an hour a day Jumping between places Jey deemed

safe. They'd dropped many of the jump points I'd used years before. The new set needed to be learned so there would be no hesitation if I needed to move fast. Sadly the bedroom on Rok was not in my daily routine.

Jey allowed me a couple local contracts on Jal. He stuck close by, acting as backup, which I tried to tell him I didn't need.

"Tough, I made a promise," he'd said and ignored any further complaints.

While the Jalvian targets weren't on par with Kess, I did feel my rhythm returning. When I asked him to let me tag along on a Kryon contract, knowing that would be a better test of my abilities, he firmly denied me. It was for my own good, but I needed more of a challenge than street corner contracts could provide. In the past, I would have sunk to begging a top contract from Marin's assassin guild, but since I'd killed Marin, and Kess had snapped up the position, that wasn't an option.

Jey worked with me as much as we dared, but even between well-practiced friends, the risk of an accident was too high for us to delve too deeply into using weapons against one another. Dummy bullets did leave deep bruises to learn from, but they weren't the same when it came to split-second reactions, and that's where I doubted myself most.

Merkief joined us for a few hours each day to go over Kess's possible next moves and to continue efforts to weave the Narvan back together. Seeing how the flourishing programs I'd left behind had ground to a halt or ended completely, pissed me off. Merkief didn't bring up our brawl, and in the interest of enjoying his occasional lapses into our previous friendship, I did my best to hide my reactions each time I answered their questions. From the hesitant looks on their faces, I wasn't doing a very good job.

Restoring communications with all of my old contacts would have provided a real feel of the situation at large, but I couldn't very well do that if I was still maintaining my dead status. Even with the link flooding my brain with information, I was isolated, just outside the big picture. I wasn't at home with my family or running Dugans. Cragtek was no longer mine. I wasn't Kryon or directly advising the Narvan. My hands wanted control but no one was willing to hand it to me. Yet, they wanted me to fix everything.

Merkief cornered me after one of our brainstorming sessions with a semi-friendly inquiry. "How are things going with your joining?"

"Not very well considering I haven't even ordered a gift yet, and I've been stuck here for over a week."

His jaw went tight and his eyes narrowed. "So do it."

"When? How? You've got me tied up here every minute of every damn day."

"I'll have Jey take you. Can't have you wandering the streets of Artor alone. What if you're recognized?"

"Yeah, a hulking Jalvian with me won't attract any attention at all." I sighed. "Jey's running ragged. You've got him babysitting me, but he's got his half the Narvan to run. Or did you forget he's doing the same amount of work as you? Give him a day off. I'll blend in much better on my own anyway."

Merkief tugged on the sides of his open coat, his fingers sliding over the latches, toying with them. For a moment I thought he might be considering being reasonable, but he said, "No, I don't think that's a good idea."

"I'm not going to run off on you. You're the one who's pushing for us to join. If you want this to happen, you've got to allow us some time."

He put his hand in one of his pockets. I could see his fingers moving over or around an object, but at that point, I was just thankful that he wasn't pulling out a gun. He stared over my shoulder for a long minute.

"I'll think about it," he said.

"Are you still adamant that Anastassia and I need to join?"

"Yes," he said firmly.

When the hells had he become so obsessed and yet distracted at the same time? I couldn't imagine how Jey dealt with him on a daily basis for as long as he had. Then again, maybe it was my presence that had turned him into this.

"Merkief, I'm trying to do what you want, but you're the one preventing me from doing it."

He scowled. "You have tomorrow."

"Tomorrow for what?" Jey asked as he rejoined us.

I turned to my ally and put on a pleasant smile. However, I didn't bother masking the dripping sarcasm. "Merkief seems to think that I can convince a jeweler to make me a joining gift in a single day, get Anastassia to accept it, and go through the ceremony. How about you?"

Jey raised an eyebrow. "Is that so?" He turned to Merkief,

shaking his head. He started to say something, but then shook it off and started again. "I seem to recall that you took two months for all that, Merkief. Two months. Not a day. If you really want him to do this, then you're going to have to make some concessions."

"No, he is. I don't have to do a damned thing. Make it work." Merkief glared at me as if the sheer force of his willing it to be so would make it happen.

Daniel had more sense than Merkief. I tried to reconcile the man who had stood over me looking overjoyed at my waking from the tank with this one. It was like he had a split personality. I wished I knew how to permanently flip him back to the other one.

"Whatever. I'm taking tomorrow off. See you both later." I formed the Jump to Rok.

Merkief slammed into me. "Don't *whatever* me. I told you to do something. Do it."

The man seriously didn't like being taken lightly. But he was so irrational that I couldn't help it. Jey stood nearby, ready to get between us again if necessary.

Stassia had said Merkief wasn't cut out for command, but I'd seen him in action during the Fragian war. He'd done well enough, even if he'd been unhappy that I'd sided with Jey then too. The techs and scientists he'd worked with while conducting the research Stassia and the Council asked for had always scrambled to stay in his favor for funding and accolades. I wondered if that was still the case, or did they whisper behind his back?

No wonder the Council didn't like Merkief in control of even half the Narvan. And Jey was under too much guilt, not to mention the lingering vestiges of their prior friendship, to push him aside and do what had to be done. Not that walking quietly into the shadows was going to be something Merkief would be willing to do of his own accord. As he'd said, he'd lost too much to do that. It was going to take force. I prayed it wouldn't have to be of the deadly sort.

"Well?" His nostrils flared and his eyes took on that same fiery cast that had led to his spewing out trash that had previously compelled my fists to bash his face.

"I'll see what I can do."

"That's better." He didn't look satisfied, but he didn't rush at me either.

"Go," Jey said, *"before I have to pull the two of you apart again. I'll deal with him."*

Chapter Seven

I Jumped to my office on Rok. Gemmen had left several datapads on my desk. With the adrenaline pumping through my system after bracing for another possible altercation with Merkief, calming down here for a few minutes before I went home seemed like a wise move. I took half an hour to take a look at where Gamnock was taking Cragtek. Gemmen obviously wanted me to know, though what he wanted me to do with the information I wasn't sure.

My walk to the tunnels garnered a few more glances than the time before as I passed through the warehouses. Men I'd known previously overcame their initial reluctance and came over to greet me, quietly, but still noticeably. The ones who didn't know me surely made note of that fact. Our cover as a buyer and his family wouldn't last much longer. I'd need to move Stassia and the kids, but I didn't know where. And I had one day. A day already full of so many tasks that I had no idea how I was going to work them all in. The walk through the tunnels brought back the edgy feeling I'd hoped to leave behind in my office.

Harmon met me at the door. "You shouldn't be seen out there more than necessary," he scolded.

"I needed a walk."

"And your kids need to get out of the house, but that doesn't make it safe. Use your jump point."

I was about to tell him what to do with his advice when I realized that made me sound like Merkief. I swallowed my initial comment.

"I'll keep that in mind."

Harmon went back to his post by the wall in the common room where he could see throughout the main level of the house.

"They're all upstairs," he said.

Damn, I'd not realized it was already evening here. To fit in, Stassia had defaulted to using planetary time rather than universal. That typically only applied to those that traveled between planets and the majority of the population in any given world didn't. Unlike Veria Minor, where the universal clock was necessary for sanity, Rok's natural day and night cycle was much shorter. I wondered how the kids were adapting to the shorter days and nights, but I'd have to wait until the morning to see them or risk Stassia's wrath by riling them up with my homecoming. I went to the bedroom to strip off my armor and most of my weapons.

By the time I was done, I heard Stassia coming down the stairs. She caught sight of me coming out of the bedroom and ran at me, grinning.

"Took you long enough." She ran her hands over my face and through my hair. "No gel this time. I take it things went well?"

"Well enough for not confronting Kess again. He's still picking at them, but pulling back a little."

"You think he's planning a larger offensive?"

"Probably, yes."

Her shoulders sagged. "How long are you staying?"

"All day. Sort of. I have some personal things to attend to here and there, but I'll be around."

"I could really use a break." She leaned into me, draping her arms loosely around my waist.

"You and me both." I rested my chin on the top of her head. "Wait, is this a headache thing?"

"Getting there," she admitted. Gemmen's been taking the kids for a few hours each afternoon so I can go work with Neko and Harmon, but it's not enough. I need you here."

The edginess compounded. How the hells was I supposed to be everywhere for everyone?

"I know. I'm trying."

"I know," she whispered.

"Come here." I led her over to the couch and sat her down in front of me on the floor. She'd taught me how to do what Strauss, her favorite doctor, had done for her when she was pregnant with Daniel. I'd gone through a lot of correction during her pregnancy with Ikeri, but I'd ended up with a fairly good grasp of which points did what and where to press and how hard. I settled my fingertips on her scalp in the beginning position. She let out a little sigh.

"So what do you need to do tomorrow?" she asked, her voice soft as I moved to the next position.

"No talking. You're supposed to be relaxing."

She made a muffled sound of assent. When her breathing slowed to the point where I was sure she'd fallen asleep, I stopped. Her head rested against my knee. I didn't want to wake her, but I couldn't very well spend the evening sleeping on the couch. It would be midday on Artor and I needed to get to the jeweler before they closed.

Darkness fell in its entirety. Neko replaced Harmon. My stomach rumbled. I realized I'd not eaten since lunch. I nudged Stassia.

"Come on, to bed with you."

Sleepily, she let me help her up and into bed. She didn't even protest when I gave her a quick kiss and walked back out of the room. Neko waved me over before I made it to the stairs.

"I know I shouldn't ask, but who is she?"

"Anastassia?"

He nodded. "She's good. I don't care how much protesting she makes about being out of practice."

"No one."

"I had a feeling you'd say that." He chuckled. "You as good as her?"

"I'd rather not answer that. It's a no-win for me."

Neko laughed and settled back into his position against the wall. "She's got you well trained."

"You have no idea." I glanced at the stairs. "I'm going to check on the kids. Then I have to run out for a bit."

He shrugged. "I'll be here."

I got halfway to the stairs before curiosity turned me back around. "How is she when I'm not here?"

"Different." He stared over my shoulder, clearly uncomfortable with divulging information on her.

"How so?"

"She's the boss. When you're not here, I mean."

I smiled to myself. Kazan was certainly still in there, as was her ability to coax loyalty from most anyone she wished.

"Good."

Neko cracked a nervous smile.

I peeked in on the kids, both of whom were sleeping peacefully. I would have to find some time for them tomorrow.

Satisfied that all was as it should be, I left my coat behind along with a good deal of my weapons and used the Artorian jump point Jey had provided that was nearest the jeweler's shop.

I wasn't comfortable with being mostly unarmed and unprotected. Funny how a few weeks ago, leaving the house without armor and only my two knives was normal. Now I felt naked. I took a deep breath and started walking, hoping to blend in with the general populace that shared the walkway. I made my way to a land transport call station and once one arrived, got in.

The transport dropped me off in front of the stone building that had stood for centuries. The weather-worn words carved above the door boasted of fine craftsmanship within. I already knew that from his work on the replacement neckband I'd given Stassia what seemed like a lifetime ago.

More important to me, was the discretion and intelligence of the jeweler within. I couldn't very well intimidate an idiot who couldn't pick up on the level of threat that I would need to lay down for this.

A young man came to the counter, and since this tended to be a family business, I guessed he was the jeweler's son. He greeted me with a large artificial smile.

"What can we help you with today?"

The whole *we* thing annoyed me. It was just me and him in the room. At least I thought so. I shook my head, hoping the paranoia so easily triggered by inane conversation would desist.

"I need a joining gift."

"Oh, how wonderful." His smile grew to a brilliant gleam of overly white teeth.

"What type of gift are we looking for?"

Not a neckband. That was the most traditional choice. She already had one of those. Rings got in the way. I didn't remember ever seeing her wear anything on her ears. Though that wasn't a traditional gift, I wondered if it would fit her.

He must have grown weary of me debating. "How about an armband? We've been doing more of those lately. Perhaps something in silver?"

I had a feeling an armband would get in the way every bit as much as a ring, but it seemed a safe choice given that I didn't know if she'd like anything else.

"Maybe."

"Would you like to look at some designs?"

He reached into the case between us and pulled out a long bar filled with bands. "These are samples only, of course. Yours would be made to order. Will you need any special sizing? Perhaps an engraved message? We can even do hidden messages if you'd like." He ran his hands over the bar, jingling the metal together with a musical tinkle.

"No messages." Nothing that would link her to me if she was caught alone. Alone, she could pretend to be anyone, but concrete evidence of my involvement in her life could lead to her becoming dinner for the blue creature that had devoured Sonia.

"Are you sure? Women love that sort of thing. Sentimental creatures, as they are."

"Quite sure."

"You only get one gift. No changing your mind later."

"Hadn't planned on it." I was losing patience with his tactics. "Give me an armband. Silver is fine."

"And the pattern?"

"I have one on file that I'd like to use."

He gave me an odd look. "Been in before, have you?"

"Yes. Can I talk directly to the jeweler please?"

"He's busy."

"So am I. Quit wasting my time."

I distinctly remembered speaking to the jeweler the last time I'd been in. Why did everything have to change while I was gone?

"Sir, there is a protocol here. You place an order with me. The jeweler makes it. You pay for it and I give it to you. There is no need for you to see the jeweler directly."

"How do I know the gift will be made by him and not come from some mass produced pile in your storeroom?"

He managed a mortally offended. "That's not the case at all, sir. Not at all. Each gift is made-"

"Yes, I know, per order, by the jeweler. I'd like to see that he exists, if you wouldn't mind."

"That isn't the way-"

"It's done. I know. Do it anyway."

"Just who do you think you are?"

Jey was right, I wasn't used to taking direction. I was the man in charge, dammit. But if I played that card in here, my efforts to blend in would go to shit.

"Just a concerned buyer. Call it nerves."

A measure of ease worked back into his taut face.

"Got a picky woman, do you?" He managed a chuckle. "I suppose I could bring you back for a few minutes. He prefers to work in solitude. You can't stay long."

"That will be fine. I don't want to keep you. I could just go into the back on my own."

"Oh, I don't know about that. My father is an old man. He doesn't like his routine interrupted. Customer visits are likely to set him off, if you know what I mean."

"I don't want to cause any trouble. I'll make the viewing worth his while."

The man's tone turned condescending. He looked me up and down. I couldn't blame him entirely. My boots were worn. My pants were comfortable, cut for ease of movement, not style, and the same for my shirt. Nothing about me screamed important, credits, or political sway; which was my intention, but still, not working in my favor at the moment.

"Trust me," I said.

"If you don't mind." He held out his hand. "It's my ears that will hear the tirade if you're not telling the truth."

I reached into my pants pocket and pulled out a credit chip. Hoping it was as adequate to the task as I intended, I put the chip in his hand. He slid it through the reader he wore on a band around his wrist. He went stiff for a second, his eyes locked on the reader.

"I do believe a tour is in order. Right this way, sir."

"I'll find my own way, thanks."

He paused for a moment then gazed at the credit chip. "Yes, of course. Right through that door."

"Thank you."

I went through the door behind the counter. A dark hallway waited for me with another door at the end. That door led to a large room filled with metal sheets in many colors and ancient equipment. Buzzing came from my left. I turned to see a hunched man with grey hair and wrinkled skin that puckered around his eyes and mouth. He sat at a bench with a circlet of golden metal in his hands, turning it methodically at a cloth-covered wheel.

He glanced up. The buzzing turned to a sudden deep thunk. The band fell to the floor. He got to his feet in a manner that I assumed would have been more of a leap had he been younger.

"What are you doing back here?"

"I paid for a tour."

"We don't do tours. You'll need to go back up to the counter," he said with polite force.

He reached for the circlet he'd dropped on the floor.

I grabbed it before he could. "I need you to make me an armband."

"You'll need to file your paperwork with Royce." He pointed at the door with a shaky hand.

I stepped toward him, driving him back to his bench. "You're going to make me an armband, silver, with the pattern I have on file. I need it in the next few hours. You will be paid for your work and discretion. Am I clear?"

His thin lips pulled into a tight line. "That's not how I work."

"It is today."

His politeness vanished. "There are laws."

"I am aware of those. We'll be bypassing them."

"There are consequences for this sort of action. I could lose my license and my business. I may be an old man, but my son will lose his livelihood. This shop has been in my family for generations."

"There are enough credits on the chip I left with Royce to buy your shop twice over. I'm sure you'll get by on the slight chance that you get caught. It certainly wouldn't happen because of me."

"How do I know you're not working with the enforcers?"

"I'm not."

There was a time I could have enforced the enforcers if it came to it, but that was the past.

"You'd say that if you were trying to test me. We've followed the laws for four generations. I'm not about to do any different today." He called out in a wavering voice. "Royce?"

"Just give the man what he wants, Father," Royce called out, keeping himself behind the door in the hallway.

"Don't be foolish. No credits will make up for our loss of integrity."

Royce remained silent.

"I'd rather not make this unpleasant if I don't have to." I reached for the gun in my waistband, hidden under my shirt.

"What are you doing?" He backed up, bumping into the seat he'd vacated. "You need to leave. We don't want your business."

"You're the jeweler with my pattern on file. I'm afraid I must insist."

His bushy brows lowered. He scooted around the seat and took a few steps to the terminal on the bench behind where he had been working. "What name is the pattern under?"

I gritted my teeth. Why couldn't it be in my name?

If I had any inkling of what Stassia would like other than what she already had, I wouldn't have to utter the words. But she wasn't Artorian, having spent her teen years dreaming up a perfect pattern. We hadn't done the traditional proposal, where I would ask her for the design. I hadn't even had time to finagle my way around that by subtly asking her to draw something up, and I didn't have the time to design something of my own. Better to play it safe and use what I knew she liked, the pattern that matched her favorite knife.

"Chesser Ta'set."

The jeweler squinted at the screen. "This account has been used already." He shook his head. "I won't do it."

"I'd say please but I doubt it would make a difference." I drew the gun.

His eyes grew large. "That's not a stunner."

"No, it's not. I believe you have an armband to make, and I don't have a lot of time."

"You'll have to come back tomorrow."

"I'll wait. Thanks." I set the circlet he'd been polishing on the bench by the terminal. "You can finish this one tomorrow."

He kept his eyes on the gun. "Those are illegal."

"I'm aware of that."

The old man darted away faster than I would have guessed he could have. "Royce!" The terror in his voice was clear.

"I'll let Mother know you'll be late," Royce called out. "The front door is locked."

The door behind us shook as Royce opened and closed the door at the front of the shop.

The old man froze. "He left me. My son left me!"

"It seems your son likes credits. Get to work and you'll be home in time for dinner. No one has to get hurt, and I'd prefer if that were the case."

With shaking legs and hands that trembled even more than

they had when I'd arrived, he made his way back to the terminal and examined the pattern records. "Since Chesser is dead. I'm guessing that's not you."

This was my gift, dammit. It wouldn't hurt to make this official, not any more than using a dead man's name. Again. "Vayen Ta'set."

He worked the terminal for a moment. "Ah yes, there it is. But you've already used your chit. With the same pattern." He studied me for a few seconds. "I remember you. Bent the rules for you last time. You were throwing credits around then too."

"I'm throwing more at you this time."

"No chit, no gift."

The disapproving scowl he bore reminded me of my father. I could only imagine the flurry of stern words he'd have hurled at me regarding this situation. Or my entire adult life, for that matter. Perhaps Geva had done my parents a favor, their early deaths preventing them from seeing what a mess both their sons would make of their own lives.

"Don't make me put a bullet in your head, old man."

Not that I would have. I needed him after all, and I rather doubted his son had the old man's talent.

I looked over the wall of metal sheets to my right and picked out a shining silver strip. Handing it to him, I stepped back to give him room to work.

"Good eye. That's the expensive stuff."

"Don't worry, I'm paying for it," I said.

"Rather attached to this pattern, aren't you?"

"It's the one I know she likes."

"These have all been for the same woman?" he asked, brushing his fingers over the sheet and looking it over with a calculating eye.

"Just work."

I sat down in the seat by the polishing wheel. The old man did his best to attempt to whittle information from me, but I cut him off every time.

Four hours later, he motioned me from my post by the wheel and sat down to put the finishing polish on the armband. Once he was satisfied, he stood and announced, "I'm late for dinner."

"Good thing Royce took care of notifying your mate."

"She died two years ago."

If that had been some secret code about informing the authorities, they would have barged in long ago. And if I'd have thought Royce was that sort of man, I wouldn't have let him leave, but I knew the greedy gleam of credits that I'd seen in his eyes.

"So what was that message all about then?" I asked.

"He thinks you're going to kill me so he can have the business. He left me here."

I didn't quite know what to do with that knowledge. The old man had done nothing wrong. He did beautiful work. It would have been a shame to kill him.

"Would you like me to do something about that? I mean, he is your son and all, but-"

His eyes went wide. "You are a horrible man, you know that?"

Some days it wasn't worth the effort to try to be nice. "It was just an offer."

"He's my son."

A son who left his father for dead. At a loss, I shook my head. "Hand it over, and I'll leave you alone."

He scoffed. "And why would you do that? My son has your bribe. I'll never see a single credit of it. I've seen you. I have your family records, know your name, and by the way, you look pretty healthy for a dead man." He pointed at the terminal. "All I need is for you to leave so I can contact the enforcers."

"If you really want me to kill you, keep on talking about turning me in. I might do Royce a favor."

He handed me the armband.

I exchanged my gun for the one pulse pistol I'd tucked into my boot. "You have thirty seconds to get out of here."

He stood up. "What are you doing?"

"If you go to the enforcers, you'll need proof."

When it was clear he was not going to make use of the time I'd given him, I fired at his terminal. The metal bent inward, buckling and curling like charred paper. The clearplaz shattered, spewing shards over the distorted bench.

"I'd get out of here. That was the lowest setting."

He gaped. "You're going to destroy my shop?"

"It would be easier to kill you, but this is my other option. Unless you plan on keeping your mouth shut?"

"I could say that I will but then make a call as soon as you leave."

"I could be back here in a heartbeat and destroy your shop."

"You know this wasn't the only copy of my records."

"I trust you'll be smart with the backup copies and keep them to yourself."

He rubbed his chin again. "Take your gift then and get out of here."

"I'll be watching the enforcer feed."

He grunted something I couldn't make out and began to brush the shards of clearplaz off his seat.

Satisfied that I'd suitably cowed the old man, I slipped the armband into a pocket and Jumped to my office on Rok. I would have gone right to the house, but I wanted to watch the feed for a bit to make sure the jeweler stayed quiet. If I had to leave suddenly, it would wake Stassia. She needed to rest.

While I was there, I sent Merkief a message, pointing him to the network copy of the jeweler's records. He didn't respond.

The jeweler may have been biding his time or he may have decided to be wise, because three hours of scouring the Artorian feeds had brought up nothing with my name on it.

The whole building shook as something exploded in the distance. A single garbled word from Harmon and a burst of terror from Daniel hit me simultaneously. I leapt to my feet and Jumped to the bedroom.

Stassia wasn't there. The sheets and blankets were all pulled back. She would have never left them like that if given a choice. I opened the door. Harmon lay still on the floor halfway between me and the stairs. A pool of blood circled his head. The front door hung open. Another body lay just inside. Fuck.

Gunfire sounded outside.

"Stassia?" My voice was strangled. Fear kicked adrenaline into my veins, speeding up time as I flew up the stairs. I stumbled over another body on the landing. A woman. Blood thudded in my ears. I forced myself to look. It wasn't her.

"Vayen?" She sounded small, quiet.

I spotted her then, slumped against the wall in the bedroom with Daniel and Ikeri beside her. Her gun lay in her lap. Blood stained her shirt.

Dammit, I should have insisted that she kept her coat, that she wore it at all times. This wouldn't have happened.

Neither of the kids moved. Ikeri held Stassia's arm, curling herself around it as if she was safe from all the danger in the world though she was in plain sight. Daniel stared at the woman I'd tripped over, his pupils dilated and mouth hanging agape.

"Are you two all right?"

Ikeri nodded.

"Daniel?" I knelt down beside him and shook him gently.

He grabbed onto me. I could feel him shaking through my coat.

"Stassia?"

"My shoulder."

It wasn't just her shoulder, but it wouldn't help matters to correct her. There were three entry wounds. One at her shoulder and the other two inching closer to her heart. And I'd just been sitting in my office, ten minutes away, screwing around with Merkief's demands to join. I should have been here.

My throat threatened to close off.

I sat down to get a quick look at the bloody mess in her shirt, adjusting Daniel so I could use my free hand. She barely moved her head. Both arms hung limply. Ikeri seemed to be the only thing holding her up.

"They didn't give him a chance. I was downstairs when they came in." She let out a hiss as I closed her shirt.

"Just the two of them?"

She shook her head. "One got out. He ran when this one went down. I did get him, but he still ran."

"Ran or Jumped?" The difference would define the level of threat.

"Ran."

"Anyone we know?"

"No."

Ikeri was even paler now.

"Are you sure you're okay?" I asked Ikeri.

"It's hard to hold her. Too much hurt," she said.

A nearby explosion shook the house. Something fell below, clattering on the floor.

Stassia looked worse by the second. We needed more immediate medical assistance than the company clinic could provide, and if assailants were roaming the grounds, I didn't trust taking her there.

I contacted Jey. *"I need help. Now."*

"Kess is attacking Rok. I'm sorry." He cut contact.

A warning from Gemmen screamed in my head. We were under attack by air forces. Ground troops had infiltrated our defenses. His warning came far too late.

Daniel squeezed me with all his might, whimpering. Outside the house, men shouted. Gunfire rang out. A rush of footsteps burst into the house below. I froze.

"Upstairs?" asked a woman.

"Yeah. Finish her off if she's still breathing. I'll get the kids," said a man.

Chapter Eight

Two sets of footsteps pounded up the stairs.

With Daniel clinging to me, I wrapped my free arm around Ikeri and Stassia and formed a Jump. We fell back into the void and tumbled onto the hard metal floor of the buried ship. Faint standby lights of the tank greeted us. I pried Daniel off and grabbed Stassia. Ikeri lay on the floor, eyes closed and limp. Stassia, in my arms, was the same. Daniel started to sob. Torn between getting Stassia in the tank and examining Ikeri, I followed the lead of my hands which seemed to be on autopilot.

Watching as if from a distance, I quickly undressed Stassia and laid her on the tank platform. I'd done this before—many, many times, a voice in my head assured me. This was no different. She would wake up and smile at me and everything would be fine again. My feet took me to the tank controls. I sat at the terminal and pulled up her profile. Stalling there, my finger hovered over the button for the final command.

Her profile was old, from before we'd left. It contained all the damage the High and Mighties had inflicted on her brain and body. So much time had passed, she'd had another child, had multiple surgeries on her brain. What would this do to her?

It would save her. I forced my finger onto the button.

The platform lifted. Time snapped back into action. Ikeri.

My daughter lay still on the floor. Daniel sat beside her, crying. Panic hit me full force. Had Ikeri been hurt? She'd looked sick when I'd found them at the house.

By habit, I reached for the gurney that always sat along the wall and pulled it alongside Ikeri. I carefully picked her up. No blood. That revelation didn't make me feel much better. Her shallow breaths told me she wasn't just sleeping and her ashen tone wasn't all shock. As I gently pulled off her clothes, I replayed our arrival onto the ship over in my head. I'd fallen backward. Daniel had rolled back with me. Ikeri had been beside Stassia, but Stassia hadn't been on her when I'd picked her up. Ikeri hadn't been crushed by either of us.

I ran my hands over her frail little body. No bruises, no swelling. Whatever was wrong wasn't something I knew how to fix. I didn't even know what it was.

Where could I take her? Jumping the three of them had depleted my immediate energy. Even if I could manage to eke out another Jump after a short break, I'd be stuck there until I'd rested, which meant leaving Daniel behind, alone and afraid while his mother floated lifelessly in the tank that might be doing her serious harm if I wasn't around to monitor her progress. What was I supposed to do?

Maybe she'd hit her head when she'd fallen. I opened the connection I shared with Ikeri, reaching out, examining the faint beginnings of her natural speech that would blossom over the next year or two. I searched for any sign that something was wrong. If it was, maybe someone at the Artorian University could help. Jey had shared the jump point he'd used to bring me there when I'd received my link.

The calm that I'd always felt when around her feathered my gentle probing. I hadn't been imagining that. But what did it mean?

"Sleep, Daddy," she whispered in my head.

She could speak already? *"What's wrong?"*

"Helping Mommy made me tired." Her voice slipped away and the connection I'd established, closed.

Daniel stopped crying. "She'll be all right," he assured me as the last of his tears rolled down his cheeks.

I covered Ikeri with the sheet and knelt down beside Daniel. "How do you know that?"

"She told me."

"When? How?"

"Just now." He sniffed.

I gripped his shoulders. "Has she talked to you like that

before?"

He nodded, looking scared. "I showed her how, but she already knew. She said Mom would be mad if we told. Are you mad?"

"No." I hugged him.

Perhaps Ikeri had ended up with some hybrid mash of Stassia's natural telepathy and my own. If that was the case, who knew what other aspects of her mixed genetics might come to light? We'd have to keep an eye on her.

Hoping I wouldn't do any further damage, I lifted Ikeri from the gurney and carried her into my room. I tucked her into the narrow bed where I'd woken in this nightmare.

"What is this place?" Daniel asked, trailing along behind me.

"Your mother's ship. Don't worry, it's safe here."

At least it had been once. I'd thought Cragtek would have been too. But Kess knew I was affiliated with Cragtek and it seemed he was sure we were there. Sure enough that he was willing to attack the whole base and planet for the chance of taking me out.

Did the Council condone his attack? Jey and Merkief had sure made it sound like the Council was against this kind of outright hostility.

"Mom has her own spaceship?" Daniel pointed to the clothes on my shelf, most of which were folded neatly. "Are these yours?"

"Yes, they are."

"Why do you have clothes here? Did you used to live here?"

"Something like that." I turned down the lights and guided him out of the room.

"What is that thing you put Mom into?"

"A regeneration tank. It will heal her."

"Like a giant doctor?"

"Yes." I led him into the compact bathroom across from my room. "Let's wash your face." Washing off the evidence of our traumatic experience would make it go away on the surface. Or make it seem less real, maybe. At least I hoped so.

"Will Mom be all right too? Ikeri helped her as best she could."

I put the cloth down and got down on my knees in front of him. "What do you mean helped?"

"She does that for me sometimes when I get hurt. Takes the hurt away. Inside." He tapped his head.

Ikeri had said she was holding her. I'd thought she'd meant holding her up, but if she'd been inside Stassia, holding the trauma and pain away, it was little wonder she was exhausted. A heavy chill settled over me. If Ikeri hadn't been there, Stassia might not be here either.

How a three-year-old happened across the abilities Stassia employed as a Seeker was beyond me. Stassia had needed training to utilize her abilities. Quite a lot of it, if half of what she'd said was true.

"Your mother has done something like that for me before."

"You got hurt before?"

I forced a smile. "Many times."

"Oh." His lips began to tremble again.

"I'm not right now though. I'm fine. We'll all be fine."

I took his hand and led him back to the tank room where I could monitor Stassia's progress.

Daniel hopped up on my lap, something he hadn't done since Ikeri had been born. He watched the stat bars slowly arc upward. "Why does this say Mom's name is Anastassia?"

"Because that's her other name."

"She has two names?" he asked.

"Yes."

"Do you have two names? She called you Vayen."

"I do." It annoyed the hells out of me that I had to admit these things to him. He should have been home playing outside, not watching his mother get shot and learning that his parents weren't who he'd thought.

"Do I have two names?"

"No. I hope you never need another name. It gets confusing."

He nodded uncertainly. "How does she breathe under water?"

"How about you just sit here with me, and we'll get her out of there in a couple hours. All right?"

"I can help?"

"Sure."

He was asleep against my chest in half an hour, as I'd expected. I sat with him there, breathing softly against me for a while before deciding to put him in Jey's bed. Which meant if I wanted to lie down, I'd be stuck with Merkief's bed.

I didn't need sleep that badly. Besides, it would be best if I stayed awake until Stassia's stats crept close to level. I hoped that if I didn't let the cycle end, I could keep some of the damage from being replaced in her system. If Ikeri woke up, she'd need me too. I could only imagine what waking in a strange place would do after all she'd seen.

With everyone taken care of for the moment, I contacted Jey. *"How's it going?"*

"Bad. I need you here." He sounded relieved to hear from me but also very distracted.

"I can't. Anastassia's been shot. Three times. No armor." I didn't bother hiding how shaken I still was.

"Holy hells, Vayen. Why didn't you say so?"

"I did say I needed help. Things were a little chaotic at the time."

I got the sensation he was glaring at me.

"I let Merkief know so he'll stay off your back. Where are you?" he asked.

"We're all on the ship. I'm trying to keep the tank from doing more harm than good."

"Come when you can. I really could use your help." He flashed me a jump point and cut contact.

When the last of Stassia's vitals crept as near normal as I dared let them go, I ended the tank cycle and set a new base profile for her.

The platform lowered, bringing her gel-soaked body within reach. I wrapped her in a sheet and carried her to her bed. I'd just tucked her under a blanket when I heard Daniel screaming.

I ran to Jey's room where I'd left him and found him thrashing around in the middle of a nightmare. I got him calmed down and took him back to Stassia's room with me. Sitting in the chair near her bed, I got comfortable with Daniel on my lap. With the door left open, I could listen for Ikeri, but I left an open connection to her just in case.

It wasn't long before Daniel's breathing grew even again. My eyes drifted shut over and over but I jerked awake each time, intent on keeping watch over them all. At least I thought I'd stayed awake, until I opened my eyes and saw Stassia watching me.

"How are you feeling?" I asked.

"Much better," she said softly. "The kids?"

"Ikeri was exhausted. She's in my room."

"But she's okay? Vayen, she-"

"I know. She told me."

Stassia sat up. She pulled her hair back behind her shoulders and wrapped the sheet around her.

"She knows what she did? How is that possible?" she asked.

I shifted Daniel's warm, limp weight so I could better face her. It wasn't often I wished he had more of Stassia in him, but favoring his Artorian side made him big and heavy compared to Ikeri, who I was more used to holding.

"You're the one with Seeker training. You tell me," I said.

She swung her feet over the edge of the bed and stood. A second later she fell to the floor.

"Stassia!" I slid Daniel off my lap and into the chair as I sprang to my feet.

"Weaker than I expected." She laughed nervously and pulled herself up.

"I didn't let the cycle end, but you slept plenty long."

"Oh. Old profile. I didn't think of that." She looked around her old room. "I have to say, I didn't expect to see this again. Did Jey help you?"

"No." I explained how Rok was under attack.

"So you Jumped all three of us again." She shook her head. "I know you had too, but-"

"No buts. There were two people in the house. On the stairs. I had seconds. I Jumped."

"I know." She leaned against the bed. "It's just that you shouldn't be doing that, not all of us at once. That had to drain you."

"It was an emergency." What did she want from me?

Her gaze dropped to her bare feet on the floor. "We shouldn't have come with you. I don't belong here anymore."

"Neither of us does, but you know it wasn't by choice."

She shot me a look that said I should shut up unless I was prepared for an argument.

"I want to see Ikeri," she said.

"Then let me help you." I wrapped an arm around her. "She's sleeping."

"How would you know?"

"I have a connection open with her."

"We didn't think she'd have your natural speech. Even so, isn't it early for that yet?"

"It is, and it's different than with Daniel. More like our bonded connection."

We stopped in the doorway. Stassia looked down at our daughter sleeping on Jey's bed.

"We've got our hands full with these two, don't we?" she asked.

"Mmhmm."

"We can't go back to that house, and we can't stay here. Vayen, if Kess staged that attack on Cragtek just to try to get to us..."

"We don't know that."

The guilt flowing from her told me otherwise.

"We can't go back to Minor. I couldn't take it if he attacked there too. Not with people we know so well," she said.

"I'll figure something out. You're going to take a shower, then you're going back to bed. I need to get to Jey so I can get a better idea of what is going on."

She backed away from my room, pulling me with her. "Harmon tried, but they burst in all at once. He gave me the seconds of distraction I needed to get to the stairs before they got to the kids." She rubbed gel flakes from her face. "Gemmen, is he all right?"

"He was the last time I talked to him. Rok is under attack, Stassia. Buildings were going up in flames when we left. I don't know any more than that right now."

"Contact him." She grabbed my shirt. "Right now."

I sighed and opened my linked connection to him. *"You safe?"*

"Holed up for now with my family. Gamnock's got the men out on the grounds. He's been gathering up a few of the invaders for questioning, but we've taken a lot of losses. Looks like the whole city has, according to the news reports."

"Any positive identifications?"

"Some old help. Mostly strangers though. The few we did know probably helped them get in."

"I want any information you get. He gets, actually. Make sure you're present. We can't afford to have you out of the loop right now."

"Gladly. Did you all get out safely?" he asked.

"No, but we'll be all right. Harmon didn't make it."

"Shame. He was a good man."

"Anastassia wanted me to check on you. I need to get back to the kids."

"Take care of them." He cut contact.

"He's fine," I reported.

"And Neko?"

"I don't know, Stassia. I didn't ask. Get in the shower."

She fiddled with the edge of the sheet she'd wrapped around

herself. "The kids like Neko."

"Glad to hear it."

I let go of her. After making sure she was steady on her feet this time, I shooed her toward the bathroom. I sat down in the hall, well within earshot if she or the kids needed anything. The water turned on, creating a soft drone.

"Vayen." Stassia shook me. "Wake up."

Water dripped from her hair. I'd not been out long.

"I'm awake." I stood up and shook out my coat.

"Could have fooled me," she said. "I thought you said you needed to get to Jey."

"I do. You need to rest though. Now that I know you're all right, I'll work through my link for now."

"Get out of here." She pushed me gently. "I'm capable of watching two kids and resting on my own."

But I didn't want to leave them. The last time I'd done that she'd almost been killed.

"We're on the ship. We're safe enough. Go."

"I thought you couldn't read my mind," I said dryly.

"I don't need to. It's written right there on your face." She wrapped her arms around my shoulders. I thanked Geva the tank had worked and that she was safe and whole and in my arms.

"All right, I will, but first, I have something for you."

She cocked her head and stepped back. "Oh really?"

I fished the armband out of my pants pocket and kept it wrapped in one hand. "I know my timing stinks, but I need to do this before I go."

She smiled softly. "Oh. All right then." She stood straighter, gazing at me expectantly.

"Quit that. You're making me nervous."

"You? Nervous?" She snickered. "What am I doing?"

I ran a hand through my hair, wishing it was long enough to cover my face. She knew she was torturing me and she was enjoying it. I took her hand in mine.

"Which people are we right now? Which name do you want me to use?"

"As much as we enjoyed being Rhaine and Isnar, I think we're going to stick with Anastassia and Vayen. That's who we were when we started this, right?"

"True. But I did honestly like being Isnar."

"I liked you being Isnar too. But I also love you as Vayen, and

I'm rather doubting I'm going to get Isnar back any time soon, if ever."

"Sorry about that. It wasn't my intention."

"I know." She squeezed my hand. "If you didn't have to become Vayen again, we wouldn't be doing this."

"Maybe we would, on our own terms."

The lines around her eyes crinkled. "Our terms were pretty set already and besides, you stopped asking."

I'd stopped asking? After her tirades? "Anastassia, you have got to be fucking kidding me."

She burst out laughing. "Maybe, yes." She quickly composed herself. "But really, if you had tried again, in the past year or two, I might have said yes."

"Might have. Or you might have ripped my head off again."

"I'm sorry about the prior head ripping," she said quietly.

An apology from Stassia in any form was a rare thing. I chose to accept it rather than question her further.

"As I was trying to say..."

"Ask, I believe you were asking."

"Right. Yes." Great Geva there was so much I was supposed to say, but with the way she was watching me, I knew I'd never get through it and Jey needed me. I skipped to the end.

"As I was trying to ask, Anastassia, will you join with me?"

"I'll have to think about it." She winked. "Those are the rules."

"There aren't any rules."

"Don't lie. I did my research."

Dammit, from the mischievous gleam in her eyes I knew that she had. "Then you know I didn't do that right."

"I'll let that go. I honestly don't remember what I was supposed to reply to half of that ceremonial crap anyway. Besides, I heard the correct words once before, even if I didn't understand most of them. At least you had the courtesy not to lapse into speaking Artorian."

I laughed. Maybe we were actually meant for one another.

"So you know what comes next?" I asked.

"Mostly." She stood waiting as if she really wasn't sure.

"I'm supposed to have a box, but I kind of forgot about that when I was blowing up the jeweler's terminal."

She snickered behind her hand and then attempted to compose herself again. "We've done the box thing. I'll get by without the opening this time around."

"Then I present you with my gift." I held out my hand that contained the armband.

She grinned. "I'm glad you had the good sense to avoid a ring. I might have had to strangle you."

"And?"

"And I accept your gift."

"Thank you." I slipped the silver band around the arm that I held and then kissed her soundly.

"It's a shame you have to run off. I think we should thoroughly celebrate this," she said.

"So you're ready to join then?"

"I didn't say that." She stilled. "Oh. Right. No sex for you until I consent."

"Um, that would mean no sex for you either, just so we're clear."

"This is true. How long did Merkief give you to complete this whole ceremony?"

"A day."

She captured me in her merry green-eyed gaze. "We're only doing this once, you and I, so we're doing it right. And dammit, I think I need some wooing."

"Seriously?"

She nodded. "Quite. I'm allowed. It's in the rules."

"More like accepted practices."

Stassia ran her fingers over the band and smiled. "Semantics won't save you."

"Merkief isn't going to like this."

"Tough. If he has a problem, he can talk directly to me." She gave me a challenging look. "So woo."

"I'm kind of in the middle of dealing with Kess and sorting out the Narvan right now."

"I realize that. I'm stuck on a small ship with two rambunctious kids. Which one of us has it worse?"

I laughed. "All right. Wooing. Anything specific?"

"Surprise me." She grabbed my arms. "The good kind of surprise, I mean. We've had enough of the shitty kind lately."

"Very true." I kissed her again. Our bonded connection flared.

"Umm, aren't you supposed to be leaving?" she asked.

"I am."

She brushed her hand over my pants. "Doesn't feel like you're leaving."

I grinned.

"Good god, don't do that now."

"What?"

She kissed me again. "You need to go."

"Jey can wait ten minutes." I picked her up.

"Oh, no you don't." She pounded on my chest. "Put me down. Jey needs you."

"What about my needs?"

"We'll get to them. Eventually. And you'll need a lot longer than ten minutes."

I loved the playful gleam in her eyes, and I really didn't want to leave, but I knew she had her mind set to play this courtship thing for at least a little while. She deserved it.

"All right then. I'll be back."

"With something for me?"

I sniffed. "I have something for you right now, but you don't want it."

She laughed so loud I thought she'd wake the kids. She threw a hand over her mouth and shook with muffled amusement. "Go," she managed to say.

I went.

Chapter Nine

Jey met me in the corner of the bunker when I arrived. "How is she?"

"Resting."

He paused a second, looking me over. "Uh huh. And the joining?"

"Has been started."

"He wanted it sealed."

"Anastassia said, and I quote, 'Tough'. She wants what's due to her."

"He's not going to like this."

"After the aggravation he's caused, I really don't give a fuck what he likes."

He scowled. "I know. So does Merkief, and that doesn't make this any easier."

"Sorry about that." Honestly, I wasn't. However, he was my closest ally in this mess, and I knew I was putting him in a tough position.

He nodded toward the crowd of men in uniforms draped with cords and metals. "You're going to be seen sooner or later so we might as well get started here."

"It's no secret that I'm still around thanks to Kess."

"True. How did he know you were on Rok?"

I should have known he'd figured it out. "He found me there once before, though on negligibly friendlier terms."

"Great. Move your family elsewhere. You can't stay on the

ship. Merkief doesn't know you're there yet, but I guarantee he won't tolerate it."

"It's Anastassia's ship. It's her tank."

"Not anymore."

I didn't like where this was heading. "Let me get this straight. What's hers isn't hers because why?"

"Because she left. You left. We needed it."

"So you touched it last. That's what this comes down to? No one is taking the damned tank away, Jey. It's ours. Hers. She's shared it with all of us. That ship belonged to her family. You can't just have it."

"Neither can you. We need the tank and not just on occasion."

"I'll move them when I can. But the ship is hers. Just so we're clear."

"So you want me to move the tank?" he asked.

"No." I took a deep breath and turned toward the projection map the others were looking at. "What's the situation?"

"Kess has several Jalvian generals in his pocket. Their ships are overhead dispatching his ground crews. My men don't want to fight back because they're all Jalvian ships and crews."

"But it's Jalvians attacking a Jalvian world. From the same Jalvian world, no less. Call it treason and take them out."

A worried look flashed over his face. "We don't take treason lightly. These men are caught between Kess's orders and mine."

"No, they're following an outsider. Rok is yours. These generals need to get a hold on their men or they will lose them. Make sure they understand that."

"They're all my men. Some of them are just confused."

I glared at him. "What happened to the Jey who led the Fragian war with me?"

He looked away. "I can't afford to lose more men."

"You've already lost them." And I was losing my patience. "Give the damned order."

Several people nearby were looking our way. I'd been trying to keep my voice down, but I seemed to be attracting attention anyway. None of them were rushing to Jey's side with offers to remove me from the room. In fact, they appeared more curious than annoyed with my Artorian presence.

"They won't follow an order like that," Jey muttered as he also noticed the suddenly quiet, milling crowd.

I tried to keep my voice down even more in light of our audience. "Don't tell me you've lost your hold on even the men in this room. Are they truly that close to a rebellion?"

"It's been hard. We've all lost people over the past few years. This thing with Kess, it's draining us. You haven't been here. You haven't seen it."

"I've seen enough. Do you know which ship he's on?"

"No."

"Find out. Now," I said.

Even the officers by the map had turned around. Everyone nearby had given up any pretense of working.

"How am I supposed to do that?" Jey hissed, clearly not welcoming the attention.

"Contacts. Please tell me you have some of those left?"

"Within Kess's forces?" he asked.

"They're yours!"

I wanted to punch him. However, doing that in a room full of Jalvians who didn't know me was a bad idea, no matter how on the fence they might be about choosing Jey over Kess.

"Do you have a list of those who have defected?" I asked.

"Generally, yes."

"Give it to me."

Jey stormed over to the nearest terminal. People flowed out of his way, maintaining an open space around the two of us. He pulled up the list on the vid and gestured forcefully at it. "For what it's worth, there you go. Enjoy."

Rather than knocking him aside like I wanted to, I waited until he moved enough that I could sit and scan the list. It was far too long. I glared at him again.

"Don't even say it," he said through clenched teeth.

"These are your people. Your own damned people won't stand behind you! How am I supposed to fix that? Put a gun to every one of their heads?"

His shoulders sagged. Jey turned away, walking into the midst of the gaggle of officers who had quickly turned back to the projection map. Conversations resumed throughout the room, though many of them were still watching me.

I turned back to the list, scanning the names more carefully. One caught my eye. My contact. Even my man had gone over to Kess. What the hells had I done, leaving the Narvan to Jey and Merkief?

Out of the corner of my eye, I noticed one of the men who

had been near Jey working his way over to me. From the amount of ornamentation on his uniform, I guessed him to be fairly high ranking but I was too busy scanning the rest of the list to examine him closely. A clerk or aide followed him. I watched their reflections in the vid as they came to stand behind me facing one another.

"Advisor Ta'set?" the officer asked, still making an effort to appear like he wasn't talking to me.

Having always operated more behind the scenes, I'd never adopted a public title. Apparently, Jey and Merkief had. I figured it was as good as any.

"Yes?"

"You probably don't remember me, but I commanded one of the Rokish ships during the Fragian war."

He looked vaguely familiar, but I hadn't been paying a whole lot of attention to everyone during that link-damaging conflict.

"Whatever the reason for your absence, I'm sure it's none of my business, but I'm glad to see the rumors of your demise were unfounded. Your presence by Advisor Te's side has been sorely missed."

"Thank you."

Finally, one person in the whole damned system understood that my absence was none of their fucking business.

"I take it you wanted something?"

He glanced over to where Jey was talking with the others. The man who was with him took a datapad from his pocket and pointed at it. The general took the datapad and half-heartedly studied it, never quite looking at me.

"We, the other officers and I, couldn't help overhearing what you said. Sir, we just wanted you to know that you have our support."

"I would hope that Advisor Te also has your support."

"Yes, of course, sir," he said quickly, but with far less enthusiasm. "If there's anything you need, please don't hesitate to ask."

He handed the datapad back to his aide. The two of them rejoined the others around the map. I watched them all in the reflection for a few minutes. They appeared to be listening attentively to Jey, but I couldn't get his last words out of my head. If I wanted Jey gone, his own people would assist me? It was too bad it wasn't Merkief here instead of Jey, I might have taken them up on it.

Refocusing my attention on my contact who had already defected from Jey, I opened my linked connection to him and was surprised to find it still active.

He floundered, stuttering, and apologizing profusely.

"Where are you?" I asked.

There was a long pause. *"In orbit around Rok."*

"Who is leading the attack?"

"I'm just following orders," he said quickly.

"I suggest you follow mine. Answer the question."

"Kess Atta."

"Give me a safe jump point and I'll overlook your lack of judgment."

He flashed me a location that looked very much like a closet. I cut contact and got up from the terminal. Jey was still busy with his men, so I settled for not interrupting him in front of them and used my link instead.

"I'm going to go harass Kess. Hopefully, I'll be back. Send some men to help clean up Cragtek would you? They got hit hard."

Before Jey could talk me out of what I planned to do, I Jumped to the point my contact had provided. The void expelled me into a small supply room filled with shelving. No noises came from anything outside the room, which I figured to be a good thing. Maybe. Cautiously opening the door, I made my way forward, contacting Mox, the Jalvian army tech who'd given me the jump point.

"Where will I find Kess?"

He flashed me the plans for the model of the ship. *"Command Center."*

My boots made little sound on the metal floor. I'd had a lot of practice with walking quietly in this sort of environment. Soldiers strode down the corridor toward me, their boots pounding out a steady rhythm. Their stride told me they were traveling with purpose.

I didn't blend even remotely—no uniform and the wrong coloring. I ducked back into a doorway and palmed the panel. It opened. I slipped inside a dark room.

"What are you going to do, just walk in there and kill him?" asked Mox. *"He's got six bodyguards with him."*

Six? Jey and Merkief were apparently more of a threat than they made it sound if Kess was being that cautious. Good thing they hadn't been on duty when I'd met with him the last time. I wouldn't have made it out alive.

"How good are his men?"

"Women. From what I've heard, he's got an Artorian, three Jalvians, and two mercs from Merchess. I'd steer clear of those two. They claim they're from Merchess, but rumor says they've both served on Twelve."

Kess was certainly covering all his bases.

"You didn't tell me he had a host of bodyguards," I said to Jey, making my annoyance clear.

"What? He doesn't. He didn't. Are you all right?"

From the confusion flowing freely from Jey, I didn't think he was lying. I wondered how long Kess had had them, and if maybe it wasn't Merkief and Jey he was worried about.

"I'm fine for the moment." I cut our connection before the chastisement I could feel him forming hit me.

Another squad of determined soldiers marched by. The floor below shook and the grating sound of hull doors clamping shut rang out. They must be launching more air strikes.

Where were Gamnock's men? Why hadn't Cragtek launched their forces, or had they already and they'd gone down before the might of Kess's rebel fleet?

The ship lurched. Sirens clanged. The din died quickly for which I was grateful and yet also annoyed that whoever had attacked hadn't done a better job.

There were no further sounds of approaching troops. I left my safe spot and made my way to the nearest lift. It took only a moment for it to arrive.

The doors opened, spewing out two Jalvians. They took one look at me before one drew a gun and the other took a heavy-fisted swing at my head. The fist connected, though with my eye rather than my jaw as I dodged the first of six bullets that sped at my head. One hit my ear. The others missed as I managed to spin and drop out of the way to use my attacker as a shield. My shield took a bullet to the neck.

I dropped him and drew my pulse pistol. The blast knocked the other man back and warped the lift doors. He landed in a boneless heap on the floor. The door wouldn't shut and the lift didn't respond. Pounding on the control panel didn't help.

Cursing the fact that there were only three blasts left in my pulse pistol, I consulted the ship's map and ran to the next lift station. This one was waiting and empty. I entered the code for the bridge and sighed with relief when the door closed and an upward whooshing sensation whisked me away.

When the lift came to a stop, it opened into a gallery occupied by a squad of armed Jalvians. Maybe this wasn't such a bright idea, but it was too late to change my plan now.

I thumbed the pulse pistol to a wide lesser beam and fired. It was enough to knock the men down, but not do any major damage. Yet, it bought me time to draw a standard pistol with my other hand and take three of them out before they gathered themselves enough to fire back. Blood ran down my ear and onto my neck, itching as it oozed under the collar of my coat. Though I didn't have time to examine it, by the raw burning feeling, I was pretty sure the upper half of my left ear was gone. I had no idea if the tank could regenerate the part that was missing.

Bullets dug into my coat, driving deep bruises into my chest. Kess must have coached them to aim for a similar target, focusing their bullets in a circle on my chest to break down the armored fabric. At this rate, it would be days before the weave regenerated.

I'd employed that trick on occasion, but I didn't enjoy being the target of it. It hurt. Quite a lot. And that made it hard to focus, and to breathe, for that matter.

Another man went down. This was going too slowly. If I gave them a chance to get a couple more shots in, I'd be Jumping back to the ship for a long dip in the tank and wouldn't have accomplished a damn thing. I adjusted the controls on my pistol, using the last two charges on a heavy wave aimed at the remaining five men. They crumpled like molten metal.

The door to the command center wouldn't open. Stupid ID locks. I tugged one of the dead Jalvians over and slapped his palm on the reader. The door slid open.

I shoved the empty pulse pistol into my coat and grabbed a second gun. The unsuspecting occupants of the room went down one after the other. Kess, standing among them, spun away from the projection map to face me. He fired at my head. I fired at his head. Neither of us connected. I ducked and took out two more bridge officers.

Someone hit me with a stunner from behind. The jolt passed through my body, making me grit my teeth in order to keep my focus on the room when my eyes wanted to close.

Kess kept firing. Bullets thwacked into my coat from all around. Why hadn't I packed a second pulse pistol? Dammit. I threw my empty gun down and drew another. Someone else hit me with another stunner blast.

His guards were well armed. As much as I wanted to bring Kess down, I had to defend myself against his guards or one of them would do more than take off my ear.

"Go for his head," Kess yelled.

The women did just that. All following the lead of the one who went for my neck. Bullets hit my collar, whizzing just past me, some racing through my hair. There was only so much I could do against bullets from five directions. Two of his guards must have been off duty. Thankfully. At least this performance far surpassed the private one I'd had with Kess.

One of the women cried out and went down. I didn't know where I'd caught her, but there were still three more and Kess to deal with. Another empty gun. I dropped it and drew my last one. I hadn't anticipated the lack of time I'd have to reload either. Plenty of ammo, no time to get to it.

I took out the last unarmored body in the room. No more damned stunner blasts. Another of Kess's guards went down, this one with a bullet to the forehead. She definitely wouldn't be getting back up.

A pulse blast from behind slammed me forward into the control panel I'd been using for cover. The sharp edge cut my forehead. Blood ran down my face and into my eyes. Fucking head wounds. No way I could take Kess out if I couldn't see him. I Jumped back to the ship.

Arriving in the tank room, I contacted Jey. *"That should slow them down a little. Hit them hard."*

"What did you do?"

"Emptied his command center and distracted Kess."

"Alone? What the hells were you thinking? What about the bodyguards?"

"There's at least one, maybe two less to worry about."

Jey was distracted for a few moments. I got the sense that he was conveying orders. While he was busy, I took the welcome opportunity to ease into the chair at the tank terminal.

When he returned his attention to me he asked, *"How'd you get in there?"*

"I have my own damned contacts, you spineless Jalvian."

"Spineless?"

"You heard me."

He spat the words, *"You have no idea."*

"Prove me wrong."

He growled in my head and cut contact.

Stassia ducked her head into the room. "Vayen?"

Daniel came running in behind her.

When I got up from the terminal, the room tilted and my legs threatened to buckle. I caught myself on the edge of the tank, leaving a smear of blood across the clearplaz.

Stassia grabbed Daniel and turned him around. "Go watch your sister." Once his footsteps retreated, she ran to my side. "What happened?"

I blinked, wiping the blood from my eyes. "Kess has bodyguards. Twice as many as you did."

She scowled. "Let me guess, you did something stupid."

"I wouldn't go that far."

"I would. Look at you." She nudged me toward the platform. "Get undressed. I'll get your profile up."

Using the edge of the tank, I made my way to the platform and sat down on it. My chest muscles hurt so damn bad I couldn't make my arms bend enough to pull off my coat.

"What's wrong?" Stassia left the terminal and came to my side.

"I might need some help with this."

She gingerly pulled one sleeve off and then worked on the other. The shirt was far worse when she lifted it over my head. I gasped and the room went black for a few seconds.

Stassia hissed. "He knew exactly what he was doing, didn't he."

"Yeah, and he wasn't the only one doing it."

Her voice hitched. "I see that." She trailed her fingers over the deep red welts and blackened patches on my chest. "Remember when I said good surprises?"

"I'll try to do better next time."

"You do that." She gave me a little push. "Lie down before you fall over."

I winced my way down onto the cold platform, immensely thankful that the tank would be taking the pain away in a matter of moments. "Hope I didn't scare Daniel."

"He thought you were invincible. Now he knows different."

"Sorry."

"He was bound to learn the truth sooner or later." Disregarding the blood, she kissed me. "See you in a while." Her fingers brushed the hair from my face.

A sharp intake told me she'd seen my ear. "That was too close."

"You're telling me?"

"Vayen, I'm serious. You have us now. You can't be out there killing yourself. What the hell would I do? What about the kids? Where would we go?"

My head hurt as much as my chest. Too many people needed me and none of them for the same reasons. "Just start the tank, Stassia." I closed my eyes, hoping she'd get the hint I didn't want to fight right now.

Her footsteps drifted away. The sensation of floating upward overcame me and then the warm gel sucked me into its healing grip.

Chapter Ten

Merkief's face loomed over me when I cracked open my eyes. "About time."

"Sorry, I was out trying to solve your problem with Kess."

"Rok isn't mine."

I sat up, wrapping the sheet around me. "It was in the Narvan last I looked. You seem to be holding lead on the System, or want to anyway. That would make it *your* problem."

He sighed and looked me over as though I were still bloody and bruised. He appeared genuinely concerned. "Was it worth it?"

"Waking up here, covered in gel yet again? Not really. Letting Kess know I'm back and proving it, yes."

"I thought we'd covered this, you're not back." Merkief's stance and demeanor went tight and tense.

A shower would have to wait. The way things seemed to be going lately, I'd probably end up back in the tank soon anyway. I got up and brushed the gel from my body. Hopefully, the cleaning bot would take care of the crumbly mess before Stassia saw it.

I grabbed a shirt from the shelf. As I pulled it over my head, I came to the unwelcome realization that, no, the tank couldn't replace missing pieces. The top of my ear had healed over, but it was missing a good inch. Yet another thing Merkief had taken from me. I stepped into my pants and reached for my boots, growing more than a little tight and tense myself.

"You clearly don't have a handle on the Narvan, and you're the one who's supposed to be in charge. Unless the two of you find some nerve and use it, I'm back. That's the only way Kess is going to fall," I said.

"The only way to make him fall is to take him out. You do that and you can go back into retirement."

"Oh really. And what are you going to do when the High and Mighties send their next candidate against you?"

"They won't," he said confidently.

"Why wouldn't they? You had plenty of opportunity to make this work. We had the Narvan generally back in order in a matter of months when Anastassia left us an unholy lurch. You've had five years. You've failed."

Merkief punched me. I shook it off. He needed to hear the truth. Whether we were friends or not anymore, I owed him that much.

"Go hit someone who deserves it. Quit letting Kess drain your forces from right under your damned nose!"

"They're not my forces!"

"I seem to recall leaving one of the Jalvian worlds in your hands."

He raised his fist again. I grabbed it and shoved him backward.

"If you hit me again, I will hit you back and we both know how that went last time."

Merkief's fists remained ready, but at his sides. He didn't back down. "Get your family off this ship. They don't belong here."

"You're right. They belong on Minor. But you fucked that up too. You're going to have to give me a few days to find a new place to move them."

Merkief stood there, red-faced and fuming. "They can't stay here."

"Don't make me have this conversation with you, too. This ship belongs to Anastassia. She can stay here as long as she likes."

"I could make her not like it."

The bond surged within me. I had him pinned up against the wall in a heartbeat. "How about I make it so you don't have to worry about using the tank ever again?"

"Let me go," he hissed.

"When I do, you're going to leave. Unless you need the tank, don't come back. Got it?"

"Or what? You're forgetting that the Council doesn't know you're back. How about I fill them in?"

I knocked his head back against the wall and loosened my

hold on him. He didn't attempt to get away.

Reason didn't work on him. Physical force had a negligible effect. How was I supposed to work with a man who was so wrapped up in his own head that nothing else seemed to matter?

"Would you like to hand the Narvan to Kess?" I asked.

"Maybe I don't care about the damned Narvan anymore."

I put more pressure on this throat. "Then I could just put you out of your misery right now. Or you can cut the shit and go do something useful."

He spat in my face.

"Who's controlling Frique?"

"No one. You, for all I care."

I let him go. "Thanks, now you can leave."

Merkief caught his breath and straightened his coat. "I don't take orders from you. Not anymore."

He took a swing at me. I knocked him aside. My time with Jey had made Merkief less effective. He might have had speed and agility on his side but he was too angry to focus properly.

He snarled and stormed out of the room.

"Daddy?" Ikeri peeked in. "Why is he so mad?"

I froze for a moment, stammering as I fought to calm myself in her unexpected presence. "He's sad. Sometimes when people are very sad they get angry."

"Are you sad?"

"Not exactly, why?"

"You're very angry," she said.

I gave her a gentle push out of my room. She didn't need to be subjected to me in this state. Ikeri deserved the father I'd been on Minor.

"Can you find your mother and ask her to come in here? Please?" I asked as calmly as I could manage.

Anastassia had been right, this life wasn't one for children or lasting relationships. Daniel would have been doomed to a messy childhood, and we would have never even considered bringing Ikeri into being. For that matter, I very much doubted Stassia and I would have stayed together very long after she'd lost her link.

She didn't do a great job of hiding her resentment at having to sit on the sidelines. Especially not since she'd had a taste of working with Neko and Harmon. Having recently been relegated to more sidelines than I would have liked, I understood her frustration.

Stassia came in as I was slipping into my web of holsters. "Did you need something?"

"Yeah, I need to find somewhere else for you and the kids, but that's going to take some time. I might be gone for a while."

She cleared her throat. "I heard Merkief wasn't happy about us being here."

"I'm sure that's not all you heard."

"No. Do you think he'd go to the Council?"

"Honestly, I don't know what he's capable of doing anymore. I only seem to find all the things he's not."

She fiddled with the sheet as she leaned against my bed. "Don't you think you're being a little hard on him?"

Even after the shit he'd pulled on us, she was sympathetic? Maybe she didn't fully understand the situation, which like everything else, was probably my fault.

"He's failing, Stassia. Miserably. And he's taking an entire system down with him. Jey's lost his balls and is following Merkief's half-assed lead. Now I have to clean it all up or hand the Narvan to Kess so we can go back to Minor in peace. So, no, I'm not being too hard on anyone."

She twisted the sheet in her hands until it resembled a thick rope. "You can't hand the Narvan to Kess. He's no better than they are."

"Maybe he's learned a thing or two. Near half the damned Jalvian forces are behind him."

She gasped. "No."

"Oh yes. They've really fucked up."

"Hey, watch it. The kids are around."

"I know! Dammit, and I can't fix that either until I figure some things out."

She stepped closer and lowered her voice. "What are you thinking of doing?"

"You don't want Kess. Merkief and Jey don't want Kess. I'm on the fence about Kess because he's got a good lead on Merkief and Jey both with the Narvan and the Council, but no one cares what I think. Merkief can't handle it. Jey can't handle it. And I don't know if Kess can handle it either. None of them can work effectively together. That rules out everyone currently on the table."

A chill settled in my gut. "We need a new option."

Her eyes grew wide. "No."

"I don't see any other choice. Do you?"

"Don't do this." She hugged the twisted sheet to her chest.

"I'll take that as a no."

I loaded my weapons and slid them into their holsters, replacing the missing guns with spares from the chest under my bed.

She ran at me, crushing me with an embrace that may have broken a couple ribs had I been her own race. "Don't."

"I'm not running off to present myself to the High and Mighties just yet. I need to find a safe place for you first." I pried her arms off me. "I need to go."

Stassia stepped back, her uncertain gaze darting over me. "I don't remember this side of you."

"You don't remember, because you were off being tortured by the Council. You said the Narvan needed Vayen. Well, I'm sorry, this is me."

I pulled on my coat and left her standing there as I Jumped to the surface of Frique. The heat roasted me like Stassia was likely doing deep down in the ship. For a moment, I felt bad that she'd had to endure my bad mood as well, but she needed to know who she was joining with. All of me.

I stood there outside the house I'd shared with Stassia on many occasions, some of which were quite pleasant. I'd cooked for her there. Made up to her there. Her family had lived in the area once. The beating sun shown down through the canopy of green leaves. Would she be happy here again? The kids would love it. But I needed someone to stand guard. And I needed to know Frique was safe.

"Jey, what's the deal with Frique?"

"Nothing? No deals, why?"

"Why not?"

Frique didn't have much in the way of extra-planetary commerce, but they did have basic resources and if Merkief and Jey needed every advantage, why the hells had they not stooped to Frique?

"The populace didn't want us. You missed dividing it in your mad dash to reassign the Narvan. Merkief and I fought over it at first, each wanting the majority, but as it turned out, even when I let him have it, their government turned up their noses and closed their doors. I've kept them in my security runs but only at distance. They've not needed us and we've not needed them."

"They're people. They have food. Lots of it. I'm sure you need to feed your soldiers."

"I have food from Karin and Jal. Rok has had some luck with an agri-project Merkief had started on Karin years ago. They've been semi-self sustaining for the past two years."

While that was news to me, it didn't answer my burning question. *"What about Kess?"*

"He could care less about Frique either. Vayen, there's nothing useful there. Just timber, prantha herds, and surly farmers."

"Thanks." I cut contact.

Frique might be my answer for now. I went into the house. Nothing had changed. Out of curiosity, I grabbed the first bot I saw and accessed its log. No one had been in the house since days after we'd disappeared. I set the bot back on the floor and went to check our rooms. Stassia's was untouched. Surprisingly, so was mine. It seemed that Merkief and Jey shared my disdain for the tiny planet.

Sitting down wasn't an option in my current state. I needed to keep moving, burning off energy before I burst. Pacing the common room with thundering steps on the bare wooden planks, I dove into my link. Twenty minutes later, I'd verified that the house had remained off the radar as far as gathering any attention. No mention of it had appeared in any records for years. If Stassia stayed close to the house, under the cover of the trees, there shouldn't be any reason for that to change. If I could keep Merkief out of the loop, I'd feel even better about it.

Since there wasn't a way to guarantee that would happen, I needed someone to stand guard while I continued to mop up the Narvan. I contacted Neko.

"I take it you're still alive?"

"No thanks to you, but yes," he said.

"Good. I need your services."

"I'm already employed. Seems this job is less dangerous than standing anywhere near you."

He sounded annoyed, but didn't shut down the conversation, so maybe there was a chance of winning him over. Starting again with a fresh guard didn't have much appeal, and I didn't have time to do a raft of interviews. I began to see why Stassia had forgiven my unannounced drunken month off early in my employment. Putting all that work into trusting and finding someone you didn't mind living with wasn't easy to toss aside.

"I wasn't even in the house when that all happened." I said, *"I'm sorry Harmon got killed in the line of duty."*

"You didn't have to be in the house. They were looking for you or her. Both of you, if rumors are to be believed."

"Which rumors are those?"

"Gemmen had me sit in on the interrogations Gamnock ordered on the men we captured. Someone guessed you'd be here, on the base. They sent in enough men to make sure you'd go down," Neko said.

"I didn't go down."

"No, you ran." He paused. *"Not that I'm criticizing that choice in this case."*

"Wise move. Tell Gamnock you quit. I'll double your salary."

He scoffed. *"You don't even know what I make."*

"Sure I do. I have access to all of Cragtek's records." Thanks to Gemmen, that wasn't an empty boast.

Hesitation leaked through our connection. *"Does Gamnock know this?"*

I threw him a little power. *"Only if you tell him."*

He paused long enough that I began to wonder if he was in fact contacting Gamnock. *"Triple it and I'm yours."*

"You're not that good. Double and if no one important dies, including you, in the next six months, we'll talk."

"Deal. Where do you need me?"

I flashed him the jump point outside the house and then let Gemmen know what I was about. No need to have him suspect Neko of defecting.

"Gamnock isn't going to be happy. He lost a lot of men in that attack. He's blaming you," Gemmen said.

"I'll make it up to him."

I spent a few minutes transferring a stash of credits to the Cragtek account. Credits couldn't replace the men who had been lost, but those resources could put new employees in their places.

Neko arrived with a bulging pack on his shoulder. He took in the house with a quick once-over. "Home?"

"For now."

I motioned for him to follow me. We went inside, and I gave him the quick tour. We spent a while at the security station, going over the controls and my strict instructions to keep everyone within the immediate treeline. The cover went far beyond that, but a boundary needed to be set. One that a single man could be expected to patrol reliably, even with all the security that we employed within the house and nearby grounds.

He sat at the controls, going over them one by one to prove he'd gotten everything I'd just thrown at him.

"You're really not messing around," he said.

"No, we're not. I'll leave you to get familiar with the place for a while. I have some work to do."

"Will your family be joining me?"

"Not tonight." I pointed him to the room Merkief had once used. "It's small but you can have that one."

He held up his pack. "I don't take much space. Will we be here long?"

"I don't know yet."

He chuckled. "Not big on the definite answers, are you?"

I'd gotten that safety practice from Stassia. "No."

"Well, there's one anyway." He headed to the room. "I'll get settled in then."

"Hold on. Give me a minute to clear it out."

A hint of hesitation feathered his words, "Do I want to know what happened to whomever's stuff you're clearing out?"

"He's still alive, if that's what's got you worried."

I cut off his mumbling about not being worried by going in and gathering up the few articles of clothing Merkief had left there. If he hadn't used anything for this long, he wouldn't miss it. After throwing Merkief's things in the garbage unit with unabashed satisfaction, I declared the room ready for Neko and let him move in.

While Neko was occupied, I spent some time on the local network, familiarizing myself with the changes that Frique had undergone in my absence. If I planned to step back into the spotlight, I couldn't ask for an easier place to start, somewhere no one paid attention to unless something major happened. I wasn't ready for anything major to happen just yet.

When I snapped out of my link trance, Neko stood nearby, waiting patiently.

"So what would you like me to do?" he asked.

"Take a walk outside for a couple hours. Let me know if you find anything at all suspicious."

While he made laps around the house in the sweltering heat, I kept an eye on the network, watching for any sign of activity relating to the house. If anyone was watching for signs of life here, they'd notice Neko.

Nothing turned up by the time he came in. The feeds stayed clean for hours after as well.

"Get some sleep. I'll be awake for a while," I informed him.

Neko nodded and disappeared into the bedroom. When his door closed, I brushed his mind with my own, just the lightest touch, nothing he'd notice, I hoped anyway. He might be a good soldier, but I rather doubted he'd had a lot of experience with probes on any level.

All I skimmed from him was that he was tired, uncertain, but excited to get a raise, and that he was at least somewhat afraid of me. That worked. Relieved not to find anything duplicitous, I vacated his mind and delved back into the Friquen government.

When the sun came up, I found a scheduled meeting in the nearest city. It seemed as good of a place as any to begin my reintegration. I took off my coat, changed into some semi-Friquen clothing, and tucked in a few weapons for good measure. Going alone would make me even less noticeable. I decided to let Neko sleep.

Jumping got me within five minutes of the city center. I walked along the streets lined with plain houses, some with businesses on the ground floor and living spaces above. Two boys came along beside me with a rotund, orange, tuber-laden hovercart floating between them, guidelines in hand. Their conversation about a prank they pulled on an unfortunate girl swirled around me until I caught sight of an open shop and slipped in. I needed to find something to make Stassia happy. I hadn't done a very good job of that so far. She liked Frique. Surely something from one of the local artisans would put a smile on her face.

The middle-aged woman behind the counter watched me through grey eyes, her dark brown hair hanging long and loose around her thin face. In some ways, she reminded me of the Verian people, resilient and simple, close to the land around them. But where the Verians embraced technology when it promised a safer and cleaner life, the Friquen people shunned it. Unless it came down to a famine or plague upon their crops, they did things the way they'd been done for generations. Even the hovercart the boys had been using, which verged on high-tech here, had to be nearly a hundred years old, as rusted and dinged up as it was.

The few shelves along the wall held jars of preserved fruits and vegetables. Food wasn't the way to win Stassia over. I peered at the clearplaz case that held a selection of metal jewelry set with brilliant red firestones and white swirled cloud beads. Expensive and well-crafted as they were, she had an armband and a neckband. Beyond those, I'd never seen her wear jewelry.

A corner contained a tower of tiny hand-woven baskets inlaid with shells. They reminded me of Sonia. I grimaced and looked elsewhere. Hand-carved boxes inlaid with three other kinds of woods sat stacked on the floor. They were pretty, but what would she put in them? They weren't the sort that allowed for locks so it wouldn't work for securing weapons.

The woman eyed me suspiciously. "Is there something I can help you find?"

"I'm looking for a gift, but I don't know what to get her."

"Maybe some of these fine scents?" She nodded to a shelf of brightly colored bottles behind her.

"I don't think she wears those."

Maybe she wanted to but never did before because definite smells would give her away when we were working. But she'd never done anything with them when we were on Minor either. Sometimes she'd come in from her Seeker session smelling like incense or herbs but that was about the extent of it.

"Don't know her well?"

"I do, but...I don't think that's what I'm looking for."

"Soaps? We have a large collection over here." She pointed at a rack of wrapped bars.

"No." Sure, she liked to be clean, but I'd never known her to indulge in specially scented soap.

"You already looked over the jewelry. How about a scarf? My own grandmother makes these on a loom that's been in our family for six generations." She reached under the counter and set three long scarves on the counter.

I picked one up. The silken fabric slipped through my fingers. It was a pretty purple, rather like the last sunset colors over Artor in fall. But what the hells would she need a scarf for here on Frique? But it was pretty. "Maybe."

"They're very fashionable right now. Many women are wearing them." She picked one up and looped it loosely around her neck. "Like this."

I could see Stassia wearing it. The style fit in perfectly with her Verian wear. Maybe she'd start a new trend, imported Friquen scarves. I could work out a deal with Frique, make a killing on shipping them over and selling them to the shops on Minor to satisfy the eager masses.

"Sir?"

"Oh, sorry. I'll think about it. What else would you suggest?"

She pursed her lips. "Come, look at these." She led me to a windowed room off the main shop filled with waist-high saplings.

"My father grows these special hybrids to remain miniature. They're covered with red blossoms every spring."

"How big do they get?"

"Little taller than you. Wider as well. You'd need to plant it outside eventually. It will be fine in the pot for a few years yet though."

The pot looked to be made of clay, glazed a deep blue like the Friquen sky. It was perfect.

"I'll take one." I went to the counter and took care of the payment. "Can I stop back by for it later? I have a few other things I need to do in town first."

"Sure," she said, beaming.

I had one last look at the pot and reassured myself that the tree was something that would put a smile on Stassia's face. Unless she complained that she had nowhere to plant it. But we had years, according to the clerk, so I'd just tell her that. She'd go with it. Maybe.

Maybe I should have found something else. I glanced around the store one last time, pondering the scarf again. What would be better? A knife? A gun? Those just weren't something that I wanted Stassia to have more of. Certainly not around the kids. Maybe a new weapon safe. But we had one sitting in the house we'd deserted on Rok. Which reminded me I'd need to get that stuff soon before Gamnock tossed it out. No doubt that man was thrilled to be rid of me.

"Was there something else?" the woman asked.

"No. Thank you." I left the store.

The meeting hall was a five-minute walk away that led me past more stores opening their doors for the day. Though I tried to find something to keep the kids busy, nothing caught my eye. What did kids on Frique do for fun? I looked around.

The streets were slowly filling with people going about their business and starting their day. Mothers with small children stopped to converse, creating knots in the flow of traffic. Any children of Daniel's age were carrying baskets, towing hovercarts or leading stock to market. It seemed once you were old enough to walk with an animal or had enough balance to be trusted not to drop something, you worked. Even the old men were working, carving, weaving or shouting directions to apprentices. Elderly women sat in the shade under awnings or trees, weaving, sewing or Geva knows what else. Frique wasn't a land of happy childhood or retirement. I certainly didn't want to live here long-term, but Stassia could visit. That would also put a smile on her face. I hoped.

The meeting hall, an unadorned, boxy plascrete structure welcomed me with as much enthusiasm as the clerk had. I fell in line with the other arriving members of the city council and public with petitions. There were still empty seats in the front row once we filed in so I took one of those. At least there, I could get a good view of the people now in charge of the city we were living near, the ones who would sell us out in a heartbeat if they thought they could get away with it. I needed to remind them of who I was and why pissing me off was a bad idea. Nicely, if possible.

Local issues were addressed first. I half-listened while getting a feel for the men and women around me. There were a few familiar faces among the elected council members, leaving a lot of unknown influences and personalities for me to observe. One of the older men sitting at the table, recognized me in short order, his eyes widening and mouth dropping open. He recovered quickly and did his best to avoid meeting my gaze.

Two hours dragged on in an endless stream of petitioners and rulings. A tall, thin man favoring his right leg and walking with a carved and painted wooden cane, made his way to the front. He stood just ahead of me and began his appeal regarding a parcel of land his village wanted to claim in order to expand their prantha herds.

Something about his voice drew me. There was nothing remarkable about his shaven head or plain clothing. He seemed no particular age or race, nor did he stand out in any certain way. Utterly ordinary among the room showcasing the vast Friquen gene-pool stew. On a planet settled by both Artorian and Jalvian outcasts, pretty much any native Narvan denizen fit in.

Yet his voice, the phrasing, the cadence, it was familiar.

As he turned to glance at the men he'd been sitting with, his blue gaze darted over mine and then snagged for a split second before looking away. I knew that voice and no absence of hair or addition of a limp could stop me now that recognition had struck. It was Fa'yet.

Far more so than Merkief and Jey, I'd never expected to see him again. Rather, I hadn't entertained the thought that he'd still be alive. Last I'd known, the High Council had wanted him dead, preferably by my hand. But I'd let him run. We'd been friends, though he'd betrayed me and cost Sonia her life. The High Council had played their games with both of us, and we'd both lost.

Fa'yet's petition was granted, and as he turned back to the aisle, he glanced at me again. His face remained calm as he passed by, however, his voice in my head was anything but. *"Vayen? I thought you were dead."*

"That was the idea."

My pulse quickened. Was he back in with the Council? Did they suspect I'd turn up here on the only uncontested planet in the Narvan? An informant at Cragtek may have alerted the Council of my presence, they'd sure been quick enough to sell me out to Kess.

He could be lying in wait, ordered to escort me to Sere the moment I showed my face. He might even be working with Merkief.

"Why are you here?" I asked.

"Living. Hiding. That's all I've got left, that and the wish that I'd died like you did rather than having to watch over my shoulder every second of every day."

I glanced backward, noting where he sat. He'd put a wall of innocent people between us.

"Are you here to take me in?" I asked, wrapping my fingers around one of the guns I had hidden on me.

"Hardly. Damned Geva forsaken ranchers elected me to show my face in public and plead their case. They think I'm good at standing up to people. I wish they'd never figured that out. I'm supposed to be dead. I'd been doing a good job being dead."

I turned back to the front after noting that my cranked around position was gaining me notice. It was hard not to turn back to gauge his face, to make sure he wasn't on his feet, either running for the door or reaching for a weapon of his own.

"I'm not the one who's out to kill you, if that's what you're thinking," I assured him.

"You were last time I saw you."

"A lot has changed since then. We're both playing dead here."

The meeting droned on around us. Another petitioner stated his request. The room smelled musty, like wet soil and old sweat. I tried to listen for any hint of Fa'yet leaving, but there was too much shuffling of feet against the bare plascrete floor to pick out anything in particular.

"Can we meet later?" Fa'yet asked.

"When?"

"Give me a couple hours to shake my companions, and I'll meet you for lunch." He flashed me a location and cut contact.

I recognized it as one of the storefronts I'd walked by on my way there. The meeting crept on, sucking up the minutes like a vast field of liquid sand. After seeing Fa'yet, my concentration was shot. I fidgeted in my seat, mulling over his situation and mine.

A bell chimed, signaling the end of the session. Thank Geva.

I stood slowly, waiting for the public to exit the room. Being in the front lent itself to me having an excuse to stand around for a few minutes without attracting undue attention.

As the public left, the council members mumbled to one another, some standing to adjust their sashes of office, about to take their own leave. I caught the gaze of the man who'd recognized me. He motioned for the others to return to their seats.

Once we were alone, I addressed the council, introducing myself to those I didn't know and praising the one I did for his loyalty during my absence. There were, of course, some questions as to where I'd been and why I'd left them to the whims of Merkief, Jey, and Kess.

Since, according to public knowledge, for those who knew where to look, I'd been attacked by Kess, I went with that angle, explaining that I had been near mortally wounded and had been recovering. They were familiar enough with his way of doing business to believe that he may just have done me that amount of damage and claimed to have killed me. No one seemed to entirely buy that I'd been recovering for five years, but they smiled and nodded all the same. I offered them any help they needed and promised to protect them from any further interference from Kess.

Just how I was going to do that remained to be seen since I didn't have a single ship or armed force beyond myself, but I did know Kess and generally were to find him.

As it turned out, I also had to promise to keep Merkief and

Jey off their backs. For neither one of them wanting Frique and claiming to have nothing to do with it, the council's annoyance seemed pretty damn fresh. Maybe they just held long-lasting grudges.

By the time I left the town hall, my stomach was churning at the thought of meeting with Fa'yet. Here I was slowly putting my foot back in the door, and suddenly I was colliding with one of the Council's inner circle. Whether he was ex-Kryon or not, selling information on me to the High and Mighties might just might buy his way back in. So would killing me. That had worked wonders for Kess.

I formed a Jump to the house three times between the town hall and the restaurant, each time talking myself out of it at the last second.

Fa'yet owed me his life. He also had every right to hate me for putting him through all these years of hiding. He'd had a nice home, a seat on the Kryon inner circle, and I'd guess, a freighter full of credits. And he'd lost it all thanks to standing up for me and Stassia and then my not killing him like the Council had ordered.

I formed the Jump to the house again. But I needed the tree. I stepped back out of the cranny I'd ducked into and headed for the store.

Fa'yet walked into the restaurant down the street. Curiosity bolstered my nerve. I passed the store and went in after him.

The simple boxy building, the same as near every other damn public place on Frique, offered no obvious threat. The few occupants didn't even glance up when I walked into the main room. Fa'yet had taken the prime seat, facing the door, back against the wall. He spotted me immediately. No backing out now.

I sat across from him, annoyed that he'd taken the good seat. The only warning I'd have would be the look on his face, assuming he wasn't in on any action against me.

I wouldn't have blamed him if he was.

"Hungry?" He pushed a menu toward me. "I don't recommend the stew."

"Been here before?"

"No, but I've been on Frique for years. I've yet to find a decent stew."

A boy tiptoed over and put a basket of crusty bread and a pitcher of what appeared to be plain water between us. He ducked away. Fa'yet pushed one of the two glasses that had been on the table at me. I poured for both of us.

We eyed each other, each daring the other to drink first. He broke and gulped down a mouthful.

"You haven't changed," he said.

"You might be right."

Which was a little sad, really. Had all those years as Isnar been neatly boxed up and stored away? Stassia still needed me beside her and our kids needed a father. The old me wasn't suited for either of those things.

"I wasn't going to come," he said.

"Neither was I."

He nodded and picked up his menu.

We sat in silence, looking over the list of five choices. Even after several minutes, I couldn't have told anyone what was on the menu. I was too busy checking the local network for suspicious activity, brushing over Daniel's mind and then Stassia's, and convincing myself I wasn't doing something stupid by sitting here. For all I knew, Fa'yet was doing much the same thing.

There were so many ways this could all go wrong. It was as if I'd turned the corner on an already crooked road only to find myself faced with a thousand forks. Geva only knew where any of them led.

"So you're working with prantha now?" I asked.

He set his menu down. "Seemed as unlikely a place to find me as any. Beats working on a long-haul freighter. I was never a fan of stasis."

"Me either." Stasis reminded me of Daniel's years trapped as an infant in a tube in the back of a lab.

"Have you been here long?" he asked.

"No."

"I might be out of the Kryon loop, but I still have ears. If Kess killed you, how'd you manage to end up not dead?"

"I gave Kess our links."

His mouth dropped open and then snapped shut. "But if that's the case, why are you still around? He's going to be pissed as all hells if someone spots you. He'll lose all credibility within Kryon!"

I gestured for him to calm the fuck down. "You're announcing it to the room isn't helping. Besides, he already knows I'm back."

"Back, back?"

"I think so, yeah."

He grimaced. "Are you sure that's a good idea? In your case, staying dead is the safer bet."

"Of course it's not a good idea, but it's necessary."

Our conversation halted as the boy came back to take our orders. When he left, I briefly explained how Merkief, Jey, and Kess were making a mess of the Narvan.

"So leave them to it. None of that concerns you."

I stared at him. "You can't be serious. That's our homeworld we're talking about."

He shrugged. "I'm sure Artor and Karin will go on without you."

"Sure, but go on how? You know as well as I do that the Council has its own direction for the Narvan," I said. "It was never one I particularly approved of."

He cracked open a heel of the bread and picked at the flaky insides. "They'll always have their own direction for systems." Fa'yet dropped the bread onto his plate and glared at me. "What can we do about it other than bend a few things one way or the other until the Council gets fed up and sends a more agreeable Kryon to end our lives?"

"I wasn't more agreeable," I said.

"You agreed to kill me. I'd say you were."

"It wasn't like that."

He gave me a dry smile. "Maybe not to you."

Fa'yet scanned the other occupants and then settled his gaze on me. "Why are we doing this?"

"Because I want to know where you stand and you want to know if she's still alive."

Fa'yet nodded. "That neatly pares it down to the bone, doesn't it?"

The boy slid two bowls onto the table and left. We both tested our food, incidentally the same soup. It was filled with a variety of beans of different sizes and colors and offered a good spicy kick.

"Not bad," I said.

"Way to avoid answering the question."

"I hadn't planned on answering the question."

He gripped the edge of the table. "I want to think you somehow managed to extract links out of both of your living heads when you handed them to Kess. But here you sit, alone and looking fairly at ease, considering. So either you've had a few years to get over her loss, you let Kess kill her to save your own ass, or she's still alive somewhere."

I took another sip of the soup.

"We were friends, dammit. Her and I. You and I. All of us. I deserve to know."

For as aggravated as he was getting, he was at least keeping his voice down this time.

"You think I'd tell you if I had a part in offing her? That would be pretty foolish. Even if you are an old bald man with a limp and cane."

"I'm not old and I'm not bald," he hissed. "Is Ana alive?"

I brushed against his link. The natural connection we'd once shared also opened. He let me in voluntarily, no need to attempt any level of probing. Fa'yet's mind was as clear and clean as one could be with the sort of past we both shared. Everything from the time he'd left Karin was right there for my inspection. Nothing stood out to me as a hint that Fa'yet was anything more than he appeared to be. Meaning, he was anxious, highly annoyed with me, carrying weapons and very, very sick of pranthas and their stinking mounds of shit.

"Yes."

Tears welled in his eyes. "I didn't dare hope."

"Do *not* cry. People are going to notice."

Fa'yet rubbed his eyes for a moment. "I wasn't. It's just..."

"I know. Common reaction. She's made a lot of men cry."

He chuckled. "I'm sure you're one of them. How is she, truly?"

"Probably cursing me right now."

The quick brush I'd done over our bonded connection had hinted at definite aggravation but whether that was aimed at me or the kids, I wasn't sure.

Fa'yet pushed his bowl of soup aside and leaned forward, grinning. "How long have you been joined? I bet she put you through your paces with the gifting."

"She's working on it."

He cocked his head. "How so?"

"We're a little behind. I just got around to the gifting part yesterday."

He scoffed. "A little?"

"Yes, well. We've been busy and it really never came up until recently."

"I'd love to see her. Is she nearby?"

"I'm sure you would. Not exactly."

His good humor faded. "It would mean a lot to me."

To her too, I had little doubt.

"I'll consider it. But not today."

"When? I'm only going to be here until tomorrow. If I stick around too long, they'll ask questions. This old, bald man with a limp and a cane has a life and livelihood to protect."

If I could verify that no one had paid attention to Neko at the house by then, I might be ready to bring her and the kids up. I imagined Fa'yet's face seeing the kids.

"Why are you grinning? That's kind of scary when you do that, you know, all broody one minute and grinning like a maniacal lunatic the next," he said.

"I was just picturing something. When tomorrow?"

"Afternoon."

Having experienced his level of utter openness, my mental wheels began to churn.

"What happened with your link? How have you evaded the Council contacting you?" I asked.

"I couldn't live without one, but I had a friend who owed me. He pulled my link and gave me a new blank one. Mine was incinerated."

"Talented friend."

"He was," he said flatly.

It seemed Fa'yet had taken no chances with covering his tracks.

"Do you have family here?"

"Not really. I've got a few women in town that don't mind keeping an old man company now and then, but I wouldn't call them family per se."

"Good, that would be in poor taste."

"Only in the way you're thinking. I get lonely too, you know."

"I'm sure you do. You're faking the old thing pretty well."

"The kick in the hip from an irate prantha when I first arrived helped tremendously. At least in that regard. Hurts like a bitch when the weather gets cold and wet though," he said.

"We're on Frique. There is no cold and wet."

"Only around here. I live over on the edge of the continent. We're only here to make our petition."

I hadn't considered that. Staying out of the big city, if one could classify anything a big city on Frique, would make him even harder to find.

My soup had gone cold. Too much talking and not enough

eating. "I should get going. I'll contact you tomorrow."

"You do that."

I slid a credit chip through the reader on the table and left. He didn't try to stop me.

The woman at the store smiled when I walked in. "Ready to pick up your plant?"

I nodded.

"Do you have a cart?"

"Uh, no."

"That pot is heavy. Did you plan on carrying it?"

I hadn't planned on buying it. "I'll manage."

She looked me up and down. A slight smile tweaked her lips. "You just might."

I could feel her watching me as I crouched down to pick up the pot. Once I found solid handholds, I hefted the pot and its contents and stood. Leaves and branches raked against my face. A twig tangled in my hair.

"Not too far to go, I hope?" she asked.

"No."

"Have a good day then. I hope she likes it."

She waved as I worked my leafy, awkward load out the door. I managed to bash a knuckle on the doorframe before I staggered out into the freedom of the street.

By the time I reached the edge of the town proper, sweat poured down my face and my arms were shaking. Why had I bought this stupid thing? The lower twigs tugged on my hair for the tenth time and had scratched up my face, neck, arms and hands. I shook myself loose and trudged onward, swearing under my breath.

It didn't help that I couldn't take a straight shot home either. Well, I could have, but my conscience wouldn't allow it—especially not with the spectacle I made of myself walking down the street as a half-man, half-tree. People were definitely watching. And snickering. I kept my glare locked onto the damned tree and focused on taking turns into less and less populated areas before finding a spot to duck into so I could safely form a Jump back to the house.

Neko happened to be rounding the house as I stepped out of the void and into the woods.

"Need a hand with that?" he asked.

What was I going to do with it? The weather was tame enough, and it was out of direct light. Stassia would know better how to care for it than I did.

"Thanks, but I'll just leave it right here for now."

"Good, because it looks really heavy."

"It is."

My legs trembled when I squatted to set the pot on the mossy ground. I wouldn't need a workout for days.

"Everything is still all clear here."

"Good." I peeled my sweat-drenched shirt off. "I'm taking a shower and then getting a little sleep."

"All right then." He pulled something out of his back pants pocket.

My muscles tensed. My hand went to a gun.

"Oh, no, no." He shook his head. "Just a scanner." He held out the black wand for me to see and then waved it over the tree and the pot. "Standard procedure at Cragtek with anything incoming."

"Right."

I knew that, I just hadn't expected it here. A cautious man, I liked that.

"Everything check out?"

He nodded and put the wand away.

"I'm off to get some sleep then. Keep up the good work."

"Will do." He offered a quick mock salute and continued his lap.

I went inside, dropped my shirt on the floor of the bathroom and stood in the cold water for a good five minutes. The water felt so good. It even numbed all the scratches the damned tree had made on near every inch of exposed skin during my trek.

Clean and much cooler, I laid in bed staring at the ceiling. I was tired, yet sleep refused to come. It didn't help that I knew the kids hadn't been outside all day and even Stassia had to be crawling up the ship's walls by now. I sighed, threw on some clothes and Jumped to the ship.

Ikeri's scream pierced the air. Daniel laughed and ran down the hall. Stassia charged after him, but I was closer. I grabbed his arm and yanked him aside. He yelped.

"What did you just do?"

"Nothing."

"Really. Let's just go back in here then," I pulled his resisting body back down the hall past Stassia who dodged out of our way, "and you can explain to me why your sister was just screaming."

"I don't know why." He tried to squirm free.

Ikeri stood in my room, crying. One of my knives lay on the floor by her feet. I opened my mind to her immediately, frantically seeking any possible wounds, but she was just scared.

I picked up the knife with my free hand. "Do you think this is a toy?"

"No," he blubbered, tears rolling down his cheeks.

"Then why the hells were you playing with it?"

"I don't know."

I shook him just enough to scare him. "Maybe you need some time to come up with a better answer."

The void swallowed us both and spit us back out in the house. I marched him into Jey's room. A quick search of the room later, I cleared out Jey's few belongings and slammed the door behind me.

The ship was no place for children. Not even ours. It held a well-stocked armory for Geva's sake. What if he'd managed to get in there? My mind showed me what that could have meant in vivid detail. I Jumped back to the ship, the only thing I could think of to get that vision out of my head.

Stassia held Ikeri, who was still sobbing.

"Come on." I held my hand out to both of them. "I have a surprise for you."

Stassia gave me a cold stare. "You're just full of them lately, aren't you?"

"What do you mean by that?"

"Nothing." She stood up with Ikeri in her arms but didn't take my hand.

"You'll like this. I promise." When she still kept her hands to herself, I got more than a little concerned for my own safety. I wrapped my arms around them both and Jumped to the new point I'd set inside the house.

The Jump with just the two of them was easier than the three all at once, but the quick succession still didn't do me any favors. Jey was right, my stamina was still low.

Stassia extracted herself from my grasp and glanced around the common room. "You're sure this is a good idea?"

"I thought you'd be happier here."

"I'd be happy somewhere safe," she said.

She was definitely pissed at me.

"I think this is safe."

"You thought Rok was safe too."

While I was happy to see that her ability to glare daggers was still fully functional, I didn't like it aimed at me. In the interest of deflecting whatever other abilities her ire might resurrect, I forced a smile. She usually liked those.

"And you were happy to stay there. I checked this place out. It's fine. Just don't go wandering too far from the house. At least the kids can play outside here."

"And what if something happens when their outside playing? What am I supposed to do about it?"

Fuck. The smile wasn't working.

"You have help." I nudged Neko's link, hoping he would save me. He walked through the door a few seconds later.

"Did you need..." He grinned, seeing Stassia and Ikeri. "Good to see you again.

Ikeri tears halted as she waved to him.

Stassia's voice softened the slightest degree. "That will help a little."

"I would think so. I've already shown him the grids and set up a perimeter. He's got things under control."

"You mean you used him for bait, checking to see if the house was safe."

"Well, I certainly wasn't bringing the three of you here without knowing."

She exhaled loudly. "I suppose I should make some dinner. Is there anything stocked here?"

"I'll pick up something. Sit down and relax. What would you like?"

"Don't ask me that right now. You wouldn't like the answer." She stormed into the kitchen.

I looked up to see Neko grimacing. He gave me an apologetic nod and then guided Ikeri over to the surveillance station where he set her on his lap.

Stassia rummaged through the cabinets and the cold storage. The icy blast rolling out the open door wasn't just from the contents inside. I kept my distance.

"Really, I thought you'd be happy here."

She slammed the door shut. "You scared the hell out of Ikeri when you took off with Daniel. She knew how mad you were at him. She can feel that, just like I can, probably more so considering her connection with you isn't damaged like mine. She thought you were going to hurt him."

"I wouldn't do that. He's just a little kid for Geva's sake."

"She felt you when you and Merkief went at it on the ship. We all heard you. She knows what you're capable of."

I stood, stunned. "You're going to have to either train her or get her some training."

"And you're going to have to guard your thoughts a lot better and maybe control your temper around our kids."

"I do have my defenses up. She's just found an in because we have a strong natural connection."

"No, you keep a connection open to her so you can check up on us."

She picked something from the cold storage and slammed it down on the counter. I wasn't the only one with a temper.

"I do the same thing with Daniel," I said.

"But it's not the same, is it?"

"Not exactly. Look, the only way I can make sure she doesn't inadvertently pick something out of my head would be to cut her off entirely. I don't want to do that. She needs to know I'm all right. She gets very concerned. I feel it."

"I get concerned too," she said.

That might have been touching if she hadn't accompanied the statement with a scowl.

"Would you like me to get something for dinner?" I asked again.

She stared at the frozen package on the counter, one hand holding onto the handle of the cold storage. "If you want. I'm not really hungry."

"Stassia, I'm really trying here."

The anger raging over our connection ebbed another degree. "What happened to your face?" She let go of the handle and edged closer as if she were finally seeing me. "And your neck and arms? Your hands."

"It's just a few little scratches."

She scowled again, but in the way she did when she was puzzling something out when working with her clients. "Do they itch?"

I hadn't given it much thought, what with wanting to see her and then dealing with the aftermath, but now that I did... "Yes. Quite a lot actually. Thanks for bringing that up." I suddenly wanted nothing more than to itch my face.

"Don't touch it. You'll only make it worse." She reached up to run her fingers along the scratch along my jawline. "Where did you get these and when?"

"A few hours ago. I was going to save this until you were in a better mood, but come on."

She seemed to know what she was onto, even if she wasn't sharing it with me. I opened the front door for her.

Stassia walked down the steps onto the mossy ground. The blue pot sat there with its lush green sapling. Stassia's scowl broke into a faint smile.

"You got me a tree?"

Maybe this had been a bad idea after all.

"Is it poisonous or something?"

The woman at the shop had seemed amused when I'd come back for it. Had she found out who I was or was she after Stassia, lacing the tree with some sort of poison that Neko's scanner hadn't registered? For that matter, as I recalled belatedly, the scanners only picked up common poisons and scanned for hidden weaponry or incendiary devices. Now I'd have to spend countless more hours in the damned tank, putting me even further behind and giving Kess a bigger lead on planning his next move against me.

"I should have gone for the soaps or one of those carved boxes," I muttered to myself.

Stassia walked over to the tree and pulled off a leaf.

"Don't touch it!"

She snapped the leaf in half and sniffed it. A full-fledged smile broke out on her face and she chuckled. "Nothing to worry about. It's a very nice specimen of quite a rare tree. You just happen to be allergic to it. It's a common reaction in Artorians."

"But why didn't the clerk say something for Geva's sake. She could have warned me."

"Anyone with Artorian blood who's been here for a couple generations has probably built up an immunity. You do blend in fairly well here, especially when you dress the part." She waved at my clothes. "She wouldn't have known you weren't native unless you told her."

"Oh."

She dropped the leaf and came to me. "That's an awful lot of scratches for just stepping outside the shop and Jumping here. How far did you carry that thing?"

"Through most of town. I didn't think to have a hovercart, and people thought I was quite an amusing sight. Took me a long time to get somewhere secluded enough to Jump."

"It looks heavy." Her fingers curled around mine.

"It is."

"I like it much better than soaps or a carved box." She kissed me.

"I didn't know what to get."

"You did." Her lips brushed over mine again.

"I don't suppose you're hungry now, because I am."

"Are we talking about food or something else?" she asked.

"You tell me." I was certainly open to either.

"I like the tree. I do. Though I almost like the effort you put into getting it here even more." She squeezed my hand. "However, we still have a few things to work out, and I'm pretty sure I'd be going way too easy on you if I called off your wooing efforts so soon."

"I'd get by." I pulled her close.

"Mmm, I sure you would," she managed to say before I pleaded my case with a long, deep kiss.

She pulled back. "Dinner and then a visit to the tank for you. That will take a week to go away on its own and it's likely to get worse before it gets better."

"I wanted to bring you here because I couldn't get to sleep. It's been awfully lonely in bed lately."

"Nice try. Go on." She gave me a gentle push.

I let her win for now and Jumped to Veria Minor. Maybe eating something she and the kids were used to would continue to improve her disposition.

When I returned to the house, I found Daniel sulking at the table with Ikeri across from him. Stassia already had the plates out. She sat next to me as I put the bag of food down.

Stassia scooped some of the fried bean cakes out for the kids and a heap of the crisp seaweed noodles she liked.

"I suppose I should bring some to Neko. He'll be hungry too," she said.

It annoyed me that we couldn't have a family dinner without a reminder that we weren't in our own house anymore. We had a guard and he had to eat. Did he normally eat with her, with my children? I'd not thought about it. I'd not been there to see. Maybe there was some other reason she wasn't as anxious to share our bed again as I was.

Stassia fixed a plate and set it in front of Daniel. "Carefully bring that to Neko. He should be through there." She pointed toward the common room.

It occurred to me that Daniel had just come out of his room and had not had a chance to explore, which was probably more of a reason for his sulking than having to face me or Stassia.

"I'll go with him," I offered.

"No, sit. You don't get to eat with us very often. I think you can stay put in a chair for twenty minutes, don't you?"

"Only if you're in the one next to me."

She shook her head, laughing. "Getting desperate for my attention?"

"Maybe."

As long as she didn't run off after Daniel to see Neko, I'd feel better.

She sat next to me and started in on the noodles.

I missed meat. Good meat that wasn't tainted by the flavor of the vegetation on Veria Minor. Even when I'd tried to deal with the flavor, it hadn't set well with me. At least Frique had excellent cuts of prantha. But this meal was for her, so I attempted to enjoy the bland noodles.

"The kids are happy to have something to eat that they recognize," she said quietly.

"I remember how hard it was to get used to that when I signed on with you. My stomach was in turmoil for months."

"Verian food was all they knew. They had just started to get used to the food on Rok and now they'll have Friquen food to deal with. I hope this won't be too hard on them."

"I'm sure they'll adapt. They're young."

She set her fork down and re-arranged the food boxes. "Sure, but what about after this?"

"After what?"

She shook her head. "We'll talk about this later. Eat."

I had a feeling that even though she'd softened, I was still going to get an earful. I tried to enjoy dinner and smile in front of the kids.

When we'd finished, I took Daniel outside and showed him exactly how far he could go into the woods. I scraped a line in the dirt and leaves.

"Go past this and you'll be in trouble. Got it?"

"Why, will something happen?"

What was I supposed to tell him? Men will leap out of the woods and try to kill you? People up in the sky might see you and come down to kill you? Lots of people might die like on Rok?

"Don't push your luck. If I hear you've been breaking the rules, you'll have to go back to the ship and you won't be able to play outside for a very long time. Neko can see everything you're doing out here. Remember that."

He nodded.

We stood outside as the evening dusk settled around us. Daniel and I discussed the knife episode in as much serious detail as I thought he could handle.

"Can I have my own knife?" he asked, making me wonder if he'd heard anything I'd just said.

"No."

Stassia claimed that Daniel acted much older than a typical full-blooded child of her own race or even the Verian children she'd interacted with in her younger years, but if Daniel was anything like my brother and me, five was still too young for a knife.

I noticed she'd come out to stand on the front step. She motioned us toward the house.

"Are we in trouble?" asked Daniel.

"Aren't we always?"

He laughed as only a child who doesn't yet understand the world can.

"You are. I'm good," he said.

"Oh right." I picked him up under one arm and tickled him all the way to the house until he was squealing with laughter.

Stassia took his hand the moment I set him down. The band on her arm caught the last of the sunlight filtering through the leaves overhead.

"You should go take care of that rash before you start itching it."

"I'll go in the morning." I started past her.

She stepped in the way and gently pushed Daniel through the door behind her. "Who knows what morning will bring. Go now while you have the leisure to go."

"I was kind of hoping to spend some time with you."

"You made that quite clear." She smirked. "We're not quite there yet."

"You're taking this whole thing a little too seriously. I'd didn't necessarily mean in bed."

"And you're not taking this seriously enough. People died because of us, Vayen. A lot of good people back on Rok. Innocent people. All because Kess knew we were there. How many people will die here?"

"I... None. How about none. We're in the middle of nowhere here. It's just you, the kids and Neko. No one to leak our location. The kids can get some fresh air. You have help. What more do you want?"

"I don't know yet." She stepped inside and closed the door.

I stood on the steps, not believing that she'd just closed the door in my face. How could she do that?

"Give her some space," Neko said.

"No one asked for your advice." I shut him out and Jumped to the ship. Getting in her face wouldn't get me any further ahead. Maybe some time to sort things out was all she needed and then she'd be back to the playful woman in my arms in the morning.

Jey's voice popped into my head. *"I need your help."*

"What now?"

"Kess made a mess of Rok. You know these people. And someone named Gamnock is demanding to speak to you. I'm assuming you know what that's about?"

I wasn't in the mood to sleep anyway. *"I'll be right there."*

Jey flashed me a jump point and I arrived a moment later.

He grimaced. "What happened to your face?"

I ran a hand over my cheek to find what had been tiny scratches were now angry, weeping welts. And they really itched. I thrust my hand down, refusing to scratch anything. At the moment, it was one of the few things I had control over.

"Nothing. Where do you need me?"

"Deal with that Gamnock first. He sounds really pissed."

"I'll be back as soon as I can then."

He looked me over again, his head cocked and brows raised. "You're meeting him face to face? Are you sure that's wise?"

"He knows who I am."

"Yeah, but he's mad. Really mad." He punctuated that last bit with a knowing and cautious nod.

"You're busy here. I'll be fine."

The command post he'd set up in a bunker somewhere that smelled deep underground from the filtered air and dampness, bustled with activity. Aides ran between officers set at terminals, madly tapping out orders or relaying coded verbal messages by vid.

"I'd rather you used a terminal if you don't have a link connection," he said.

I sighed and waved my hand at him. "Fine."

"Bad day?"

I didn't bother with a reply as I went to find an empty terminal. Once I'd settled in, I contacted Gamnock. It took a few minutes to establish a direct vid connection. He gave me a narrowed-eyed stare from what appeared to be an office similar to Gemmen's.

"What's the problem?" I asked.

"Problem? My base has been attacked, my men slaughtered, my ships destroyed, one of my best men killed, another ran off, and my father deems to tell me, with a smile on his face no less, that you and yours have survived unscathed."

"Not true, but we did survive."

I took a moment to review the company records since the attack. "I sent you credits to cover the loss of men. Why haven't you hired anyone?"

"No one wants to work for me! It seems Cragtek is too dangerous. Entire families were slaughtered in their homes. The families of my employees, in homes where they'd lived safely until you arrived. Are your credits going to erase their deaths? Will they clean up the blood and dispose of the bodies?"

"Kess is the one who attacked you, not me. I don't see him offering to do anything for you or your people."

"Actually, he has."

My heart missed a beat. "What do you mean by that?"

Jey's cautioning me to interact by vid suddenly seemed like a good move. Not that I planned to thank him for it since it was half his fault I was in this mess to begin with.

"He's providing me with new employees. For my father's sake, I hope you're well hidden wherever you are. Don't come back here." He cut contact.

Fuck. There went what little friendly help I had in the Narvan. If Kess had any confirmation of Stassia and the kids from Gamnock or his own men, I could only hope Kess remained smart enough not to mention them to the High and Mighties. Then again, he'd had plenty of time to get over any lingering affection he still might have harbored for Stassia. I had a sinking feeling that handing her over to the Council, with or without the kids wouldn't be near as much of a credibility issue as my own reemergence. However, it would be the perfect way to punish me.

I hoped he wouldn't stoop to that, but my hopes were holding on by thin threads these past few days.

"You don't look so good," Jey said. "I'd say go, but I do need you here."

"I can wait."

For a little while. A very little while. My meeting with Fa'yet tomorrow took on a whole new sense of urgency. I prayed that it wouldn't be too late.

Chapter Eleven

After six intensive hours of helping Jey sort out Rok, I finally made it to the tank. I woke up on the platform, cold, naked and alone. A quick shower to remove the gel and a change of clothes later, I Jumped back to Frique to find everyone sound asleep. Even Neko, though he was at the surveillance station, kicked back in his chair. As angry as I was to find him asleep, I realized he was just one man. He needed his downtime too. I'd need another guard. Or to be here, reliably, in order to give him an off shift. I laughed to myself. Little hope of that.

I'd need to find someone else to help out. That I trusted. On short notice.

And I needed real sleep. The two hours I'd gotten on the tank platform hadn't done much toward bringing me back to full awareness.

I peeked in on Daniel asleep on Jey's bed and then checked Stassia's room, expecting to find Ikeri or her, but it was empty. Confused, I checked my room. They were both sound asleep in my bed. Ikeri had one of my shirts wadded up in her arms where she lay next to Stassia.

As much as I wanted to join them, Stassia had laid out the perfect deterrent. I couldn't bring myself to wake Ikeri by moving her to another bed. We all needed sleep. I had little doubt tomorrow would be a busy day.

Sunlight breaking through the leaves and shining directly at my eyelids brought me out of sleep. Someone came between me and the light before I had a chance to focus. I leapt off the couch and onto my feet. Ikeri toppled backward in her rush to get out of my way.

"Sorry." I scooped her up and plopped back onto the couch.

"Didn't mean to scare you," she said, planting a tiny kiss on my cheek.

"And I didn't mean to scare you."

She giggled.

I glanced around. The doors to all the bedrooms were open. Everyone seemed to be up but me. How had I slept through all that?

"Where is your mother?"

She pointed to the door. "Outside with Daniel and Neko."

"Shall we go see what they're doing?" I stood and turned to pick her up.

"No. Stay." She tugged on my arm.

I sat back down.

"What would you like to do?"

She pouted. "There are no toys here."

"I'm sure we can find something."

Stassia found us in the kitchen stacking the bowls, plates, and cups into a precarious tower. She rolled her eyes.

"I can't tell which one of you is the kid."

"Me!" Ikeri shouted and ran to give her a hug.

"We need to talk," Stassia informed me, nodding toward my room. "Ikeri, why don't you go outside with Neko and Daniel?"

She ushered Ikeri to the door where it didn't shock me to see Neko waiting. He had another one of his apologetic nods ready to go. I wondered if he practiced them in front of a mirror.

"Yes, we do," I said as soon as the door closed. "I have another surprise, one I think you'll like even more, and I'm not allergic to this one. Maybe it will make you feel a little more secure about staying here."

She opened her mouth and closed it again as if I'd totally derailed whatever it was that she'd been going to run me over with.

"You're giving up this foolhardy idea to dive back into advising the Narvan?"

It was my turn to gape. "Um, no. But I still think you'll like this. Hold on." I contacted Fa'yet and found him eagerly awaiting me. I flashed him a jump point. He arrived a blink later.

Stassia jumped back. Her eyes went wide as recognition sunk in. "Isnar?"

"Indeed." He hugged her tightly, cane in hand.

Over his shoulder, she gave me a questioning glance.

"You wanted wooing. I didn't know what else to get you."

"I'm a gift now?" Fa'yet laughed. "I suppose there's a first time for everything. I hope I'm the right size and color. I know how picky you are, Ana."

She burst out laughing. "You're fine. Just what I wanted."

He was what she wanted? Why did he get the hugs and laughter when I got the scowls and 'we need to talk'?

They'd been good friends for years. Very good friends. I knew that, but I couldn't help myself. And I was Isnar. That's the name she'd called me for all the years we'd lived together, the one she used when she smirked in bed, the one she used when she cursed me for being late, the name she called me in front of our children. Not him. Me.

They both looked at me as if I'd spouted a third arm from my chest. Fa'yet stepped away and Stassia grabbed my hand, putting herself between me and Fa'yet.

She looked me in the eye. The calm of the bond washed over me, clearing my head.

"I suppose you'll be wanting to give Isnar the full surprise?" she asked.

"Why don't you go prepare it and give us a minute."

She looked between us. "Will you please remember the part about not doing anything stupid?"

I glared at her. She hurried out the door.

Fa'yet cleared his throat. "Well, I see you two are getting along splendidly."

"Yeah."

"And you chose now to try the gifting and joining?"

"We were fine until that all started. And it wasn't my idea."

"Hers?"

"Oh hells no."

He held up his hand. "I probably don't want to know. How about you explain why you sent her scurrying out the door?"

"How badly do you want out of the prantha business?"

"In a safe and alive manner?"

I nodded.

"Pretty badly."

"Would you miss your bed warmers?"

"I'd get by. What do you have in mind that doesn't entail me going back to Sere or showing my face anywhere the High and Mighties might see me?"

"My family needs a second guard. I think you're qualified, even with the cane."

Fa'yet smirked. "Is that so? And who's the first?"

"Neko. Anastassia has been practicing with him."

"Qualifications?"

"He came recommended from Cragtek. He's proven himself fairly competent."

"Doesn't sound like a stellar endorsement," he said.

"I'm rather short on options at the moment. You'd both need to sleep sometime."

"This is true." He nodded sagely. "And you'd feel better not having her alone with another man."

It wasn't a surprise that Fa'yet saw right through me in that regard. He'd been the one to spot the bond in the first place.

"There is that."

"I don't know as you trust me either," he said.

"I do. It's just..." I raked a hand through my hair. "Things have been less than ideal lately."

"Relationships take work, sometimes extraordinary amounts of it. And even then, not everything will be ideal."

"Thanks. That's just what I needed to hear," I grumbled. "You want out of the prantha business or not?"

"I haven't told you my fee."

"Does it involve more than credits?"

He rubbed his chin. "I suppose not."

"Then consider it covered."

"Oh, one other thing," he said.

There was always one other thing. "What?"

"Don't ask me to inform on her, and I'll do the same for you. Whatever is between you two stays there. I don't want to be in the middle."

"Done."

I had the kids to fall back on if I really needed to know what was going on in my absence.

"Good." He grinned. "Then I want to see the full surprise."

As we walked out the door I heard Stassia announce the arrival of Uncle Isnar to Ikeri and Daniel.

Neko looked to me. "And who is this?"

"A friend. He'll be helping you from now on. I imagine a bed would be more welcome than a chair every night."

His gaze dropped. "Sorry about that. I must have dozed off."

"Can't say as I blame you. This time. Don't let it happen again."

Fa'yet frowned. "Vayen? Kids? Really? My fee just went up. I don't do kids."

"They're not that bad."

"They're your kids. Yours and hers. Of course they're bad. They can't help it."

"I didn't think I'd like kids either, but they grew on me," I confided as we walked over to them.

"They do that when they're your own. So I've heard, anyway."

"Take the night shift. They'll be sleeping. There, problem solved."

Daniel came running over. "Now I have an uncle and a grand-father! I'm Daniel," he said proudly.

Fa'yet wore a pained smile. "Lucky me."

"You are!" insisted Daniel. "And this is Ikeri. She's three. She likes hugs."

"I'll keep that in mind." He backed away. "I'll just wait inside. I'm not really dressed for this inland heat."

I let him go. He was wearing the same clothes he'd had on yesterday and likely the day before. The ones that he'd been perfectly comfortable in. The kids would grow on him, but he'd need time to adjust. The man had lived a mostly solitary life since I'd met him. Even dealing with the other three of us adults in the same small house would be a big adjustment. Which made me realize that we wouldn't be able to stay here long. We needed something larger or Neko and Fa'yet were likely to be at each other's throats, or Stassia at mine after having to trip over them at every turn.

Stassia came up to me. "Is he all right?"

Neko and Daniel walked away, likely following the perimeter I'd set up.

"He says he doesn't do kids."

She laughed. "Oh, he will. I'll make sure of it."

"He's going to take the night shift for now."

She nodded. "And where is he staying?"

"My room, I guess. Or Jey's."

"Daniel has already claimed Jey's room. I'll keep Ikeri with me. Isnar can have my room."

"And just where will I sleep?"

"Where ever you are. I doubt it will be here," she said stiffly.

My stomach churned. "And what does that mean?"

"It means you're busy. You survived the night on the couch. If you happen to be here, so is the couch."

I'd had more than my fill of couch sleeping during our first couple years on Veria Minor. My back ached at the thought of another night on that narrow perch. Sitting on it was one thing, but it was built for people her size, not mine.

"That wasn't what I had in mind. I want to be here."

"No, you want to run off and save the Narvan. You're just dragging us around with you." Stassia took off, walking in the opposite direction Neko and Daniel had gone.

She'd said she would have joined with who I had been on Minor. But that's not who I was now, and I didn't know, even if we did get back to Minor, if I would ever be able to settle back into Isnar's skin again. Could I stop imagining Merkief and Jey in our house there, threatening us? Could I be satisfied with running Dugans instead of the Narvan? Would I be able to relax at my desk in my office without feeling my life run out of my body?

I ran to catch up to her. She didn't slow down.

"Stassia, I'm doing everything I can to make sure the three of you are safe. I didn't ask to get involved in this mess. You know that."

I needed her support, her mind, and her comfort when things went wrong. I'd seen the spark of Kazan in her back on Rok. She'd been excited. I knew it, felt it. But now that was gone. And all I got were glimpses of the Stassia I loved. The rest was a woman who was angry all the time, and I didn't know what to do to fix it any more than I had when she'd far too slowly transitioned to Rhaine on Minor. Great Geva, I couldn't go through that again.

"Why are you being like this?" I asked.

"Because you can do this, be Vayen again. Without my link, I can't help you. As much as I wish we could do this together, I'm holding you back. We all are. You belong here. It was your choice to leave it behind before. I appreciate that you did, and I know I didn't always show it. That I was...what was your word? *Impossible,* much of the time." She wrung her hands and seeming to see that I noticed, instead clasped them firmly together. "This was our dream to come back here, to be like we were, and I've tried. I really have. But we have a family now, and, more than that, I'm not able to be everything I once was." Her path began to arc back to the house. "Thanks for bringing Isnar in. I do feel better having him here, and I've missed talking to him."

Maybe he would be able to reason with her or coax a bit of Kazan back out, help her find her place here again. He'd always been the one either of us could talk to.

"I thought having him here would make you happy."

"It does. It's just-" She waved her hand around as if she could pull the words out. "I need some time to think."

"About what exactly? Talk to me."

"About you. Me, us. This." She tinked her fingernails against the armband on her wrist.

"What is there to think about? I love you. Like you said, we have a family. What else is there?"

"It's not just that, Vayen. What you're doing, what you intend to do, it impacts all of us. It certainly impacted all those people on Rok."

She came to a stop and looked out into the trees. I stood beside her but gave space. Our bonded connection overflowed with a slow-moving sadness that threatened to drown me.

Half-turned away with her arms crossed over her chest, she said, "There was a time when I sat in this same house and went about my own business, mildly aware of the residual consequences of the actions that I felt were necessary. But now, I'm just one of those residuals. I'm not calling the shots. I'm hoping that everything works out, but I don't have one damn bit of say in any of it."

I knew she was having a hard time with staying behind. Hells, I was having a hard time with it too. I wanted her beside me, and if we couldn't be working together, at least consulting with her when I was home. She didn't have the benefit of a link or even her natural mind speech to help occupy her time or stay in the loop. It was one thing when we were both stuck on Minor, making the best of our lives there, but now she had to watch me getting back to living mine.

"I'm sorry." I stepped closer. She didn't move away. Progress, I hoped.

Stassia leaned her head on my shoulder. The scratchy surface of my coat didn't seem to bother her in the least. "I know you're doing what you think is right. I even agree with you for the most part, but I don't know if we can... If I can do this," she said.

That sounded an awful lot like I was on the verge of losing something big, and I didn't like that at all.

"What do you want me to do? Do you want me to walk away from the Narvan?"

Even as she shook her head, I continued, hoping to find the answer. "We could try running. I don't know if we could evade Merkief or Jey, but we'll try if that's what you want."

"As if you're in this for either of them?" She laughed bitterly. "If you really think that, you're fooling yourself. Granted, you were at first, but I heard you with Merkief that last time. You're back. Jey could rough you up a little, sure, but this is between you and Kess now. The only danger from Merkief is the possibility of him spilling information to the Council. If he does that, we're all dead."

"Then you see why I still need to play along with helping them."

"But you're not playing." She smacked me on the chest. "You're in this. You're going to end up on Sere in a fucking private audience and either get your head blown off or sucked back into being manipulated by the Council. Neither of those works with this." She hit the armband again.

I took her hand and gently gripped her wrist. "But I want this."

"I know you do, but you can't have everything you want."

That hurt. A lot. My throat closed and my pulse thudded in my ears. I didn't know what to say. I let go of her hand and swallowed hard.

"What should I do? Tell me."

Stassia focused her gaze on the trees beside me. "As long as you have a link, Merkeif or Jey can find you. At least eventually, but I couldn't ask you to give your link up again. I wish to all your hells that I could get one too. That would make this easier."

"I wish you could too."

A distant smile tinged her face before a shadow of her old work mask slipped into place. My heart leapt to see it.

"Wishes aren't going to get us anywhere. We have to face reality. We both do."

"Stassia-"

She shook her head. "The Narvan needs a firm hand. It always has. That hand can't be mine. It has to be yours. But that also means you can't be here." She kept her impassive gaze locked just over my shoulder. "No matter how much either of us wishes you could be."

I wanted to strangle reality just then.

She hugged me. Despite how level her voice was and the lack of emotion on her face, I could feel her shaking. Or maybe it was me. I held on tighter, not knowing what would happen once I let go.

"I need to breathe," she whispered.

"Sorry." I grabbed her hand before she got away, but I didn't know what more to say. I kissed her instead. It wasn't the same as before, missing the warmth and peace I usually felt when I was so close to her. It was desperate this time, pleading.

Shoes on leaves entered my awareness. Neko and Daniel were back. I reluctantly parted ways with her lips. When I tried to catch her gaze, she stared at my feet.

"I guess...I should go?"

She nodded slowly.

Maybe the answer to this shitty reality problem would present itself if we had some time apart. I released her hands.

Her steps were the visual definition of hesitant, but they slowly gained velocity as she followed Daniel and Neko into the house. I stood there, outside. Even with her side of our connection greatly diminished, the waves of emotion flowing from her hit me hard. Maybe it was less the strength and more the degree of anger and frustration. She wanted to be beside me just as badly as I wanted her there. I wasn't the only one cursing the Council, Jey and Merkeif, and all the gods and men who had driven us to this.

Chapter Twelve

I filled a week with helping Jey recover from the mess on Rok and even meeting with Merkief. I figured I'd better stay on his good side as much as I could, given the threats that had passed between us. At least until I was able to topple Kess and get back in with the High Council.

With the week away, I also hoped to give Stassia the time she needed to figure things out. Maybe it would allow Fa'yet a chance to talk with her, and I wouldn't have to be present to see it.

The bond cried out to go home, but I stuffed it down and concentrated on work. Lots and lots of work. Jey had invited me to stay at his house on Jal. While I didn't like it there, I had a bed surrounded by four walls to hide behind while I laid awake in it.

Jey crossed the bunker and stood beside me with a raised eyebrow. "How many stims are you on today?"

"Only one, why?"

He pointed to the two data pads on the table in front of me and the projection map floating beside me. "You just ran more simulations in the past eight hours than I could put together in a week."

"They seemed fairly straightforward."

"Maybe to you." He studied the current conflict playing out on the projection map. "You really think Kess will try for Moriek?"

"It's the least protected Artorian world. If he got a solid foothold there, he'd be well on his way to converting enough Artorians to his cause to unseat Merkief. Merkief's hold over the Artor is tenuous at best. Honestly, the Premier is jealous of Karin because it's doing better than the damned homeworld. They'd rather have you supervising them, and you're a fucking Jalvian. That's how pathetic the situation has become."

Jey scowled. "Don't hold back or anything."

"Holding back has never one of me strong points."

"Thanks for the reminder."

I shook my head. "We'll need to strike at Merchess. That's Kess's major source of credits. Quit licking your wounds and go on the offensive for once."

"We tried that before."

"Yes, well, you have me now. We're doing it again."

His brow furrowed. "With what ships? What forces? Whose credits?"

"Yours, yours and mine. You want the Narvan back or not?"

"Yes," he stated firmly.

"Then prep your fleets. Quietly. Round up your best and most trusted men and send me a bill."

Jey took in the map and the men around us. "You better be good for it. If I default on this, I'm done."

"I'm good for it."

"One other thing while I have your attention for more than thirty seconds."

I tore my gaze from the map to look at him.

"Merkief wants to know how you're joining is progressing."

"Funny that he didn't have the nerve to ask in person. When he does, I'll answer."

Neither of us would like that answer.

I turned back to the simulations and willed Jey to go away. I missed my office at Cragtek where I could work alone, uninterrupted, for as long as I wanted.

Though I did my best to look busy with the datapad, my thoughts were elsewhere. It took a few minutes to catch Daniel's attention but when I had it, he answered in a clear voice. His natural speech was growing stronger every day.

As was usual in Daniel's quick reports, Neko was awesome in all things, but I could hear the worship in his voice when he spoke of Fa'yet too. I had a feeling Fa'yet was softening to dealing with the kids. There could be no other reason that he agreed to teach Daniel the basics of wielding a knife days ago.

I wasn't too happy when Daniel had first told me about it. A great amount of excitement had overpowered his initial trepidation of the admission, but the more I thought about it, being able to defend himself at least at some level was perhaps a good idea. As long as he didn't advance to guns. And he kept everything away from Ikeri. I rubbed my temples.

I missed my little girl more than the any of the rest of them. Well, that wasn't entirely true. I missed Stassia differently. Each day felt wrong without her there beside me. Not even just physically beside me, but supportively. I'd always known, from the day I signed on as a naïve idiot, that I could depend on her to have my back. But now I was adrift and the shore remained out of sight.

Ikeri brought her own brand of peace, glowing like a little beacon in the night. How would her abilities manifest themselves when she grew up? If we got her back to Veria Minor, perhaps we could entrust her to a full Seeker for training. They weren't as stringent on Minor as they were on Prime, where Stassia had only been able to receive half the required training.

The small doses I allowed myself of Ikeri were enough to tire her speech in short order. She told me she'd been working with her mother, practicing what I imagined were the slightest of the Seeker arts on our guards, who had turned into very willing subjects. It seemed both of them enjoyed relaxing even if, for Fa'yet, it came with the cost of dealing with a three-year-old.

Hours later, Jey interrupted my preliminary battle planning by loudly clearing his throat. He'd probably been standing there for awhile.

"Why don't you go home for the night. You look like you could use some real rest. You're certainly not getting it at my place."

"You just want to take credit for my plans."

He chuckled. "These men know me and my recent failures. Besides, they've seen you hard at work over here for days. I wouldn't get away with it. Now get out of here."

He shooed me off.

"All right."

I got up, collected my datapads and Jumped to the point outside the house to avoid startling anyone. It was the middle of the night and pouring rain. I swore profusely and tried to get the datapads under my coat before they got ruined. Either Fa'yet or Neko noted me standing there because the exterior light came on. Everyone would be sound asleep. But, Jey was right, I could certainly use some sleep, too.

The door locks clicked as I approached. Fa'yet met me with a questioning glance.

"Just here for some sleep. And to dry off, now. Damned rain."

He nodded at the black sky. "Good timing then."

I wasn't in the mood for his humor. Walking past him, I took off my coat and hung it up by the door. Water ran off it as I pulled off my boots and left them there too. At least there would only be one muddy puddle for Stassia to be pissed about. My clothes were dry enough. I set the datapads down on the table by the couch and sat. The couch must have triggered something in my body because suddenly I could barely keep my eyes open.

Fa'yet threw a towel at me. I hadn't even noticed him getting up to go in the bathroom to get it. I really did need to sleep.

"Thanks." After a moderate effort to dry my hair and face, I tossed the towel aside. "How are they?"

Fa'yet smiled sadly. "They miss you. Beyond that, I can't say."

That didn't bode well but wasn't unexpected. The dim night-time lighting over the surveillance station wasn't enough to keep me awake. I stretched out on the cushions.

"Aren't you even going to look in on them?"

"I'll see them in the morning. Don't want to wake them." My eyelids slipped closed and sleep settled upon me.

꙾

"Vayen!" Merkief's voice pierced my sleeping mind. I sat up, half asleep, only then realizing his voice was in my head.

"What's the emergency?"

"I've been hit. I need help."

I wiped the sleep from my eyes. Damn, I wasn't usually so out of it when I woke up. Then again, I hadn't hardly slept in a week.

"So Jump to the tank."

"I can't." He flashed me a jump point.

I took a deep breath to clear my head and slipped into my still damp coat and boots. I'd get some dry boots on the ship after I got Merkief in the tank.

Fa'yet watched me.

"Gotta go."

He nodded. "I'll tell them you were here."

It would only piss Stassia off more and prove her right. I couldn't even spend a whole night on the couch for Geva's sake.

"If you think it's worth it."

"It is," he assured me.

My link sense flooded back to full awareness. I'd only been out three hours. No wonder I was fuzzy-headed. The void swallowed me and then spit me out in a factory filled with whizzing bullets. This was the last place I needed to be as exhausted as I was.

"Where the hells are you?"

I ducked and dodged, returning fire while looking for Merkief. Whoever was after him was a pretty accurate shot. A couple bullets bit into my coat but most just missed my head by a hair, and I had to keep my focus on every damn breath and movement to keep it that way.

"He's over there," someone said.

Seconds later, bullets sprayed at me from a second direction.

Why the hells couldn't Merkief give me a jump point right next to him if he was hurt so damn bad? I reached for his mind but it was muddled, distant.

"Where are you?" I yelled.

Three people called, "Over here." One of them was Merkief but with all the noise, I couldn't pinpoint him. My nerves were singing. Every bullet that thankfully whizzed past me made me tense up more. This was not going to end well if I didn't find him soon.

A little voice in the back of my head told me I should leave him to his fate. But we'd been friends. He'd saved my ass several times. My conscience demanded that I find him.

I gave up trying to fire back and concentrated on staying hidden while I searched. A hand tugged at my pants as I rounded the end of what looked like some sort of turbine.

Ducking down, I discovered Merkief wedged underneath. Blood pooled around his side. His face was pale and his eyes held a glassy sheen. It was a sad state of affairs if he'd truly alienated himself to the point where I was the one he called when in dire straits. What would he have done if I'd still been back on Minor? Although, I couldn't blame Jey for not coming to his aid. This opportunity did present a simple answer to reducing the number of hands on the Narvan without firmly placing blame on him. Or myself. I could leave, pretend I'd not answered either.

His concern upon our unexpected reunion in my office at Dugans and on the ship when I'd awoke from the tank, shown brightly in my mind. He had been genuinely glad to see me. He'd been that same way a few times since, the man I used to know. But he was also something else. Different, disturbed, issues I'd had a hand in creating. Maybe something I could fix once I got Kess out of the picture.

"Come on." I clamped a hand on his shoulder and Jumped him to the ship.

Within two minutes, I had him stripped and the platform rising into the healing gel. I glanced at the pile of bloody clothes and his armor. Hoping for some clues, I went through his pockets. I didn't find anything unusual, an almost empty stim tin, a few weapons. It wasn't until I reached all the way to the bottom of one pocket and came out with a ring that I was hit with the need to sit down. He'd opted for a ring as his joining gift and now he carried it with him. I stared at it for a long while, wondering what the woman who had worn it had been like.

It took a good deal of searching, but I found record of his joining on Artor, along with a still frame of the two of them documenting the occasion. They stood side by side, grinning, hands clasped together. She, a pretty woman in an Artorian military dress uniform, looked straight at me. He, the man who had been my friend, younger and clearly happy, had his gaze locked on her. I wished I could have been there in person to see them together. If I had been, she would probably still be alive.

It must have been utterly devastating to lose her. What would it feel like to lose Stassia? Even thinking about it made me ill. I got up and put the ring back in his pocket.

When I sat back down at the terminal, I checked the information from the initial scan. How had he managed to take a bullet so far on one side? He'd been wearing armor. He would have to have had his coat wide open for a bullet to catch him there. And the wound itself wasn't immediately critical. He'd been bleeding for a while, and from the size of the puddle, lying there bleeding.

Why would he do that with people firing at him? And why hadn't they closed in? And why the fuck had he given me a jump point so far from his location? He could have Jumped himself to the tank long before I got there.

When his attacker had said 'he's over there', I'd thought they'd spotted Merkief, but they'd been firing at me. Merkief hadn't been firing back, he'd been on the ground in an undisturbed puddle of blood. The gunmen had been good enough to easily have been Kryon. And they'd been waiting for me.

I shot to my feet and slammed my hand on the wall for lack of Merkief's face. He'd made plenty of mistakes lately, but this one could have outright killed me. Why hadn't he warned me when he'd called for help? I needed to know who had sent him there and why.

Remembering how weak Stassia had been when I hadn't let the tank cycle end, I opted to do the same to Merkief. It would cost him some extra tank time to set a new baseline later, but I didn't care. I wanted answers.

As soon as the gel had done its work on the critical damage, I stopped the tank and cycled him out. My link kept me busy with reinvesting and sorting credits in order to finance Jey's upcoming attack. I was in the middle of untangling a particularly convoluted investment chain mired in layers of aliases and businesses that had changed names and hands during my absence, when Merkief woke up on the platform.

He glanced around until he spotted me. "I'm used to this treatment on my own, but I was looking forward to a bed since you were around."

I was at his side with a gun to his head before he got any further. "Why didn't you warn me about the live fire, and why the hells didn't you Jump long before I got there?"

He groaned. "Of course you'd assume I had tried to off you."

I shoved the barrel into his forehead. "Actually I assumed you were just stupid, but now that you mention it..."

"I'm really regretting all that time I gave you with Jey. You should have been easier to kill."

"Excuse me?"

"Oh don't look so shocked. You know how the Council works. They order. We do. Jey said you were exhausted. I thought this was outside the box enough for the plan to work, but apparently not."

I couldn't believe how matter of fact he was. 'Yeah, I meant to kill you, but it didn't work out.' No apology, no scrambling, he didn't even seem to care about the gun I had at his temple. I jabbed it against his skull to remind him.

"Oh please, we both know you're not a trigger-puller. If you were, you would have taken Kazan out and saved us all a lot of trouble."

"It seems you're not either."

He looked away. "So what now?"

He'd fucking tried to kill me. That wasn't something I could fix. No amount of dwelling on good times or glimpses of the possibility of regaining them could make me forget what he'd done. What he'd planned. What he'd wanted.

I needed to put the gun away, to sit down, to have a little time to process this. What would Merkief do if I let him up? Certainly not wait around.

"Was this a unanimous Council decision?"

"No."

"You told them I was alive."

"They already knew from Kess, but yes. Some of us follow through on our threats."

That sounded far too much like words I'd heard from the Council before. I still couldn't believe he'd gone so far as to tell the Council about me. I didn't want to believe it.

He pushed my gun aside and tried to sit up. His muscles strained before he got halfway. He fell back on the platform.

"You might want to stay down. You're only alive enough to wake up and talk to me."

He finally had the grace to look a little worried. "Well, that's unexpected."

"I'm working on it." I put the gun away. "So what was the payoff for offing me?"

"Jey's planets. They're sick of him."

"Funny, you were the one lying in a puddle of blood. What if I hadn't taken your bait? Think one of your Kryon friends would have taken care of you? You're prepared to give the Council the tank?" I shook my head. "I dare bet it's you the Council is sick of."

"I knew it was a gamble," he said quietly.

"Did it pay off?"

"I did leave Anastassia and the kids out of it. You can thank me for that. Kess hasn't mentioned them either."

But when Kess's people had hit Cragtek, they were after the kids. If he hadn't told the Council about them, he meant to use them against me himself. At least Merkief hadn't gone that far.

"That's something, I suppose. I might have to let you live."

He snorted. "You will. You're dependable like that too. You'll probably hit me a few times, but you'll toss me back in the tank when you're done."

"That's actually a good idea."

An emptiness sat where my rage should have been. Each blow

felt hollow, ungratifying in any way. He didn't fight back, even as bones shattered.

Once he was unconscious, I started the tank cycle again. I might be predictable, but dammit, I needed time to think. If I changed my mind about killing him, I'd still have plenty of time before the tank fully cycled him out.

Needing someone to work through this with, I contacted Jey.

"Do you have a minute?"

"Not really, why?"

I explained what had just occurred.

Jey arrived on the ship seconds later, the veins in his forehead ready to burst. "He did what?"

"You heard me. He said you told him I was exhausted."

Jey held up an empty hand. "I told him that so he'd leave you alone for a while. You needed to sleep. I had no part in this."

I didn't think he would have, but I was glad to see his reaction seemed honest.

"This isn't just you being all paranoid and blaming him for fucking up?" Jey asked.

"No, this is him telling me he was trying to kill me and working with Kryon to make that happen."

"Well, fuck. I had no idea he'd sunk so low. Get him out of the tank. We'll kill him."

"I dare bet that the Council played him completely. They'd pick you over him any day."

"They'd off him?"

"After he served his purpose? Yes. He'd only be in the way and whining otherwise."

He made a face. "That's harsh."

"Hey, I didn't kill him, did I?"

"Not yet, but we have to," he said.

"We need to know who he's dealing with and how much of the Council is against me. If I've already lost the majority, we need a new plan. If there's still a chance I can step in, then I need to know who to avoid. Not to mention that if the Council knows I'm alive, Kess has to be deadset on completing the job this time around."

"All right then, we'll hold off, but don't let him out of your sight." Jey looked like he was ready to Jump.

"My sight? I'm kind of busy and I do need to sleep. How about some help?"

He shook his head. "I'm the one that's alive and running things. You've got a few hours to rest before he wakes up."

I sat back down at the terminal after Jey left. As I stared at Merkief's stats and listened to the faint drone of the air scrubbers, my vision blurred. I jerked awake twice before taking note of how long he'd be in the tank and estimating recovery sleep. I had a good seven hours, even with giving myself one less than my initial estimate just in case. Arriving only to find he'd woken early and run back to his Council contact would do me no good at all. Neither would falling asleep here and having him kill me when he woke up before I did.

As tired as I was, I didn't trust myself to wake on time. I needed a living alarm. Like Stassia or Neko. Fa'yet would be off duty by now. It had to be day on Frique. In preparation for a visit topside, I went into the bathroom and washed Merkief's blood off my face and hands. Nothing to be done about the swollen knuckles. Again.

Maybe I could see the kids for a few minutes before getting some sleep. In a bed, since everyone else would be up, maybe even my own that smelled like Stassia. I smiled to myself and Jumped to the mossy yard in front of the Friquen house. At least it wasn't raining this time, but it was still damn humid.

As Daniel barreled into me once again, I began to think he'd made it a personal mission to see if he could catch me off guard enough to knock me over. I staggered back, catching both of us before he accomplished just that. He laughed. I didn't.

Ikeri came running out the door, her little legs pumping as fast as they could go. She squealed with delight and wrapped her arms around the lower half of my coat, pinning me in place.

"Nice to see both of you too." I patted Daniel's shoulder and picked up Ikeri.

"She's inside," said Ikeri.

"Are you picking up thoughts again?"

"Not trying," she said shyly.

Maybe Stassia was right. I'd need to seal off my connection with Ikeri until we ironed out some boundaries. But not today. I'd be sleeping for most of my visit and she was so happy to see me.

Daniel followed us into the house. Stassia glanced up from whatever she was cooking in the kitchen and gave me a tight-lipped smile. I set Ikeri down and walked over to Stassia.

I got as far as a quick hug before she slipped her hand into mine and led me to my bedroom.

"Keep an eye on that, will you?" she said to Daniel just before closing us inside.

My heart pounded faster. Had staying away worked? Had she come to terms with our situation? My exhaustion vanished in the hopes of a different sort of relaxation in my very near future.

I tried to kiss her. She dodged aside.

"I hear you tried to stop by last night."

"I did. I slept for a few hours. Figured I'd let you sleep too." I tried again.

She batted me away. "This is exactly what I was saying. You can't even stay here for a few hours without being distracted or called away. What kind of life is that for our children? They can't depend on you to be here in the morning, or any other time of day for that matter. Neither can I."

"Stassia, come on. It was one night."

"The one night in eight that you deigned to grace us with your presence."

"You didn't want me here!"

Her fire guttered out and she sagged against me. I wrapped my arms around her.

"Tell me how to make you happy because I'm at a loss. Every time I try, I end up deeper in the hole."

"No, you don't." She sighed. "It's just that it seems like there is no road to happiness where we both get to share it."

I kissed the top of her head. "I thought that before but it turns out there was."

"How about now?" She looked up at me with such hope in her eyes that I really wished I had an answer.

"I don't know yet."

"I was afraid you were going to say that." She leaned against me again. "So where did you have to run off to last night? Isnar said you looked horrible when you showed up."

"Saving Merkief's ass." That sounded better than the truth, and it was, in itself, partly true.

"And?"

"What do you mean and?"

"The rest of it? I can tell when you're lying, idiot."

"I wasn't lying."

She leaned back and regarded me with an unwavering gaze.

"Fine. Merkief set up an ambush with other Kryon wherein he meant for me to die, but I didn't, and then I saved his ass from myself. For the moment anyway."

She went stiff. "He didn't. Not Merkief."

"Oh, he did. He admitted to it."

"How could he do that? To you?" she asked with a whisper.

"The Council is playing him, Stassia. Just like they tried to do to me. He's not totally at fault."

Stassia shook her head and scowled. "So the Council knows about you."

"Thank Merkief and Kess for that. Though for the moment, you and the kids have been left out of the revelations."

She didn't appear all that relieved. If anything, she looked more pissed off. "It was his decision to follow their orders. He could have found a way out. You did. Why couldn't he do that? Why would he agree to kill you? He's been demanding that you help him! After all the shit we've gone through thanks to him and Jey, how could he do that?"

"That's what I'm going to figure out. Which is why I'm here. I've slept all of five solid hours in a row in about a week. I'd like my bed, if you don't mind."

She let me go and stepped aside. "So you're just going to sleep on it? Where's Merkief? Is Jey watching him?"

"Merkief is in the tank. He'll be there for a while yet and then have to sleep it off. I'd like to be a little more alert before he wakes up."

Disappointment shown on her face. "I see. So you came back to sleep."

"No, I came back to see you and the kids. And sleep. In that order."

"And you've seen us." She made a little mock wave. "We need to figure something out, Vayen. This isn't working for anyone."

"I know. I'm doing the best I can."

She nodded and kissed me on the cheek. "When do you need me to wake you?"

"Six and a half hours."

"That's it? You need more. I'm sorry, but you do look horrible."

"Thanks. I wish I had time for more, but I don't."

"All right then." She gave me one last forlorn look and then shut the door.

The only consolation was that the sheets smelled like her. When I closed my eyes, I pretended she was lying there, just out of reach.

That was the problem. Everything was just out of reach.

Chapter Thirteen

My wakeup call was less personal than I would have liked. It was amicable enough, but there was a definite barrier building between us. The closeness we'd shared as Isnar and Rhaine was quickly becoming a pleasant memory. At least her hostility had faded.

The kids were outside playing, which made the meal she insisted I eat quite silent. I methodically shoveled the food into my mouth. She stood in the kitchen not quite watching me and doing her best to look busy doing much of nothing. We said a goodbye without words, without touching, with little more than a resolute nod really.

When I returned to the ship, I found Merkief still asleep on the platform. I tossed a sheet over him and sat back to wait.

He stirred awhile later. "Sure, this time I get a sheet and no gun? Diverging from the predictable?"

"Trying."

He sat up apprehensively. "So I see you decided to let me live, though Jey informs me that he's not in agreement with you on that."

"Who's your Council contact?"

He swung his legs over the side of the platform and secured the sheet around his waist. "Does it matter?"

"Yeah, as a matter of fact, it does."

"I suppose you're going to tell me I owe you an explanation, and you'll help me out of whatever the Council is holding over me to make me do such a horrible thing."

"Are they holding something over you?"

He stood up and stretched as if he were in no particular hurry. "No you moron, they offered me Jey's half the Narvan, like I told you. I don't have anyone left for them to hold over me. They offered, I said yes. That's pretty much it."

"So what was all that with demanding Stassia and I join? How the hells did that play into your plans if you meant to off me?"

"My plans changed when Kess went to them about you before I did."

I went cold inside. He had planned to go the Council from the start. Even after this attempt on me, I didn't want to believe he'd be that devious, that he'd be that fucking cruel.

"If you don't mind, I'd like to take a shower now," he said.

I planted my palm on his chest. "I mind. Maybe you should share your new plans before I-"

"Before you what? Beat on me again? Send me to the tank again? I'm sick of this, Vayen. Really fucking sick of this game. Either kill me or let me go."

He seemed to be trying awfully damn hard to make me angry. "Do you want me to kill you?"

The nonchalance vanished, leaving a defeated and miserable man before me. "I don't see why you wouldn't. It would be the wisest move."

"I know how the Council works. They played me too, so cut the shit and tell me what they're holding over you."

"Why?" He sighed. "She's probably already gone. I failed. They know I failed."

"So who is it?"

"Not going to let that drop, huh?" He leaned against the platform and gazed at the empty chair by the terminal.

"Hadn't planned on it. Unless you have something else to offer me?"

"Her name is Devora."

"Kryon?"

He nodded.

"She's been helping me on contracts for a while now. Since shortly after Jey and I parted ways in that regard."

I checked with Jey, seeing if he knew of Devora while Merkief and I talked.

"And what did the Council do to change that?"

"Reassigned her. Out of the system. Out of Sere," he said.

"And they'll bring her back if you do as you're told?"

"That's what they said."

"You know that's a lie, right?"

He bowed his head.

"I've got nothing," said Jey.

"Why doesn't Jey know about this woman?"

"You think I'd trust him with anything after the last time?"

"All right. Still, you managed to keep your relationship with her a secret from him for a couple years?"

"It seems I'm better at keeping secrets than advising even half a star system."

"Any other secrets I should know about?" I asked.

"Not at the moment."

"And how did you keep Devora a secret from the Council?"

"I didn't. They've known about it from the beginning."

"Who is your connection with the Council?"

He gave me a defiant stare. "You don't get to ask that."

"I'll let it go for now, but if they send you against me again, I want a name. Got it?"

"Sure."

"I also want to know exactly what they're asking you to do."

"Starting when?"

"Right now." Because I was seriously considering hitting him again.

He smiled. "Well, since that attempt failed, I'm supposed to attempt to befriend you and agree to cooperate. How am I doing so far?"

Fuck. I really had to something about being so damn predictable to those who knew me well.

Wait. That meant that whoever was in the faction against me, knew me. I searched through names and cloak-covered faces. Would Deep Voice want me out? He'd been on my side once. Chandi was dead but her cohort in crime, Shoulders, would undoubtedly like to see me dead. Beyond that, no one particular Councilmember stood out. Could they be basing their assumptions on my prior experience? I knew the Council kept accurate records on those they had under thumb.

"Who's your contact?" I asked again.

"Or what? You won't help me find Devora?"

He was ruined. The light in his eyes had gone out. My beatings had instilled no fear or sense of threat. He was just going through the motions. Puppeted motions. I needed to know who held his strings.

"Of course I'll help you find her. You claim I owe you a life or two. I'll do what I can to repay that."

"Do you mean it?"

Damn, I couldn't tell if he cared or not. Was he dragging me into some other High Council plot? Was he taking Jey down with me? I couldn't afford to cut Merkief loose. I'd have no idea what the Council would be up to next.

"Yeah, I mean it."

"Because we're such good friends?" The sneer on his face made it clear enough that he was mocking me, but playing me was something he seemed to be good at. So what was his goal this time?

"We were once."

He rolled his eyes again. "Maybe you thought so."

"We were."

He snorted. "Yeah, you ordering me around all the time, standing in your shadow and then Jey's shadow too. Those were good times. I really miss those days."

"It wasn't always like that, and you know it."

"That's how it ended and that's what matters. I was a good kid when I was younger, had a bright future, but look at me now. Which one matters?"

"The man I left behind was still a good one."

"He's gone. Accept that and maybe we'll find some common ground again."

"Maybe I want that man back."

"Vayen, give up already. You killed him. He's gone."

"I killed him? When I left, you were waving and wishing us well."

"And then you wiped his memories clean and cast him adrift in a mess he was never meant to handle. He did what he could but he drowned, and now I'm all that's left."

"Have you been drinking? That's damn melodramatic even for you."

He scowled. "Look, you want to help me find Devora, fine. Cut your ties with Anastassia and let's go."

My mouth dropped open and my tongue fumbled to form words. "Do what? I can't!"

"You can, you just don't want to. But you will if you want to save them."

A chill ran up my spine, making the hairs on my neck stand on end. "What do you mean, save them?"

"I mean I'll buy you a week or two but then you're going to want to be on your own. You're going to Sere."

"Why am I going to Sere?"

"Because you want to know who I'm dealing with."

I didn't like how this was going. Was there even a Devora to find? Had he fed me a quick answer to throw me off balance? "I want to see her. Devora. Show me."

"I'd love to."

His eager response made me shrink back even more. I steeled myself against whatever he was about to throw at me and opened my mind to his.

A woman, thin in a wispy but willowy sort of way with pale skin and short black hair looked straight at me. Her pale blue eyes bore a chill that made me wonder if there was, in fact, anything between her and Merkief beyond a work partnership. She didn't appear to be the sort of woman who was looking for a man to work with. She looked like she'd rather kill him and go get dinner alone.

I tried to mesh this woman with the one he'd joined with. They couldn't have been more opposite. For as long as I'd known Merkief, he'd never gone after a woman like Devora. This woman would eat him alive. My gut told me he was lying.

"Was the sympathetic story part of the Council coaching too?"

Merkief shrugged. "I told them you'd see through it, but they were convinced the image would sell it. Guess I still know you better than they do."

As things stood, that revelation was not a relief. "What are you getting out of screwing with me? Is this fun for you? Are you enjoying yourself?"

His deadpan stare filled me with unease. "I was buying you time, but now you've ruined it. And no, this has never been fun, but it was necessary. The more I give the Council, the more they give me."

"What do you mean? What are they giving you?"

"Information on Kess mostly. But there was a new offer on the table. They said they'd tell me who killed my family."

Rather than literally knocking some sense into him, I grabbed his shoulders and shook him. "They did, you know that, don't you? The Council ordered it. Merkief, they're just screwing with your head. Don't listen to them."

For a few seconds, his attention wavered. When he came back, couldn't have looked more destitute if he'd tried. His head wobbled about loosely, arms limp. "You're right." He focused on me, but didn't resist my hold in the least. "They lied."

"What did you give them for that?"

"Everything."

My mind reached out to Fa'yet in a panic. Our connection was far more solid than what I had with Neko. *"High alert now. I'll be moving all of you as soon as I put a new location together."*

"Anything specific we should watch for?"

"When I know, you'll know." I cut contact.

I forced myself to swallow. "What exactly is everything?"

He hopped back onto the platform and sat there. "This ship. The tank. All the jump points I had Jey give you."

The floor dropped out beneath me. My words came out a ragged whisper. "You gave them the tank? How could you do that? You've just killed us all."

He shrugged again. "I'm already dead. You said as much. Why does this surprise you?"

I left him there and fell into the seat at the terminal. The edges of my vision turned black. "You gave them her ship. Her tank. How could you do that? It wasn't yours to give."

"It isn't mine. It isn't yours. She can't use it without you, so it's really all sort of a grey area, isn't it?"

"You gave them what I nearly died for. What Anastassia kept from them for years and nearly cost her her life, too. You just handed it to them!"

"If you want to still pretend she's dead, I suggest you delete her profile so they can't see she was here recently."

"How do I know they haven't been here already?"

"Because I just gave it to them a minute ago." His smile had the most unnerving quality to it. He sat on the edge of the platform, kicking his feet as if he didn't have a care in the universe.

The records were all there for the taking if anyone knew where to look. And I was sure they did, thanks to Merkief. If I didn't make peace with the Council, they'd remove the tank or take me out while I was floating helplessly in it. Even if I made some arrangement with the High and Mighties, I'd be subjected to their demands and whims like every other Kryon member. The moment I pissed them off, the tank would be gone. And what about Jey? I contacted him, warning him about what Merkief had done.

He swore in my head and arrived seconds later. "Where is he?"

"Where?" I pulled my attention from my frantic wiping of records to glance around the otherwise empty room. "Fuck. All he had was a sheet. I didn't think he'd go far."

Jey ran towards Merkief's room and was back before I'd entered the deletion commands. I noticed Merkief's armor was missing from the pile of bloody clothes.

"He's gone. Do you think he really gave them the tank?" Jey asked.

"Since I can't honestly say that I don't think he would have, I have to believe that he did."

"That leaves us totally screwed, doesn't it?"

"Yeah."

I made one last sweep through the records, making sure I'd voided all mention of Stassia since our disappearance. They already knew I was here so I didn't waste time with mine.

"What if he's just scaring us off?" Jey asked, pacing the tank room.

"He's doing a good job." I eyed the gel-filled tank that had saved my life so many times. The tank had saved all our lives over and over. "They're not getting it."

Jey turned from the tank to me. "What are you thinking? You can't destroy it. What if he's bluffing?"

"Then we make sure he's screwed too."

I pulled open the panels on the front of the tank base to examine the internal system. Not much of it made sense to me. The mechanics of what went on behind panels had never been in my realm of expertise. "You know what any of this is?"

Jey shook his head. "It doesn't look like anything I've seen before. The writing on the parts isn't in any language I recognize."

"I wonder if Anastassia knows."

If only I could contact her directly. In case we would still have access to the tank, I didn't want Fa'yet or Neko knowing about it either. I contacted Daniel.

"Are you near your mother?"

"Yes?"

"Ask her which parts are vital to the tank."

"What does that mean?" he asked.

"Just repeat what I said to her."

"But I don't know what vital means."

I took a deep breath and let it out. *"Please, just ask her."*

His attention wavered and then strengthened. *"She's saying bad words."*

That made two of us. *"Tell me what she says after she's done with the bad words."*

His voice shrunk in my head, dimming, quieting. *"I'm scared."*

So was I, but I was doing my best not to let him feel it. *"Why, what's going on?"*

"I don't know." His hold on our connection snapped.

Ikeri was in his place before I had time to panic. *"Mommy said to show you this."*

The image of what was behind the panels popped into my head. The picture zoomed in on four components and then was gone. So was Ikeri.

I showed two of the items to Jey and worked on removing the others myself. I only hoped both of us could remember how to put them back in if we ever got the chance. Then, in a fit of 'what if' I made Jey show me how to reinstall the two components he'd removed, and I showed him the two I'd done. That way if just one of us survived this fiasco, we'd still have a chance.

"Where should we put them?" Jey asked.

"Take yours to your house on Jal. Find somewhere I'd know but they'd be hidden. Don't tell me where they are. I'll hide mine in the Friquen house. That way if either of us is probed, we won't know where the other parts are."

"What if we're both probed?"

"Then we're fucked."

He nodded. "Pretty much, yeah. All right then. What are you going to do about Merkief?"

"I'm moving Anastassia. He said something about giving me two weeks before dragging me to Sere, but who knows if I really have that long."

"I'd guess more like two days. He's too unpredictable," Jey said.

"You don't know the half of it. If you'd have seen him here earlier." I shuddered. "It's like he's become unhinged."

"I wish I knew what to tell you." He sighed loudly. "So you're moving your family again?"

"Seems the safest plan. As far as I know, he hasn't told the Council where they are. But if he's dragging me to Sere by whatever force or reason, I don't want to be the one to lead some desperate Kryon member straight to them."

"You're not going to take that mind-wipe stuff, are you? I know I said you should have but," he shook his head. "Having seen the two of you together, and with the kids, I wouldn't want to see you put yourself through that."

"I don't want to do that either, but I can't know where they are. I'll figure something out."

"I'll leave you to it then. Let me know if you need me," he said solemnly.

"I will."

He Jumped.

What to do about moving my family yet again? I spent the next hour keeping half an eye on Frique and the other half flitting all over the known universe for an unlikely safe haven. One stood out as a viable option but it was damned far away.

The bond begged me to go home and be near Stassia so I could think with a clear mind. For once, I agreed. I picked up the two components and Jumped to the surface.

"Back again so soon?" Neko asked.

"I might even stay awhile."

He chuckled. "I'll believe that when I see it."

"Yeah, me too, but I'm going to try."

He waved me inside and continued his walk around the house. I went in and quietly hid both of my tank pieces in different places. When I was done, I found Daniel was in his bed and Ikeri tucked into mine. Stassia sat on the bed beside her.

She glanced up as I walked into my bedroom. "How'd it go?"

I opened and closed my mouth, trying to find words to describe what had happened far below in the ship. "Can I pick your brain for a bit?"

Stassia nodded and started out of the room.

"No, in here. Privately. Put Ikeri in with Daniel for tonight."

She gave me a wary look.

"Please. I need your help with this."

"All right."

She picked Ikeri up and carried her into Daniel's room. I followed with a blanket and a pillow and laid them out on the floor for her. After Stassia set Ikeri down and tucked her in, we went back to my room.

"How long until Fa'yet's on?" I asked.

"Any time now, why?"

"Because I want this between you and me. Neko won't be curious about it, but Fa'yet might."

"His name is Isnar. You could call him that."

"That's your thing. He'll always be Fa'yet to me." And I wished to Geva that he was to her too. Every time I heard that name come from her lips, for just a split second, I thought she was talking about me, but then reality would smack me in the face. The real man, the one who truly bore that name was living with us, spending time with Stassia and my children. There wasn't room for two Isnar's.

"If you say so." She shook her head. "So what was all that with the tank?"

"That's part of what I needed to talk to you about. Thanks for your help. Using Ikeri worked perfectly."

"I wouldn't say perfectly. She's a little girl, Vayen. We don't know what's going on in that head of hers."

"We won't make a habit of it."

"Agreed." She brushed her hand over my armored sleeve. "Are you staying long enough to take off your armor?"

"That's the plan, yeah." I took the hint and stood to take off my coat. Hanging it up on the hook by the door, I pulled off my boots and sat on the bed next to her.

"Plan on needing these?" She tugged on one of my holster straps.

Was she trying to undress me? I slipped out of my holsters and draped them individually over the table beside the bed so I could put them back on quickly if I needed to.

"That's better," she announced as she moved closer, her hand sliding into mine. "So then, what do we need to discuss and why were you needing vital tank parts?"

I closed my eyes and ran through what Merkief had said. The smile on his face kept popping up behind my eyelids, taunting me, threatening worse than any words. I knew what had to happen but I didn't want to say it. Not yet. Not with her sitting so close by and in a relatively good mood.

"It can wait a little while. Tell me about your day."

"My day?"

"Yes. Your day."

"Well..." She rubbed her hands over her face. "Daniel is progressing nicely with his speech lessons. Isnar has been helping. I can't pick up where you left off with him, but I can generally tell what he was doing. Ikeri, frankly, scares me a little. She's got a very strong gift for as young as she is. I'm doing the best I can to work with her, but I'm worried that I'm either giving her too much or not enough. And I can't tell, because I can't talk to her like you can. So Isnar has been helping with that too."

"Sounds like he's taking my place nicely."

She scowled at me. "That's not funny."

I hadn't meant it to be, and I was surprised she hadn't picked up on the bitterness that I'd thought had been quite clear.

"And what about Neko? Have you still been working with him?"

"Yes. It helps break up the day. I miss having my clients. I miss my Seeker sessions. I miss feeling useful on any level. Vayen, this hurts more than I know how to express with words."

She opened her mind to me as much as our truncated connection allowed. Waves of unhappiness hit me like a storm building over an ocean. Fa'yet may have been helping with many things, but helping her find her place here wasn't one of them.

It broke my heart that the strong woman I knew now felt she had no place or purpose. I'd done this to her, selfishly wanting her by my side again. She'd found peace on Veria Minor, but that was gone. Her dream of becoming semi-Kazan again had been shattered by the massacre on Rok. She was lost, floundering, and I wasn't the anchor I'd once been just as she was no longer my cornerstone.

She wiped a tear from my cheek. "You understand, don't you?"

I nodded. The conversation I'd wanted to put off was the one she needed to hear.

"Merkief gave the Council the tank, our jump points, everything."

Her mouth dropped open.

"He claims he didn't tell them about you or the kids. Yet. But quite frankly, I can't believe anything he says. It's not safe here. I don't want another Rok just as much as you don't."

She nodded solemnly. "So what's the plan?"

I didn't particularly want to give voice to the plan. I wanted to stay there and pretend nothing was wrong, that Merkief hadn't betrayed us all, that I wouldn't be facing the Council with no hope of using the tank again.

"I was thinking." I cleared my throat, hoping to quell the tremor in my voice. "That it might be best for the five of you to go away for awhile. Settle down somewhere that is actually safe and far away. Away from this mess and me."

Her hand gripped mine with what felt like all the force she had in her body. "Where?"

"I've been investigating a well-established colony on a planet called Pentares."

"I've never heard of it. How far away?"

"Six months by freighter."

"Why would we take a freighter? Can't you just Jump us there?"

"I'm not going, and I don't want to know where you are."

"In case you get probed." Her voice shook.

I nodded. "I don't have a solid jump point for Fa'yet or Neko, not that I want to have one floating around in my head either. I want you to travel. Take your time. Be between here and there for a good long, safe while."

"What do you plan on doing during those six months?"

"Whatever I need to do. Whatever I have to. But I'll know you're safe and untraceable while I'm doing it."

"Won't they find records of us boarding here?"

"Not if you bypass the port. Fa'yet and Neko can Jump the three of you to the freighter. It's just outside Narvan space, following the standard trade route. I'll give Fa'yet the name and he can take care of the details from there."

"But how will you find us?"

I made myself look at her until she met my gaze. "That's the question, isn't it? Do you want me to find you?"

Her fingers ran over the silver armband, tracing the etched surface. She bit her lip and pulled the band from her arm. My gift rested in the palm of her hand.

"Maybe you should take it."

My voice broke but I didn't care. "Why?"

"You worked hard for it. You only get the one, right? That's how it's supposed to work, you said. You'll find someone else, someone that can wear it and give you an answer faster than I can."

"Stassia, there won't be anyone else. It's yours. I don't care how long it takes you to answer, as long as you eventually say yes."

A sad smile tugged at the corners of her lips. "Are you sure?"

I took the armband from her palm and slid it back onto her wrist where it belonged.

"I want you to come for us. To us. Wherever we are. You'll do that, won't you? You'll do what you have to do and come back to us?"

"I will."

She grabbed me then, wrapping her arms around me. I joined her, glad that I'd removed everything she'd asked so we could be together as Rhaine and Isnar for a little while. But we weren't that either. Even when she'd had her first horrible headaches, been angry and frustrated with our leaving the Narvan behind, and when she'd had so many physical problems while gestating Ikeri, I'd never felt the fear and sadness that I did now.

Though I wasn't physically tired, thanks to the hours of sleep I'd had while Merkief had been in the tank, I was emotionally drained. We fell asleep, her tight against me and my arms around her. It was the best and worst night of sleep I had in weeks.

When we woke, the sun had barely risen, shedding just enough light to lend us silhouettes. I stole glances at her until I caught her watching me too.

"So you'll be gone for at least six months then?" she whispered as if she were afraid Fa'yet might hear us where he surely sat out at the surveillance station.

"I don't know for sure, but let's plan on that for now."

Her hand snuck under my shirt as she rolled towards me. "I don't suppose, since we've put the joining on the back burner for now, that we could-"

"Without affecting the joining, right. Sure. I think we could make that happen."

"Good." She kissed me and both of us made quick work of the clothes we'd fallen asleep in.

&

Fa'yet did his best to look elsewhere when we eventually made our way out of the bedroom. Though Stassia had started the morning whispering, she'd given up the effort to be quiet rather quickly under the circumstances.

"Hungry?" Stassia asked.

"I may have worked up a hunger."

And I'd missed her cooking, crazy as that was to admit. I'd grown used to it. Watching her move around the kitchen reminded me of our years on Minor and brought a smile to my face.

"Someone's in a good mood this morning," Fa'yet said only half to himself.

"Don't worry, Isnar, I'll make sure you're fed too," Stassia assured him.

"No offense, Ana, but I'll make myself something when you're done in there."

She shook her head. "You'll come to appreciate my cooking eventually."

"It does grow on you," I said.

"Oh shut up," she chided.

It was still early and the kids were sleeping, so I took a few minutes to check in with Jey.

"How are the fleets doing with their preparations?"

"They'll be ready to go tomorrow. Will you?"

"I'll be there."

"I'll send you a jump point when we're ready to launch." He cut contact.

"What are you planning?" Stassia asked.

"Planning? I'm planning on eating. How long is that going to take?"

She rolled her eyes. "Vayen, you know how long eggs take. What were you just doing?"

"Talking to Jey."

"Things still all right between you two?"

"Yeah."

"Good. Did you talk to Isnar about your plan yet?"

"No." I ignored his questioning glance. "After I eat."

I wanted some semblance of a regular morning. Was that too much to ask?

"Well, tell me about this place then. I'm curious," she said.

"Stassia, can it wait?"

"Neko's asleep and so are the kids. It wouldn't kill you to speak out loud to Isnar in front of me."

Sighing, I turned my chair so I could see both of them at once. "Fine. The five of you are taking a trip."

"One way or return?" Fa'yet asked.

"That remains to be determined."

His lip curled and the rest of him didn't appear any more

enthused. "What kind of trip?"

"One I'm told lasts about six months using the standard trade route jump gates. You'll go by freighter. I want you mobile and away from action for at least that long."

"You realize these sort of trips for five people are costly, right?"

"Not a problem."

"Didn't you spend a single credit in all the time you worked for her?"

"He invested. Widely." Stassia said, waving her spatula in the air. "And no, he lived off me the entire time."

"I did not. I paid for dinner when it was my turn."

She pointed her spatula at me. "But you never bought a house, or several, or paid off surveillance satellites, or bribed the locals."

"Well no, you had that covered. I did buy my own clothes and weapons."

"Some of the weapons. Most of those came from my arsenal." She slid a plate in front of me. "Your breakfast is served. Now tell us about Pentares."

I took a bite and chewed the spicy eggs slowly, buying time. Both of them looked at me expectantly. Apparently, I was allowed no semblance. Normal was a thing of the past.

"There's a good-sized human colony there. I thought you might like to be among your own kind for once."

She looked puzzled. "I haven't ever been, now that I think of it. The Verian station had a sizeable population, but many of them left when the trouble with Jal started. What's the population mix then?"

"Human and probably a few outside consultants."

"Wait, you're sending me off into completely foreign territory?" Fa'yet looked almost panicked.

"I did ask if you'd miss your bed warmers."

"But come on, Vayen, we're talking no natural conversation at all, not to mention the other implications. I don't know as I'm okay with that. I'm not the celibate sort."

"I'm sure you'll make do. Who knows, there may be other Artorians there."

He shook his head. "No, I'm pretty sure you'd mention it if you knew that for a fact."

"So you'll be released from your obligations when I return."

He stared hard at me. *"You know that's not an option I can bank on. You wouldn't be sending us off like this, not to a place like that if you really thought you'd survive whatever it is you're planning."*

I looked away. *"You'll work something out."*

Fa'yet chose to drop that line of protest for now. "The only natural conversation I'll get is from your children? Do you know how cruel that is?"

"They need your help, so does Anastassia. Will you do it or not?"

He bowed his head. "You know I will, but I don't like it."

"I'm not paying you to like it."

Stassia interjected herself between us, sitting down across from me, with her back to him. "What about the kids though? Shouldn't they be around your people?"

"Why shouldn't they be around your people?"

She cocked her head and took a bite. "I suppose that's true."

"See, I'm not an idiot all the time."

Stassia chuckled. "So what kind of colony is it?"

"Research. Plants mostly. Alternative crops for deep spacing vessels and tough climates. Thought it sounded right up your alley."

"If what my father always griped about is true, the majority of my people's technology is far behind yours. If Pentares is truly that far away, they'll likely never have heard of anything we have here."

"That was the idea."

She twirled her fork as she chewed. "So I could sneak in a little Artorian tech knowledge and help my people while still appearing useful on my own merit. Hmm, I just might not be opposed to that."

"I had a feeling you wouldn't be."

"Maybe you do know me pretty well after all." She winked.

"I like to think I have a clue or two."

Fa'yet rolled his eyes. "If you two are done mooning over each other, I'd like some more details on this trip we're taking. When are we leaving?"

Stassia turned back to me, waiting for an answer.

Merkief said two weeks. Jey said two days. I had an attack to lead tomorrow. I couldn't think of a worse distraction from a major offensive than worrying if Merkief had led the Council to my family. But then, I didn't know if he realized they were here. I'd outright asked him about Frique. Did that make the choice too obvious or hide them in plain sight?

I hated all this not knowing and people who should have been on my side, acting against me. It all felt so wrong.

"Tomorrow. I'll let Neko know too."

"Not big on the advance warning are you?" Fa'yet said.

"Remember what I said about High alert? This is all sudden to me too and directly related."

"All right then." He threw his hands up in the air. "I guess I should get something to eat and then pack. You're a rotten boss, you know that?"

"I've heard. I'll get you the freighter information as soon as I have definite details. No, better yet," I transferred what little I had to him. "You set it up. I don't want to know the details."

"You'll contact me? After you've taken care of this threat, I mean?" he asked.

I shook my head. "Best we shut all connections down. I'll make my own way to you. If that's possible."

"You're not going to demand I have my link removed, are you? Because that's not going to happen."

"No. I remember what it's like not having it. You don't need that level of distraction, and I'd prefer you able to Jump them elsewhere if needed. I'm sure you know what you need to do."

"Yeah, set up alternate locations, I got it. Just make sure you don't lead any of the High Council to my head and we'll be set."

"That's why I want all connections severed."

He nodded. "I'll leave you two to your morning then. Your monsters should be up any minute."

Once he'd grabbed a few things from the kitchen and had gone into his own room, I turned back to Stassia. "He's okay with them, isn't he?"

She laughed under her breath. "They're converting him. Slowly."

"What about you? Are you okay with him being around all the time?"

"It's different. I'd rather it be you, of course, but we're working around the both of us needing space thing. It helps that he's out of his element too."

"And Neko?"

"He and Isnar have gotten into it a couple times. Patience was never Isnar's strong suit and he's always preferred to work alone. Neko's still learning. I've been helping him where I can, as far as training that is, and slipping him hints to keep the peace between them."

"I'd hoped that splitting their shifts would prevent that."

She shrugged. "There has to be some overlap or they'd never share information."

That was true, but I wished I'd been around more to enforce them getting along. Hopefully they weren't as bad as Jey and I had been when we were first hired.

"I'd find you another if I had time," I said. "Three would be best. That worked well before."

"We'll get by. Besides, I don't think I could handle another stranger around. At least I know Isnar. I'm afraid all this juggling people and houses isn't good for the kids. They've been asking for Gemmen for days. They were very attached to him."

"He was attached to them too." I pushed my empty plate away. "Look, that's not a good idea. We burnt that bridge. Not with Gemmen necessarily, but with everyone else there. He's not the one calling the shots anymore. It's best we cut our ties."

She put her fork down. "Have you received threats from Gemmen's son?"

"Can we not talk about that right now?" I glanced at the closed doors across the room. "I wish the kids were awake."

Her eyebrows shot up. "That's the first time I've ever heard that out of you. You must want to avoid the topic pretty badly."

"Yes, but I'd also like to see them for more than five minutes. It's been awhile, and we don't have much more time together."

"Oh." She bowed her head. "I hadn't thought about that yet. How are we going to tell them that you're leaving?"

"I don't know. What do you think?"

"You're the one leaving. You tell them."

"So I have to be the bad guy and the one they might never see again? I'd rather not."

"Don't say that," she whispered.

"You tell them. After I leave. I'll be out of here before you will. I have to meet Jey at some point tomorrow."

"Oh no, we're not lying to them. Ikeri will sense something's off."

"Then I'll block our connection."

"Don't, not until you have to. She's going to have a hard time with that."

"I'll have to when I leave. Can you handle her?" I asked.

She crossed her arms over her chest and stared at her own plate. "I don't have much choice, do I?"

"Fa'yet can help you."

"Isnar doesn't even like kids. He's trying, but Vayen, this would be easier with someone who doted on them. Like Gemmen."

"Gemmen has a family of his own. He has wives and kids and grandkids. He's got a whole Jalvian dynasty going over there. And he's on the outs with his son. I wouldn't ask that of him. They'd never take him back."

Her shoulders sagged. "I know, it's just hard not be selfish, you know?"

"Oh, I do. Trust me, I do."

I got up and went to the wall of windows in the common room. The sun shone through the leaves. Morning had come full force and the last day with my family was underway.

Stassia came up behind me and wrapped her arms around my chest. "Sorry, that was a stupid thing to say." She pressed her cheek against my back. "Are you ready? Shall I get them up?"

"No. I'll do it."

She let go and backed away to the couch where she sat down to watch the trees she'd once loved so much.

"I'm taking the sapling with us," she announced.

"Won't that just get in the way?"

She looked at me, drilling the statement in. "I'm taking it with us."

I nodded. "I'll let you work that out with Neko and Fa'yet then. They'll be thrilled, I'm sure."

"I don't care."

Her determination made me smile inside. I kissed the top of her head as I passed behind her to go to the room where the kids were still sleeping. They both woke when I opened the door.

We spent the morning playing. Stassia sat with us on the floor on occasion, but she often found somewhere else she needed to be.

I spent lunch outside with Neko, walking in the sweltering heat, explaining about the trip to Pentares, and what I'd need him to do there. He was young and excited by the idea of leaving everything behind, much like my first few hours on the job with Stassia when she'd been Kazan. That had ended soon enough with gunfire and overwhelming fears of inadequacies. I hoped Neko would have a better time of it.

We told the kids, or more, Stassia sat next to me on the couch as I told the kids that they'd be going on a trip. Daniel was all smiles, much like Neko.

"Will there be new races for us to see?"

"I'm sure there will be," I told him. "You'll be on a freighter, a real spaceship. They'll be stopping by ports throughout the systems they pass through. And jump gates too. You'll get to see all kinds of new things."

He jumped up and down, clapping his hands, eyes glowing with excitement. "Will we get our own rooms on the ship?"

As much as I wanted to grant his wish, knowing how he missed his own room on Veria Minor, that would be far too expensive. They'd need the majority of the credits I'd set aside for them once they got to Pentares. I had to plan for the fact that I might not be coming back for them, that they'd be living there for the rest of their lives. I wanted them to be set and comfortable, along with the two men that I was trusting to watch over them, neither of which came cheaply. Between providing for my family and financing the offensive for Jey, my credits were dwindling. I either needed to start earning more or have the action against Kess pay off immediately. Since Kess was controlling some of our very own forces, I didn't expect to have a lot of spoils to offset the cost.

That meant I needed to work. And work, the sort that paid what I needed it to pay, meant slinking back to Sere and rejoining Kryon. If they'd have me.

I'd know soon enough.

"No, you'll probably have far less room than we do here, but you'll be able to walk around on the ship. You won't be in your room very much, I'd imagine. There are usually lots of things to do on a ship like that. It's what they're made for."

"Like what?"

I grabbed him and tickled him until he was squealing. "You'll just have to wait and see."

Ikeri, in stark contrast, sat staring at me, tears welling in her eyes. "You're not coming with."

"No, I'm not, but Fa'yet and Neko are. They'll keep you safe. And your mother."

"But not you." She got up and walked into my room.

I watched the door close, knowing she was curled up on my bed, crying. I could feel it. I looked to Stassia.

"Let her be for a few minutes. You won't be here to run after her, she'll have to get used to that."

"I don't run after her."

"You do. All the time." She squeezed my hand. "It's sweet, really, but she'll have to adjust."

I didn't want her to have to adjust, dammit. If this was the last time I would get to comfort my little girl, then I was going to do it no matter what Stassia said. I got up and opened the door to the bedroom.

Ikeri lay on the bed, hands gripping the rumpled blanket, which in itself made me smile. Stassia had been so off-kilter this morning that she'd not made the bed. It was a rare thing indeed and something of a matter of pride that I'd distracted her so badly.

Ikeri turned to look at me, sniffing. "Why are you happy?"

"I was thinking about your mother." I sat down next to her, rubbing her boney back. "You need to eat more."

She stuck her tongue out. "I don't like the food here."

"You know what? It was never my favorite either."

"Really? Mommy said you liked it, and that I should eat it too."

"Did she now?" I laughed. "Well, I suppose you should listen to your mother then." I leaned close to her ear and whispered, "But I never did like the food here very much."

She giggled and snuggled up next to me. "Will I like the food on the ship better?"

"I honestly don't know. I've never been on a ship like that before."

Her eyes grew round. "You haven't?"

I shook my head. "You're going to do something that I've never done. You'll have to remember everything so that when I see you again, you can tell me all about it."

"Okay." Her hand wriggled into mine. "Mommy is sad."

"I know. So am I." I pulled her onto my lap. "Let your mother be sad, all right? Don't try to fix her? You'll just wear yourself out, and I don't want that. You hear me?"

"Yes, Daddy."

"Promise me."

She looked solemnly into my eyes, so adult, yet only a tiny girl. "I promise."

"Good."

"You promise too."

"What am I promising?"

She leaned up, pressing her round, rosy cheek against mine. "Always wear your coat so you stay safe."

"That, I will certainly do. I promise."

"Good." She sat back down and snuggled against me.

I sat there with her for a while, growing sadder by the minute, already missing all of them even though I'd not yet left.

Dinner came from Veria Minor. I'd hoped that our last big meal together would seem like we were back home, but it was far from it. Stassia wouldn't meet my gaze. Daniel asked a hundred questions about the ship and the colony. Ikeri barely ate a thing and remained utterly silent. Everything felt wrong. I wanted this day to go on forever and yet to be over immediately. Dinner ended in strained silence.

I suggested we go outside for a bit so the kids could play in the last light of the day. They'd be boxed up on a freighter for months. Fresh air would do them good. Daniel ran around like he had all the energy in the world. Ikeri made an effort to keep up with him, but I guessed it was only because she knew it would make me happy to see them playing together one last time.

Stassia sat beside me, her hand in mine, yet a thousand miles lay between us.

Fa'yet kept a watchful eye over us all. I felt him sitting at the station behind us, probably cursing himself for getting involved with me again. Soon I wouldn't have anyone watching over me. Jey beside me, perhaps, but no one at my back.

I squeezed her hand. "Have you talked to Fa'yet about your headaches?"

"No."

"Neko?"

"Definitely not. He might live with us, but I hardly know the man. You remember how long it took me to trust you with knowing about the tank?"

"Yes, too long. You need to tell them. You'll be out there by yourself. I won't be able to help you. They need to know what to do."

"I have warning, Vayen. It's not like they strike out of nowhere."

"But I won't be there."

I'd taken care of her when she was down since before we'd left. It really grated on my nerves and the bond to know I wouldn't be there when she needed me. And she would. The stress of knowing I was out of the picture, living in even closer quarters with Neko and Fa'yet, the kids underfoot, it would all get to her. Very likely sooner rather than later.

"I'll figure it out." She got up and walked inside.

She would. I just wished I'd be there to see it.

I ran around with the kids, playing until the shadows grew thick under the trees. When we went in at last, we found Stassia on the couch. She'd been watching us through the window.

She got up and went into my room. I put the kids to bed, doing my best to hide how sad it made me, knowing that it could well be the last time. I had little doubt that Ikeri saw through me, but she smiled when she kissed me goodnight. Daniel was still asking excited questions when I cut him off and told him to get some sleep.

Stassia was already in bed, staring at the ceiling when I came in. "You could come with us."

"We've been over this. I can't."

"I know," she whispered as she rolled over, putting her back to me.

I slipped into bed next to her and wrapped an arm over her. She stayed facing away and remained silent. And so passed our last night together.

≈

Jey's voice woke me. *"We're launching in an hour. I'd say you have another two before I need you to Jump aboard. Thought you would appreciate a little advance warning."*

"Thanks."

I yawned and cut contact. For getting a full night of sleep, I sure didn't feel rested. I was still yawning when I returned from the bathroom after a quick shower.

Stassia sat on the bed, forlorn eyes watching me dress. "You're leaving?"

"Very soon. Yes."

She nodded and got up, dressing and braiding her hair back in a matter of minutes. "I suppose you'll want breakfast before you go," she said as if it were any other morning that I'd be leaving for my office on Minor.

"That would be nice."

I followed her out of the bedroom and into the kitchen. Like well-oiled gears, we went about getting breakfast ready together, much the same as we'd known one another's moves back when we'd worked contracts.

Fa'yet watched us eat from his seat at the security station. "You should pack soon, Ana," he said finally.

She got up and went to the bedroom. I let her go and went to wake the kids. I made them breakfast and sat there while they ate, cataloging every tiny detail for the days and months ahead. I found myself in a silent conversation with Geva, bargaining everything in the hopes that my family would never come to harm because of me.

Daniel looked around, and seeing Stassia was out of the room, he leaned toward me. "I'll still be able to practice with Uncle Isnar, right? On the ship? Will there be room for that?"

Why couldn't they have chosen to just call him uncle? Or anything else, for that matter. But no, they'd followed Stassia's lead.

Teaching him how to use a knife should have fallen to me, not Fa'yet. Sneaking behind Stassia's back was our special thing. Not that I thought we pulled it off near as neatly as she let us believe, but it's what we did together.

When I looked to Fa'yet, he shrugged.

"I'm guessing the two of you could find somewhere to make that happen. Your mother will probably find out though. She doesn't miss much. In fact, it wouldn't surprise me if she knew already and is only remaining silent to make you sneak around." I winked. "She's like that."

There, they'd been warned. Would Stassia be as tolerant of their antics as she was of mine when I was with Daniel? I might never know.

Fa'yet laughed. "She *is* like that. But we'll be careful anyway." He shared a conspiratorial grin with Daniel.

The kids were definitely growing on him. I only hoped that Fa'yet proved to be a good influence on Daniel. With Stassia and Chesser's blood in his veins, the boy would likely end up a stubborn bundle of trouble. For that matter, I hoped I'd been a good influence on him too.

At least I'd grown up with a fairly normal childhood. It wasn't until the war with Jal had begun to suck Artor dry that violence really touched my family. I'd hadn't been aware of what the news vid feeds were really about until I was several years older than Daniel. The poor kid was already living the stuff of news feeds.

Stassia came out of the room with the things I'd recovered

from the Cragtek house all packed. She set a bag on the floor and went to the room the kids had been sharing.

"We're leaving today?" Daniel jumped up from the table and ran around the room, whooping with glee.

"I doubt Neko is going to thank you for waking him up like that," I said.

Daniel froze. "Sorry. I forgot."

Neko's door flew open. The disheveled man stood in the doorway, glowering at Daniel. "You better be sorry."

Fa'yet scowled. "And you should be up and alert. And dressed. And armed. Get yourself together." He grumbled to himself and stalked over to have a private word with Neko.

"We're almost ready," Jey said in my head. He flashed me a jump point.

"I'll be there shortly." I cut contact and focused on Stassia. "I've set credits aside for you. There are separate accounts for Fa'yet and Neko. Pay them as you see fit."

She glanced at the men across the room. "You trust them to guard us but not enough to pay them upfront?"

"Did you ever pay me upfront?"

"True. How am I supposed to access these accounts?"

I slipped a folded sheet of paper into her hand. "All the information is here. Once you're onboard, have Fa'yet transfer everything into your name."

"Why don't you just put it in my name?" she snapped.

"I did, I mean your new name."

Her anger wavered as she swallowed hard. "Maybe I don't want a new name."

I kissed her forehead. "Do what you need to do, Stassia. The credits are yours. The kids will need things on the freighter. They're likely to grow two sizes before you arrive. You'll need things too. And a place once you get there. There's enough there to keep you set for a very long time."

Her voice hitched. "I don't want to be set for a very long time."

"But you will be if you have to be."

Why did she have to fight me every step of the way? This was hard enough already.

"Make sure you convert the credits as you pass through ports. Pentares is very far from the Narvan, as are ninety percent of the other places you'll pass through. Keep your assets available."

She sighed heavily. "I will."

"Good." I kissed her forehead again. "I should pack too."

I went to my room to find my few things folded neatly on the bed. I found a spare bag in the kitchen and tossed my extra clothes into it. Who knew if I'd be coming back here, or if I'd ever want to. I spent the next fifteen minutes going through the weapons chest in my closet, making sure my coat was stocked and everything was in working order. Fully armed and armored, I emerged from my room.

"You're leaving then?" Stassia asked.

"It's time."

Ikeri ran to me. I knelt down and hugged her. "I'll always miss you," she said. "Remember your promise."

"I will." I kissed her cheek. "You remember yours."

She nodded and stepped away, tears running down her rosy cheeks.

Daniel approached me next. He hugged me tightly.

"Take care of your mother. And listen to her. Got it?"

He nodded.

"Promise me."

"I promise," he said solemnly.

"And you better listen to Fa'yet and Neko too. And watch out for your sister. Can you do all that?"

"I promise."

"Good."

He sniffed a little as he backed away.

Fa'yet emerged from Neko's room. I stopped him with a hand on his arm. "You'll take care of them all?"

"You know I will." He clapped me on the back. "You take care of yourself, all right?"

I nodded, unable to speak through the lump in my throat.

Stassia came to me and took my hand. She led me outside, where we were alone. Her voice was filled with desperation. "Promise me you'll come for us."

There were an awful lot of promises being tossed about. This was one I couldn't make. "If I'm alive..."

She punched me in the chest. "Lie to me, dammit!" Tears filled her eyes but refused to fall.

"You've always said I was no good at lying to you." I tried to smile but failed.

"Do it anyway."

I took a deep shuttering breath. "When it's safe, I'll come for you."

Stassia stared at me in much the same way as I imagined my face had looked when I'd watched the kids eat breakfast earlier. I pulled her close and kissed her. I didn't need to see her. I needed to feel her. That was the thing I most wanted to hold onto, the peace of the bond we shared. The thing that would be gone when she muffled her end of our bonded connection, as only she could.

Stassia's hands fell to her sides. I let her go.

"I'll be waiting," she said.

I took one last look at the little house on Frique with Stassia standing in front of it and my children waving at me through the window. When I'd etched into my memory, I closed my eyes and stepped into the void.

Chapter Fourteen

Jey met me in the room he'd given me as a jump point. I'd caught him in the middle of changing into the Jalvian military uniform he preferred to wear when on official business. He cocked his head and looked me over.

"You all right?"

"No."

Though I'd just stepped away from Frique a minute ago, I knew there was no going back. I'd set my feet on the path they needed to be on for better or worse.

Before I did anything that I didn't want Ikeri picking up on, I sealed the connection we shared, walling her off. Daniel was easier, he didn't have the emotional neediness of his sister. Before I could decide what to do about Stassia, she did it herself, sealing off her end of our bonded connection. I wouldn't be able to establish it again until we saw one another.

Neko went next. Were they all standing in a circle, letting each other know who was shutting me out when? Had I started the cascade myself when I'd shut Ikeri out? Likely I had.

Fa'yet went last. He sent a final burst of encouragement and then our linked connection went dead. Our natural one blinked out seconds later as if it had never existed.

I let them all go. Emptiness filled my stomach. Only Jey's presence and the faint connections with the few contacts I'd reestablished kept me company. Merkief's connection sat on the edges of my awareness. I'd been avoiding it at all costs.

"You want to wait here for a few minutes? You look like you need to sit down."

"I'll be fine. What do you need from me?" Sitting down would only lead to wallowing. I needed a distraction.

"Use your link if you want to. Hang out here. You don't look the part right now."

"What do you mean by that?" If he expected me to get into a Jalvian uniform, he had another thing coming.

"No offense, but you look ready to break down at any minute. That's hardly something my men are going to respect."

"I'm not." I forced my work face into place.

"That's better. Come on then. You can always come back here if you need to."

I followed him out into the corridor. We took a lift up to the command center which was brimming with milling officers and specialists going about their business.

"Sit here," he said, pulling out a stool for me at an empty terminal. "This should have everything you need. The map is behind you in the middle of the room."

"Can I get one at this station?"

"What is it with you and maps?"

"I like to have a full grasp of the situation."

"You have maps in your head, you know." He thwacked me on the back of my head. "Use those."

"I like the visual at hand."

"Get up if you need to, but don't you dare fry your link again."

Grumbling, I set about getting the terminal configured how I liked it. Once I had that ready, I sunk into my link and connected with the few contacts I had throughout the Jalvian fleet.

Mox, my tech spy on Kess's ship, verified their location. Using the information he fed me, I tweaked my plans and set up our initial line of attack. It didn't mesh with what Jey had planned, but once I pitched it to him, his eyes lit up.

"This is why I wanted you here." He clapped me on the shoulder.

We were able to catch Kess unsuspecting, firing bombs from orbit directly into the strongholds he'd set up on Merchess. It bothered me to strike at Merchess, a planet that we'd overseen for years. I knew people there. I'd lived there. Stassia and I had some very good times there.

I crushed the thoughts of Stassia. That was exactly the sort of distraction I didn't need.

These people had converted to Kess's rule. They were the enemy now. Still, I tried to strike targets that would yield low casualties. If we managed to knock Kess out, I didn't want too much of a mess to clean up afterward.

Kess's ships did not fare well. We picked off the smaller ones one by one as they streaked through the atmosphere and into space where we were waiting. The larger ones that swarmed us from the family ports in orbit were more of a threat. We boarded those we could and subdued them from the inside. Many of the Jalvian ships that Kess had taken were following the orders of a few officers. The main contingency wasn't opposed to surrender and pardon. We took out those we couldn't sway to see reason.

My Jalvian spy confirmed that our attacks were pissing Kess off. His men were grumbling, unhappy at being caught unaware.

Kess had gotten lax with his defenses. Jey and Merkief hadn't been this aggressive in years.

When Merchess seemed mostly subdued, we called off the attack. A hole in the dome above the Nikera city had claimed the lives of thousands before it had been sealed. Those that had died were slaves. They'd had no part in choosing Kess and their deaths did not sit well with me.

The ships still in the spaceports stayed in their bays. The remaining Jalvian ships that had opposed us, submitted their surrender. We boarded them, removed the offending officers and incarcerated them for later action. Our troops spread throughout the fleet, commanding men who hadn't been to their homeworld since joining Kess, to return to their homes and families. Once they reintegrated, I had a feeling the remaining unrest on Jal would end.

The rest of the damage Kess had wrought would take time to erase. Of Kess himself, there was little sign. Perhaps he'd fallen back to Twelve.

I got my answer when two men appeared in the command center the instant Mox shouted a warning in my head. Our connection went dead.

The two men whipped out automatic weaponry. Men fell, screaming, writhing on the floor. Blood splattered on the controls. Jey fell as one of his own men shoved him forward onto the floor and threw his body over him. No one came to help me.

I ducked for cover and helped myself with a gun from my coat.

Nothing near as large as what they carried, but good enough for a headshot if I dared to take the time to aim. The bullets they fired were huge and high powered. It would only take one or two of those to get through my armor, not to mention the damage they would cause even if they didn't.

The man atop Jey jerked as bullets sank into his back. I prayed Jey was unharmed since the tank wasn't currently an option.

While they were focused on Jey, I leapt up and took out the two men before they caused any further casualties. They'd also done a fair amount of equipment damage. The officers snapped into action, ordering power and systems to be re-routed. I pulled the dead man off Jey. Blood covered the back of his head.

I contemplated being alone against Kess, Merkief and the High Council, and I shuddered.

Men ran to Jey's side, knocking me out of the way. He rolled over, looking stunned from hitting the floor face first, but got to his feet seconds later.

Relief flooded through me. I announced, "We have a spy."

Jey nodded. "I'm on it."

A careful look around the carnage-filled command center made it clear who Jey's immediate contacts were. Three men, all officers, eyed the remaining survivors with suspicion, glancing from one man to the next in rapid-fire succession.

One of the techs who'd been near me got up. Without looking at anyone directly, he headed for the door, following the men who were carrying the one who had saved Jey. Before I had to say anything, the three officers converged on the man. He didn't struggle when they grabbed his arms, he smiled. His jaw jerked as if he were biting down hard. Ten seconds later he went limp. Kess had some very devoted help.

"If he's got one, he's likely got more," I said.

Jey went to discuss the issue with the officers. A swarm of crewmembers barged into the room, surveying the damage and beginning triage.

Merkief's unwelcome voice penetrated my head. *"You've been seen. If you want any sort of upper hand with the Council members who hadn't known about you until just now, I suggest you get to Sere while Kess is distracted."*

It seemed Kess wasn't the only one with spies onboard. Or maybe Merkief had thought this was the perfect time to lure me into another trap. Regardless, if I wanted a chance that didn't involve me being dragged to Sere at gunpoint, this was it.

"I need to go," I informed Jey.

His head whipped around to face me. *"No. Not yet. Don't do this."*

"It's not like I'm running off on some suicide mission like Anastassia did."

Jey's eyes narrowed. He stalked his way though the bustling crew. *"The circumstances might be different, but yes, that's exactly what you're doing."*

"They know I'm here. If I don't go, they'll either try to take me out or take me in. I'd rather not have any more lives endangered on my account. If I go of my own accord, I might be able to strike a deal at least somewhat in my favor."

"You really think they'll deal with you?" His tone implied that he didn't.

"This is what the two of you wanted. What you demanded, when you barged back into my life."

"It's what Merkief wanted. Not me."

"Well, you weren't doing much to stop him and now he's getting his way. I hope you're both happy." I ran my hands over my coat, double checking all the lumps and bumps. *"Kess should be down on his luck for a bit, take full advantage of that."*

He caught me in a hard stare. *"I will. You better take care of yourself. I'd rather not face Anastassia's wrath if this goes wrong."*

"I'll do my best."

"And you're coming back to help grind Kess into the ground, right?" He started edging his way closer, eyes clearly judging the distance.

"Wouldn't miss it." Before he got close enough to physically keep me from leaving, I formed the Jump to Sere and stepped into the void.

⁓

Sere greeted me with the sudden attention of four grey-suited guards which quickly became a private escort. They herded me, not to one of the private rooms where I'd met with Deep Voice and the others years before, but to the room where trials were held. The room where I'd lost the woman who had been fully Kazan.

They unceremoniously shoved me into the single metal chair in the middle of the room and then took up positions around me.

I knew better than to ask them what was going on. Either they were being controlled like puppets by High and Mighties or they were merely following orders. They wouldn't be swayed to any manner of helpfulness by pleas or bribes. These were vacant souls, husks of men and women with nothing to gain or lose.

Three more grey-suits joined us within minutes. They looked directly at me with intent that went far beyond their vacant faces. These were the puppets.

"Mr. Ta'set," one said, inclining his head. "I'd say we were surprised to see you, but that's not entirely true."

One of the others, a woman, stepped forward. "You look fairly fit for a dead man."

Fairly? I resisted the urge to glare at her.

The remaining puppet stayed back, letting the other two work me over with their hollow gazes and implanted words. The woman said, "How is it that Kess Atta came to have your link and that of Anastassia Kazan?"

"I gave them to him."

She raised her brows, the most expression I'd seen on her face since arriving.

"You chose this exile?"

"You didn't leave me any choice."

"There are always choices, Mr. Ta'set," said the third puppet whom I knew immediately from his tone to be controlled by Deep Voice.

"And I made mine."

"Then why are you here?"

"The Narvan is a mess. Someone needs to clean it up."

"And you would be that someone?"

"I'm here aren't I?"

"You held the Narvan before. Then you died, vanished, stepped away to leave your people and our resources floundering. Why would we trust you again?"

"Because you don't trust Kess, Jey, or Merkief. If you did, you'd have picked one and set him up to advise the system years ago. Instead, you've let them nibble at each other while advancement on all fronts has ground to a halt. You've got no one to blame but yourselves."

"Big words from a dead man," said the woman.

"You should have remained dead if you wished to remain living," said the man. He signaled to the four guards, one of whom raised his gun and aimed it at my head. "We cannot abide by this sort of behavior. An example must be made."

"Now wait a minute," said Deep Voice, knocking the man's hand aside. "We're not in agreement here."

The three figures lost their spark of life. When they returned a few minutes later, I was grateful that the first thing they did was motion for the guard to lower his weapon. However, when a cloaked forth figure entered the room, I began to sweat in earnest. This one was an actual High and Mighty in the flesh.

"I'm glad to see you back among us. You still owe me a meal," said the figure in a rasping hiss of a voice.

Oh Geva, anyone but him. Anyone but the blue creature I'd watched devour Sonia. I gripped the arms of the chair, and regardless of the fact I was far outnumbered, contemplated the odds of being able to Jump from the room before getting my head taken off. They weren't good, but if we'd still had access to the tank, I might have taken them anyway.

"You will call me Arpex. Where is Kazan?"

"Dead."

"You seem well enough for it," said the woman.

"How long ago?" Deep Voice asked.

What would they expect of me if she were truly dead? Should I be sad but distant to account for the time I'd had to cope or cold, having given her link to Kess?

What had Kess told them to cover his ass? If I gave him partial credibility, maybe he would be more willing to work with me toward putting the Narvan back together.

They were all looking at me, waiting. I cleared my mind of everything but the room and its occupants.

"Kess killed her at the Artorian University where she was seeking treatment. He and I had a deal. He let me go in exchange for my link."

The blue creature hidden beneath the cloak hissed.

"What sort of deal?" asked Deep Voice.

"You wanted her dead. I couldn't kill her thanks to the fact that you bonded us together. But you had your demands. Kess had been after her for years and was more than happy to take her out for me. I'd planned to stay and partner with Kess as his payment, but after the job was done, I couldn't. Thank your forcing of the bond for that." I let out the snarl I'd been holding back.

Deep Voice's puppet closed in on me. His manically animated eyes blinked off time from one another. "You voluntarily had your link removed and vanished?" His fist caught me in the jaw. "You left this mess in your wake to do what? Weep and wallow? Do you have any idea how many lives were lost, how much time, research, resources," he shook his fists, "while you were doing nothing? You let that happen! You. It's all on your head. Not ours."

The magnitude of his accusations threatened to swallow me. The men, women, and children who'd died in Kess's attack on Rok were only a small fraction of the lives that had been lost so I could enjoy my freedom with Stassia. The Narvan had been brought to as much of a near standstill in my absence as it had before Kazan had taken over. The peace my brother had died for, that I'd killed for, rationalized all of the High Council's demands for, was gone, squandered for a few years of happy memories.

But it wasn't all my fault. They'd bonded me to Stassia and then demanded the impossible. The High and Mighties had stood aside, their factions betting on Merkief, Jey, or Kess. Their indecision had cost far more lives than my single brash decision.

The coldness I'd been seeking to sell them on Stassia's death settled over me. But it had nothing to do with her death and everything to do with theirs. It was their games that had sent my family into exile, deprived Merkief of his, and killed so many countless others. I'd always thought the High Council had direction, some sort of level of protection for my homeworld and the system as a whole, for all the worlds and systems it controlled. But if the Narvan was anything to gauge the situation in the known universe by, that wasn't the case at all. The Council was nothing more than a bunch of self-important cloaked bastards pulling the strings of others for their own amusement and gain.

A newfound certainty filled me with burning purpose. We'd be better off without them.

"Mr. Ta'set," said the man. "You are at fault. You must be punished for your actions before we can consider your proposal."

If they were going to consider my proposal, they didn't mean to kill me, but I still didn't like the word punishment being tossed around.

Arpex made a chattering noise beneath his cloak. Its claws clacked together. My resolve almost faltered as the memories of Sonia's screams echoed in my head. But then I remembered

Stassia's calming touch and her mind meshing with mine, creating a balm over the terrors I'd witnessed. She and the kids were gone. Safe. Far from me, the Council, and Arpex's winged jaws of horror.

I breathed deep through my nose and mustered all the bravado I could find. "How about we postpone the punishment and focus on getting the Narvan back in working order. We've all wasted enough time already."

"You seem to have forgotten your place."

The woman gestured to one of the guards beside me. I heard him raise his arms and braced for a bullet. There was a brief moment of realization of an impact on the side of my head. The room went black.

Chapter Fifteen

I came to in a tiny room I didn't recognize. The hum of a stun field penetrated my awareness. The tiny part of my head that wasn't throbbing informed me I was in a holding cell. The thin mattress on the plascrete floor that I found myself lying on implied that my punishment had already begun. The fact that my coat and weapons were gone reinforced this dire realization.

Sitting up slowly, I gingerly explored the side of my head. A sizeable lump, but no blood. Jey needed to know what was going on. I opened my Link to him.

A shrieking wail ripped through my head, blossoming into a pain that tore through every nerve. I fell back on the mattress, gasping, wanting to scream but lacking the breath to do so. Within seconds, the wave of agony subsided to the degree I could breathe, but the throbbing in my head and every muscle kept me on the mattress for another ten minutes before coherent thoughts again began to form.

The bastards had activated the restrictive field they'd developed during Stassia's incarceration. Until I found a way to escape it, there would be no Jumping, no using my link or my natural speech. Fucking hells, I was stranded Geva knows where under the direct attention of High and Mighties themselves. Maybe Jey had been right. I should have hidden and made them come after me. Though, I doubted the end result would have been any more in my favor.

I reached for my tin of stims, only to remember they'd taken my coat. That's when I realized they'd also taken my clothes and left me in a fucking grey suit. The same damned suits their zombies wore. If this was where my punishment was heading, I didn't like it one bit.

"I see you've discovered that the field is active," said a male voice from beyond the humming blue light.

I forced myself to my feet and approached the crackling wall, hoping for a glimpse of the speaker. "It's even better than I remembered."

"Glad to hear it. We hope you'll keep it's usage to a minimum. We'd rather have you coherent during your time of service. And we both know what its overuse can do to a brain. That would be a shameful waste."

Was this a friend or a foe? The semi-transparent wall kept me from getting any solid visual details.

The grey suit was soft and fit well enough, but it made my skin crawl. "Just what kind of service are we talking about?"

"You need to be reminded of your place among us. You are to follow orders, not give them. You were good at that once. We have hopes that you will be again."

The frequency of the hum rose and then the wall crackled and dissipated with a clap of static that made my hair stand up as the jolt passed through my body.

"You should really get that looked at. The dissipation should be far smoother and without the static," I said, once I'd recovered from the shock.

"No, it works just fine," said the broad-shouldered form beneath a cloak.

My heart sank. Shoulders? Really? Were my favorite High and Mighties lining up to get a crack at me?

"I suggest you follow me and don't cause any trouble. Arpex has been waiting for you."

"And just what does Arpex want with me?"

"It has chosen you as his servant. Lucky you." Shoulder's chuckled. "He ate the last one."

Servant? Me? I gritted my teeth and followed him down the twisting corridor. Hours ago, I'd been off leading an army, now I was a servant to the blue-shelled bastard?

"It better not consider eating me."

"I'd love to reassure you that it won't happen, but I'm not going to. It could. Your, we'll call him your benefactor for the sake of maintaining anonymity, is on the same tier as Arpex. Neither has power over the other and the upward tiers are waiting to see how you perform before making any decrees on your behalf. I suggest you don't disappoint them."

Shoulders stopped in front of an archway covered with a mesh door. He stood aside, waiting for me to enter.

The fixtures overhead emitted a harsh yellow light that made me doubt the actual colors of anything within Arpex's chambers. The door led to a short, arched hallway that opened to a large domed room, the top of which loomed several stories overhead. In the middle of the room stood a cupped platform on a thin pillar. It must have been three times my height to even the bottom of it. The room was hot, almost rivaling the heat of Frique. If the heat bothered Shoulders, his cloak covered any sign. Sweat trickled down the sides of my face.

Shoulders made a clicking noise. A rustling came from the platform above us. I caught a glimpse of green. The wings I'd seen devour Sonia, that had encased me once as well, snapped open. Arpex swooped down and landed before us. Its wings folded back against its shell. The clicking came from within its body. I couldn't tell where exactly as it seemed to echo throughout the shell. It began an exchange with Shoulders, the meaning of which I dreaded to learn.

When it had told me I could call it Arpex, I'd assumed it was a name, but Shoulders made it sound more like a race or perhaps a title, so I wasn't sure. I wasn't sure of a lot of things at the moment.

Arpex switched to the raspy voice that I was familiar with, the words emanating from the black box strapped around its upper shell. "I am hungry. You will go retrieve my meal. Then you will clean my plate and do whatever else I ask of you. Do you understand?"

I nodded.

"Speak."

"Yes, I understand."

"Good. Go now." A bold invasive presence entered my head, implanting a jump point.

Shoulders clamped a thick, brown-skinned hand on my arm and Jumped us both to the location I'd been given.

Great, I wouldn't know when the field was active and when it wasn't. I guessed that unless one of them told me to Jump, I'd find myself rolling on the floor in agony.

The sky above had an odd green cast, as if a storm was about to strike. Barren rocky ground surrounded us. Ten figures stood by an outcropping a short way off. Shoulders strode over to them. I followed.

"Who are these people?"

"Stock. Don't concern yourself with them. You are here to do a single task: select a meal for Arpex."

The rolling in my stomach made my voice flat. "By meal you mean one of them."

"You've killed for us hundreds of times. This is no different." He pointed to the ten people, whom upon closer inspection, I saw to be in chains. "Pick one."

Their skin was a light brown, smudged with dirt and only washed clean beneath trails of tears. They appeared fairly well fed and though their clothes were also dirty, they weren't ragged. A basket of fruit and bread sat in the shadow of the rock and a cistern brimmed with water. While I was heartened to see they had some supplies, by my quick estimate, it didn't appear enough to sustain them all for very long. Then again, not all of them would survive.

Some regarded me with defiant eyes. Others pleaded in a language I didn't know. It wasn't anything my link could translate either, which indicated I was far from home.

Their outstretched hands shook beneath the weight of the thick chains and cuffs around their wrists. Even without understanding their words, it was clear they were begging for their lives.

I'd hoped to find someone elderly among them, someone sick, anyone that would make my task easier, but they were all young and healthy. I walked up and down the line, trying to make a choice I didn't want to make. Some of the men and women had seen hard work, visible from the calluses on their hands and muscled bodies. One was a little girl with matted curls. She was probably no more than five years old. I couldn't look at her without thinking of Ikeri.

"How long have they been out here?"

"Since sunrise. They will remain for ten days. Those you do not select for Arpex during that time will be set free and then new offerings will be placed here."

"How many meals does it need?"

Shoulders shrugged. "It is not your place to ask. Only to do."

I could save some of them. I changed my selection process to choosing those who I desperately wanted to survive. Oh Geva, I wanted them all to survive.

Shoulders came up beside me. "You're taking too long. Choose." He followed a step behind as I stopped in front of each offering.

The first, a woman, shook her head, babbling. She tried to stand in front of the younger woman next to her, but the chains only let her move so far. I passed them by.

The third, a man, older than the rest, strained in his chains, gaze burning with hatred. That was far easier to bear than the tears and pleading. I marked him as a possibility.

Fourth and fifth were two teen boys, one a few years older than the other. Their terrified gazes darted between me and the ground. The boys deserved to go back home to their families, to find some measure of happiness before they met their end.

Sixth was a woman with braided hair. It was the wrong color, but the glob of spit she hurled at me reminded me of Stassia amidst one of her tirades. Her hands curled into fists and she shook them at me from waist level. Blood dripped where the metal cuffs raked against her skin. I had done everything to keep Stassia out of the barbed jaws of the Arpex and I had no intention of feeding this incarnation to him either.

Seventh was the little girl. She looked between me and the woman next to her with frantic eyes, whimpering and falling back into the shadows as much as the chains allowed. The nightmare I'd prayed to Geva to save me from danced before my eyes with the vision of this tiny body encased in the slavering winged-jaws of Arpex.

The woman yelled louder. Blood dripped down her arms.

I had to make this end. "Him," I pointed to the angry man.

"As you wish." Shoulders produced a key from somewhere in his cloak and handed it to me. "He looks like trouble. Keep him in check but conscious. Arpex likes a little fight in them. Makes them sweeter."

I grimaced and took the key.

"I trust you'll Jump him back to your new home." He relayed a solid jump point. "If you don't arrive with that man within minutes, we'll be forced to follow the tracker we implanted while you were out, and you'll be punished further. Do you understand?"

"Yes."

"Good." Shoulders vanished into the void.

Once I was sure he was gone, I kept the key in my hand but merely stood before the doomed man. The least I could do was reduce his awareness of the upcoming agony. I sought out a natural connection with him.

His eyes went wide. Though he possessed no telepathic abilities that I could find, he certainly knew I was in his head. I dove into a full probe in the few minutes I had before Shoulder's came after me. The words and meanings in his mind were near impossible to follow in my reckless plundering, but his visual memories were simple enough.

As Shoulders had said, these were a race of people the Council unmercifully used as stock. They were chosen by their fellows to be sacrificed, placed at this rock never to be seen again. I wondered where those who were not chosen were released since they never found their way home. Perhaps they were placed on another world. Of this world, I caught little information. These were simple people, subjected to a rough life on a barely habitable planet. They knew little comfort or wonder and didn't even have the sort of technology that backward Frique took for granted.

Faces sped before my mental eye, a couple I recognized as Council zombies. It seemed not all were chosen as food. If I had not come, would one of their own have been forced to choose the next offering?

I did enough damage in my mental rampage to severely impair the man's cognitive abilities. He'd still be on his feet and would likely put up a fight given basic survival instincts, but at least he wouldn't be overly aware of his cruel end.

He didn't struggle when I unlocked his cuffs. The chains fell to the rocks with a clatter. The others stood quietly as I took a moment to study him and form the Jump for both of us. We arrived in front of Shoulders. He stood, arms crossed over his chest and tapping a foot loudly beneath his cloak. Arpex, who I couldn't tell a thing about other than it was still the same sickly green color under the garish light, wasn't hissing. I guessed that was a good sign.

I pushed the man toward Arpex and waited for the barbed jaws to snap out from its back. The man looked around the domed chamber and then seemed to notice the creature standing before him. The wings remained in place.

Shoulders glanced at me and backed away.

"What did you do?" demanded the raspy voice that boomed

from Arpex's box.

"I brought you a meal."

"No. You brought me spoiled meat!"

The Arpex turned toward Shoulders, now standing by the door as if he'd been discovered in his plan to escape from the room. "Take this empty creature to someone who can use him."

Shoulders walked back over to us and led the lack-witted man away. Once the door had closed, the Arpex skittered at me with unexpected speed. It caught my left wrist in a claw and clamped down. The rough edges cut into my flesh, pressing deeper and deeper with a slow, steady pressure that took my breath away. What air remained to me leaked out in a low anguished cry as bones shattered.

I watched in horror as my severed hand fell to the floor. The tank. I needed the tank! I lunged for my hand as I formed a Jump to the ship. The restrictive field sent a new burst of pain through my head and body, knocking me to the floor where I laid gasping as blood spurted from my wrist.

The hand that had so often saved my life and taken so many others lay inches from my face. How in the nine hells was I supposed to recover the Narvan with only one hand? How could I defend myself? I needed both hands, dammit!

It occurred to me, as my thoughts somewhat cleared, that the tank wasn't operational. I couldn't use it if I wanted to, especially now that I couldn't even contact Jey to help repair it. Then again, as I'd learned with the chunk of ear that I'd lost, the tank could heal around, but not regenerate the large areas of missing tissue. I needed a surgeon.

Arpex had to know that I'd need my hand if I was to take the Narvan back for them. This punishment phase was temporary. They'd said as much. Wherever the hells we were, the Council had to have a top-notch medical staff. They wouldn't trust themselves to anyone less than the best.

It was just teaching me a lesson, I assured myself as weakness overcame me and my eyes threatened to slip closed. I'd wake up in a med clinic and find my hand reattached. This was all some twisted joke to them.

But Arpex hadn't moved. I didn't hear anyone rushing into the room to help me. Though the effects of the field slowly wore off, what little energy I had left seeped from my arm. My eyelids blinked once more and then refused to open.

❧

Someone kicked me in the ribs. "Get up. You have work to do."

Work. Right. My shift. Why the hells was I still so damn tired? I slid a leg over the edge of the bed but it hit the floor after only a few inches. Anastassia was going to be pissed if I wasn't suited up and ready before Merkief or Jey went off duty. Which one was I replacing? Probably whichever one had kicked me. But that would mean they'd been standing on my bed. And the voice that had woken me didn't belong to either of them.

I cracked open an eye. Bright yellow light seared into my retinas. I squeezed my eyes closed.

The foot caught me in the ribs again, this time with a crack and the familiar sharp pain I'd come to associate with a broken bone. There would be no trip to the tank to fix it. The thought of having to endure long-term pain did nothing for my ambition to regain full-consciousness.

"You left a mess on my plate. Clean it up or you'll be punished again."

When I opened my eyes for the second time, I was vastly dismayed to find the Arpex looming over me, one of its four feet gearing up for another strike. I held up my hand to fend it off but it didn't work. There was nothing at the end of my arm but a poorly wrapped bandage.

"What did you do to my hand?"

"Nothing. It's still on my plate. Get up and clean the mess."

"You took off my fucking hand!"

"You brought me an empty meal," it said as if that was a total justification for its action.

"I need my hand!"

"I need to eat."

Arpex kicked me again, this time its sharp-edged, hard-shelled foot caught me in the face, opening a deep gash along my cheekbone. Blood ran down my cheek, soaking into the shoulder of my grey suit. There was nothing in reach to staunch the flow of blood.

It hissed. "You are making another mess! Vile weak-skinned creature."

Weak and shaking, I made my way over to where my hand lay in a puddle of dry blood. A trail of fresh wet drops followed me.

Artor had skilled surgeons who may have been able to reattach it even now, but I wasn't on Artor. In fact, I had no idea where the fuck I was.

Shoulders entered the room, perhaps summoned by the Arpex or just gifted with impeccable timing. "I see you haven't been eaten yet."

I held up my stump. "You better be here to fix this."

Shoulders came closer. "No one ever said Arpex made good medics. We'll get some better bandaging on that. Can't have you getting an infection. That would spoil the meal almost as badly as a vacant mind."

"I don't mean bandages. I need a fucking replacement. And I'm not talking some low line model either. If you expect me to retake the Narvan, I'll need to be in full working order."

Shoulders laughed. "We don't need you to retake the Narvan. Your strike against Kess Atta has given your partner the edge he needed to take the lead. Events are progressing nicely without any further interference from you. You're ours until someone else says otherwise. Or you die. At the rate things are going, that seems the more likely outcome."

He pointed to a bucket on a counter next to a sink. "You may have gathered by now that Arpex dislikes a mess on its plate. You will dispose of any scraps in that chute." He pointed to a small square door in the wall near the counter. "Go on, pick up your hand and put it in the chute."

I looked down at the hand that had held my children, that had explored every inch of Stassia's body, that had been with me every day of my life. It was not a scrap to be tossed away.

"Do it," bellowed Shoulders.

"No."

"Arpex, it seems our obstinate charge requires another lesson. Maybe make this one a little less messy?"

Arpex chittered. "Your Kazan, how did you meet her?"

Its question, so out of the blue, caught me off guard. "As a kid or when she hired me? I'm not sure what you're asking." With as much blood as I'd already lost, I didn't want to lose any more.

"When you were hired. Gather all the details in your mind and then we will begin," said Arpex

"Begin what?" The hotel room where Stassia and I had met burned brightly in my memory. It was one of the safe things in my head that I didn't have to worry about hiding from the Council.

I could feel myself smiling as I remembered how nervous I'd been upon walking into the room. Seeing her there, I'd realized how much she'd changed from the woman my brother had gifted years before. Her nails had strummed across the tabletop as I'd weighed her offer of employment and the hinted threats lurking just beneath the surface. The enticement of all I'd be able to do for my homeworld and the system had far outweighed the dangers, and her smile reminded me of the woman I'd briefly known before. My brother had trusted her and therefore so could I.

Something sharp pricked my brain. My thoughts scattered as if they were a bubble that had been popped, vanishing in an instant and leaving me with only the vague recollection that I'd seen something wonderful. Whatever it had been was gone. The hole niggled at me, driving me inward, searching for what had filled the space.

"Mr. Ta'set, you were going to tell me about how you came to work with Kazan."

"I..." There was nothing there. I remembered getting a message from her with an invitation to an interview. I'd kept it a secret from Sonia and traveled...I didn't know where. The next thing I remembered was meeting Jey and hating him on sight. Stassia had been there. What had happened in between?

"What did you do? Why can't I remember?"

"I just had a little snack," said Arpex smugly, in as much as a thing without a face could be smug. "I eat memories as I also eat flesh. They flavor the meal. They are not as filling but are still very enjoyable. Do you have another I might devour, or are you ready to be compliant?"

Stassia had once told me that the blue creature could get inside her head and force her to Jump when they were developing their restrictive field. Had it eaten some of her memories too?

Geva only knew what memory it might extract from me next. How much was I willing to lose and for what?

I looked down at the hand on the floor. They wouldn't reattach it. The longer it lay there, the worse it would get. I knew how much flesh stunk when it was no longer living. If I gave them this one thing, maybe they'd see to the deep, throbbing gash on my face and the stump and give me something for the pain. I'd have killed for a stim or three.

Cringing as my broken ribs protested bending over in any degree, I gingerly reached down to the floor. Even though I'd touched, transported, and disposed of plenty of dead bodies it was rather surreal to pick up my own cold fingers. I kept my eyes on the door to the chute and when I reached it, opened the door and tossed the thing I carried into the darkness.

Cleaning up blood was also a task I was very familiar with. We'd all made a mess in the tank room on countless occasions and often doing some preliminary cleaning was preferable to waiting for the bots to get to it. Doing it one-handed, however, was new. I kept my seeping and throbbing arm against my chest, praying I wouldn't bump its vacant end against anything while I worked. Progress was slow. Shoulders left after only a few minutes of watching me work. Arpex stood guard, looming over me.

When I emptied the bucket for the last time, it clacked its claws. "You will now go find me another meal and you won't ruin this one. After you have again cleaned my plate, you will be allowed to eat and then I will have someone repair the holes I have made in your weak flesh. You still have the key?"

The fact that it kept referring to the floor I stood on as its plate made me shudder. Lightheaded and hurting, with no hint of an end to my punishment in sight, I felt the front chest pocket of my suit. The key was still there.

Though I didn't want to see Arpex eat, I knew I needed rest, food, and painkillers and the Council could offer me these things. The longer I stalled in returning to the rock and its chained victims, the longer I'd have to wait for any sort of relief. I bowed my head and Jumped.

As with last time, the field didn't stop me and I'd felt no change in the room to indicate its status. If I entertained any notion of escape or retribution, I'd have to find a way other than testing their field at random. My writhing on the floor would alert the High and Mighties to my lack of appreciation for their hospitality, and I'd be in for more blood loss. Or maybe eaten.

The miserable people chained to their rock couldn't help me other than to come peacefully to their end so that I could gather my strength and devise a way to bring the Council down.

The cursing and pleading started up again as I came closer. I ignored them this time and chose the first woman, granting her wish to spare the younger woman next to her.

Unlocking the cuffs and restraining her at the same time proved to be difficult. She quickly discovered that slamming her elbow into the seeping stump that I attempted to hold her with was an excellent defense.

I gasped and nearly let her go. Pinpricks of light swam in my black-edged vision. It was fortunate that I was much larger than her or she might have gotten free. I didn't want to dwell on what sort of punishment that offense might have held for me. As it was, she smashed her head back into my mouth several times while I was trying to form the Jump. I swallowed blood as we stepped into the void. When we arrived in the domed room, she caught me again, this time in the cheek. The newly opened wound bled profusely. I shoved her toward the waiting Arpex and wasn't particularly sorry about it. My duty done, I tucked the key into my pocket and fell onto my mat. Lying there, I closed my eyes and did my best to block out the screams as Arpex's winged jaws snapped around the woman. They grew muffled and strangled and finally ceased.

A nudge to the ribs startled me awake. I must have passed out because falling asleep didn't seem possible. A cloaked form loomed over me. Shoulders held a bowl in his hands. "You need to eat. Then get cleaned up, we have another task for you."

I sat up, realizing the pain had ebbed. The dressing on my stump had been changed and much improved. Upon examining the cut on my face, I found a bandage there as well.

Shoulders nodded toward the counter. "There's a change of clothing for you. The bathroom is right there." He nodded to a narrow door near the counter. You've got half an hour. Then I want you at the jump point on Sere. Got it?"

"Yes." I reached for the bowl, knowing that as much as I would have liked to fling it in his face, I needed the strength the meal would offer.

With my stomach full of bland mush, I retrieved a clean grey suit. Arpex must have been on its platform or gone as I saw no sign of it.

I made use of the tiny bathroom. It was far too small for Arpex to fit inside. Not that the room offered anywhere to hide. I changed quickly and then reluctantly looked into the narrow mirror on the wall. Someone had washed my face when they'd bandaged it, but the horrible yellow lighting made my bruised and split lip look extra painful. Dried blood was caked in my hair along the side where my cheek had been cut open.

I looked like utter shit. I wasn't used to this long-term discomfort thing. The tank had always taken the pain away, put me

back together, and spit me out in need of nothing more than a little rest and a hot shower. This was the crap everyone else had to
deal with. No wonder Kess was so bitter about all the downtime
he'd suffered because of us.

Where to put the bloody clothing? The chute seemed as likely
a place as any. I tossed it in and Jumped to Sere.

Three grey-suits glanced at me upon arrival and then looked
away as if I didn't matter. Great Geva, I was one of them.

What would Stassia think of me now? She'd probably laugh
sadly and say 'I told you so'. She'd never been one to shy away
from rubbing things in.

But I wasn't fully one of them. Not yet. Not ever, if I had any
say in the matter.

Another grey-suit approached, this one with an intent look
that told me a Councilmember had his strings in hand. "You will
escort the soon to be arriving Kryon to this meeting room."

Directions to a room flashed into my mind.

"You will not speak in any manner to anyone. You will not pay
them undue attention except to guide them to the room you have
been shown. Violation of these orders will result in punishment.
Do you understand?"

"Yes."

The man's gaze dropped to my bandaged stump. He scowled.
"We would prefer that you follow orders to avoid any further
damage."

"I would also prefer to avoid any further damage."

"Good. We do have future uses for you." He turned and walked
away.

Shoulders and Arpex must not have been in the same loop as
this Councilmember, which made me wonder how many loops I
had around me. Did they form a chain or were they a tangle that
would sort itself out?

I stood like a good zombie with the other three grey-suits.
Having seen them in action hundreds of times before, I knew how
to play the part. Look vacant, don't answer any questions, crowd
the incoming Kryon and herd them to the directed location. Easy
enough, and it sure as all hells beat serving up offerings to Arpex.

Merkief arrived first. Had he been hiding all this time or had
Jey decided not to kill him after all?

I should have known the Council would have placed me here
for a specific reason rather than general service.

"Vayen?"

Since I had nothing to say to him, playing dutiful zombie wasn't too hard. At least, not initially.

"I thought they'd kill you, I swear. Not this. Oh Geva, not this." His voice shook, but without looking at him directly, I couldn't tell if he was angry, distraught, or just fucking with me again. The only consolation I had was hoping that my continued presence would torture him one way or another. Holding on to that, I kept my gaze forward as we led him to the room I'd been shown. When he entered, I followed my counterparts back to the jump point.

Kess and Jey arrived within seconds of each other. Kess laughed. Jey gasped. Both of them were in my head immediately. Though I would have loved to answer Kess's taunts and Jey's pleading for me to show some sign I was still aware, I maintained my silence.

That this was a test, I had no doubt, and being a test, someone would be observing every minute detail. What would they take next, a foot, more memories, something else? If I wanted the chance to speak to Jey, I'd have to wait for another, less observed opportunity.

We marched our charges to the specified room and when the door opened, we again turned to leave. To my surprise, we were invited inside. My three fellow zombies had weapons, which were ordered to point at the heads of Jey, Merkief, and Kess, who were seated before a Council puppet. I stood behind everyone, wondering who exactly this show was for.

As the meeting progressed, it was clear Jey was the chosen one, deemed the winner of the Narvan. For that, I was grateful. Kess and Merkief were chastised, made to promise to behave like good Kryon and support Jey. There would be no more infighting or there would be punishment. They were directed to turn around.

I was the example of punishment.

Keeping my gaze locked on an invisible point over the Council puppet's shoulder, I clung to the fact that the Narvan was now safe in Jey's hands. He was the lesser of the evils before me. If I couldn't guide my homeworld, he was my second choice. But I wished he was a lot more of the old Jey instead of the beaten one who had submitted to Merkief. The old Jey would have told the High Council to screw themselves, grabbed me and Jumped me to the tank. Granted, he would have done that, not to save me, but to beat and berate me for my stupidity and letting down

Anastassia and the Narvan, but it still would have been welcome, given the alternative.

Jey sat meekly, nodding and making promises to do the Council's will. He tried our linked connection again, begging for any sign that I could hear him. It took all my concentration to keep my focus on the wall and maintain silence.

The Council puppet finished his decrees, relegating Kess to his own advisory position of the Nebula territory and supporting Jey as requested. Merkief maintained his hold on half the Narvan but was placed under Jey as a clear subordinate. From their tight voices and what I caught in my peripheral vision, Merkief and Kess weren't pleased on any level. They were dismissed.

When they were gone, the Council puppet also left the room, leaving me with Jey and the three armed grey-suits who lowered their weapons and put them away.

What were we supposed to do now? I waited for them to clue me in but they just stood there, apart from me, backs turned, still facing the spots where their charges had stood.

Jey glanced around the room and made his way past the idle grey-suits to stand in front of me. The test had just gotten harder.

They were still watching. I could feel it just as I always had when I'd met privately with the High and Mighties. Did Jey know?

He kept his voice hushed. "Vayen, come on, please tell me you're in there. Don't let them do this to you."

Without the Council puppet to focus on, it was much harder to maintain my good behavior. I desperately wanted to answer him.

"She's going to kill me. Come on. Snap out of it."

She. Geva save me. I'd not considered that Jey or Merkief would leak the truth about Stassia living past my corroboration of Kess's version of events. Not like this. If the Council latched on to his comment, Arpex could fish for more details on her. This would be worse than taking the Fragian memory wipe pill. Arpex would take its time eating the memories of my children, of our life together, of Pentares. I'd never find them again.

Jey shook me. The jarring motion did my stump, ribs, and face no favors. Whatever medication they'd given me was beginning to wear off.

The bond screamed, beating at my brain from the inside. I wanted to shake him back, to yell, 'the Council is listening, you naïve bastard!', but I kept my silence. Better to not show anything at all than confirm any further ammunition for the Council to use against me.

"I can see you fought them. Come on, dammit. Don't let them do this to you." He punched me in the stomach, nothing like the beatings we had recently exchanged on the practice mat and not near a Shoulder's punch, but it made my ribs ache even more. It was more than enough to get my attention if I'd have been willing to give it. But I wasn't.

"Merkief will pay for this. I swear to you."

More vengeance on my behalf was exactly what I didn't need. I needed Jey's full attention on the damned Narvan. The urge to speak became overwhelming. Keeping my face blank and my mouth sealed was one of the hardest things I'd ever done.

He whispered, "If they can do this to you, they can do it to any of us."

An intense pressure burst into my head, propelling me into the shadows of my own mind. My mouth moved of its own accord and spoke in a voice that wasn't mine.

"Bear that in mind before you make threats against your friends."

Though I fought as much as I could, the force within me stared at Jey, making me see the anguish I'd heard in his voice.

"Merkief is not my friend. You took care of that. Now you took care of Vayen too. Explain to me why I want to work for you again?" Jey asked.

"Would you like to see yourself in grey?"

Jey looked me up and down, his gaze lingering on my missing hand and then rising back to the eyes that weren't mine. He swallowed hard.

"No."

"Then you have a job to do. I suggest you get to it before we change our minds."

The hate I'd seen burning behind his bright blue gaze before we'd found our own middle ground flared. I wanted to smile, but even if I'd dared, control of my body wasn't my own.

The presence in my head seemed to sense my traitorous thought. It stomped hard, grinding me into the darkness.

Chapter Sixteen

When I came to, I found myself on the mat in Arpex's domed room. I must have been out for a good while because the medication had fully worn off. I sat up slowly but was struck with the sensation of swimming through a murky mire. Everything in the room spun, including the stranger's face that appeared over me.

"Lie down until you get your bearings. You'll only injure yourself further."

"Who the hells are you?"

"Arin. There was probably more to that once, but I don't remember. Like you, I served Arpex when I first donned the grey."

Great, they'd assigned me a mentor. Spy or helpful, I didn't care at the moment, I just wanted to be alone with the ache in my head so I could attempt to sort out what had happened in the meeting.

"Leave me alone."

"Can't do that. I've been assigned to assist you until you accept your role here. And heal, that's important too." His head bobbed. "I was like you when I came into Arpex service."

I blinked a few times and poured my wavering energy into clearing my vision. He was a thick man, likely heavily muscled once, Jalvian by the fair looks of him. Long scars marred the sides of his face, jagged, some thick and some thin as if whatever he suffered, it had been repeated over an extended period of time. He had two hands.

"You're nothing like me. Go away."

"You should thank me. I fed the Arpex for you and cleaned his plate. I never wanted to come back here. I don't want to be here. I don't." His hands clenched before him. "A lesson, they said. Help him, they said." He shook his head and scrunched his eyes closed as his whole face wrinkled up as if he were in pain. "I don't want to be here."

He relaxed after a long moment and he peeked up at the platform overhead. Leaning in close, he whispered, "I remember not remembering. The holes, the gaps, they get bigger until everything starts to unravel."

Unraveling also apparently made one insane. I needed all my wits about me. Defiance would turn me into Arin, and that wouldn't do anyone an ounce of good.

"Who were you before? Why did you end up in grey?" I asked.

Arin glanced around the room, keeping his head bowed, peering left and right out of the corners of his eyes. "Kryon. I wanted something that didn't belong to me, someone, and I wouldn't listen when they told me no. Now I wear grey."

"How long have you worn grey?"

"Years." His blue eyes lit up. "Oh! I knew your Anastassia." He wiggled his eyebrows. "At least you got what you wanted before you ended up here."

I grabbed his arm, the closest part of him, and squeezed it with all the strength I had in me. "I most certainly did not get what I wanted."

I'd wanted to bond with Anastassia of my own accord if we'd ever reached that point on our own, not because some drug lulled me into it. For her to accept me as her equal so we could run the Narvan together, not because she had to after the Council had ruined her link. I'd wanted to work with her again, but that could never happen because of the damage the Council had done in her head. Living out our days in peace on Veria Minor would have been a welcome alternative, but Merkeif had fucked that up. Now, she and my children were well on their way to the far side of the known universe without me.

"Don't say her name again."

I let go of his arm and sank back into the mat. Of course, they'd send me a helpful spy that had known Anastassia. They'd caught that scent thanks to Jey. I'd have punched something if I'd had the energy.

"Calm, calm," Arin said, patting my shoulder. "The first hosting is hard on the body and yours wasn't in good condition to begin with. Come," he held out his hands. "I will help you to the bathroom, and then we'll eat and get you something for the pain."

Without much alternative, I took his hand and let him mostly carry me to the bathroom. When I was done, he took me back to the mat and offered me a bowl of the same tasteless mush I'd had before. And I'd thought Verian food was bad.

Whatever was in the patch he put on my neck afterward was enough to knock me out until my body demanded to use the bathroom again. That was when Arpex deigned it was time for its next meal.

"Take him with you," Arpex ordered.

Arin Jumped us both to the rock where six offerings were still chained.

"How are you feeling?" he asked.

"I'm fine." Truthfully, I could barely stand on my own. Whether I was fooling him or not, I didn't know.

He gestured toward the offerings. "Your choice. I picked the last one."

Without allowing myself to dwell on it, I pulled the key from my pocket and fumbled with the cuffs of the person standing beyond the little girl. When the locks finally opened, I put my hand on their wrist. I realized it was a young man, barely a man, but it didn't matter. The Arpex needed to be fed and I needed time to regain my strength.

"Why him?" Arin asked.

Ignoring Arin, I Jumped the meal back to the domed room. After shoving the manboy toward Arpex, I went back to my mat.

Arin arrived seconds later and settled down next to me. That's when I realized that he had his own mat and it lay head to head with mine. Escaping him wasn't an option. In an effort to find some privacy, I closed my eyes and draped an arm over my head to block out some of the sounds of Arpex feasting.

I'd meant to do some thinking, but when I woke to Arin shaking me, I realized I'd fallen asleep instead. That's all I seemed to do. My body needed to heal, but all the wasted time seemed so, well, wasteful. How did other Kryon get anything done without access to a tank?

No wonder the Council had favored Stassia and I.

I got up with a little less help from Arin and looked for a clean suit on the counter. There wasn't one. When I asked Arin about it, he shook his head. "No one's getting messy for a few days. It's gorged itself. It will let us know when it needs to feed again. Until then, rest."

Resting wasn't a problem. My body demanded it. Days passed in a blur of bowls of mush, Arin muttering about not wanting to be there, and walking ten steps to the bathroom and back to my mat to sleep.

I'd lost track of how long I'd been in the sweltering dome when Arin woke me to say, "It's time. We must release the remaining offerings."

"Can't wait."

My face hurt less, but my stump was still throbbing and my ribs ached. Spending any amount of time trying to use my stump was not likely to put me in any better mood. Though, the thought of setting five of the ten free made the whole situation slightly less repulsive.

Following Arin's lead, I Jumped to the rock. Those that remained were dirtier than when I'd first observed them. The ground stank where they'd had little choice but to void their bodily wastes mere feet from where they stood. Their eyes had sunk into their gaunt faces. The food that had been there on my previous visits had been eaten and the cistern was dry. The girl and the two younger boys sat on the dirt and didn't rise when we came closer. The other two did but their protests were weak and their hands seemed to lack the strength to raise the thick chains.

Arin froze and glanced at me. "I'm sorry."

"For what?"

He went vacant, empty as I'd seen so many Council puppets look when they were devoid of a host. When he reanimated it was the rasping voice of Arpex that spoke.

"Which would you choose?" it asked.

Of those standing, only one man remained. If these people were to be set free somewhere away from their established community, he'd be needed to help provide or protect them. It had to be the woman then. "That one."

"Why?"

"Does it matter? You're hungry. Eat her."

"It matters." Arin walked up and down the line, peering at the remaining offerings. "You will learn to choose the ones that have the most vivid memories. Barring that, you will choose the ones that will create the most vivid memories for another. Do you understand?"

"Yes."

It wasn't enough that he meant to digest these people, he wanted the most terrified of the bunch. Sonia must have been a gourmet feast. My fists clenched. At least I imagined the missing one did where it lay somewhere at the bottom of the refuse chute, buried beneath a bloody grey suit and buckets of Arpex slobber.

Could I rip its blue shell apart with only one hand? How bullet-proof was it? Could it withstand a direct pulse wave?

He stopped in front of the little girl. "I want this one."

"No," I said without thinking.

Arin half-sneered half-smiled. It was a painfully awkward expression from a creature who didn't possess a face of its own. "You would seek to save her from me?"

"I would. She will be set free."

Arin chuckled and pulled a gun from a pocket on the leg of his suit. He held it out to me. "Go ahead then. Set her free."

"That's not what you said. What your friend said, I mean. He said they were released."

"And so they are—released from this life. Take it and save her if that is your wish." He tossed the gun at my feet.

"No."

"Come now, I spared your primary hand. You are able and you know what must be done. You've done it for us countless times before. Would it make you more agreeable if you were paid per head?"

"This is different." It had to be. This wasn't who I was.

"This is following orders. No different than before."

"And if I don't?"

Arin went vacant again and the Arpex stepped from the void in all its blue-shelled terror. Its four legs made quick work of the distance between us.

"Tell me of your mother."

"No."

I shoved all thought of my childhood deep into my mind, protecting my mother's smiling face, and her angry one, her voice as she asked me about my day at school and the one that yelled at me for trampling seedlings in her garden. With each moment I sought to shield, came a sharp sucking sensation. None of my defenses meant a thing to Arpex. Memories slipped through my fingers and vanished as if they'd never existed.

"Mr. Ta'set, tell me about your mother."

"I..." I knew things were missing, there were blanks in my childhood beside my father and brother. Someone else had been there.

How many memories had Arin lost before he'd become unhinged?

"Pick up the gun," said Arpex.

I did. I fired directly at the blue nightmare. The bullet hit the shell but deflected and hit the rock. Pain took hold in my mind, on par with the damned restrictive field but still allowing me to breathe and remain on my feet. Though it seemed that was more by the force of Arpex's will than my own. It filled my body as the other Councilmember had at the end of the meeting with Jey, but utterly foreign and lacking any finesse.

My hand aimed the gun at my foot and fired.

I felt the pain but it was distant. Worse than the pain I didn't feel, was the Arpex impressing the thought on me that it would let me suffer without treatment until someone else interfered. It thought I was weak and not worthy of all the effort the other Council members were investing in me. It didn't like the Narvan except that Frique would make a lovely nesting ground. The rest should be stripped for resources to be given to more compliant and beneficial races. Arpex wasn't getting its way and wanted me to pay for it.

It backed off enough that I regained some control of my body. Letting go of the gun wasn't an option. My fingers remained firmly wrapped around it no matter how hard I tried to throw it down.

"Kill the girl."

I couldn't afford hesitation, not with the Arpex already riding along in my head. I aimed and fired. Years before I'd saved a Ka'opul girl on Merchess after she'd suffered a gunshot by a Kryon out to get me. This girl reminded me of her. At least that was the safe thought I clung to as tears streamed down my face.

"The boys. I'll have one of them," the Arpex declared.

The boys in question scrambled away from me as far as their chains would allow. They cried as I unlocked their cuffs. "Which one?"

"You choose."

I shot them both. It was a far cleaner death than they would have received otherwise.

"What did you do?" Arpex hissed and invaded my head again.

"I chose."

"Tell me about your father."

Did something so alien truly know what memories it took or did it just know which prompts had the most flavor? It was worth a try. I thought of Gemmen and all our conversations in the past, how he'd helped me and the respect we'd shared for one another. Each thought of the years we'd worked together was sucked up by the vacuum of Arpex's mind.

"Tell me about your father."

Though I knew something was gone from my mind, my father's face was still there. I laughed. I wasn't defenseless after all.

My head exploded. I tasted dirt. The explosion went on and on like someone had found the exact spot in my mind to grasp all of my nerves at once and twist them with an iron grip. Something ripped at the side of my face as if trying to let the pain escape. I became dimly aware it was my own fingernails raking at my flesh. The agony went on for what seemed like hours.

❦

A cool cloth on my face woke me. Arin dabbed delicately, rinsing and then wringing out the cloth to start again. I groaned.

"Quiet," he whispered. "You found the way to win?"

"What?" Nothing I remembered resembled winning in any degree.

"The memories." He tapped his head.

"Oh, that." Not that I particularly counted my subterfuge as a victory given the pain I was in.

"I wish I'd have found the way as quickly as you did. I might remember more of who I was." Arin grinned. "Rest now. I'll tend to Arpex while you recover. Then you'll owe me. Jumping the remaining bodies for disposal left me drained. But so is Arpex. It may not emerge for a day or two. You wore it out." He beamed down on me proudly.

I closed my eyes and let Arin and the new drug patch he stuck to my neck work. The whimpers of the little girl and cries of the young boys gnawed at me as I lay there. I let the pain wash over me and through me, seeking some form of absolution but finding none. Eventually, I fell into a drugged sleep.

True to his word, Arin took care of Arpex and let me recover.

However, it wasn't until Shoulders showed up, four days later that I was allowed out of the domed room to have my wounds truly seen to.

"You'd do best not to anger Arpex again," Shoulders said as he led me back to the room.

As if Shoulders actually cared. I limped along behind him, glaring at other grey-suits who passed us by. Mindless idiots.

"We'd hoped you'd be past this by now."

"Sorry to disappoint you," I managed to say, though talking or moving my jaw in any way, strained all the cuts and gouges on my face.

"You will be glad to hear that the Narvan is on its way to recovery."

"It never should have needed to recover. I left the Narvan with able-bodied replacements but you cloaked bastards decided to make a game of it instead."

He spun around and punched me in the stomach. At this rate my ribs would never fully heal.

Shoulder's had always seemed to favor that region. Maybe he enjoyed the breath-sucking gasp his full-force slug elicited. For once I was glad he liked my gut because my face didn't need any more aggravation. I kept my mouth shut and ignored him the rest of the way back to the Arpex dome.

Chapter Seventeen

We'd gone through eight cycles of offerings, four more episodes of me scratching the piss out of my face and neck, three bouts of desperation where I'd reached out to test my link access and found myself wracked with the shrieking field of agony, and no excursions from the room except to Jump to the rock before Shoulders showed up again. By that point, I'd grown used to seeing my scabbed and scarred face in the mirror and wearing a grey suit.

The mush came reliably twice a day and it gave me the energy I needed to heal and go about my duties. I made sure to never pay as much attention to the faces of the offerings as I had that first time. There were enough people haunting my sleep as it was.

Between my hand, and my perpetually torn up face and bruised ribs from being kicked near every morning, I'd become more inclined to let Arpex have what memories it asked for unless it was something truly important, and my definition of what that was narrowed considerably as time wore on. My acquiescence seemed to take the thrill out of the process, and after a while, it stopped asking.

That was good, because in spite of me trying to keep a running list of what it had asked for so I could keep my shit together, the words were no longer associated with anything and that made them difficult to remember. I knew I was forgetting some of them. The more I tried to remember my list as I lay on my mat at the end of each day, the more frustrated I got.

I didn't recall ever seeing such a mess of a zombie as I appeared to be, but if Arin was to be believed, he and I weren't the only ones to live through Arpex duty. Those who had, all bore similar scars.

Shoulders saved me from release day when he showed up to pull me from Arpex's dome. He Jumped me to a point similar to the one on Sere. This one had a single grey-suit in attendance. She ignored us as we proceeded down the hallway.

"Some feel it's time to move you to a new form of service. However, if you show any signs of noncompliance, you will return to your previous task."

I nodded, grateful for the chance to escape the yellow-lighted nightmare I'd been living in.

"Arin will join you tomorrow once the offerings have been released. Until then, you will be on your own."

I wished they'd not kept the release day weapons under such close guard. Arin and I were only allowed to carry them to the offering rock on that one day and then they had to be surrendered immediately upon our return to the dome. If I'd had it on me right then, I would have taken Shoulders out.

Whatever was under his cloak, I could only hope it was less bullet-proof than the Arpex's shell. But they'd kill me for that, and I'd have only rid the universe of one High Council member, and a lower tier one at that. I sighed inwardly. Finding a way to take out as many as possible would be far more beneficial.

Shoulders led me through five minutes of corridors before pulling open a thick, metal door. A loud clank reverberated through the narrow room as we entered.

"You should be familiar with this sort of duty," he said, pointing to the wall of vids and the chair sitting before a control panel. A sleeping mat lay against the wall opposite the vids. Another lay against the wall on the other side of the door.

"Who will I be watching?"

"These are feeds from all our bases. The system will automatically cycle through all available feeds. You can control the selected audio feed here, pause the rotation here and capture here." He indicated the controls for each. "You will capture anything of interest. Your selected feed will be evaluated and acted upon at our discretion."

The current feeds featured views of Kryon quarters, some vacant, some occupied, meeting rooms, one of which I recognized from Sere, another jump point similar to the one on Sere, and several corridors where cloaked Council members or Kryon went about their business.

"If you see anything that requires immediate action, speak here." He pointed to a button and a vocal relay on the panel.

"One of you will be on duty at all times. Food will be delivered twice a day. Bodily functions will be dealt with there." He gestured to a small sink and open waste unit in the corner. "A cleaning bot is assigned to this room and clean uniforms will be provided every other day. Do you require anything else to begin?"

"No."

"Then begin." He turned and left.

The door clanked closed. A bolt thunked into place. Then there was only the single audio fed and the lit wall of vids to keep me company. Not that I wanted company, but I had grown used to Arin's presence, and part of me was grateful that he'd be joining me. He may have been off in the head and reporting on me, but he was an evil I knew, one I was comfortable with, in as much as one could be comfortable as a prisoner of the High Council. Seeing and hearing Arin served as a reminder of what would happen if I let them win.

At one time, being on duty for a full day and night wouldn't have been a challenge, but my body was weak. I could see muscles melting away each time I changed my grey suit. Without even an offering to wrestle into submission long enough to Jump, my physical decay would be even worse.

Were they watching me now? I sat in the chair and cleared my mind, flipped through the feeds, and scanned the audio of anything that looked interesting. After a few hours of feeling nothing like what I normally experienced in the meeting rooms themselves, I decided I was truly alone.

The room was too narrow to do much and the floor space limited. Stripping off the top half of my suit, I fumbled for a few minutes before managing to tie the sleeves around my waist with one hand and my stump. Yet another reason I missed Arin. He helped with simple tasks without me asking or being overly affected when I snapped at him for doing just that.

Stassia's daily tirades during our first months on Minor were much easier to understand now. Getting used to life without her link or the natural telepathy she'd relied on had been hard on her, not to mention losing the Narvan and the work she knew. She'd taken it all out on me. Constantly.

Arin bore the brunt of the aggravation that escaped my tightly reined in emotions with a bowed head and slumped shoulders. His defeated stance hadn't made me feel any better. Worse, actually. I couldn't become him. I needed to survive so I might eventually see my family again.

I managed to do as many rudimentary exercises as my trembling body and single hand would allow while still keeping half my attention on the vids. Sweating and tired, I took a long drink from the sink and then settled back into the chair. Once I'd cooled down enough, I fought my way back into the suit. I supposed it was high time I started figuring out how to do everything on my own. Who knew how long Arin would be with me or what kind of service they'd ask of me next.

The vid feeds rotated through room after room, some occupied and some empty, as well as corridors with people walking here and there. Nothing stood out to me as suspicious and nothing I overheard sounded interesting enough to report. Though, I did enjoy hearing snippets of progress in various systems and noting new races in the other High Council bases I now had access to. A few spoke languages I knew at least to a rudimentary degree, many did not. Testing to see if my link was functioning just so I could translate wasn't worth the likely spike of pain.

Some Kryon had bodies as strange as Arpex, which made it difficult, if not near impossible, to guess what they might be talking about. I decided that unless someone whipped out a weapon, I'd skim over those and concentrate on what I could actually understand.

My gaze danced over the vids, scanning and watching. Everything froze when a familiar room rotated into my view. Our Kryon quarters. Rooms I hadn't used in years, though Jey and Merkief surely had. Cameras I'd never known were there, and dammit, I'd searched, we all had. The view flipped from room to room. They were empty, but when it flashed to Stassia's room, I paused the feed.

Her personal things were at a minimum here, a rock she'd told me was from Frique, an ancient book her father had given her and a candle. It didn't matter where the candle was from. As I'd learned in the years she'd acted as a Seeker for the Verian people, it was what she used to focus, to cleanse her mind before beginning the purge of troubled thoughts. I would have given anything for one of her Seeker sessions right then. For that matter, I would have given quite a lot to see her in any manner right then, but her safety came first and that meant not thinking of her at all.

She was dead. Ikeri, my little center of calm, didn't exist. Daniel, my rambunctious partner in mischief didn't exist. Fa'yet and Neko, who were watching over my family while I was stuck here, serving Geva knew how much time rather than healing the Narvan like I'd planned, didn't exist.

As far as the Council was concerned, I didn't exist anymore either. I was nothing more than one of their countless grey-suits, one mostly subdued zombie among presumably hundreds. I released the pause button and let the feed speed on.

Arin arrived late the next day, relieving me so I could sleep. It came easier without the heat of the Arpex's room and knowing I wouldn't wake up to a blue shelled foot kicking me in the ribs. Nor would I have to retrieve living meals.

The exercise, little as it may have been, had put my body at ease enough to rest without too many nightmares. By morning, what I considered morning anyway, I'd only woken in a cold-sweat twice. Not counting the times I'd been unconscious, it was the best rest I'd had since my imprisonment had begun.

Arin took his turn to sleep when I replaced him at the vid wall. When his breathing sunk into a steady rhythm, I chanced another round of floor exercises but left my suit on. The bolt sliding within the door brought me to my feet in a sweat-dripping panic. I wiped my face on my sleeve and slid into the seat just as the door opened. A fellow grey-suit entered with a tray bearing two bowls of white mush. He studied me for a second and then handed me the bowls and left with the tray. The door locked.

Had he known I was hiding something? Why was I hiding my physical activity anyway? What would they do if they knew? Well, idiot, I said to myself in a mockery of Stassia's peeved voice, they'd know you have an ounce of will left and they'd do their best to crush it. If I meant to maintain my efforts, I'd need to learn the cycle of this new prison.

I gave myself ten minutes to cool down before waking Arin to eat. He took his bowl, and as we only had the one chair, sat back on his mat.

"So who's stuck on Arpex duty now?" I asked.

"No one. It's in a semi-torpor state and will remain that way for six cycles. The stock will be left in peace until it needs to feed again. That's not to say that the Council couldn't rouse it at any time if Arpex's skills are needed."

"But I was told that I'd have to go back there if I didn't do well here."

"It's not the only Arpex within the Council. They'd likely assign you to one of the others. Best not let that happen." He gestured to the room around us. "This is as good of a job as it gets around here. It's where I was when they sent me to assist you. Took me years to get here. Be grateful you rose to it already."

I swallowed the last of my mush. "This? This is the best I can hope for? Being locked in a room barely big enough for the two of us for Geva knows how long and two meals of crap a day?"

Arin scraped the last of his meal from his bowl with his finger and licked it with relish. "There's no blood on our hands, no one is in our heads, and we get to see and hear what is going on in the rest of the known universe. You won't hear any complaints from me."

He had a point, but the situation was still far less than optimal. I nodded toward the wall of vids. "Do you know where some of these other places are? Have you been there?"

"To some of them, yes. We go where we're told."

"Can you tell me about them?"

If I could get information on the other bases, I might be able to find a way to cripple the Council. The vids would also provide me with possible safe jump points if I studied them well enough— assuming the restrictive field wasn't in place if I got it in my head to Jump anywhere.

Arin stared at his hands. "You should sleep now. I'll take over."

"Did they tell you not to talk to me about the other places?"

"Those places don't matter. Please, just sleep now."

"They're not watching us here. We're alone. You can tell me."

His bowl clattered to the floor as he shot to his feet. "Stop. Just stop! We will do our jobs and that's all. Do you get it? Do you understand? This is where we are now. Unless you'd rather go serve an Arpex, you will accept it."

"I only wanted-"

"I know what you wanted. You still think you can get free. You can't. You belong to them now, just like the rest of us."

He stormed over to me, a burning shadow of the formidable Kryon he'd once been. "You think you're the only one to end up here against their will? No one wants to wear the grey. No one. You're not any different, and I'm sick of cleaning up your blood every time you think you are."

I stood, facing him eye to eye. "And I suppose you'll report to them that I asked you about the other bases."

"If they ask, yes. I know better than to lie to them. One of these days you'll learn that too, and what is left of your body will thank you for it."

"I'll keep that in mind."

Arin shouldered me out of the way and plunked himself down in the chair. I went to my mat. The audio feed droned, merging snippets of conversations into a bizarre dialogue that numbed my mind. The blessed moments of silence where the feed happened upon an empty room were few and far between.

The lights in the observation room were far less harsh than the yellow glare in Arpex's dome, but I longed for a night of sleep in total darkness. I'd searched for light controls when I'd been alone in the room but found none. Arin hadn't arrived with any solutions either. He seemed perfectly content to sleep with the lights on. If I'd had a blanket, I would have used that to cover my head. Or a pillow, but I had neither. The mat was comfortable enough, and the room a pleasant temperature, but I missed sleeping in a bed. And sharing it with someone. I closed my eyes and threw my arm over my face, seeking what little comfort I could find.

Days melted into weeks of monotonous duty with Arin. I refused his help and he stopped offering. Our conversation consisted of scant words to wake each other and hand over meals. He did tell me one day that there were other observation rooms and not all were at our location. I suspected that moment of chattiness was only because he hoped to quell any remaining ideas I might have of sneaking around or escaping.

Despite Arin's negativity on the matter, I began to catalog jump points in my mind using the vid feeds. It gave me something to focus on other than the fragmented list of lost memories I struggled to repeat to myself each night.

I named the jump points, making sure to keep them all straight and avoid duplicates. From what I could tell, there were seven bases. All of them mostly indistinct from one another except by the varying races of their grey-suits. Those seemed to consist of the majority of that area's population. I'd noticed some overlap, but it wasn't enough to mask the pattern that slowly emerged in the wall of flashing vids.

Sere, I knew well enough to have a fairly reliable map in my head. I began to compare what I knew of that layout to what else I saw, wondering if the Council used copies or similar maps for their other bases.

I'd come to suspect that three of the seven bases were primarily used for housing Council members. One of those was where I'd attended Arpex. I'd yet to ascertain if my new prison was there, on Sere, or at yet another base.

Our room didn't have a mirror, but I didn't need one to feel the last of the scabs from my final nerve-twisting, face-rending Arpex encounter flake away as I washed myself one morning in the small sink. I had only to look at Arin to know what had been done to me. Of course, he didn't have the puckered scar along one cheekbone from a serrated Arpex foot or ache in the foot that made me limp if I stood for any length of time. If his ribs bore the same lingering ache as mine, he masked it damned well. The flap of synthetic skin they'd sealed my wrist with was healing nicely but the stump was still sensitive.

I didn't think of myself as old, but when I woke each day, my body told me otherwise. Sure, I'd gathered a few scars in my service to Anastassia and the Council, but the tank had kept me vibrant, whole, and in much better shape than I had any right to be, considering how I'd abused my body on a daily basis. Even during our time on Minor, I'd exercised near every day and ate well. The life-sustaining mush the grey-suits fed me wasn't doing me any favors, and the half hour of limited physical activity I snuck in every day only did so much.

Thanks to the lack of actual chatter with Arin, I had intense imaginary conversations with Stassia and Jey while trying to stay alert when I was on duty.

Stassia was convinced I was getting what I deserved for leaving her, but she'd always remind me that I'd promised to find her again when I was done here. I kept telling her that it didn't look like I'd ever be done. She'd tell me she was waiting anyway.

Jey would thank me for straightening out the Narvan for him with the Council. He'd tell me all the plans and programs he was changing, implementing, and considering. I'd tell him they were all wrong, but he'd never listen. He'd tell me the Narvan was his now and it was too damn bad if I didn't like what he was doing with it.

Merkief showed up now and then, sometimes laughing at me, telling me this was what he wanted all along, other times begging for forgiveness. Part of me wanted to kill him for his betrayal. The other half wanted my friend back, the one who knew me too well, that I could talk to and laugh with.

Fa'yet would dance around the edges of my wavering awareness, usually as I drifted off to sleep. He'd pat me on the shoulder and thank me for all the credits, saying they almost made up for all that I'd taken from him when I'd sent him into hiding. He'd thank me even more so for handing his Ana over to him, subdued, tamed, and ready to settle down. Ana was so comfortable calling him Isnar thanks to me and she was the only one capable of keeping him company in an otherwise non-telepathic society. He was the dependable one. I'd left her.

Whenever Fa'yet came, I had no power to banish him. Every protest I could think of only made his eyes sparkle with merry laughter like it used to when we'd share a bottle and commiserate over Stassia's issues and Kryon woes. I never slept much when he was around.

The reports Arin and I gathered seemed trivial. He added much more to it than I did. Most of the incidents I recorded were Kryon bashing the Council when they thought they were alone in their quarters, sometimes there was interesting gossip on other Kryon and possible contract information leaks. What I found most intriguing was overlapping information on separate contracts that it seemed someone should be made aware of before Kryon inadvertently found themselves against Kryon. Was the Council really so sloppy that they relied on their hidden observers to point these things out?

As I'd always suspected, the private meeting rooms were on the vid loop. We were privy to many Kryon bully sessions. It was somewhat heartening to learn I hadn't been the only one to be blackmailed, strong-armed, and outright threatened into acting against my will. As Arin had said, I wasn't any different than the rest of them, Kryon and grey-suits alike.

I'd tried to grab the cleaning bot once in the hopes that it would have some useful parts with which to make a weapon. The damned thing's metal casing was so hot it burned my hand. I swore under my breath and let it go about its business. For the next week, I'd had to hide the blisters from Arin.

My workout sessions were relegated to when I was sure Arin was sound asleep, and before our second meal, though that wasn't as reliably timed as I would have liked. Our attending grey-suit caught me in a heavy sweat more than a few times.

Months drifted by until I'd lost track of them completely. Then one day our door opened at an unexpected hour during my sleep shift. The noise of the bolt and door opening brought me awake in an instant.

A cloaked figure stood there, demanding my attendance. For once, it wasn't Shoulders.

I got to my feet and glanced at Arin, sitting at the vid wall, but he revealed nothing that led me to believe he had any idea what this was about.

The Councilmember grabbed my arm and Jumped me to one of their regular meeting rooms. Except this time it wasn't for standard zombie duty procedure.

Jey sat in the single chair. Two of my fellow grey-suits stood behind him with guns in their hands. There, only a couple yards from Jey, my escort released me and stepped forward to join two other cloaked figures that stood between us. One of them pointed back at me with a gloved hand. I made sure to keep my gaze off Jey, but since no one was directly watching me, I focused on the grey-suits behind him rather than avoiding him altogether. I'd been alone with Arin in that room for so damn long that seeing a familiar face, even in the periphery, was like visiting home.

"There. You've seen him. We will tolerate no further demands. Now do your job or it will be handed to Mr. Atta. He was more than willing to do what we asked of him."

"I'm sure he was," Jey spat back at them. "Kess also has no idea how to deal with Artor or any of its subsidiaries. The Jalvians don't trust him now either. You hand the Narvan to him and you're right back in resource chaos. I highly doubt that's where you want to be, given your demands."

This wasn't the Jey I'd been talking with in my imagination. I liked this one much better. This one was on the verge of telling the Council to go fuck itself. I felt my lips curling.

Jey's posture changed, straightening, stiffening, and for just an instant, my gaze dipped to investigate. He was staring at me. His knowing gaze locked with mine for a split second, sending a jolt of excitement through me. I blinked and slipped back into my blank zombie gaze.

"You have had time to rebuild and reestablish." The Councilmember said. "You will now fulfill your part of the agreement and expand beyond your system. There are four unsettled regions within reach of yours. Using jump gates and installing new ones as Artor provides them, you will explore, conquer if necessary, and absorb these territories."

"You know damned well that Fragia is going to require conquering before we expand further outward. We're not ready for that yet. I said I needed two years."

"You've had one. That's enough. Perhaps Mr. Ma'tep could have done better."

Fuck. I'd been here a year already? Panic threatened to surge to the surface. That was twice as long as I'd told Stassia. I had to get out of here. I had to leave. To get home. Now.

Heart thudding, I struggled to keep my breathing even, to play the good zombie. If I fucked this up now, gave the Council any indication that I had somewhere other than the Narvan to be, my story, Kess's story, would go to shit. I had little doubt that Arpex and I would have a sudden reunion. I'd lose my family forever.

Calm, I needed to remain calm. I breathed in and out, listening to Jey's welcome, familiar voice.

"He might have at one time, but there's only so much a man can take," said Jey. "You fucked with his head one too many times and now he's not good for much of anything."

"This one thought he could put off our demands too." A female voice with a melodic ring said, gesturing over her shoulder at me. "You see what good that did him. He could have been in your position right now, powerful, free, and on the verge of taking on new territories for his people, but he made the wrong choices."

Jey looked ready to burst. "You think I'm free? In what universe are any of us free? You want us to run off into war, not because we have to, or want to, but because you demand it."

"Vayen, please, I know you're in there. Help me."

I'd been allowed to Jump in, and Jey could use his link, the field couldn't be active here. Still, bracing for the pain I'd endured too many times, I tentatively opened my link to him. The pain didn't come.

"They're watching. Always. Be careful."

"We have the overall picture. You are nothing but a lowly system advisor. It is not your place to question," said one of the cloaked figures.

"No one is watching you," Jey said. *"They're just screwing with your head. Talk to them. Make them understand."*

"Everything on Sere is watched. I watch for them now. Look where talking to them got me."

"So I should just do as they say? I should drag our people into war and Geva knows what else? If this was going to be easy, they wouldn't need the force of the Narvan. They'd have no interest in what's out there. They know damn well what they're sending us into."

"Stall them."

The cloaked member that had brought me there turned around. "Mr. Ta'set you are dismissed. Return to your duties."

Knowing I had only seconds before I'd be banished back to my field enclosed room, I took my time walking to the door.

"Stockpile explosives. Small, powerful, in packaging able to be Jumped."

"For what?"

"We're taking out the Council."

"You're insane," he whispered even in my head.

"I'll contact you again when I can."

The door closed behind me, and daring no further disobedience, I closed off our connection and waited. The cloaked figure exited a minute later. They Jumped me back to my narrow, vid-lined prison.

Arin glared at me as I came in. The lock clicked back into place seconds after the door closed.

He turned back to the vids. "What was that all about?"

"A meeting. Someone demanded to see me."

His voice rose, "You're not special. Remember that."

"How could I forget with you here to constantly remind me?"

I went to my mat and rolled toward the wall so he couldn't see me grinning. Maybe I was insane. Maybe Jey would dismiss my plan and finally write me off.

But maybe he wouldn't.

Chapter Eighteen

Without the use of my link and stuck in constant light, I eventually lost track of how many days it had been since the meeting with Jey. One shift blended into the next. No one came to knock at our door other than to deliver our meals and retrieve our bowls. The bot scurried in and out of its maintenance tube on its own irregular schedule.

Arin seemed content with this tedium, but it wore at me, making me edgier with every passing shift until I wanted to claw my way out of the room by sheer force. Enough of me was still aware that futilely wearing my remaining fingers down to the bone on the heavy door wouldn't help anyone—except to perhaps give Arin some amusement. That wasn't the sort of incentive I was looking for.

Even my memories wouldn't talk to me anymore. For all I knew, Jey had caved to the Council's demands and was off crushing the shell of Fragia we'd left standing years before. He'd been a formidable force during our previous joint effort against Fragia. He could handle this.

Or he could have lost the spark I'd seen in him however long ago our last meeting had been. The Fragians could have easily crushed the man who'd let Merkief and the Council dominate him. Fragia could have rebuilt their fleets and replenished their forces. Jey could be long dead and the Fragians could be stripping my homeworld while I sat in this tiny room, watching glimpses of the known universe flit by.

The only benefit to this surveillance duty was getting a better grasp of how much of the known universe the Council had their claws on. They seemed to always be expanding, recruiting new system advisors from the Kryon pool, and shaping those systems into new forces able to expand outward. As Stassia and I had learned, to our utter frustration, the betterment of those systems was not a priority. I witnessed a couple other meetings similar to the last one with Jey. The Narvan wasn't the only obstinate one. As much as I wanted to assist the opposing side, all I could do was try to point out where the Council was expanding against or too close to itself. Where they too blind to see it or too eager for more territory to care?

There was no news of Merkief or Kess. Were they supporting or hindering the expansion? I hated not knowing. Though I scoured the feeds for any news on the Narvan, nothing of consequence presented itself. Maybe our feeds were specifically tailored to keep me in the dark. Arin was less than helpful when I ventured to ask if he'd heard anything either.

"The Narvan no longer concerns you. Just do your job," he scolded.

Attempting to hold what little sanity I had left, I continued verifying my catalog of jump points, learning what I could of the other Council bases. It wasn't much. The Council was very good at keeping the feeds mixed and from angles that only showed a single room or corridor at a time. It was a true puzzle to sort all the bits out and fit them together into a viable map, especially when I wasn't even remotely sure that I was working with all the right pieces.

I had nothing to write on, no notes, no sketches, only what I was able to hold together in my head and even with that, I grew more concerned as the shifts went by, that I was becoming more and more like Arin. The more I tried to piece together what I was missing or connect events around the terrifying number of gaps, the more uncertain my past became.

❧

It was Deep Voice who finally broke the monotony. His cloaked form arrived at our door and silently beckoned me out.

Hesitantly, I left my chair and walked quietly into the hallway.

"I have something for you," he said once the door had closed, gesturing for me to follow him.

I paused outside the door. "Arin will wake soon and wonder where I am. Shouldn't I wait until he's on duty? What if something happens on the feeds?"

"According to his reports, you don't even like one another. Why are you concerned if he wakes and finds you gone?"

So he had still been reporting on me. That wasn't too surprising. Regardless, I would have been alarmed to wake and find him missing. There were too many uncertainties outside our room. We'd been each other's only constant for however long we'd been together. Leaving felt uncomfortable, wrong.

"We don't, but I'm also leaving my post unmanned."

"Your sense of duty is touching, truly. It's why we keep you around. Some of us anyway." He waved me onward. "You'll be back soon. While your reports do have a unique angle we certainly appreciate, the system is redundant. If there is anything concerning afoot, we'll know about it."

I followed him down corridors I'd not been in before. Other cloaked members passed by, ignoring us. When we came to a door with a blue symbol mounted on the wall beside it, he palmed the panel. The door snicked open, allowing us inside. It was one I recognized from the vid feeds—a common room in which many members of the Council dined. Various sized chairs and tables of different heights were scattered throughout the room. It must have been eight times as large as my prison. I could breathe here, stretch my arms out wide without coming near any of the walls.

The room was otherwise unoccupied and the kitchen area was empty and dark. Deep Voice chose a table of comfortable height for both of us.

I'd never seen grey-suits in the room before. Jey was nowhere in sight. The room was suddenly too big, too open. I didn't know what was going on. I was alone with Deep Voice. As curious as I was about the reason for this excursion, I wanted to be back in my prison.

"Why are we here?" I asked.

"Relax. I thought we could talk."

Councilmembers didn't talk to zombies. They ordered.

"About?"

"Several things. First though, since you have adjusted well and have been so helpful, as I anticipated you would be, I do have something for you."

Well, that was somewhat promising. I shoved my unease down and tried to remember who I was, that I had goals, a life I wanted to get back to.

"A new hand?"

"Sadly, no. Wait here."

Deep Voice got up and went over to a metal door on the wall. He opened it and returned to the table with two boxes. They were familiar boxes, ones I'd used for years and never given a second thought to. Take out boxes. He set them on the table and pushed one in front of me.

"I've heard you don't appreciate the nutritional base that sustains our workforce."

The smell wafting up from the box brought saliva rushing to my mouth. I swallowed it down and opened the top to find a steak as big as my hand, half a loaf of warm bread and a tumble of cubed vegetables. Steam rose up, caressing my face. How long had it been since I'd had hot food? I grabbed one of the orange chunks and tossed into my mouth. My eyes closed as I chewed, my senses overwhelmed by the earthy flavor. Chewing, oh Geva, it felt so good to chew. I grabbed another chunk and then tackled several bites of the bread.

Deep Voice handed me a fork. "I trust you'll behave with this?"

I grabbed it and stabbed the thick slab of meat so I could gnaw off a bite. Goosebumps rose as I savored it, juices trickling down my throat.

"One might think we'd been starving you," he chuckled.

"You have. What is this meal going to cost me?" I asked around a second mouthful of steak.

"Some answers."

"Start asking then. I don't want to get in too deep and find out I owe you."

I tried not to stare, Council members didn't like that. In fact, I found myself looking at the table or my meal rather than the cloaked figure talking to me. It was curiosity that tugged my gaze up to see the fork disappear into the hood and come out empty. Did they ever get sick of wearing those damned cloaks? I could see why Chandi had chosen to toss her anonymity aside. Though, that hadn't worked in her favor in the end.

"Is it true you've still been exercising each day?"

Took them long enough to bring that up, not that it did much good. I was still wasting away, but a few months of meals like this would put some meat and muscle back on my bones.

"Yes."

"Why?" He asked, enjoying his meal at a much more sedate pace.

"Why not?"

"That isn't an answer," he stated flatly.

"Isn't it?"

"Mr. Ta'set, I'm not here as your enemy. I suggest you stop fucking around or you'll take this meal to the refuse chute and return to the Arpex. It's been asking for you, seems it finds your memories particularly tasty."

"It's all you've left me," I said.

"The fucking around or the exercising?"

"Both." I shoved a hunk of crusty bread into my mouth.

"I'd say I'm glad to see you haven't changed, but that isn't completely true in this regard." He sighed. "The territory over-laps and contract oversights you spot, those have proven to be especially useful. Is it because of your Kryon background or the fact that you fulfilled so many contracts on your own that you are able to see them so clearly?"

"You're not the only ones who can grasp the bigger picture, you know."

"You'd be surprised."

He ripped small bits of his bread apart and popped them into his mouth as he talked. At least he was eating regular food and not people—something I'd never considered the need to appreci-ate before wearing grey.

"We glean our workforce by various means and from a myriad of races, but few perform as well as you have. When it became clear that you would wear the grey, I pushed for you to attain this assignment from the beginning. I knew you'd do well here. It was unfortunate that I didn't have the numbers on that particular vote. The damage done to you could have been avoided."

"Is that your version of an apology?"

Deep Voice put his bread down and went silent for a long moment. I clutched my fork, ready to use it if necessary.

"We don't all agree with the Narvan plan that the majority have demanded." He pushed back the hood of his cloak.

A twisted part of me held out hope for a face I might recognize, but other than the fact he was Artorian, at least in part, he was just a man old enough to be my father. Granted, he was a man in infinitely higher standing within the High Council than I was.

It was the scars along the sides of his face that made me forget to chew the food in my mouth and choke.

He waited to speak until I'd sorted out the mess in my throat. "I held out hope for your eventual promotion once. It would have taken years, but you were on the right track."

His dark eyes regarded me thoughtfully. "As you can see, you wouldn't be the first to rise up from the workforce and don a cloak. If I could make that happen, would you stand with me against them?"

I almost choked again. "You'd put me on the High Council?"

The thought of never seeing Stassia again and burying my bond forever hurt like all nine hells, but infiltrating the Council was a worthwhile trade. Geva, the things I could do for my people, for people all throughout the known universe. I'd never imagined this option. Never hoped for it. Never had an inkling it had been on the table. But here it was, like Geva handing me a shining out to the otherwise bleak future I'd screwed myself into.

"We've discussed your promotion, yes."

"Your tier?"

The scars along the side of his face rippled. "You know about that?"

"One hears things."

In the wake of his announcement and the coherent corner of my mind running projections of this opportunity, I realized I'd stopped eating. I finished as much as I could before this turned unpleasant, as my meetings with him usually did.

He nodded. "The Arpex?"

"And his friend."

"Neither of them are friends."

"I heard that too," I said. "How large is your tier? Do they honestly stand a chance of opposing this endless expansion? That can't sustain itself forever. Those systems must be allowed to maintain themselves, to grow naturally. The Narvan isn't the only one to near crumble apart from the inside."

Deep Voice cut several slices off his steak with great precision. "Finish your meal. I can't block the feeds for too long before someone discovers the interruption."

"How large?" I asked again.

"Answer my question."

"Of course I'd oppose the demands of the other tier, or faction, or whatever you're calling it. It's what I've been doing all along."

"But do you have the nerve left to do it?"

"You took my hand, not my spine."

He nodded. "Good. I'll discuss it with the others."

Deep Voice knew things. He was Artorian, at least in part, for Geva's sake. He wanted to prevent my system from falling apart. He'd been my ally of sorts before. If he wanted my help now, there had to be a reason. I prayed it wasn't something too terrible, something that set my homeworld back even farther than the mess between Jey and Merkeif and Kess had.

"Can you tell me how the Narvan is doing?"

He put his knife down but kept his hand on it. "I think it's best that I don't."

My mouth went dry and the heavy meal churned in my shrunken stomach. "Why? What's wrong? Is Jey all right?"

"You'll need to let these personal attachments go if you wish to join me. We need you to focus on the bigger picture."

It was hard to keep my frustration under control, to keep myself in line now that I had tasted a hint of freedom. But he was giving me a chance at something huge. I couldn't afford to piss him off. While I did keep my hand from pounding on the table or his person, I couldn't keep the aggravation from my voice.

"How in the nine hells am I supposed to focus on anything if you don't give me the information I need to make decisions?"

"You'll get what you need when the time comes," he said.

"When will that be?"

"When it does. That is all I can tell you for now."

As though I'd been drowning for so long and finally got a full breath, I couldn't sink back under the water. I couldn't spend another day with Arin, doing nothing.

"Don't make me go back there. Please."

My plea went unacknowledged. Deep Voice replaced his hood and got up to clear the boxes from the table. When he came back, he held out his hand. I reluctantly turned over the fork.

"It's time to return you," he said.

We left the common room and made our way back down the corridors. Every step made breathing a little harder, like a heavy weight settling back onto my chest.

"How will I contact you again?" I asked.

"You won't. The field covers your section of the complex. Be patient, Mr. Ta'set. Do your job. Do it well so you can remain where I can reach you. I'll come when we're ready to move forward."

Deep Voice led me back to the room and opened the door. Arin sat at the vid wall. He turned as I entered, mouth open as if ready to voice his displeasure. His eyes widened when he saw the cloaked figure next to me.

He spun back around. Even after the door closed and the lock slid into place, he didn't say a word.

I lay on my mat with my stomach full and my mind spinning. If Deep Voice managed to get me on the Council, I'd be able to do so much more for the Narvan than I could by blowing everyone out of existence. I could meet with Jey and offer him the help and guidance he needed. The Council would be allies instead of puppet masters.

Sleep washed over me with dreams of standing beside Deep Voice in a shadowy room and telling Arpex and its supporters that the Narvan wouldn't be going to war now or ever again.

Shift change arrived with a stomach ache. My body didn't remember what to do with the big meal I'd had the day before. Trying to recall how good it had tasted helped get me through most of the shift full of discomfort, but by the end of it, my body purged what remained of the offending solids.

Had the meal been worth the aggravation? I wanted to think so.

"Whatever they told you, they're lying." Arin tossed over his shoulder as I went back to my mat.

"I have no idea what you're talking about."

"They're only going to use you. You're not special," he said adamantly.

"Someone thinks I am."

"They're wrong. Go to sleep."

When sleep finally came, I dreamed my cloaked form sent Arin to the Arpex dome. Permanently.

Chapter Nineteen

As days passed, I began to think Arin might have been right. A week went by and then several more until I lost count again. How much talking did Deep Voice have to do if his supporters had already discussed this move? He'd evaded my question on the size of his rebellious tier. Were their numbers high enough to accomplish our goal?

When I flipping through the audio feeds, I overheard a Kryon mention the ongoing Narvan expansion and a Fragian conflict. My finger froze on the button. It was already happening. Any interference on my part was far too late. Jey was off to war.

No Council opposition from the new guy would reverse what had been started. If Deep Voice's faction had ever stood a chance of doing that anyway. Surely, he knew that I'd glean this news at some point and be concerned. He would have given me some sort of reassurance if his offer was still in the works.

Deep Voice hadn't come. He hadn't sent a message.

Worse yet, Jey would be fully occupied with this expansion. No explosives were coming. If they ever had been. He'd probably discounted my plan as insanity from the start.

All my research had been for nothing. Both of my options for a future had gone to shit. If I'd have had anything to throw, I would have hurled it against the wall. Instead, I pounded my remaining fist on the control-free section of the panel in front of me and muttered curses under my breath.

Had Deep Voice meant anything he'd said? Stassia's specter

laughed and shook her head sadly, telling me the Council had only been fucking with me.

'Do your job', he'd said. Of course he'd wanted me to continue to point out the Council's errors so they could fix them before anyone else noticed. Wanted to make me feel special, useful, to dangle hope in front of me so I'd keep trying to earn their favor. They'd played me.

The damned Council would never let me join their ranks. I was never going to leave this room. I was going to die in grey.

Well, fuck them. Fuck them all.

The next meal came. I left it uneaten.

Arin got up to replace me. I lay on my mat but sleep refused to come.

When he went to sleep, I took my place in the chair. When his breathing became slow and steady, I stayed in the chair. My reports were only that, the bare minimum of my job. They no longer included any extrapolations of what I'd seen or heard. I threw in the occasional obvious oversight on their part, but only through captured footage, and only because I didn't want to live out the rest of my days in Arpex's dome.

My stomach demanded that I eat when the next bowl of mush came. The second one went uneaten.

Arin didn't question my untouched meals. As shifts passed, he seemed less abrasive than he'd been in a long time. Not that we had anything to talk about, nor did I have the urge to even if we had. My life became an endless loop of work and sleep. My reports grew even shorter, only something to do pass the time until my eyes were weary enough to close again.

There were days I considered not reporting anything at all. At least Arpex would offer me an end, an out to this prison. Pissing it off would be easy enough. Except it would probably consider me tainted meat, not protesting, not terrified of death. Shoulders would lead me off to some other form of lingering half-life in Geva only knew what form of service.

My ribs ached whenever I thought of Shoulders. Cringing, I maintained my minimum of duties, staying mostly awake during my shift, reporting little. My waking hours were filled with the need to return to my mat where I could close my eyes and get lost in a life where I was still alive with my family, sometimes on Minor, sometimes in hiding on Pentares. Keeping track of which reality was the dream grew harder and after awhile, it didn't matter.

Arin and I were one.

❧

It was the sight of Merkief standing in our old Kryon quarters that reignited a spark of life within me. I couldn't grasp how long it had been since I'd seen his face. Trying to remember made me feel ill.

Was I angry to see him? Relieved? I didn't even know. Rubbing my hand over my scarred face, I fought to clear my mind of the memory gaps and the knowledge that I'd lost far too much time locked in this room to be of any use to anyone.

The last time Merkief had popped into my life, he'd ripped it apart. There wasn't anything left to ruin now.

We were the same. Neither of us had anything left to lose. I'd never considered that we'd have anything in common again, that we might have something to talk about. Hells, that I might ever want to talk to him again.

It was his fucking fault I was here. His fault I'd lost my family, my future, my life. Everything.

Everything. He'd said that the last time we'd talked, when he'd failed to kill me, when he'd vanished after giving the Council...everything.

My brain lurched through memories, bridging holes where Arpex had feasted, shoving my face in the realization that it was indeed me who had ruined his life, taken his everything. Merkief's actions were far more intentional, but the end result was the same. And he blamed me.

Rightly so.

Were we even now?

My insides were too warm, twisting about, different from what I vaguely remembered hunger felt like. My body shook silently and my cheeks were suddenly wet. I wiped the dampness away with the excess sleeve over my stump.

Had I atoned enough?

I rolled the wet cuff back with thin shaking fingers on a hand that looked far more like it belonged on Gemmen than on me. I'd given up trying to catch glimpses of my reflection long ago. There was nothing there I wanted to see.

See. That's what I should be doing. I wiped at my eyes again and focused on the vid in front of me.

Merkief appeared to be talking, but no one else was there. Maybe he'd lost his mind too. I made sure Arin was sleeping and turned up the volume.

"Jey said you could hear me, dammit. He said you were watching." Merkief paced around the room, glaring at the ceiling and the corners. "Where the fuck are you?"

Jey had sent him? An unfamiliar sensation rippled through me. Was this excitement? I'd forgotten the feeling of my heart pounding, an electricity that brought life to my worn and aching body.

I had to know why he was there.

With the field in place, using my link or natural speech was out of the question. I couldn't Jump to the room. I couldn't use my link to access the system controls enough to even blink the damned lights to show him I was listening. The vid panel offered no alternate controls or ability to speak to anyone other than the Council in my reports.

"Jey sent me with a message. If you want it, you'll have to come get it. If you're even there." He slumped onto the couch. "He was probably making that shit up just to get me to put my drink down."

Merkief left the room. I clutched the edges of the control panel. He returned a minute later with a bottle in hand. He spun around slowly, gaze darting over the walls. "Maybe you can hear me. I wouldn't blame you for not answering." He took a long pull from the bottle. "I'm sorry, all right? Please. Dammit, let me know you're still there. We need you."

They needed me. Oh Geva, someone actually needed me. I had absolutely nothing to lose.

I released the feed. As the vids plodded along with their display rotation, I got down on my mat and closed my eyes. Knowing how much it was going to hurt, it took me a good ten minutes to sink into the deep meditative state that I would have used to dedicate my total attention to my link, but instead, I slowly cracked open the natural connection Merkief and I had once shared. More than a few times, Stassia had chided me about sinking too deep into my mind, fearing I would lose myself there. This time, when the pain of the Council's field threatened to rip me apart, I sunk lower, leaving the agony of my body behind.

I didn't plan on going back there anyway.

I slipped into Merkief's head. *"I'm here. Put your hands over your face and don't look up. What is the message?"*

His voice was hushed and filled with wonder. *"Can you really see me?"*

"I can't hold this connection long. Hurry."

"Jey has what you requested. Do you have the jump points?"

"Where is he?"

"Obliterating Fragia. Do you have the jump points or not?"

Was Merkief spying for the Council? Did they know that I was up to something with Jey? Would he report everything back to them, ending any chance we had of taking out the Council?

"Why are you here instead of helping him?"

"He doesn't want me around, not after what I did to you. I need to get you out of there. Please. I'm sorry."

He sounded sincere, but he'd also proved he could fake that pretty damn well.

"How will the devices be Jumped?"

"We have volunteers," he said.

"There will be casualties beyond the Council, Kryon and those like me. Are your volunteers prepared for that?"

"We knew it would be all or nothing."

Pain edged into my awareness, shaking my hold on our connection. I flashed him the thirteen solid jump points I'd formed, hoping the secondary points would cover any miscalculation on my part.

"There will be a field in place on some points. Your volunteers will be able to Jump in, but they will be incapacitated and they won't be able to get out. They will need to be armed and ready before Jumping in."

"Got it. Do you have an exit plan?" he asked.

"I'm not leaving."

"You have to. What about Anastassia and your kids?"

"They're away, as if their safety means a damn thing to you."

Our contact threatened to buckle any second. I scrambled to maintain it long enough to totally sever the connection with my body. Just a few moments longer and I wouldn't have to go back to that room ever again.

"It does."

"I think I'm here, for what it's worth, but it will be too late." I flashed him the jump point that was my best guess for where I'd been imprisoned.

"Dammit, I need-"

Despite my desperate clinging onto Merkief's mind, my hold snapped, shooting my awareness back into an agony-ridden body. My last thought was a prayer to Geva to make the explosives detonate any second to save me from the torment.

❧

I woke up in some sort of medical facility with a blurry greysuit looming over me. I really didn't know why I bothered to pray. Geva hated me.

"He's awake."

A cloaked figure took his place. "How much did he fry?"

"The majority of his link functions from what the scans show. We won't know if there is any permanent brain damage until he's fully alert. We've begun to initiate repairs as per your request."

"You have horrible timing with your suicidal efforts, Mr. Ta'set. I have the numbers we talked about."

My thick tongue and distant lips tried to form words. "Fuck off."

"What did he say?" asked the cloaked man.

"Nevermind," said the grey-suit. "He's going to be in and out for a while yet. We're bringing him out of the coma slowly so we can better monitor any complications."

Coma? I'd been in a coma? For how damn long? Where was Merkief's squad of suicide bombers? If he had ratted me out...

"I'm going to kill him," I muttered.

"You're not going to be killing anyone for a long while." The cloaked man patted my arm. "Rest now. You'll be joining us when you're well."

Joining them? Numbers. A majority. The overwhelming taste of a steak filled my mouth. A cloak of my own. Memories slowly slipped together as creeping warmth stole my awareness and sucked me back into sleep.

When I woke again, alarms were clanging. A single light shown down from the ceiling. I could make out another one down the hall. Emergency lighting.

I was alone.

My bed shook and then stilled. Someone shouted in the distance. I sat up, only to suffer a blinding pain in my head that made me fall back onto the pillow.

The bed shook again. Screams filled the hallway nearby.

I slipped a foot out from under the sheet and let it dangle until it found the floor. Sitting up slower, I made it to the edge of the bed before my vision started to spin. Tubes ran from my body to silent equipment. I yanked them out and discovered that I was wearing nothing more than a thin yellow shirt that hung to my knees. Ties down the front held it loosely closed.

Using the bed for balance, I made my way to the nearest wall. With the solid surface at my disposal, I stumbled to the door. The floor shook. Something buzzed in my head like a pesky insect that I couldn't shoo away. I blinked away a wave of dizziness. Hand on the wall, and moving slowly, I made my way out of the clinic.

"Vayen, you need to wake up and Jump," said a familiar voice that sounded so very far away in my spinning head. The buzzing came again.

I focused on the voice. *"Who is this? What's going on?"*

"You need to Jump. Now."

Jump, he'd said. I needed to do that, but where, and what if the field was still active? If it hit me again, I'd be out for Geva knew how long, and what had the grey-suit said about my link being mostly fried?

With my back against the wall of the corridor, I took a deep breath and fought to clear my head. Merkief, it had been his voice. He hadn't been lying. The bombing had begun. Too late to get my own cloak now.

If I wanted to live, I needed to leave.

Had the Council really had put a tracker in me? If they lived through this, they were welcome to try and hunt me down.

I closed my eyes and formed a Jump to Jey's house on Jal. Nothing happened. While I was relieved to not be subjected to another round of agony from the restrictive field or even more of a headache than I currently had, I'd just verified that my link was indeed fucked.

A cloaked figure ran by, knocking into me and sending me to the floor. Whatever they were running from, I figured it must be in my favor. I got up and continued to make my way forward.

When I rounded the next corner, a faint explosion sounded in the distance. Maybe Merkief and Jey had sent more than one person in. There might be someone who could help me.

I reached out to Jey, but all I got was louder buzzing in my head. Two more turns brought me to a hallway that ended abruptly in a charred pit. I kept my hand on the wall beside me and peered over the edge. Wherever the original explosive had detonated, it had taken out what appeared to be the central shaft of the entire compound. Downward lay only darkness and smoke. Upward, I could see stars. Thankfully, the Council had chosen a location with a breathable atmosphere. Frigid air flowed in from the hole above. My breath created white puffs and my skin prickled in the cold.

Bright light and an ear-shattering explosion ripped through a level above me, spilling debris and more smoke out into the pit. A body plummeted past. The stench of burning flesh filled the air. I coughed and backed away, waving at the thick smoke.

The structural girders separating me from the destruction above creaked and groaned. I needed to get out before the whole damn place collapsed. There was no help here. I needed to go up.

Making my way back the way I'd come, I tried to find anything familiar to associate with the maps I'd formed in my head. The flickering lights and groaning above and below lent an unhelpful level of panic. A woman screamed. Another explosion sounded above me. I stumbled over the mangled bodies of two fellow grey-suits in my rush to find an exit.

There had to be lifts or stair access to the upper levels somewhere. I ran down the hall passing several more bodies, some cloaked, a few more grey-suits and a woman in armor of a race I'd seen in the vids but didn't have a name for. Pounding on door panels as I passed by finally paid off when one opened to a twisting, narrow stairway.

Taking them two at a time, I bounded upward until I lost my breath. I tried the level door. It wouldn't open. I dragged myself up another two turns of stairs and tried that door. It opened far enough for me to wedge myself through. I tripped over the tattered remains of several people, sprawling onto the blackened floor. Laying there, facing the burnt and bloody face of a woman, I wondered if this is what it had been like inside the storm shelter we'd destroyed on Syless years ago. Was this Geva exacting her justice?

Scrambling back to my feet, I fled. I'd just reached the first corridor intersection when I came face to face with a singed and wide-eyed Merkief.

"Vayen? Great Geva, what did they do to you?" He glanced over his shoulder and shook his head frantically. "You're not supposed to be up here!"

"I can't Jump," I managed to say. My body was numb and no matter how many times I blinked, nothing seemed quite in focus.

An explosion ripped through the hallway he'd run from. Merkief pushed me down and threw himself on top of me, his coat fell open and spread over us both. Heat flared around us. The stench of burnt hair and scorched flesh hit my nose. I made my eyes open and looked up into a face full of explosives. Merkief was covered in them. There were several gaps where the silver, fist-sized balls were missing from their rows.

"Jey is coming for you. I've given him your location," he rasped in my face as he pushed himself up. The back of his coat was smoldering and the burnt stench was definitely coming from him.

"Get back to your family." He grabbed my shoulders and grimaced. "It wasn't supposed to be like this. I swear. I should have listened to you, but I couldn't..."

"I get it. Are we good now?"

"Yeah," he said, his voice breaking. "We're good."

"He can get both of us then. Sit down. You've done enough damage here."

"Tell Anastassia I'm sorry and give your little girl a kiss for me." He let go and staggered toward the stairway door.

"Wait!" I yelled after him.

Seconds after he was gone, another round of bombs rocked the building.

Jey stepped out of the void next to me. He clamped a hand onto my bare and handless arm. I waited for the void to swallow us, but it didn't. Jey swore. His words were difficult to make out with the echoes of explosions in my ears. He shook my arm and then let go. His gaze took on an irate and yet horrified cast as he took me in from head to foot.

Merkief reappeared in the doorway to the stairs, yelling something unintelligible, pointing behind us. We turned to see someone with a gun.

A pulse blast ripped down the remains of the corridor.

Suddenly I was no longer on my feet, but airborne. Jey had one hand on me, hoisting me upward, but the other was covering his face with an armored sleeve.

A figure in a ragged cloak emerged from the smoky haze just as the pulse activated Merkief's arsenal. The last thing I remembered was an orange glow and being pierced by a thousand barbs.

Chapter Twenty

"He's coming around," said a female voice.

I cracked open an eye, expecting to see the ordered ceiling of the Council's med clinic where I last remembered being. I'd been in a coma. My link was fried. Deep Voice had been there telling me my timing sucked. That he finally had the numbers to control the Council. It seemed like there was something after that but it wouldn't come to me. Had Arpex been snacking on my memories again?

"Vayen?"

That wasn't right. Grey-suits and Councilmembers never used my first name. The lighting overhead was all wrong too, long glowing tubes, like warehouse lighting.

I tried to see who was talking but it hurt to lift my head, and for some reason, my right eye wouldn't open.

"Where?" was all my dry, rasping voice managed to say before I started coughing.

"Get the man some water for Geva's sake."

I knew that voice. "Jey?"

"I'm right here."

Someone held up water to my lips. The cold liquid burned all the way down my throat. It tasted like there was something metallic in it.

Jey crossed over to the other side of the bed where I could see him. Scabs covered his face and neck, jagged lines, some larger and some nearly healed. He wore a hodgepodge of clothing, most of it straining to cover his Jalvian bulk.

"I hope I look better than you do."

Jey shook his head. "Don't bet on it."

"You should sit, sir. You're not ready to be on your feet," said a woman. From the little I could see of her, she wore a long blue tunic. The scrape of a chair along the floor preceded its arrival behind Jey. He sunk into it. The blue tunic swirled at the edge of my vision.

"I won't be in your way?" he asked.

"You'll be better suited to help him with his hand. I need to figure out why this eye isn't activating. It should have opened when the natural one did."

An eerie feeling settled over me. "What is she talking about? And why does my voice sound off?"

Jey put a hand on my arm. "You want the good news or the bad news first?"

"Just tell me what the fuck is going on and where we are. Where's Merkief?" I started coughing again.

A comforting warmth swirled into my veins and crept inward.

"You better not have fucking sedated me. If one more person knocks me out..."

"Keep him alert, Nessa. Just help him relax."

"If you say so. You're holding him down if he gets out of control."

"I've got him," Jey said.

"Why can't I see her?"

"You took some shrapnel in your right eye. And most everywhere else, for that matter. That paper-thin thing you had on didn't offer much protection."

I'd been standing in a corridor. Merkief had been there. He'd knocked me down and shielded me. Pieces of memory fell back into place. I reached out to the connection we'd shared but nothing was there.

He was gone.

I wanted to close my eyes again and wake up somewhere else, with both of them beside me. They could even be looming over me with angry faces, just as long as they were both there.

"Why did you let him do that?" I asked.

"I didn't *let* him. I put him in charge of finding volunteers and coordinating the attack with you. I was off taking out Fragia, which seemed the more sane option. But you two pulled it off."

He shook his head. "I didn't know he'd signed himself up until I got his panicked demand for me to Jump you to safety."

He rubbed the bridge of his nose and looked away. "The first day he saw you in grey, he changed. That meeting crushed him, I mean beyond everything he'd endured before. A clean death was one thing, but seeing you like that..." He shook his head. "He refused Kryon work, gave up on his planets, and well, gave up. It was like he was wearing grey too. He wanted to make it up to you. I guess he found his way."

"He's dead." Another wracking cough hit me.

Jey nodded. His grip on my arm tightened. "You need to stay calm. You've," his gaze wavered, "changed. It took me longer to Jump you than usual and you swallowed a lot of heat. That's why you sound like this. Coughing is only going to aggravate your condition. If you keep it up, I'm going to let Nessa knock you out again."

"Don't do that. Please." A twinge, like a split-second shock, passed through the right side of my face.

"Well now, looks like we got that working. Can you see me clearly?" asked a woman with pale blue skin. White specks crept up her chest onto her neck and over her face in a flowing pattern. Golden flecks in her yellow-green eyes seemed to twinkle. Two braids of white hair hung at her temples, leaving the rest of her tall, oblong head bare. She wasn't unattractive, I supposed, just very different.

"If you're supposed to be blue, then yes."

Nessa bared her pointed teeth in what I hoped was a smile. A high-pitched trill came from her throat. "You didn't tell me he was funny."

Jey rolled his eyes. "He's not. He's a self-centered, mostly insane, ill-tempered Artorian."

"That's not what you said before," Nessa said.

"Let's not repeat what I said before. His ego doesn't need to hear it. Don't you need to test his hand or something?"

"I have a new hand?"

I picked up my left arm. Rather than the stump I expected to see, an oversized, grey-skinned hand with thick fingers and black nails wiggled at me.

"Please tell me the rest of me does not match this hand."

"You're not quite as bad off as that." Jey kept his grip on my arm but let me hold up the new appendage to get a better look at it.

My feeble effort to shake him off didn't work. "You can let go."

"It was part of the deal to wake you. Nessa is worried that you'll inadvertently hurt yourself."

I jerked my arm away from him. By the fact that my arm shook just from the effort of holding itself up, I was pretty sure it was more that he reluctantly let go rather than any degree of me overpowering him.

"Not that I'm not grateful, but really, this was the closest match?"

"I'm so sorry," Nessa bowed her head and averted her gaze. "We're a lowly trade freighter. The best we have are modified replacement limbs meant for mercs at the fringe. They're not picky out there. We take what we can get at a good price."

After being the obeisant one, it was rather disconcerting to be the recipient once again. "It beats a stump, I suppose."

The gold in Nessa's eyes flared when she smiled. "See, he's not ill-tempered."

"Don't let the mostly insane part fool you." Jey turned back to me. "That is the ugliest hand I've ever seen. However, Nessa tells me it's been modified with black market enhancements. You should be able to crush just about anything. Might be useful."

"And where are we going that crushing anything would come in handy? I want to go home."

"You will. I needed you awake before I could leave. I'd offer to Jump you, but I think you'd be better off here and traveling on your own."

"We could repair the tank, we have the parts. Get me there, I'll help you."

"That was the first thing I thought of when I woke up," Jey said.

"Couldn't you find my half of the parts?"

"I did find them and I went to put the tank back together now that we don't have to worry about the Council, but we have bigger problems. At some point, someone had a fit and destroyed the control panels and cracked the tank itself. We lost more than half the gel. If I can find someone to do the repairs, it will still be a long while before it regenerates enough gel to fill the tank again."

"Merkief?"

"Or one of the Council. Either one would have been pissed to find out what we'd done. Doesn't really matter now. Fixing it will take time. I wish I could spare you the long healing. Looks like you're used to it though."

"You do remember that I can crush most anything with this new hand, right?"

Jey snickered. "Nessa's quite skilled. She'll take good care of you. Her father was smart to invest in her medical training."

Nessa turned a darker shade of blue. "He said the mercs would pay more if we offered a full-service operation. We're still working on the medical facility." She glanced around what looked to be a partially furnished warehousing bay.

"I'm sure they will appreciate your services. You did a spectacular job on Vayen here. He was quite a mess when we came in."

"Thank you. You're very kind." She ducked her head and stepped back. "Now that you're both awake, I'll see about getting you some dinner."

I watched Nessa leave, not that I could see very far while flat on my back in the bed. Once I was sure she was out of earshot, I turned to Jey. "Kind? You? Come on, she's our medic. Are you really trying to get into her bed?"

Jey grinned. "I'm scarred, not dead. You've got to admit, she's cute."

"And you've told her who you are. Of course she's going to fall all over you."

"Sadly, she's falling over you far more than me."

I tried not to cough, but my throat itched so damn bad, it was hard not to. It helped to keep my voice low, but the raspy words that came from my lips didn't sound like me at all.

"The one woman I have is tough enough to deal with. Speaking of which, the ship and our destination?"

"We happened upon this freighter just outside one of the jump gates on the way to Fragia. I came aboard to check out their merchandise in case they had anything that might be of use. Turned out they didn't, but the captain was an amiable man and offered to wait in order to set up a trade deal within the Narvan when we returned. I was here meeting with them, on our way back, when Merkief called me in. It was the first place I thought of to Jump you back to. I knew they had a medic on board and no other patients."

"You didn't think of Artor? Their medics are far more skilled and their replacement parts of far higher standards."

"You're dead there. I thought you might want to keep it that way. Besides, Nessa really is good. She could easily work at the University. Other than the make of the hand and eye, they couldn't have done much more for you than she did."

"My link?"

"Nessa scanned it but doesn't know much about it. You know you can't Jump. Can you access the network here?"

I opened my link. I could see the information around me but it was difficult to reach, as if some of the translation connections were missing. I'd barely touched it, but I could already feel a headache coming on.

"Slow, but yes."

I reached out to Jey's Link but got only buzzing.

"Nothing? I can feel you trying," he said.

"Remember when Anastassia's link was going? It feels like that."

"You really did a number on it. On the bright side, there's no sign of infection or damage within your brain. Nessa said she found signs of repair nanite activity but there weren't many in your system."

"Not surprising. The bastards wouldn't want me to heal too quickly."

He nodded. "Give them time to work. I'd offer to get you a new link, but the LEs wouldn't touch you in this condition. Your body needs time too."

I didn't want to wait. I wanted to be on Pentares immediately. However, I didn't relish the thought of being knocked out again, nor did I trust anyone with my head long enough to perform the damned link replacement. And I didn't have a jump point to get to Stassia anyway.

"Nessa also removed something from your neck. It was tiny but obviously didn't belong there. Some sort of tracking device, maybe?"

I nodded. "The Council."

"I don't think there's any of them left to hunt you down, but she destroyed it just in case."

"You look much better off than I feel."

Jey shrugged. "I was wearing armor. I tried to get you above the pulsewave. Thank Geva you're much lighter than you use to be. But when the blast hit, it threw both of us down hard. Nessa repaired your spine, and she promised me that you'll have a full range of motion. I hope she's right."

"How come you're still here if you're up and about? Why not at least get to Artor or Jal and get fixed up properly?"

"Once I was able, I did Jump back to Jal for a consultation, but to be honest, they were pretty impressed with Nessa's work and didn't have much more to offer. Without the tank we're both stuck with the natural recovery route. Besides, I wanted to make sure you were all right here. Anastassia said she would kill me if I didn't make sure you got back to her in one piece. Since you're missing a few, let's hope she wasn't being literal."

I laughed, which quickly led to coughing. Jey helped me with the water again.

"When you reach your family, will you be coming back? I could use a hand keeping the system in line. Your choice, obviously. If you want to vanish, I'll gladly deny any rumors of your brief reemergence."

"I need to talk to Anastassia first. We didn't part on the best of terms."

He shifted uncomfortably. "Right. Of course."

I let him squirm for a few well-deserved minutes while I sipped the water. It may have had some sort of medication in it, but there didn't seem to be enough cool and wet to soothe my throat.

"So you're keeping the system?" I asked.

"They know me. As far as they're aware, the Council never existed. Then there are the remaining Fragians. You think I'm letting Kess oversee them? Besides, someone's got to keep my people playing nice with yours."

"True."

My eyelids demanded to close. Nessa arrived just before I nodded off. I managed a few bites before I gave up and went to sleep.

When I woke, Jey sat beside me, wearing his own clothes and armor. The faraway look on his face told me he was deep in his link, probably managing the system while I slept.

I reached out and tapped his arm. He snapped out of his trance and blinked a few times.

"You sleep a lot." He sounded annoyed, though he looked relieved to see me awake.

"Making up for lost time."

"Nessa says it's good for you. She's been hovering over you since the moment we arrived."

"Tell her to stop."

Jey chuckled. "She even did your hair for you. Lucky man."

"What? You've got to be fucking kidding. Give me a mirror. Now."

"See, why aren't you like this when she's around? You're just trying to make me look bad in front of her."

"You don't need me to make you look bad."

He laughed me off and searched around until he turned up a mirror and handed it to me.

I took a deep breath. I hadn't really seen myself since I'd left Arpex's service. A silver-irised eye blinked back at me beside the usual dark one.

"At least that's a better match than the hand," I said.

"It's entirely artificial. Your fellow Artorians wouldn't like that either. Nessa was able to save the surrounding tissue. It was only the eyeball itself that was destroyed."

"Great, it matches my hair. When the hells did that happen?"

"Between the first time I saw you in grey and the last."

I picked at the silver strands sprinkled throughout the dark ones. My hair had grown well past my shoulders again. It hadn't been that length since I'd first arrived on Veria Minor. To be truthful, I didn't mind the braids Nessa had plaited at my temples to match hers. For the moment, it kept it out of my face and saved me the trouble of tying it back myself with my ungainly new hand.

Scars like Arin's lined my face, though thankfully I had fewer than he'd sported. Due to my single-handedness, they were mostly relegated to the right side, but they traveled down my neck too. A white line marked my cheekbone where the Arpex had kicked me, and like Jey, fresh scabs ranging from pinpoints to thick jagged lines marred my face and neck. From the sore spots on my scalp, I guessed them to be in my hair too. I peered under the blanket to see they also covered the rest of my body. I swallowed hard and handed the mirror back to Jey. I didn't need to see that again anytime soon.

"Don't they have any version of healing gel out here?" I asked.

"Her gel is as good as Artor's, and yes, she used it. The damage was just that bad. Your back is the worst. Take my word for it. You've still got bandages back there. Nessa wouldn't be happy with me if you got up to look."

"Can you do me a favor?"

"Depends what it is," he said.

"Get me some damned clothes. My own clothes. And nothing grey."

He chuckled. "You got it."

By the time Nessa returned to check on me, Jey had helped me dress in clothes that hung loose on my far thinner frame. Good thing I was confined to the bed because the pants would have fallen off.

"You dressed him?" Nessa scowled at Jey.

"He demanded I do it. He's like that."

Nessa nudged him out of the way and went about her scanning, probing, and medicine administering. She rubbed a new layer of healing salve on my face, leaving me coated in a sticky glaze. When she was satisfied, she backed away, giving us a little privacy.

Jey turned serious. "You go where you want and do what you need to. If you decide to come back in whatever capacity, just let me know."

"I will. You're leaving?"

He held up a hand. "You have weeks of recovery ahead of you yet, and I can't watch over you and the system at the same time. You might have been willing to leave the Narvan behind for Anastassia, but sorry, we're not like that."

I burst out laughing. And coughing.

Nessa was right beside me in an instant. She glared at Jey and grabbed the glass of water.

When I could breathe again, I restrained myself to a chuckle. "Then get out of here before you kill me."

"Are you sure? I can check in if you need me to."

"Jey, I'll be fine. Go. Take good care of my people."

"Your passage is paid for. Just tell the captain where you need to go. He'll find it. He promised me he would."

"I'm sure he will." I knew how Jey's persuasion methods worked.

He turned to Nessa. "You'll get him back in full working order?"

She nodded. "He's got a lot of physical therapy ahead of him, but he looks the sort to be up for it."

Jey wiggled his brows and grinned at me.

I just shook my head. "Don't you have somewhere else to be, Mr. System Advisor?"

"I do. Keep in touch, on your terms, all right?"

"I will." I waved him off.

Jey gave me one last long look before he stepped into the void and vanished.

Nessa smiled and came closer. "I thought he'd never leave."

Chapter Twenty-One

I spent the next two weeks evading Nessa's attention as much as one stuck in her care could. Even after I'd explained that I wasn't interested and was with someone else, she still insisted on flirting and heavy innuendo. Either she had a thing for exceptionally scarred men or Jey put her up to it. Someday I'd have to ask him and pay him back if that was the case.

The captain had come to see me the day after Jey departed. He seemed far more in awe of Jey than Nessa did so I made sure to tell him that I'd contact Jey immediately if I so much as suspected that they were trying to head anywhere but my destination. He'd made sure to pepper every conversation we'd had since with plenty of 'yes sirs' and sharp nods.

The day I could stand up on my own and make it ten steps away from the bed and back, I quit being nice and demanded a room elsewhere on the ship. The only thing I kept of Nessa's where the braids she'd given me.

There was no shortage of women, who could have been Nessa's sisters for all I knew, offering to wash and braid my hair for me, along with anything else I might need. I had the distinct feeling that Nessa's father put a serious emphasis on services of one particular variety. One I didn't have any interest in.

They seemed to have an abundance of clothing and they offered me a good deal of it when they caught on that I only had three changes of oversized clothing to my name. That was all I let them do for me.

For the most part, I kept to myself. Being around people, interacting them or maintaining polite banter beyond a sentence or two was uncomfortable. Their lighthearted air was difficult to tolerate and made me even more edgy. I was used to Arin and none of these people were him.

The room they'd given me was four times as large as the one Arin and I had shared. It took me weeks to get used to the walls being so far away.

Sleep was hard. The cold-sweat terror that had plagued me during my imprisonment had briefly subsided while in Nessa's care. Most likely because she'd kept me medicated or outright sedated most of the time. Now that I was on my own, it was back. The room was too dark. Too quiet. I was far too alone. As much as I disliked Arin, I missed him. His breathing. Knowing he was right there. I'd taken comfort in the fact that he woke up in a sweat as often as I did. His half-asleep muffled screams assured me that I wasn't alone in what had happened. He understood as no one else could. Now he was gone.

Merkief haunted my sleep as well, sometimes the cold, demanding man who'd torn me from Minor, sometimes the despondent one he'd been in the end. He kept warning me that not all of the Council was gone, that there were other Arpex out there. His warnings carried over into my waking hours and made my skin crawl, made me watch every shadow, jump at every unexpected sound.

Considering what scant weaponry the ship currently carried, I asked the captain for a knife, which, from his sideways glance, I gathered was an unexpected request. But he found one that suited me and insisted that it was free of charge. I kept it with me at all times.

It wasn't enough. I needed my body back.

My energy level took its sweet damn time returning so that I could start getting my muscles back in any sort of shape.

The women seemed to be taking turns bringing me meals, each doing their best to try to get into my room like it was some sort of contest. None of them got an invitation.

Getting my stomach adjusted to solid foods again took time too, but I had plenty of that. There wasn't a lot of variety, and I didn't recognize any of what they served me, but it beat the hells out of tasteless mush.

The change in my voice was the hardest to get used to. Every time I did speak to someone, it sounded like someone else saying what I was thinking. As the months of travel passed, I stopped coughing constantly, which was a major improvement.

My passage to Pentares was a month shorter than Stassia's had been since my ship made a minimal number of trade stops, and those only along the direct route. That was a good thing because the more I let myself believe that I was really going to see my family again, the harder it was to have any semblance of patience. Every day was another closer and yet one too many to wait.

Each day I got a little stronger and the horror of my days in grey faded in faint degrees. The repairs within my link progressed slowly. When I did try to access it, I had to get past an instant reflex to cringe while I waited for the pain of the inhibitor field to hit me.

Eventually, I worked up the nerve to count the days I'd been gone, discovering I'd wallowed in the Council's clutches for nearly three years. Add to that the travel time and...my heart sunk.

I'd told Stassia six months. Was she even on Pentares anymore? Had they given up on me and gone elsewhere? Geva only knew what names they might be using by now.

The decision to demand that Fa'yet close off all connections to me when they'd left, was one I regretted very much right then. It had been the right decision, but still, it didn't make the uncertainty any easier to bear.

Had she found someone else? Maybe even Fa'yet himself. They'd always been close. If he'd found no other Artorian women out here, Stassia was the next best thing, even in her telepathically damaged state. He'd be lonely, she'd need comforting. The kids needed a father.

Paranoia drove me to access any network I discovered along the way for as long as I could stand. As slow and often painful as the process was, I eventually found her, the kids, and Fa'yet and Neko, though only after a good deal of time untangling records based off of their arrival date. They were still on Pentares, though only Geva knew in what dynamic.

The Pentares network was archaic compared to what I was used to accessing. Nothing was stored in a logical place. I didn't want consider what that meant for the living conditions of the colony.

Comforted by the knowledge that she was at least there, I

devoted my final weeks to preparing myself for meeting her and far too many hours of every night speculating how that could go wrong. It seemed like each night I fell asleep with the lingering question: What if she had found someone else or if she hadn't, saw what was left of me and wanted out?

Merkief continued to accost me at night, as did Arpex, and Deep Voice. If the level of destruction of the base where I'd been was anything to judge the others by, there wouldn't be many survivors. The ones that haunted me were no doubt dead. But it was possible that a few had Jumped to safety or that I'd missed a base. Jey knew enough to watch his back. Anyone in their right mind wouldn't consider that I'd survived, not when I'd been in the clinic with my link in shambles. I should have felt safe, tried to convince myself that I was. I was on a ship, halfway across the known universe from where I'd been. Nothing had happened here in months. Yet, I kept my knife in reach at all times.

Arin was different than the rest. He turned up in my room one day and slowly began to appear more the closer we came to Pentares. Leaving my sleeping hours to the others, he talked to me while I was awake, telling me I was still in a coma in the clinic, that this was all a dream.

"You're no one special. Why do you get to escape?" he said over his shoulder while he kept his attention on the empty wall across from us. "Enjoy meeting your family. They're not real, but I don't blame you for thinking they are. Rest now. Arpex is waiting."

"Shut up." I waved him away.

As usual, he didn't leave. The only way I could escape him was to leave my room. I hated leaving my room, too many people to watch on the ship. Too many people watching me. I would never blend in again. Anywhere.

My physical appearance might not have been something I'd paid much attention to all my life, but I certainly wasn't fond of what I saw now the few times I hadn't managed to avoid a mirror. The gel had left me with a fine patchwork of scars that covered my entire body. While that was far better than what I'd first seen when I woke up in Nessa's clinic, it wasn't me.

Had Stassia felt the same way when she'd been released years before? Not that the wounds she'd suffered were near as obvious.

The gel hadn't done anything for the scars I'd gathered while in service to Arpex or fixed the ache in my foot, my ribs, or my back from how I'd landed after the pulse wave had ignited the explosives Merkief had been carrying. And it certainly hadn't made the grey in my hair go away.

From what Jey had said of my condition, Nessa had done a miraculous job getting me back on my feet with my back straight, but stiff, yet generally working as it should. But I missed the tank. Though, even that couldn't have fixed the damage I'd suffered in my imprisonment. Geva was collecting payment on all the injuries I'd avoided in prior years.

I spent long, frustrating hours alone, working with my hand until I was able to pick up fine objects without crushing them. The silver eye provided the same visuals as my natural one. On one sleepless night, I discovered that it also allowed me to see in the dark. Both of those things might have come in handy if I'd planned to go back to working in the Narvan, but they were also another strike against me on Artor. Unnatural enhancements were highly frowned upon.

Truth be told, I looked far more like a tattered merc from the fringe than any semblance of the man I used to be. Mercs were nothing unusual to the crew of this ship, but they were avoided by the general populace of any planet I'd ever been to, including Kess's rough territory beyond the Nebula. Would there be enough shadows to hide in on Pentares?

When I couldn't take being my room any longer, I wandered the ship. The stacks of storage containers of all sorts made me feel a little more at home. If I was going to have a chance with my family, I needed to learn how to tolerate people again, to remember how talk to them in a civil manner. Could I keep Arin at bay and my patchwork of memories in enough order to appear like I had my shit together? The crew provided an ample testing ground.

The captain found me offering advice to a few of his men on how to better organize their stock. We ended up sharing a couple meals together. I gave him some names within the Narvan as well as pointing him toward Cragtek, hoping the new business would help redeem my standing with Gamnock in some small way.

My coat and weapons had been lost. When I mentioned it, the captain offered to give me a coat of common quality from his stock. As much as my nerves would have liked the comforting weight of armor, it would have only solidified my merc-like appearance. To his confusion, I declined his offer.

I hoped Pentares was as peaceful as I'd first believed it to be when I'd sent my family there. The knife wouldn't make it through port security. Without being able to Jump to the surface, I had to play by the rules of the real world.

If Arin was wrong...if this wasn't the dream.

I prayed this was real. It had to be.

Chapter Twenty-Two

When docking day finally arrived, I was at the bay doors with my bag of donated clothes in hand before we were even clamped in. The captain wished me luck, pressed a credit chip that he informed me was pre-converted into my hand, and got out of my way.

The trade station itself offered nothing unusual, a mix of races and the general din of too many languages being spoken at once. Graffiti offered some color to the otherwise worn walls of the central hub. Automated movers went about loading and unloading freight, their beeping and squeaking gears only adding to the chaos. A handful of beggars held out their cups to new arrivals. Merchants held up their wares, waving over anyone with whom they could make eye contact. I bypassed all of them and found my way to the next ship going to the surface of Pentares.

The flight down to the planet itself was uneventful. From the sparse occupancy of the ship, I gathered Pentares wasn't a popular destination. Those who did join me on the downward journey sat far from my seat. The only people that spoke to me were the woman checking baggage and another who verified the identity Jey had provided. Those two couldn't get away fast enough.

I realized the crew I'd traveled here with, who routinely interacted with my ilk, hadn't adequately braced me for the new reality of my appearance. Not even remotely. There were too many people here and they were all very aware of me, where exactly I was, what I looked like.

Could I endure the sideways stares and whispers for the rest of my life? Would my family look at me the same way? I rubbed the thick fingers of my new hand, assuring myself that I wasn't as broken as I had been. In the quiet of my mind, Arin laughed.

"Do you remember your list? All the memories Arpex ate?" he asked. "They're going to know."

"They won't," I whispered to my reflection in the window.

"You can't hide it. You don't even remember what you've lost," he whispered back in a mockery of my raspy voice.

I squeezed my eyes shut and willed him gone. When I opened them again, we'd entered the atmosphere.

The surface of Pentares reminded me a little of Veria Minor, scattered colonies connected by trade lines. With no domes and no visible planetary engineering, it was downright Friquen in its natural state. Beyond the colonies, Pentares was mostly wild tangles of dense jungle threaded with rivers, yielding very little habitable land.

On the ground, the port city swarmed with a myriad of babbling, most of which my link couldn't translate. The signs were in a language I couldn't read either. No one responded favorably to me asking directions. It took me a while to hunt down what sufficed as a transport hub.

What little information I'd dug up had provided me with Stassia's address. She was only a two-hour ride on the surface trade shuttle from the main port city. Again, though the shuttle was fairly full, the seats around the one I'd chosen remained empty.

It was strange to be surrounded by so many people like Stassia. But they weren't like her. I hoped. The whispers and hastily averted gazes accosted me throughout the ride.

When the shuttle came to a stop at the station, I grabbed my bag and quickly departed. Unfortunately, hushed comments followed me along the twenty-minute walk to her building. A couple men broke from the others to hurl insults at me in Trade. At least I could understand them. One feint in their direction and they took off. My appearance did have its benefits. Not that I wanted to be known as that kind of man here, not if I was going to stay with my family and attempt a life like we'd had on Minor.

Two sturdy women wearing dark blue uniforms with badges I could only assume were local enforcers, followed me for a couple blocks, one madly typing on a datapad, while the other kept her eyes on me. Eventually, they dropped back.

The colony where Stassia lived was quite large compared to Veria Minor, more like a smaller city on Artor, but without any of the amenities. The air was heavy with the oily smell of poorly adjusted personal transports. The high humidity level didn't help, but I supposed that was needed to support the surrounding habitat. That's where the plants were that so many came to study, the reason why Stassia was here too.

All the buildings seemed primitive, made of poorly engineered products that might last a century or two before requiring extensive repair. The traffic system was a mess and traffic itself, loud.

If I hadn't seen the jungle coming into the colony, I would have never known it existed once the tall outer ring of buildings filled the skyline. I couldn't spot any single family homes. Like Jal, it appeared that height was sought after for status. The upper floors boasted open-air patios with pots full of brightly colored flowers or maybe it was food, it was hard to tell from the ground. The units on the lower and ground levels bore small windows and not a visible speck of plant life. Everything down on the ground was hardscaped and even that wasn't done well. There were cracks in the walks and lines didn't match up. A myriad of materials butted up against one another haphazardly as if the same area had undergone multiple bursts of development.

The multistory structure bearing the symbols I'd been searching for towered upward, though thankfully not to the degree of a Jalvian plex. Tinted clearplaz windows might have offered a decent view from above, but from my vantage point, they offered no hints as to what might be inside.

A creaky lift delivered me to her floor. The hallway closed in as I located her door. I set my bag down and knocked. My heart thundered in my chest and my throat went dry.

The door slid open. Fa'yet stood there, a gun in his hand.

"Who the hells..." His eyes went wide and his mouth dropped open. He lowered the gun and stepped back.

"You could say hello," said the rasp that wasn't my voice.

His voice shook. "Hello."

He'd given up his old man act and let his hair grow back in. He wore his curls short and swept back from his face in a style I'd noted on other men on my walk here. I didn't see his cane, but he was still favoring the one leg, and he wasn't wearing armor. An overturned book, the ancient kind, sat on the arm of the chair he edged toward.

I walked in since he made no move to stop me and took a good look around. It was a large apartment, taking a third of the level of the public housing complex. I supposed the expense was worth giving them all the separate spaces they needed. A hodgepodge of furniture filled the large open room, most of it looking like it belonged in a museum due to the primitive materials.

"I'm glad to see you," Fa'yet said finally.

"I can tell. Where is she?"

"Clearly, victory didn't come easy."

Why was no one running out to greet me? The damned rooms were silent.

"Where are they?" I asked again.

"Daniel is at school. Ana's working. Neko is out. Ikeri is here, but I don't know as-"

"You don't know what? She's my daughter, dammit. Ikeri?"

Little feet tiptoed down the hallway toward us. Her footsteps stopped dead for only a second before she barreled into me. Her mind opened to mine, reestablishing the deep connection we'd previously shared.

"Daddy," she said with a sense of reverence.

I picked her up and held her tightly. Tears slipped from my natural eye and ran into her soft curls. I'd expected to feel her rummaging through my thoughts, but she kept her mental fingers to herself.

"I'm learning," she said.

"I see that."

Yet she still knew what I was thinking. Maybe she was just learning to be more subtle about it rather than learning not to do it at all.

"I missed you." She kissed my cheek and then pulled back.

I set her down. Her brown curls hung almost to her waist and she stood taller than mine. I was sad to see that she had truly begun to grow up, her face had thinned, losing the round rosy cheeks that I remembered so fondly. My inspection stopped there with the narrowing of her eyes as she looked me over as well.

With her hands on her hips and a disapproving frown, she looked me up and down.

"You didn't wear your coat like you promised," Ikeri stated in Anastassia's most disapproving tone.

I couldn't help myself, I laughed. I laughed so hard that I had to sit down in one of the small chairs that was just as uncomfortable as it looked. A smile eventually broke through Ikeri's disapproving glare. She giggled.

When I felt someone beside me, I looked up to see Fa'yet laughing too.

He clapped me on the shoulder. "It is good to see you again." His mind opened to mine, reforming our natural connection.

"Don't bother with the link. Mine's still recovering."

He gave me a solemn nod. "You'll be wanting to see Ana, then?"

"Any reason why I wouldn't?" Recent months full of paranoia flooded my mind with plenty of reasons.

"No, it's just that your reappearance is, well, unexpected."

"Sorry to surprise you by living."

He licked his lips and glanced at Ikeri. I couldn't even begin to guess what they were saying to one another.

"That's not what I meant. We had no warning that you'd be arriving," said Fa'yet.

"Did you need warning? I wasn't expecting a big party."

"No, of course not." He cleared his throat and stepped back. "Here, I'll show you where to find her."

Fa'yet went to a terminal mounted on a desk near the dining table. From the ancient look of it, I was amazed it was still operational. No wonder the local network was such a mess. If all the terminals were like this one, they couldn't handle anything more.

He pulled up a map of the colony. Ikeri was suddenly at my side. She reached for my hand and then, seeing what she was reaching for, dodged to my other side and took that one.

"I'm glad you're here," she said, then gave Fa'yet a mischievous smile. "We shouldn't tell Daniel. He needs a surprise."

Fa'yet chuckled. "That he does, and this just might do it." He pointed at the map. "This is where you'll find her. She's been pretty wrapped up in her work for the past couple years."

"She always was."

Even on Veria Minor, she'd spent just as much time in the little shop she'd set up to do her Seeker therapy as I did at my warehouse. It hadn't mattered if the kids had gone with her, she'd mostly given herself over to her task. It was Fa'yet's lack of immediate response that made me wonder if this time was different somehow. Ikeri squeezed my hand.

"We'll stay here, if you don't mind," Fa'yet said.

"I'll be back." I gave my little girl one last hug and dashed out the door.

The lift took me down to the street level where I made an effort not to plow through the people who stood in my way. They may have been taller and of a more similar build to me than the Verians we'd lived with on Minor, but they still seemed small and frail, like some distant and primitive offshoot of Artorians.

While I'd been around her people on the Verian station. I hadn't realized there was such a wide variation in their appearances until I saw so many of them together here. They'd certainly not latched onto any genetic ideal or even hint of a plan for their race.

Given a few generations with some Artorian help, they'd be well on their way to a more solid and better-built future. Then again, from the few hints Stassia had dropped over the years, not everyone, which I now directly took to mean her own kind, appreciated the orderly and upward goal of genetic precision.

A moving walkway took me under the street and into the building's lower levels on the other side. I hadn't known such things were still in manufacture. Though, I supposed someone needed the rest of the civilized universe's junk.

I stepped off the walkway at the point Fa'yet had specified. It was a short walk to the security checkpoint that stood in front of the research facility where she worked. The security guard took one look at me as I approached and tapped a button on her desk.

She held up her hand and spoke. I shook my head. My link had slowly been accumulating words during my few hours on the surface and working out translations for them, but it would be weeks before I could begin to rely on its accuracy.

She switched to a rough version of Trade. "Wait here."

"Why?"

"You have clearance to enter?"

If I had needed any sort of clearance, I was pretty sure Fa'yet would have mentioned it. I was in no mood for delays.

"No, nor do I need any. I'm unarmed." I leaned in real close. "And you're going to let me through now."

She was trying very hard to maintain her composure, but I could see her trembling. "What business do you have here?"

"I'm here to see someone. My visit is a surprise, and I'll be very angry if it doesn't remain that way."

"I see. Chuck will escort you." She said something in her own language into a small triangular device pinned to her collar.

A slender young man wearing an identical beige uniform strode toward us. I scowled. He grimaced and didn't even try to hide it.

"Is there a problem?" he asked in a tone that said he knew there was and he was only attempting to be polite.

"Please escort him inside. He's making a surprise visit."

"I see. This way." He gestured for me to follow him as though he wasn't sure I'd understood what he'd said.

We made it into the building and out of the public eye before he drew what looked like a stunner. At least Stassia's people were civilized in that regard. I sighed, jabbed him in the face with my rock-solid new hand, and waited until his unconscious body hit the floor before continuing on my way.

It had been far too long since I'd seen Stassia. Though part of me dreaded it, I needed to see her true reaction when she saw me. I didn't want her warned, primed, or armed with a fake smile. I needed to see the truth in her eyes. Had she really been waiting for me, and now that I was here, was I still welcome in her life? I sure hoped so because the moment after I saw her face, I needed to be alone with her for a very long while. Part of my body that I'd long ignored, assured me it was very much alive and anxious to see her again.

In order to avoid any further attention or delay, I evaded everyone I could and ended up taking a detour before I found my way to the door Fa'yet referred to as her lab. A narrow slit of a window gave me my first glimpse of what lay inside.

The sapling I'd given her on Frique sat lush and tall in its pot next to an unoccupied desk. Two rows of long counters filled with various containers, clear tubing, potted plants, leaves, flowers and ancient observation equipment littered the countertops. Somewhere in the vast room, Stassia laughed. My stomach clenched.

I palmed the door panel but it refused to open. Damned thing. Knocking politely was out of the question, someone else might answer the door. I went to work on the lock, thankful that I'd spent so much time working on fine movements with my new hand.

A man said something in what sounded like Trade. I'd never heard Stassia speak the language they used here. She was probably more comfortable with Trade too being that she didn't have the luxury of a link.

Another man laughed. A third, too close to be either of the voices I'd already heard, passed by the door and froze when he saw me. My efforts with the lock paid off when it clicked and the door opened. I walked in.

The man backed away, stammering. I followed him, coming to a corner in the room, where it opened into another section of long counters that I hadn't been able to see from the door.

Stassia stood there, leaning over a stand lined with glass tubes filled with red-brown liquid. She pointed one out to a tall, brown-skinned man who stood beside her with one arm lazily draped across her lower back as he leaned in to take a closer look.

"Anastassia," the man who'd seen me finally managed to say.

The as yet unseen man, who was busy paying attention to something in his hand, walked into the one who had alerted Stassia. Those two scrambled out of the way as I strode forward intent on ripping the arm off the man who was touching her.

Stassia glanced up. She appeared frozen, unblinking, maybe not even breathing for all I could tell.

The man beside her pulled her behind him and stared me down with dark eyes. His somewhat broad and muscular form blocked her from my sight, which did nothing to calm me. If she'd been looking for a replacement for me within her own people, she couldn't have gotten much closer.

"Who the hell are you?" he asked in much more fluent Trade that the security guards had used.

Nothing more coherent than a snarl came out of my mouth.

Despite his best efforts, Stassia leapt in front of him. "Vayen?" she choked out.

Her protector looked at her in disbelief. "You know him?"

"He's my husband," Anastassia said more steadily.

"You said he was dead."

"I said I *thought* he was dead."

She walked hesitantly towards me. One hand reached out toward my face. I could see her eyes taking in the scars and my new eye.

"My god, what happened to you?" She finally dared to touch me, her fingers running lightly down the long, mostly grey braid beside my face.

I wanted nothing more than to wrap my arms around her, but my fists wouldn't unclench. My arms remained woodenly locked to my sides to keep from attacking her or him or anyone else that was stupid enough to come near me.

"Everyone out!" Stassia ordered in a tone that verged on Kazan.

The first two men scampered for the door. The third, however, strode confidently to her side and worked up a threatening stance of his own.

"I'm not going to leave you alone with him. He looks ready to hurt someone."

"That would be you, Raphael. I'm amazed he hasn't killed you already." Stassia shoved him toward the door, keeping her eyes on me until we both heard it shut behind him.

During all I had endured, it was Stassia and protecting our children that kept me going, the thought of being with them again. But now that we were finally together, I couldn't move.

She had found someone else, someone like her, who was whole, who had a shared interest in her job, and who was there when I was not. Fa'yet had tried to warn me, subtly, in a way that wouldn't set me off in front of Ikeri.

"I shouldn't have come."

She stood there, stammering silently.

All the scenarios I'd imagined alone at night in my room on the way here played in my head at once. I'd never come up with an answer of what I'd do if she turned me away.

"Vayen, it's been years. Isnar searched as much as he dared, but we'd heard nothing from you or about you. I didn't know what to think anymore."

She looked no different than the day I'd left. They'd been safe here, going about their new normal lives and I'd crashed into them, upsetting the balance they'd found.

"You made me promise to find you," I said, finding my voice again.

"I did." Her gaze darted toward the door. "Raphael and I work together. That's it. I swear."

"We worked together too. I remember how that went."

She took a deep breath and let it out, then looked me right in the eye. "He's wanted that, but I keep putting him off. It didn't feel right." A hesitant smile edged her lips. "Maybe that bond of yours rubbed off on me after all."

She'd called me her husband. I dropped my gaze to her neck to see that she still wore the neckband I'd given her. The armband still adorned her wrist Our bonded connection swelled to life as her mind opened to mine as much as it was able. I'd known

I'd missed what I felt around her, but when the peace surged over and through me, I didn't remember it being half as beautiful as it was in that moment.

Stassia slipped her arms around me and rested her forehead on my shoulder. "I can't believe you're here."

"Most of me, anyway." My arms remembered how to move and my hands unclenched so I could hold her.

It felt so good to have her there, to smell her, to have her hands on me. Arpex hadn't taken what mattered most. Only that blue bastard and Geva knew how many gaps there were because I'd fed it something else in order to keep Stassia, but they were worth it.

"You really need to stop thinking I'm dead every time we're away from each other," I said.

Anastassia let out a sharp hysterical laugh. She pulled back enough to look me over again.

Rather than answer her unspoken questions, I kissed her. And once I'd got that little taste, it was all I could do to not push things farther right there.

"Where?" I managed to break away long enough to ask.

"Not here," she said just as breathlessly. "Raphael will probably be back with security any second."

"Minus one, unless he's awake by now."

She smacked me on the chest. "What did you do? We live here, you know."

"I don't have any weapons on me. I only hit him once. He was slowing me down."

She shook her head and sighed. "Come on, we better clear this up before it gets any worse."

"I have other things I'd like to clear up right now." I tried to kiss her again, but she ducked away.

"You have a one-track mind, you know that?"

"It's been years, I'm allowed."

"I know exactly how long it's been, but still." She reached for my hand and came up short. "That's new."

I held up my grey hand and flexed the thick fingers. "It's not pretty, but it's useful."

"I thought Artor would have better-"

"I wasn't on Artor."

Raphael thundered into the room with four security guards right behind him.

One of them addressed Stassia. "What's going on here?"

"Nothing. He didn't mean to scare anyone."

"Ma'am, he attacked Chuck. We have it on vid if you don't believe me."

She gave me a disapproving glance before refocusing on the guard. "Oh, I believe you. Is Chuck all right?"

"We're having a medic look him over," said one of the other guards as they began to fan out around us.

Stassia stepped closer to me. "As you can see, my husband has had a few rough years. He's having a hard time adjusting to civilian life. I'll keep my eye on him. It won't happen again."

"We'll have to see if Chuck will be pressing any charges before we can dismiss this."

"I'll talk with Chuck," Stassia said. "He won't be pressing any charges."

The guards looked at one another. "As you say, ma'am." They walked away.

Stassia's head snapped to Raphael. "I'm taking a few days off. See that work progresses while I'm out."

He glared at me. I glared right back.

"Of course. Enjoy your time off," he said quickly.

Stassia took my other hand. "Come on, it seems I need to have a quick talk with Chuck before we can get back to addressing your one track mind."

We walked to the main doors. The downed guard sat against a wall with another man on his knees beside him. He wore a grey suit.

I froze. My next breath refused to come.

Arin laughed. "Enjoying the dream?

The medic looked up as Stassia approached. He was human, like her. I'd not seen any other human grey-suits.

"Vayen?" Stassia tugged on my hand. "What's wrong?"

Breathe. I needed to breathe.

"It's not a dream. She's real," I told Arin. "Go away."

The pressure on my chest eased as Stassia filled my field of vision, blocking the men on the floor.

"Nothing," I managed to say. "Sorry about..." What was his name? I needed to be normal, to prove I wasn't on the verge of losing it. Her concern began to buffet my mind. She needed to know I was all right. What the fuck was his name? "Chuck."

She squeezed my hand and let go, returning her attention to

the medic. I made myself look at him again. He wore grey pants, black shoes, and a open-necked grey shirt. Not a suit.

"Nothing appears to be broken. Lots of swelling though, probably will have a nasty bruise," the medic said.

He backed away, giving Stassia space to speak to the wounded guard privately. I was glad to see that she had found a place here, one where she was in the lead. She was always happiest when she was in charge.

A couple minutes later she got up and returned to my side. "All right then, that's taken care of. You can take us home."

"I'd love to, but I can't. That part of my link hasn't recovered yet."

We made our way to the walkway. With her beside me, it was easier to ignore the stares and whispers.

"Anything else lost or recovering that I should be aware of?"

I pulled her out of the flow of foot traffic. "Stassia, we lost Merkief."

She looked up at me uncertainly.

"It wasn't me. He blew..." I couldn't get the memory of his face lit by the burst of explosives out of my mind. The stench of charred flesh wafted around me. I shook my head. "He said to tell you that he was sorry."

Tears welled in her eyes. "Do you want to talk about it?"

I slipped my arm around her. "Other than to ease your mind with the fact that the High Council has been eradicated, no."

Her hysterical laughter returned. "You did what?"

"Suffice it to say that they look far worse than I do. If any of them managed to escape, that is."

She stood there, staring at me, mouth hanging open. "You're not kidding. You took them out?

"Merkief and Jey helped." I tugged her hand, urging her toward the apartment.

"You'll have to tell me what happened."

"Another day." Maybe once the nightmares stopped plaguing me, I'd be more willing to talk about the reality that had birthed them.

"All right." She wrapped her arm around me. "We might as well pick up Daniel while were out. It would save Isnar a trip."

"Seriously? I'd rather Isnar took a trip."

"Vayen, I'm sure your son would like to see you."

"He can see me later." I had Stassia right next to me for Geva's sake and that made everything so much easier. Better.

Arin was quiet for the moment. The paranoia that had held me so tight in its grasp on the long trip here was only a soft whisper. Pentares was new, unfamiliar, I'd have plenty of excuses to fall back on if I screwed something up due to my missing memories. The air, the smells, Stassia next to me, it was all real.

We were almost home, near a bed and a door and privacy.

She snickered. "From what I'm picking up from you, later will be days. You might want to get this out of the way first."

I sighed and let her lead me down another street. "Why can't he walk home by himself?"

"Because, like his father, he gets into trouble when he's by himself."

"Oh."

Her voice softened. "Also like his father, he has a legitimate excuse. He's out of his element here. Some of the other kids don't like him because he's telepathic. No one else here is. They don't understand it and it scares them. And beyond that, Daniel scares them. Also, unfortunately, like you, he's come to enjoy that fact."

"Oh."

"I remember you being more articulate," she said with a smile.

"Sorry, I'll talk to him."

"Isnar tried. I tried. Neko tried," she said. "I hope you fare better."

"Look at me. I've kind of cornered the market on scaring people."

"Well here's your chance." She pointed to a shaggy-haired boy who towered over the others around him. The shadow of a fading black eye added to his glower. He'd be nine by now, but his Artorian build made him appear several years older than his classmates.

When he spotted Stassia, he started toward us. He cocked his head and scowled as he got closer, looking me up and down. "Took you long enough."

"I'm sorry, I was busy trying to stay alive. What happened to your eye?"

"Someone's fist, I imagine. What happened to yours?"

"Something far more unpleasant than a fist." I tried to wrap my mind around the fact that the mischievous boy I'd left behind had turned into his true father right down to the dry demeanor and bad attitude. No wonder the rest of them were hoping I could reel him in. "I suggest you start walking."

Stassia dropped behind us as we headed back to the house. I put my new hand on his shoulder. He gave it a glance and kept walking. Apparently scaring and intimidating wasn't going to work. As Stassia said, we were both out of our element here. Maybe I needed to change tactics.

"That's one ugly hand," he muttered.

"That's what Jey said." It made me smile to think about it.

"What happened to your real one?"

"Something sharp, I imagine."

He looked at me and grinned.

"So I hear you're getting into trouble."

"They're ganging up on me. I'm just trying to get home."

"How many?" I asked.

"I beat three, but there were four last time."

"Impressive."

"Vayen," Stassia said from behind us.

I cleared my throat. "Right. I'm sure your mother has told you what you're supposed to do if the other kids are picking on you?"

Daniel bowed his head. "Yes."

"Well, do that."

I reestablished the natural connection between us. *But I'll show you how to beat four. You know, in case the other option doesn't work.*

He stopped in his tracks as soon as we entered the housing complex and hugged me. "I'm glad you're home."

Stassia eyed me suspiciously.

"What?" I asked over Daniel's back.

"Remember how you're terrible at lying to me? Your innocent routine isn't much better."

I winked at her as the three of us piled into the lift. When we entered the apartment, Fa'yet got up and took Ikeri's hand. He motioned for Daniel to follow them as he reached for the door we'd just walked through.

"Where are you going?" Stassia asked.

"I remember you two together. There aren't enough sound dampeners in this apartment. We'll be back in a few hours." The door closed behind them.

I turned to Stassia and pulled her close. "Now then, where in the hells is our bedroom?"

She threw her head back and laughed. I took that as an invitation to kiss her throat and work my way up. The bond blossomed between us as her mind further opened to mine in very pleasant ways, flooding it with warmth. When I reached her mouth, she kissed me back with such intensity that I gave up making any progress toward another room.

Then she pulled away.

"What? I assure you all the important parts are very much in working order."

"I felt that." She grinned. "There's just one thing first."

"You're killing me here. What now?"

"Our joining, is that still on the table?"

"I'm about ready to put you on the table."

She glanced from me to the table and smirked. "Is that a yes or no?"

"Definitely a yes." I pulled off my shirt.

"Well then." She took a step back. "I'm afraid we can't have sex until I consent to the joining. That is how it works, right?"

"Anastassia, you had better be kidding." I covered the distance between us in a single step and reached for her shirt.

She batted me away. "What about my wooing?"

"Not funny."

"Don't be so sure." She snickered and then composed herself. "Fine, if I'm not going to get any wooing, then I suppose we can skip right to the consenting."

"Yes?" I asked.

She nodded. "Yes."

I grabbed her and kissed her and made quick work of all the damned clothing between us.

"The bedroom is over here." She tugged at me.

"The table is over here." I picked her up.

"You're an idiot, you know that?"

"But I'm your idiot and you love me."

Stassia laughed and held on tight. "I do."

About the Author

Jean Davis lives in West Michigan with her musical husband, two attention-craving terriers and a small flock of chickens. When not ruining fictional lives from the comfort of her writing chair, she can be found devouring books and sushi, weeding her flower garden, or picking up hundreds of sticks while attempting to avoid the abundant snake population that also shares her yard. She writes an array of speculative fiction.

She is the author The Narvan series and of several standalone books including *A Broken Race*, *Sahmara*, *The Last God* and *Destiny Pills and Space Wizards*. As an author who's been both self-published and traditionally published, she appreciates all reviews as they help readers discover good books.

Read her blog, *Discarded Darlings*, and sign up for her mailing list at www.jeandavisauthor.com. You'll also find her on Facebook and Instagram at JeanDavisAuthor, and on Goodreads and Amazon.

CPSIA information can be obtained
at www.ICGtesting.com
Printed in the USA
BVHW041003010320
573478BV00008B/102